CONTROL BURN RESIST
The Submission Series Book Two

CD Reiss

*everafter*ROMANCE

The Submission Series

EverAfter Romance
An Imprint of Diversion Publishing Corp.
443 Park Avenue South, Suite 1008
New York, New York 10016
www.DiversionBooks.com

For more information, email info@diversionbooks.com

First Diversion Books edition July 2015.
Print ISBN: 978-1-68230-019-0

Contents

control.

The Submission Series
Book Four

Chapter 1

Monica

"Get on your knees."

Even through the phone, I could tell Jonathan was using his dominant voice. I got nervous that I would dampen the expensive panties so badly the protective paper at the crotch would curl and peel off. "Yes, sir."

Facing the dressing room mirror, I got to my knees. The black garter and stocking I was trying on looked as though it had been taped on me. The black satin belt slung low on my hips held the straps that dropped down my thighs with silver rings.

"How does it look?" he asked.

"I think you'll like it."

"How does it make you feel?"

"You really want to know?" I asked.

"I'm sitting in the back of my car, thinking about you. It's wall-to-wall traffic. So, yes, I want to know how it makes you feel."

I heard women outside the dressing room door. Their soft conversations and laughter were muffled by the clothing draped around the room, lingerie with bows and clasps and metal rings set into lush satins and elastics. Every piece I'd tried on aroused me, and when he called, the addition of his voice to the mix brought me near tears.

"How do I feel?" I asked. The carpet dug into my knees, and I was goose bumped from the air conditioner, but that wasn't what he meant. The black satin bra's cups were made of two panels that could be moved for access. It felt so comfortable, I didn't even know I had it on. The curves of the underwear accentuated the length of my pelvis. "I feel like fucking."

I heard him take a breath. I did enjoy shocking him. "Tuck the phone under your left ear."

"Done."

"Done?"

"Done, sir."

"Put your left hand on the mirror," he said. "Lean on it."

"Yes, sir." My hand spread on the mirror like a starfish. It would leave a mark.

"Put your right hand between your legs."

"Jonathan…"

"Do it."

My cunt clenched with anticipation. I stroked lightly through the string of cloth, sucking air between my teeth from the tingle of the touch.

"Get under the fabric," he said, as if he could see I hadn't put my fingers on my skin.

"Yes, sir." The word *sir* seemed to vibrate not just outward, to him, but inward, down a thick nerve connecting my vocal cords to my core. When I slipped my fingers under the panties, I shuddered.

"You wet?"

"So fucking wet," I whispered.

"Your legs spread?"

"Yes."

"Look at yourself in the mirror."

I did, and I was greeted by a face slack with arousal, flushed with sex. "Yes, sir." I watched myself submit to him, in that outfit, as if I needed to be more turned on. Outside the door, I heard a throat clear.

"How do you look?" he asked.

"I look like I can't stay in here much longer without someone coming."

"You got that right," he mumbled. Papers shuffled on his side. He was working while telling me to finger myself. A true multitasker. "Stroke your clit and all the way down to that beautiful hole." I groaned, my cheek caressing the phone. "Keep going. Work your clit. Go around it twice, then over the top."

I did, and the heavenliness came as much from my own touch as the knowledge I obeyed him. "Oh, Jonathan."

"Put two fingers in."

My pussy clenched around my fingers, kissing them, sucking them in. The heel of my hand found my clit as I pushed my fingers in and out.

He whispered, "Tomorrow night, when I see you, I'm going to put my fingers in you and lick you until you beg me to stop. Then I'm going to squeeze your clit with my lips until you come again."

"I want you."

"You will have me."

"May I come?" There was a distinct possibility he'd say no, and I was so far gone, holding off my orgasm would hurt. "Please let me come." His silence tormented me. "Please, sir." I smiled a little. I never thought I'd actually want to call a lover *sir*. But it felt good, and right, and fun.

I heard his smile as he said, "You may."

I pressed my whole hand along my wet cleft, feeling everything from the tingle around my pussy to the powerful ache at my clit, back and forth, slowly. My breathing got hard and short. I had to keep it down. If I could hear myself, someone else could as well. I closed my eyes and buckled. My hand left the mirror as my back arched, encompassing me in heat from my knees to my waist. I bit my lip to keep from crying out. My hips pumped as pleasure washed over me in impossibly long waves. The phone dropped to the carpet.

Chapter 2

Jonathan

I heard the phone hit the floor, and her groans fill the room. I looked out the window onto the parking lot otherwise known as the 710 freeway and imagined her touching herself. I imagined her expression, her smell as she writhed on the floor enough to drop the phone, all while wearing some elastic and satin configuration. A shiver went down my spine. I felt connected to her when I commanded and she obeyed. It was as close to touching her as I could get.

"Jonathan?" she whispered.

"How are you feeling?"

"I want to curl up next to you and go to sleep."

"Have I told you how amazing you are? You please the hell out of me."

She didn't answer right away. My little goddess of Echo Park must have been smiling. "Wait until you see the underpants I just made a mess of. They're gonna please you plenty."

"Buy everything."

The next pause wasn't as pleasant. "I want to talk about this."

"We can talk tomorrow. I'll pick you up at five."

"Are we going to lie in bed and watch the Dodgers lose game six?"

"You're not supposed to ask a man where he's taking you." She grumbled. My goddess was a big baseball fan. She probably thought I hadn't noticed or had forgotten.

After she'd left the previous morning, when I drifted off to sleep with her humming and stroking my hair, I leaned back in my office chair, looking out the window and thinking of her. Hours later, I called her and asked her on a date.

"A real date?" she'd asked. "Like dinner or a movie or something?"

"I know a nice place. We'll have some wine. Good food. You know, like people do." I'd looked out over the Hollywood Hills. I had to see her again. I had an ache for her that phone calls and texts wouldn't satisfy. It started the minute she left and had grown to uncontrollable levels in the hours since.

"Well, that's fine and all," she'd said, "but just so you know, I don't fuck on the first date."

I'd been laughing when my assistant came in. I indicated she should sit and took the schedule she offered me. "I need you to get something to wear," I said into the phone.

"Oh, not again."

"Again and again. I'm in a meeting." I looked over my schedule for the next day. "Can I text you?"

"You're avoiding my refusal."

"I won't be late. So be ready. *Dressed* and ready."

"Thanks for the clarification."

"You're welcome."

I'd tossed the phone aside, glanced at my schedule, and glanced at Kristin. "I have a meeting with my ex-wife at six thirty?"

"You said to take any meeting she wanted."

"I did. Cancel the meeting and cancel the standing order. She goes on the schedule like everyone else." Kristin shook her foot and nodded, her body a barrel of emotional tells. She was so transparent, I had no idea how she'd gotten through Vassar without those bitches eating her alive. "Yes?"

"Are you making your lunch with Eddie tomorrow, or do you want to meet Gerald Deritts from Council 12? He called and had an opening on the mixed-use ordinance."

"Cancel Eddie."

"Sheila's stuck on the 405. She's added this to the agenda." She'd handed me a folder.

"Ah, our trust," I'd murmured as I flipped through it. When we got engaged, I set up a trust for Jessica that provided for everything she needed. Though she had taste and social standing, she couldn't manage a dollar. When we divorced, I'd intended to revoke her benefits, but never had. I'd been such a pussy. I'd told myself she hadn't taken a dime from me because I needed to believe it. The withdrawals didn't hurt me, but she'd continued to take money from the trust, and I owned the building her studio was in and didn't charge her rent. There were other incidentals I'd probably forgotten. "Tell Sheila I want to review all my financial entanglements with my ex-wife.

Book that for next week."

Kristen had pursed her lips. I could have asked her what was on her mind, but it wasn't worth a conversation. Her crush was cute when I'd hired her, but it was getting less so. I'd said no, I didn't want to sleep with her. Further conversation about that, or why I wouldn't bend over backward to see Jessica anymore, would be unproductive.

After dismissing Kristin, I'd tried to get back to work, but my thoughts were consumed with Monica. In anticipation of our date the next day, I opened an account at Bordelle for her. When I texted her the info, she shot back...

—*An account? For all the girls?*—

—*Just opened it. Go. For me.*—

The next day, she called me from the dressing room to thank me, and I couldn't help it. I had to have her, and I did. She got on her knees when I told her to. She slipped easily into play and out again, becoming her witty, intelligent self seamlessly. She wasn't intimidated by me. She teased and challenged me. She kissed like she meant it, and from the very first night, she enjoyed fucking without reservation or shame.

Monica was, in a word, perfect.

Chapter 3

Monica

I was bag laden as I walked to the café. Jonathan had called Bordelle and told them to wrap up everything I'd put in the dressing room. So I went to Nordstrom's and got my own goddamn dress. I hoped he liked it because it set me back two weeks' tips, a lot of money for something that would end up draped over the chair on his porch. But I needed to feel right with myself. I accepted him as a dominant in bed, and that worked out very well for us. In the outside world, I was my own woman.

Except for the eight hundred dollars in lingerie.

I rushed to the entrance of Terra Café. Yvonne sat at a patio table with her fourteen-month-old, scooping ice cream out of a cup.

"Girl," she said as we hugged, "where the hell have you been shopping? And what's with the shoes?"

I tipped my foot to make the red sole visible. I wore the shoes I'd gotten at Barney's more often than I should, but letting them sit at the bottom of my closet seemed a crime. Yvonne looked at me sidelong while she scooped ice cream. Her afro was teased to four times the size of her head, her eyes lined with gold, and her lips painted the exact chocolate color of her skin. She was simply gorgeous.

"You like them?" I asked.

"I know what they cost, so I know where you got them. So whether or not I like them depends."

I sat down and ordered a green tea and a chocolaty cake thing. Aaron, in his striped shirt and overalls, sat with his mouth open. Vanilla ice cream dripped out of the corners of his mouth like he was a dairy vampire.

"I'm sorry about your friend," she said. "Were you close?"

"She was like a sister to me." I felt a little hitch in my throat, a sob pushing up from my gut. I swallowed it. I didn't cry in public. In private, the past few days had been a rush of tears and beaten-back sorrow. "Anyway. It's fine. I'm dealing with it. Still haven't cleared out her room. But anyway... how's school? It's your last year, right?"

"Tryna get my thesis accepted. Thinking about doing gender instead of race. Something with women's bodies and politics."

"Sexual intersections." My tea came.

"Oh, that's good." She scraped the bottom of the cup. "Now, I didn't ask you to lunch to talk about UCLA."

"The weather, then?"

"My boss? Your former boss? The hot motherfucker? Six two? Medium build? Reddish brown up top... and down below?"

"Not in front of the baby."

"I hear he's a freak." I spit my tea. "Well," she continued, "word gets around. So..." She slithered in her chair. "What. The. Fuck?"

"Yvonne, really. Totally inappropriate." I looked at her over my cup, wishing for a quick and painless death. I'd known she wanted to ask me about Jonathan, but I didn't know she was aware of his proclivities.

"He's really private about who he's..." She stopped herself. "... who he's spending time with. But we all saw your picture from the L.A. Mod show in the paper. And it was no secret at your friend's wake."

"I don't know what you'd call us at this point," I answered. Aaron made a long *aaaaaahhh* sound of pure delight. He kicked under the table and the silverware bounced. "He's cute, this baby. You made him?"

"Me and that creep. Can't deny he's a good-looking creep."

"Is he still stalking you?"

"Cops had to come last week. He put a camera at my bedroom window to watch me sleeping. Isn't that sweet? Oh, and he got my bank account information 'to put Aaron's child support right in there' to save me the trouble of going to the bank. I said, man, I hope narcissistic personality disorder isn't genetic."

"I'm sorry to hear that."

"I called you so you could help me with a little escapism, and so far you're a big fail."

I knew she'd ask, and I had prepared boundaries, but she immediately broke them down by revealing the freak rumor. The thing was, I wanted to tell her. I had no one to talk to. Darren didn't want to hear it. Gabby was dead. Debbie and Jonathan were friends. I knew some of my girlfriends better

14

than Yvonne, but none of them had asked about the handsome man at my side at Gabby's wake. They'd raised eyebrows and introduced themselves. I got phone calls, roundabout questions, and invites to parties and gatherings. I refused everyone but Yvonne, probably because she was very up front about demanding information.

"We're having sex," I said. "Tomorrow night, we have a date, which we haven't done yet."

She put a board book in front of Aaron and leaned toward me, folding her long, skinny arms. "You're *having sex*? Who are you, grandma? Come on. I hear he's into whips and chains."

I pressed my lips between my teeth. I would have to deal with the rumors at some point. "I've never seen him hold or use a whip or a chain. Nor have I observed either one of those things in his house or his bedroom. However…" I let my voice trail off and sipped my tea, leading Yvonne along. "I won't deny there may be some truth to those rumors."

"Girl," she said with no little excitement.

I shrugged, wanting to play it off, but Yvonne had come to dish. She wasn't leaving with generalizations and vague admissions. "How is it?" she asked.

"It's incredible."

"Tell me." Her whisper was hoarse with anticipation.

"I can't," I whispered back. "It's not cinematic. It's not exciting unless you're in it. He speaks to me. He tells me what I want before I know it and before I can deny myself. I'm free with him, but not in the way you think." I turned my teacup around in the saucer.

I stopped. I could have said more. I could have told her he dominated me, and I submitted by letting go of everything I expected of myself. I ceded all control, all emotion, all physical boundaries, and in doing so, I found sexual honesty. I felt closer to him than I felt to anyone else because he saw parts of me I didn't. The quivering, weak, fearful parts that I denied existed, he brought out and caressed. Thinking about his demands made me want him again. I crossed my legs, convinced Yvonne wouldn't understand.

Her expression told me I was right. Her face was still, disentangled from the drama surrounding my adventures with a rich man. She wasn't exactly concerned as much as apprehensive. "So where's it going? Serious? Steady thing? Just sex?"

"I don't know."

"How do you feel about it?"

She was definitely not getting an honest answer to that. "Taking it slow. I like being around him. I'm trying to not get too attached, but I don't know if staying detached is working."

Aaron fussed, and Yvonne pulled him out of his chair. He rested his head on her shoulder. "You buy yourself the shoes and underpants?" she asked.

"Of course not. The shoes alone…" I pursed my lips. I didn't like where she was going, and I didn't have the heart to slap her the way I'd slapped Darren.

"I'm gonna ask you something because I like you. You can get your panties in a twist if you want, but you shouldn't."

"I may not answer."

"He abusing you?"

"No!" I cried. "God, Yvonne, what part of what I said makes you think *abuse*?"

My reaction was offense, not for myself, but for Jonathan. She didn't know him. She didn't know us together.

But I couldn't hold her to my level of loyalty. The twisting web of rage in my chest surprised me, though. Was the rage caused by her implication that Jonathan was an abuser? Or because I'd just found out he had a reputation?

Yvonne, who couldn't see my neurons pulsing like machine gun fire, continued, "Kink is often a disguise for abuse and exploitation. I know it's not that way yet. But if you get uncomfortable, will you call me?"

"No." Not only was I not calling her, I wasn't calling anyone. What Jonathan and I did, and how we did it, was private. Having even one person know was making me very uncomfortable.

"Sure, you will. Look, I know how a nice guy can turn into an asshole on the turn of a dime, so all I'm saying is…" Her expression changed, as if what she wanted to say fell dead on her lips. She smiled instead. "I'm totally jealous. If he's *not* abusing you, I might have faith in men again. That's all."

I exhaled a long, lung-emptying breath, as if I'd been holding it. I'd been unfair and insensitive. Yvonne's history included a brother who fondled her and a boyfriend who locked her and their son in the house when he went to work. Of course she was attuned to possible abuse when I came along with bags of expensive clothing and a man who tied me up and spanked me for our pleasure. I pushed my cake toward her. "Eat, please. I have to stay skinny if I want to look good in this shit."

Chapter 4

Jonathan

Long Beach was the absolute last place I wanted to be. The sky was the color of a handful of quarters. Without the sun to warm the air, the wind off the ocean hit cold and hard.

I had to be quick. I had a meeting with the deputy mayor in Century City in two hours, and then I had a date. A real date, where I'd wear a suit and behave myself.

At the Port of Long Beach, the *Faulkner Coalmine* was set to be cataloged, packed up, and sent to a warehouse in Europe, never to be seen again. I'd bought it the night of the Eclipse show. Eclipse shows only ran a week, so the minute the show closed down, my dealer, Hank, had a team in to collect it. Wainwright was surprised, but the check cleared nicely. He showed up at the closing to chat up my dealer, trying to sell more work. Fucking hustler. Obvious how he got her into bed.

Lil pulled up to the warehouse. Hank strode out to meet me. He was six feet tall, early sixties, bald, and wearing a four-thousand-dollar suit. He could tell shit from chocolate, negotiate a deal, take up space at an auction, and determine true worth from hype. More importantly, he understood my taste, which was why he'd been so surprised I wanted that piece.

"Jaydee." He held out his hand. He had on a few big rings and a clunky watch, and his voice was thick with New York. He looked more like a truck driver than an art dealer, and that's why I liked him. He snuck up on people with his knowledge and erudition, and by the time artists and agents realized they weren't dealing with a rube, I had what I wanted.

"Hank." We walked through the warehouse. My companies used the space as a logistics hold for construction materials and imported food. The offices for the people routing it all over the world were inside the warehouse, too.

Hank waved his arm dismissively. "What the fuck did you buy this piece of shit for? You want something to spend your money on, I got a girl with a studio in Compton. Tears in your eyes. Tears."

"You called *me*. And not to question my taste, I presume."

"I question your taste every day."

"Really? Never would have guessed."

Hank stopped outside a conference room door. "It's good work, no question. But I don't know how much of it you saw before you went overpaying while I wasn't looking."

"Almost none."

"Fan-freaking-tastic. Can we not do that any more?"

"I have my reasons."

"Fine," Hank said, obviously annoyed. "Everything's here. All the documentation, the sketches, inspiration, all the history and work that went into the installation. That's what you bought, sight unseen."

"Can we go in now?"

Hank remained in front of the door. "Look, artists are crazy. I never met one who wasn't a little scrambled. Maybe they all got bit by a shithouse rat when they were babies. This? That I got behind this door? I'm thinking of calling the LAPD just so they can have a record of it. But I need your okay first."

"You've really intrigued the hell out of me, Hank."

He opened the door. The room was outfitted with a long table and black office chairs for impromptu meetings with the logistics staff, importers, and customs officials. Every surface was covered with sketches and tiny, three-dimensional mockups. Some cutouts, some collages, some mounted, all numbered to match the catalog.

"I left the good shit on the table, under that black matte," Hank said.

I moved the black cardboard. It was about the size of a placemat, but it hid something bigger than its actual size.

The top sketch was a black quill pen spaghetti scrawl, and only by looking at it carefully could I discern a woman with her throat cut and a blood-spitting dick coming out. The woman had dark hair. I knew who it was.

Next in the stack: her face split open and a target inside.

A gun in her snatch. A dozen knives pinning her to the wall. Hands choking her. Squeezing her breasts blue. Pulling her vagina out. It got worse. The things he fantasized about doing to her body were sickening.

"Is this actual blood?" I asked.

"Your guess is as good as mine. The catalog says 'mixed media.'"

"Thank you for showing me this."

Hank slipped the black cardboard over the drawings so the violence didn't take up the whole room. "Should I shove it up his ass?"

"No. I want you to photograph it first. Then I'll tell you when to burn it."

"Do you know what this cost you?"

"Yes, I do."

He regarded me for a second. "You know the girl."

I held my hand out. "Thanks again, buddy. Make arrangements with your Compton girl if you think it's a fit."

"Will do."

On the way back up the 710, I couldn't think straight, much less work. I'd never wanted to hurt anyone as badly as I wanted to hurt Kevin Wainwright just for putting those images in my head. But he'd done nothing wrong. The purpose of his work was to exorcise his demons. He couldn't be held legally or morally accountable for its content. If he was angry at Monica for walking out on him, he had every right to draw her slashed open if that gave him closure.

So I couldn't call the LAPD, and I couldn't tell Monica. I'd have to admit I bought the thing behind her back, and she wouldn't think well of it. Worse, I could scare her for no reason. I didn't want to scare her. I wanted her to be the same, proud little goddess I knew. I was just going to have to watch her more closely in case they were more than just drawings.

Chapter 5

Monica

I wore one of my new garters, a purple so dark it could be black. Over that was the black lace dress I'd bought at Nordstrom's. The skirt fell just above my knees and the satin lining stopped just above the hem. The neckline was modest, and the sleeves covered my upper arms. It was skin tight but comfortable and classy. He could take me anywhere. I was only a slut underneath the dress.

I braided my hair. I tried to make it special, but I simply didn't have Gabby's skill, and my arms ached by the third try. I did my best, though, same as every day since she died. I wore my hair as a remembrance to her, as if I could call her back and whisper in her ear *I loved you.*

I didn't have a roommate to answer the knock at the door. Times like that made me feel gut-twisting loneliness. I ran out, winding a band around the bottom of the braid. Even though I knew it was Jonathan, I had to look out the window to check first. He leaned on the corner of the porch, looking at the opening of the crawlspace. His brown leather jacket hung over a suit and tie, and his expression was dead serious.

"See something you like?" I asked when I opened the door.

"Your foundation's slipping."

"Have you noticed the hill? And gravity? How they conspire?"

He glanced back at me without moving his body. Fuck, he was gorgeous. "I can get someone to fix it. I'm a real estate developer, you know. I've got guys."

I strode over to him and put my hands on his back. He looked at the foundation critically, as though he was doing calculations in his head. He looked at me again, and I put my fingers in his hair. We stood like that for a second as I drank him in.

"You're beautiful," I said.

"I was just about to say that." He turned and leaned on the railing with his legs spread. I stepped into the opening. He slid his fingers up my thighs, past my hemline, leaving my skin tingling in their wake. When he got to the lace tops of my stockings, he put his hands beneath my ass and stroked me gently.

I leaned down until my nose touched his, gasping when he fondled between my legs lightly. "Jonathan," I whispered, "what are you doing?"

"I just want to know what barriers I'm dealing with here."

"You always stick your hand up a girl's skirt on the first date?"

He caressed the insides of my thighs, keeping his touch soft. "I haven't bothered with an actual date for about nine years." He angled his face so his lips met mine. I put my hands on his neck and kissed him. The tip of his tongue found mine, and we weaved our mouths together until I was a ball of heat and desire.

"I hate to break this up," he said, "but we're on a clock here."

I groaned. I had no idea how I would make it through dinner.

"And you have to get a change of clothes," he said. "Jeans and a jacket."

"Why?"

"Can you let a guy surprise you?" He slapped my ass and pointed to the front door. "Go."

Still smiling from the delicious sting on my butt, I gathered up clothes, stuffed them into a bag, and ran back out to the porch. He'd parked the Jag in my driveway, right behind my little black Honda. He opened the passenger door for me and closed it when I got in. As he drove up the 101, I put my hand on his, stroking the top of it.

"You working tomorrow?" he asked. "Because I have the day off."

"Work, then Frontage."

"Without your partner?" he asked, then waved his hand. "Sorry. Obviously."

"Yeah. I wanted her on the piece with me and the boys, too. But, shit, I miss her."

"What boys and what piece?"

"I'm collaborating with Darren and Kevin."

The car swerved too far right, and he almost had an accident. A horn blared and a middle finger was raised. Jonathan waved in apology. "You were saying?" he asked.

"Don't have an accident." He pulled off at Los Feliz Boulevard. "Where are we going?" I asked.

"Small place in the hills." He turned up into Griffith Park.

"You're not just taking me to your house, are you?"

"No, not *just* my house. I have things planned, and they include my place. Initially." He glanced over at me. "I didn't suggest a date so I could take you back to my room and pin you to the bed."

"Are we going to watch the game from your bed?"

"Nope."

"Damn. Brad Chance is pitching."

"Why bother watching? He's going to overuse his screwball and wear out his elbow by the third inning."

"It's fun watching guys swing at them. Especially Den Adler. He practically falls over," I snickered.

"So," he said definitively, stopping at a light, "you've avoided this 'piece' thing for exactly three minutes, and I've been very good about it."

I put my hands on my knees. "Kevin asked me to collaborate on a thing with him for the B.C. Modern. We're on a tight deadline. I brought Kevin and Gabby in." The light changed to green, and I was relieved of the weight of his stare.

"Why?" he asked.

"Because they're family, and I like working with them."

"Not as a buffer between you and Kevin?"

"No." I wasn't sure if I lied to him or myself.

He pulled the car to a wide space on the side of the road and put it in park. He faced me. "Why did you agree to work with him after what he did at the Eclipse show?"

Layers of emotion masked his face. The top was a cold calm, an understanding bordering on parental. Under that, something wilder, but laser focused and powerful, pushed to the surface. I took a nervous breath. He was pissed, and I'd never seen that before. Goose bumps rose over my arms, and I rubbed my thumbs against my forefingers. I wondered if he could hear the clatter of my heart.

"Having music at the B.C. Modern could make my career. Everyone will hear it. Everyone will review it. It was like being handed a gift, and if I'd refused, I would have regretted it the rest of my life."

"Your ambition outweighs your sense."

I tried to match his anger with my own, but I felt puny and unjustified.

"We were pretty clear that my work is my work. That hasn't changed." I kept my eyes level with his even though I felt the weight of his stare. He didn't like Kevin. I knew that, but I wouldn't abdicate my right to live my life as I pleased.

"Everything's changed, Monica."

"Not that."

With those few words, I felt two wills pressing against each other, hard, straight, still. Nothing moved. No friction was created between them. His hands clenched the wheel, and mine were wound into fists. I couldn't bear it. I touched the top of his hand.

He grabbed the back of the neck and pulled my face to his, drowning me in a kiss so hard and hot, I almost forgot what I'd seen in his expression. What had he seen in mine? That my heart could be broken? That I was falling in love with him, and if I tried to stop, the inertia would crack me in two? I pulled my face off his.

I said, "I know you don't like Kevin."

"Understatement of the year."

"He's harmless. And I'm trustworthy."

"The latter, I believe. But men know other men." He stroked my cheek. "Can you not be alone with him? Can you promise me that?"

It was a lot to ask. Darren was involved, but who knew what situations would arise? I covered his hand with mine. He needed me to make an honest effort. I could do that. "Yes."

"Thank you." He kissed me and got back onto Los Feliz Boulevard. We made the rest of the trip in hand-holding silence. Whatever anger had manifested in his face got pushed away. He pulled into his driveway, and the gate shut behind us with a clang. He walked around the car and opened my door. I had never seen his house in daylight, never seen the art deco woodwork on the windows or the detailing of the roof shingles. He took my hand and led me up to the porch. The front door was open, and he went in, expecting I'd follow. But I stopped at the threshold.

"What?" he asked. "Cat got your feet?"

"I've never entered your house with my clothes on before."

"Ah. Well, first time for everything." He tugged on my hand until I crossed into his house. The living room was as it had always been but bathed in light from the setting sun. If the room could look warmer, more inviting, I didn't know how. He looked back at me and the sunlight dashed off the tips of his eyelashes as he pulled me through rooms and out to the backyard.

The pool was a huge, bean-shaped expanse in the center of the yard. Close to the house, a flower garden, sectioned by paths of flagstones, spanned from the main house to the pool house. Smaller, cozy areas with benches lined the right hedge, and on the left, wall-sized sliding glass doors opened into the sitting room where I'd had tea.

Aling Mira approached us in a modest black suit, carrying a tray of white wine.

"Hi," I said when I took a glass. She nodded and walked toward a little table set for two. A middle-aged man lit the last candle on one of the flagstone paths and then the two on the table. I told Jonathan, "You have a nice yard."

"Come walk with me." He held out his arm, and I took it. We headed toward the pool on the candle-lined path. "Aling Mira cooked a Filipino specialty for you called kare-kare. It's made from—"

"Oxtail stew?"

"You've had it?"

"I live in Los Angeles."

He smiled and squeezed my hand. "She saw you slept in my room. So she's very impressed with you."

"How long has she worked for you?"

"A long, long time. She's seen it all. She wants me to be happy as much as my own mother. Well, maybe an aunt or something."

We strolled around the pool while the staff set up dinner. The sun was setting fast, and the candles lining all the pathways became more visible as the sky darkened.

"You lived here with your wife?"

"Yes. Why?"

"The bed?" I cringed. "Was that…?"

He laughed. "New bed, don't worry. You're the only woman I've had in it, actually."

"I feel like a groundbreaker."

"You've broken some ground on a few things."

"Such as?" I swung to face him.

"This date?"

"And?"

"And showing you off at the L.A. Mod."

24

"And?"

"And taking care of you. And wanting to see you again and again. And dressing you for my eyes."

"You're making me feel very, very good." I kissed him gently and breathed in that leather and sawdust smell that was his choice, not his ex-wife's. "I have to talk about you dressing me."

He put his arms around my waist and pulled me close. "Yes?"

"It makes me uncomfortable when you buy me expensive stuff."

He kissed my jaw and neck, as if to belie my discomfort and turn it into heat. "But the diamond was all right?"

I pursed my lips. "No, it wasn't, but before I could think about it, stuff happened. So you got that one in under the wire. Don't let it happen again."

He put his lips to my ear and said, "I have a piano. A Steinway. Would you play it for me after dinner?"

I kissed him and whispered, "I'd love to."

"And you'd sing for me?"

"Yes." I dragged my lips across his cheek, listening to him breathing and feeling his hands at my waist. The idea of making music for him was so intimate, so arousing, I didn't think I'd be able to make it through dinner.

"When we met, you said you wouldn't," he said.

"Things changed."

"So, you'd take this talent, gifted to you from birth, and use it as an expression of how you feel about me?"

I pulled away. "Aren't you clever."

"Money is a blunt tool for expression. It's vulgar compared to art, I agree, but it's all I have. I want you to accept it. It would make me happy."

I didn't know how to argue without making the gifts he was born with somehow coarse and ugly, while mine were worthwhile enough to give. He really had me cornered. "You just did a number on me," I said.

He bowed. "Captain of the debate team at Loyola."

"Ah, a good Jesuit education," I said, walking away. "I suppose now I get to wear all my new underwear without guilt."

He grabbed my hand and pulled me back. "You said you were Catholic, so you have guilt somewhere."

"Only until eighth grade. I performed 'Invictus' for my graduation recital and earned my escape from parochial school. I entered Los Angeles Unified guilt-free."

He took me in his arms and kissed me. "'Invictus.' Classic. We did that in sixth. Eighth grade was Kipling. 'If.'"

"Oh, that's a long one."

"I had to recite it with *feeling*."

I smiled. "Yes, me too. '*Out of the night that covers me, Black as the pit from pole to pole—*'"

He completed the stanza. "'*I thank whatever gods may be, for my unconquerable soul.*'" He grabbed the base of my braid and pulled my hair as he drew his mouth to mine. He was so sweet. His kisses were hard and passionate, a controlled lack of restraint in every flick of his tongue, every grasp of his fingers. I pushed into him, feeling his erection against me. He pulled away at the sound of a throat clearing.

Aling Mira stood behind me. "I'm sorry to interrupt. You said I should let you know when dinner is ready."

"Thank you," Jonathan said. He rattled something off in Tagalog. Aling Mira nodded to each of us and went back to the middle-aged man who stood in a secluded area.

"What did you say?" I asked.

"I thanked her and gave her the rest of the night off." He put his hand on my back. "I'm perfectly capable of spooning you stew. And I'd like to."

We strode slowly to a table set with silver and porcelain. On the side table was a full setting with stew in a silver serving bowl. Aling Mira and the man went to a back gate.

"Who's the guy?"

"Her husband, Danilo. They live in the back house."

The metal gate clacked behind them, and we were alone in the yard. Jonathan pulled a chair out for me. I stood in front of it, between him and the table. I was ready to sit, but I wanted another kiss. I tilted my face to him, until I felt his breath on my face, and parted my lips.

He reached for me, and I thought he would put his arms around my waist. Instead, he met my lips with his and leaned into me. In one wave of his arm, he yanked the tablecloth, knocking the dishes off the table. They clattered everywhere, smashing and spinning. His weight continued forward, throwing more plates out from under me, until he pinned me to the table.

I opened my legs, wrapping them around him as we kissed. My dress rode up to my waist. I pushed into him. His cock was so hard, like a tight fist against me. He groaned into my mouth, then pushed his fist of a dick into me again. He fingered under the garter belt, twisting his fingers in it.

"I want you to wear these all the time. Under jeans. To bed when I'm not there. I'll buy you more. You be who you want when we're not together, but under your clothes, this is the reminder that you're mine. Understand?"

"Yes."

He unbuckled his pants. A shiver went up my spine as I watched him take his dick out. My panties were no more than a damp string at my crotch, and he pushed them out of the way, handling me roughly. His fingertips probed for my soaked opening. He jammed two fingers in me. I cried out in pleasure and spread my legs farther, kicking a bowl and sending it crashing to the ground.

"You're ready," he growled, sliding his fingers out and jamming them in all the way. He ran his finger across the front wall of my hole until I felt a shudder I'd never felt. He pushed, stroking, curving his finger over a hard nodule of nerves inside me while pressing the heel of his hand on my clit. I went weak with a radiation of pleasure.

"Do you want it?" he asked.

"Yes, Jonathan. Please, fuck me." He removed his fingers and lodged his dick in me. "Oh, God," I said, barely coherent.

He moved above me, his every stroke hitting the mark, bringing breaths of gratification. He put his fingers in my mouth, and I sucked on them, tasting myself. His dick spread me, pushing against my clit, the edge of my opening, and sending shockwaves through me as his thrusts found their rhythm. He removed his fingers and pulled my leg over his shoulder. He went so deep, I cried out. I pushed forward, wanting him inside me, a part of me. I was so close, and as though he could sense it, he slowed down.

"Take it easy, little goddess."

"Oh, I can't. I'm going to come."

"No, wait."

"I can't." I was desperate, on the edge of a cliff, a rope tied to my ankle and a boulder. The boulder was tipping over the edge of the cliff, and I would follow it to the bottom of the crevice.

"'Invictus.' Second stanza, Monica." He leaned over, still moving his hips. "Do it. '*In the fell clutch of circumstance...*' Slowly and with feeling, or you start over." His voice was a beacon of control and sense in the chaos of his every stroke, every inch a burning fuse to an explosion.

"You're joking," I gasped. "I can't recite 'Invictus' now."

He leaned down and sucked my nipple, leaving a trail of saliva when he looked up and said, "Do it."

Oh, God, how could he expect me to recall eighth grade while getting fucked on a dinner table? I had to stare through the pressure to give in to my orgasm, hold it back to remember. "'*In the fell clutch of circumstance, I have not winced nor cried aloud. Under the bludgeonings of chance.*' Oh fuck, Jonathan…"

He pinned my hands over my head and started on the next line. "'*My head is bloody…*' And no rushing, baby." His thrusts got faster, deeper, more willed.

I picked up, "'*But unbowed. Beyond this place of wrath and tears, looms the horror of the shade, and yet the menace of the years…*'"

"Ah, Monica. Go. Make it." His face was reddened with effort. He wanted to come too, and that, coupled with his searing thrusts, sent the boulder over the edge.

"'*Finds and shall find me unafraid,*'" I cried to the heavens. He moved to the rhythm of the poem as I continued, watching that boulder get smaller in the distance. "'*It matters not how straight the gate, how charged with punishments the scroll.*'"

He said the last stanza with me. "'*I am the master of my fate. I am the captain of my soul.*'"

"Yes, Monica."

"Yes!"

I was dragged off the cliff first. I cried out his name as I fell into a chasm of blackness and tingling lights. I clenched my thighs around him. My arms wanted to flail, but he had them tight as my pussy ignited, clutching for him, pulsing for him to be deeper. The orgasm came from deep inside, undulating up my spine and down the backs of my thighs. I lost myself in it.

I heard him grunt, miles away, then moan into a snarl of satisfaction. I gasped as he tightened above me, the base of his cock pulsing as he came. His eyes squeezed shut and his arms bent as he let go of my wrists and fell on top of me.

We twitched together, spent, still breathing in the rhythm of a poem.

Chapter 6

Jonathan

I'll cop to having plenty of sex, much of it of the "wild" variety. I'll admit I have memories that would beat most men's imaginations. I'll tell you I've had beautiful women do exactly as I tell them and we've gotten off on the control. But that? That was a new classification of fucking.

"Jonathan?" she whispered from under me. Her uttering my name brought me to my senses. I pulled my face out of her neck and kissed her collarbone.

"Monica."

"Are you all right?"

"No," I said.

"Really?"

I put my nose to hers. "Joking." My shifted weight made my cock drop out of her.

"Ah," she moaned as if she'd miss it. "I should use the bathroom."

"I'll set up dinner in the kitchen."

She smiled, and my world went on fire. "Let's eat it this time."

I got off her and she sat up. Her hair was falling out of her braid and the hem of her dress was bunched around her waist. One shoe had fallen off. I found it and slipped it back onto her foot, then helped her off the table.

"Thank you," she said.

"My pleasure." I kissed her because I had no choice. When she walked toward the house, I touched her neck as if I needed to tether her to me for another second. I brought the stuff on the sideboard into the kitchen and set the table. I had a handful of silverware and stopped myself.

Fork on the left, spoon above.

Or if it was a soup spoon, did it go on the right?

If she noticed I'd done it wrong, she'd tease me. I'd like that enough to throw her across the table again, which was not what I wanted to do. We didn't have all night, and I wanted to actually share a meal with her. I put the spoons on the right and set the tureen between the bowls.

I liked her. She was great. Outstanding. Gorgeous and smart. All those words seemed cheap, though. My rejection of them alarmed me, because they weren't good enough. I was losing control, and I needed to figure out why.

The lack of a condom was definitely something, but only part of the story. The fact that we were far enough along to feel each other's skin spoke volumes. Her looks were something also. She was beautiful, but not my type. I usually went for blondes, so maybe not. Her singing that night at Frontage ticked it up a few notches for me, but I had fucked other artists since Jessica. Monica was honest, real, and honorable. Those were commodities I didn't see every day, and those were words worthy of her, but those qualities didn't seduce the mind or calm the heart the way she did.

I forgot where the napkins went. Fuck. Where was Aling Mira when I needed her?

The issue with Monica was obvious, but I wouldn't allow myself to utter certain words, even in my mind. Certain commitments and feelings were simply inaccessible and needed to stay that way. I'd rejected my ex-wife, but the passions she'd thrown away were dead. I regretted that, grieved their loss, because if anyone deserved true, deep feelings, Monica did.

An honorable man would have given her up before she fell in love, choosing a small hurt over a bigger one later. But I wasn't that honorable. I wanted her more than I'd wanted anything in a long time, and I would have her until she couldn't bear it any longer.

I felt like an animal.

I heard her clopping down the hall in those cheap, sexy shoes. When she came into the kitchen, I sighed. Her hair was down, except for a thin braid at the side of her head. She was well put together, yet she looked like someone had just fucked the shit out of her. I held out my hand and she took it.

"I'm starving," she said.

I pulled out the chair for her. She glanced at the setting and said nothing. Instead, she tilted her head to see what was inside the tureen. What made me think she even cared where soup spoons went? She made me unsure about the simplest things.

She sat. "That looks good."

I ladled her stew, and then mine. She put her napkin on her lap and waited for me to sit before she took a scoop and blew on it.

"I'm sorry. I think it's pretty cold," I said.

"Ooh, good, she used banana blossoms." She pointed her spoon at a smaller dish. "Is that pinakbet?"

"Yes." I speared a piece of okra and held it to her lips. She parted them, allowed the fork in her mouth, and slid it out, her teeth barely scraping the silver tines.

"That's nice," she said, chewing.

"Have you been to the Philippines?" I asked.

She smirked. "I've been to Mexico."

"No farther?" I placed another forkful of pinkabet before her.

"No." She took the food I offered.

I poured wine for us. "I'm surprised. You seem more... worldly than that."

She shrugged. I noticed a little redness around her ears. "I'm not sheltered. There're plenty of ways to get into trouble in a thirty-mile radius."

"Do tell." She shrugged and took a spoonful of stew. "Come on," I said. "We'll make a trade. I'll tell you something that will make you run away if you tell me how to get into trouble in Los Angeles." The way she glanced at me made me think she had something more than a harmless exchange of stories on her mind. She obviously didn't realize the depth and breadth of the stories I could tell without touching the things I didn't want her to know.

"Deal," she said.

"Ladies first."

She took a sip of wine and straightened her shoulders, as if daring me to think less of her. Then she swallowed a little too hard, and I knew that down deep, she was afraid I might. I tried to remain impassive, but I was jumping out of my skin.

"One time..." she said, then paused.

"Go on."

"I shot up heroin."

I tried not to choke on my wine. "How was it?"

"Incredible."

"Really? And just the once? I don't get a whole story? Just six words and an adjective?"

"I'm gauging your reaction."

"I went to private schools. My friends financed dealers and producers to ensure their own product flow. So," I poured more wine, "how does a beautiful Catholic girl end up with a needle in her arm?"

"I've been tested since, you know. I'm clean."

I didn't say another word. I held out another bit of pinkabet, which she took. I was going to feed her until she told me about this tiny crevice of her life.

"Ok, well." She swallowed. "It was, like, the core of a laugh. You know that wavy good feeling you have inside before the laugh comes out? But the laugh is a release from that feeling, and when you're done laughing, it goes away. So without the laugh, and the release, it got huge. It kind of started in my heart and worked outward like a supernova and stayed there. Imagine that feeling, that happy feeling before you laugh, being big and *staying*. I was lying down, but I was flying, and at the same time. Well, at first it was just the good pre-laugh feeling, but then the tension came and I wanted it released, because it was painful. Emotionally painful. Like, if the tension got too much, and it broke, so much sorrow would come out."

She paused and took a sip of wine, not looking at me. "When I came down, I puked and I felt like crap. I mean, who wouldn't, right? But I knew the first time is the only really great time, and I didn't want to end up some sick addict. Not even to be Janis Joplin."

"But why do it in the first place?"

"Kevin… I know you're his biggest fan. He and I used to do things just to experience them. Just to see, you know, if there was something to it, or if we could translate it into our work. So we did some stupid things."

"But he never tied you to a bedpost?"

"No."

"He's a sad man."

She laughed. "We ran with our eyes closed. We walked through downtown barefoot. We slept on Skid Row a whole weekend."

I think I let the silence go a little too long. I was thinking about her huddled in filth under an overpass, broken glass underneath her, and strange, unstable people within arms' reach.

"What?" she asked, sipping her wine.

"Did he *sleep*? When you were on Skid Row?"

"I guess."

I took her hand. "I couldn't sleep knowing you weren't a hundred percent safe. I couldn't walk you into danger or watch someone put a needle full of drugs in your arm. I couldn't rest."

"Well, good, because the piss smell kept me up and I was hungry. Speaking of, I'm going to eat more oxtail stew, and you're going to tell me something that makes me want to walk out. Except I won't."

She took a spoonful of stew and glanced at me, so sure her feelings could survive any revelation. I had so many wonderfully juicy stories that wouldn't even half nudge her out the door. So many others would require a discussion that would ruin the evening.

I asked, "Are sexual escapades on the table?"

"Sure." She looked into her bowl. Maybe that was a bad idea. I didn't want her to get bent out of shape. If she told me a story like the one I intended to tell her, I'd get bent out of shape.

"Are you sure you're sure?"

"As long as your wife isn't in there."

"Why? Besides the fact that she's not the escapade type?"

"I'm not going to pretend your ex-wife's my favorite person ever. But to me, what goes on sexually in a marriage, you don't talk about. So—" she put her hands over her ears "—la la la, don't want to hear it."

In the five minutes I had to decide what to tell her, I'd prepared a story of bedding three women at once. It was absolutely true, terribly unsexy, and funny all at once. But she'd thrown me by respecting a woman who'd lied to her and caused her hurt, by honoring a vow she'd had no part of. Monica deserved better than a canned story I'd told a hundred times at the club.

I took her wrists and pulled her hands from her ears. She smiled at me.

"I agree," I said. "You're safe from my marriage bed. But not the rest." I took my hands away and picked up my wine glass, taking a deep breath. "There's a difference between a dominant and a pig."

"Really?"

"My father," I said, leaning forward, "is a pig." She looked as though she was ready to choke on her oxtail stew. "You all right?" I asked.

"I'm fine. I sense an example coming?"

"I hit puberty early," I said. "By thirteen, I was done. Close to my fourteenth birthday, my father wanted to know why I hadn't gotten laid yet."

She chewed, then gazed up me with those big, chocolate disks. "Okay?"

"He set me up on a date with a girl. Woman. Rachel. She was a couple of years older than me. That was my first time. And guess what? Turns out, she was his mistress."

She swallowed hard. "How old was she?"

"The math you just did in your head was correct."

"Wow. He whored out his underage mistress?"

"To his underage son. Like I said. Pig. And you should see the look on your face." Her heartbeat was practically audible. She pushed food around and I worked to control my nerves.

She sighed heavily. "Honestly, I didn't expect you to even have a story like that."

"You think rich people don't have sick shit in their houses?"

She raised her eyebrows and swirled her spoon in her stew. "Something like that."

I laughed. Partly because I was nervous about voicing a fragment of the story, and partly because I was relieved she hadn't run away. Not yet, at least.

She put her spoon down and sipped her wine. "Did you see her again?"

"I did but on different terms. It was messy for a while." I cleared my throat. "She died."

"Oh, I'm so sorry. How?"

"Car accident. I was about sixteen when it happened."

I should have shut up way before mentioning the accident. If she looked into it, I was deeply fucked. So I stopped talking. Just stopped.

She waited, slid off her chair, stepped over to me, and put her hands on my face. "You know you have to tell me the whole thing, right?"

"There is no more." I put my hand up her skirt until I felt the lacy top of her stocking. "You're going to have to take the dress off for where we're going next."

"Upstairs?"

I put my fingers under the lace and up the garter straps. "Nope."

"Where?"

"Have you finished dinner?"

"Yes."

I pulled her down, kissing her hard. She tasted of lovingly made Filipino food and cold white wine. I wanted her all over again, but we had someplace to be.

Chapter 7

Monica

I slipped into my jeans, keeping my fancy underwear on. I felt filthy, sexy, sensual with garters under denim. When I reached the front foyer, I found the door open and a loud rumbling in the driveway.

Jonathan straddled a matte black rocket of a motorcycle with red touches at the rims. The back seat was suspended by nothing but air and the promise of velocity.

"Well," I said as I clopped down the porch stairs in my heels, "is this new or is it some old thing you found in the back of the garage?"

"I got rid of the Mercedes and saw this." He handed me a helmet in the same matte black as the bike. "You've ridden before?"

"Yeah." I slipped on the helmet. I'd dirtbiked with Kevin in the Sequoias until mud covered me from knee to toe and I walked like a cowboy coming home from a week on a feisty mare. Once, in freshman year, Ivan Ikanovitch took me out to Ventura on his new BMW. Needless to say, I had to take a cab home.

"Let's go then, little goddess. This trip usually takes forty minutes, and we have thirty five."

I slid onto the back seat and put my arms around his waist. "You shoulda let me recite 'Invictus' as fast as I wanted. We'd be on time."

The gate slid open as if by his thought waves alone, and we took off, my legs clenching the seat and my arms clutching his waist. When we stopped at a light, I heard his voice in my head.

"You're cutting off my circulation."

The clarity of his voice was shocking, and he turned to me, tapping the helmet.

"There are microphones in here?" He nodded. "Fancy."

The light changed, and we took off. We didn't talk much as we zipped onto the five, turning onto the 110 freeway. I tried not to squeal when he went really fast since he could hear me. Instead, I leaned on him, enjoying the softness of his leather jacket and the way it creaked against mine. Even though it was early November, the air was warm as it whipped under my clothes.

Another piece of the puzzle fell into place. He was fourteen when his father loaned him his mistress. His first sexual experience was coated in familial ties and discomfort. He went to the institution when he was sixteen, right about when she was killed. He'd given me a portion of the story. His time in the institution had something to do with his father's promiscuity and penchant for young girls, as well as his absurd expectations of his son's virility.

I was still missing some puzzle pieces. Something was very seriously off, but his explanation was a start, and I felt a sort of relief knowing that eventually, when he was ready, he'd fill in the blanks.

We traveled eighty miles an hour past the industrial tinkertoy skyline and outlet malls with their blindingly bright, sky-high screens, blasting high above neighborhoods still burned out from the riots, and back to a middle-class residential zone.

I slipped my hand under his jacket, then under his shirt. I felt his taut stomach and the little hairs on it, the warmth of his skin making me feel safe and cared for.

"Are you making a pass at me?" he asked in my head.

"Not at this speed."

"Okay, because I'm having you in a couple of hours."

"I know." I leaned my head on his back. "You're a big ho."

"Only for you these days."

I hoped my sigh wasn't audible through the microphone. I knew I was choosing to believe him, and that choice was conscious, and thus, fallible. I knew he could walk out on me at any minute, for any reason. If he really was over his wife, he could look for a more permanent mate with whom he had more in common, like money, and social standing, and similar friends and interests.

But I chose, maybe unwisely, to believe he wanted me for more than a short time because it made me happy to think it.

I was screwed.

He turned off the freeway at Carson, and after a few more quick pivots, he slowed in front of a grassy, floodlit field where a blimp was parked.

"We made it," he said, pulling up to the chain-link fence around the field's perimeter. A man in a white shirt and vinyl jacket approached us with a clipboard. Jonathan took off his helmet. His hair was a complete wreck, a school of wild-armed starfish backlit by floodlights. He fingerbrushed it and faced the man with the clipboard.

"Mister Drazen?"

"Yeah."

"You just made it. Park the bike in the lot to the left. Have fun."

"How are they doing?" asked Jonathan. I took off my helmet. I could only imagine what my hair looked like. A bunch of broken strings in the same backlighting, no doubt. And the little braid I'd left coming from my part probably looked like a dreadlock.

"Down two in the second. Having trouble getting men on base," the man with the clipboard said.

Jonathan shook his head and started the bike again. We cruised to the center of the lot and parked by a sheet metal trailer held up by a cinderblock foundation. He put the kickstand down and leaned the bike over until it was stable.

"What was that?" I asked, dismounting first. "The game? They're losing already?"

He got off and set the bike straight. "Apparently."

"Are we going on the blimp?"

"If you're good."

"And we're going to Dodger Stadium? Maybe? I don't want to assume, but the second blimp always comes about the fifth inning." I was trying to keep my shit together, but I'd lived my whole life in the Stadium's backyard and had never found a way to even get into a playoff game. When I knew the right people, the team had been in the basement. During good years, I'd been hanging with people who didn't "do" sports because organized team activities were uncreative, uncivilized, and boorish.

"Yes," Jonathan said. "We're going to see the game from the sky if you move that tight little ass. They won't wait."

I jumped on him. I couldn't help it. I'm only made of flesh and blood, and that blood is Dodger blue. I kissed his face and wrapped my legs around him. He caught me, hitched me up by the backs of the knees, and started for the blimp. The white noise was deafening, and before he let me down, I said in his ear, "Thank you."

He took my hand, smiling as if he was pleased to see me so happy, and we ran across the grass to the huge machine. It was bigger than I'd imagined. Massive. Overwhelming. A tire company's name was written across it in letters two or three times my height. I couldn't hear any of the men who greeted us, but I put on my customer service smile. In this case, it couldn't have been more genuine.

We were hustled into a gondola with six seats facing front. The two at the windshield were pilot and copilot. Jonathan and I were guided in behind that, and behind us were two men who appeared to be businessmen. We were surrounded by windows, but Jonathan made sure I got the seat closest to a view. I jumped in. I wanted to talk to him, but it was simply too loud. The copilot gave us headphones with mikes on them.

I heard Jonathan say, "Can you hear me?"

"Yes," I replied. "Can you hear me?"

"Loud and clear."

"Baby," I said, smiling until I felt my face might snap in two, "I'm a sure thing tonight."

Everyone in the cabin cracked up. Of course they could all hear me. Jonathan put his arm around me and pulled me to him, kissing my forehead while he laughed. I buried my head in his chest.

"Don't worry, miss," said the pilot, his voice loud and clear. "We get that a lot." After a pause, he continued. "I'm Larry. This here is my copilot, Rango. We'll be heading for East Los Angeles in a few seconds, set to arrive at Dodger Stadium in about forty minutes. Hold on, takeoff can be a little jarring for first timers. Buckle in."

The noise got even louder. I found my buckles and strap. Jonathan helped me click in, then he took my hand. Seconds later, I felt as if I was being launched from a rocket. Larry turned a wooden steering wheel set between his seat and Rango's.

"I'll have the game on," Rango chimed in. "We're in the bottom of the fourth against the New York Yankees. Cashen is pitching for the Yanks as we speak."

I closed my eyes and heard Jonathan's voice. "Open your eyes. These flights are hard to get, even for me."

I opened them and looked at him in the darkened cabin. He touched my cheek and smiled, and I felt protected and secure. Even if it was an illusion, knowing he was there made me feel less like I was shooting out a cannon and more like I was on a fun trip I wouldn't have dreamed up for myself.

The city spread beneath us in a blanket of lights made of a plaid of streets, freeways, and floodlit parks. I couldn't tear my eyes away. We were low enough to see cars and people but high enough to turn them into dots of velocity and intention. Everyone was headed somewhere, and we were above, passing in the wind.

The game wasn't going well for my team. I listened without discussion as another inning went by with three men stranded on base, a pitcher who threw balls that were fouled off until I knew he must be exhausted, and a beaner that may have left star hitter Jose Inuego with a concussion.

I felt Jonathan leaning over me to see the window. He rested his chin on my shoulder, then his lips landed on my neck. Leaning there, we looked out the window together. The gondola chilled as the minutes went by, and though we had jackets, I put my hand on his and found his fingers icy. I moved one of his hands between my knees to warm it and folded the other in mine. We stayed like that, looking out the window, his chest to my back, his chin on my neck, and his hands warmed by my body, until I saw Elysian Park. I probably could have picked my house out from there.

"Look!" I sounded like a kid. "I can see it!"

It seemed to take as long to get over the stadium from the moment I saw it as it took for us to get to Los Angeles from Carson. Another blimp passed us, heading away from the game. Larry and Rango waved at the pilots. I was filled with contentment and a feeling of rightness, of being a part of something bigger than myself. I'd only felt that during orchestra practice in college, and only when everything was going right. The percussionist was spot on, the conductor spoke in a manual language as easy to understand as the written word, and we all followed as if lifted by the same tide.

As the feeling slipped away, I wanted nothing more than to recapture it. I pulled my headphones off and faced Jonathan. His eyes were visible from the lights on the pilot's dashboard. He pulled his microphone out of the way. I kissed him, and I didn't care who saw. I molded my lips to his and fed him my tongue. He took his hand from between my knees and put it to my cheek, warmed from my body, gentle to the touch. I extended that feeling of rightness for another minute until the gondola seemed to blaze with light.

I opened my eyes. We were right over the stadium. I took one last look at Jonathan and mouthed the words, *Sure thing.*

He mouthed back, *I know,* and I smiled.

I'd never seen a game like that before, and I found it disconcerting initially. I was used to television, where I could see every twitch and nod of the pitcher, and live games from the bleachers, where I could tell the direction of the ball from the sound it made coming off the bat. From the blimp, the players looked like white flowers on a perfect lawn.

I put my headphones back on and leaned into the window. The announcer was going on about pitch counts and men on base, and I heard the guys in the gondola doing much the same. The Yanks were up. Men on first and third. One out. Harvey Rodriguez was on deck.

Larry cut the engine, and the noise reduced. "We're gonna hover until a commercial, then fire it up again."

Jonathan put his lips to my ear. "Rodriguez is a lefty. They're going for a double play. Watch the infield." The shortstop and third baseman took two steps toward first. "They step toward right field because a lefty pulls that way, and forward to get the ball on the jump so they can pop it to second on the force play. And they're playing it a little forward because there's a guy on third who can go for the steal on a wild pitch or a sac fly."

"But what if the fly is shallow? They'll miss it, and it'll be a mess. The outfield just came in a little, too. I mean, Rodriguez barely has to work to sac a guy in."

"You take your chances. They're down by two, so if a guy strolls home on a sac fly, it's a bummer, but there's not much difference in the middle of the game between being down two and down three. There's more to gain with the double play."

Rodriguez walked. Bases were loaded. Some moments in a ball game were more important than others. They weren't the grand slams or the fat, bobbling errors at shortstop. They were the bases-loaded, one-man-out moments where either someone scored or someone was stopped dead. They were unpredictable, uncontrollable, and oftentimes silent as death. Like the one extra foul ball that would have been a third strike. Or the pitcher catching the line drive that would have sent a man or two home. Or a walk to load the bases.

"I can't watch." I covered my eyes. I couldn't see anything from up there anyway. I just saw dots move around and heard the broadcast. But Jonathan reached from behind me and took my wrists, pulling them down.

"Come on. Play with me. Don't bail."

"Yes, sir," I said, joking on his use of the word *play*. The infield moved way in, practically to where the dirt met the grass, and Jonathan's arms tightened. His hands, now warm, draped over my crossed forearms. "I know they're playing in to catch the guy at home plate if they have to," I said.

"Yes." He kissed my neck once, twice, three times, each one softer than the one before. Each lingered longer than the last. I tingled all over, and it took all my self-control to keep from bending my head back and leaning into him. I would have looked exactly like what I was: a woman in heat.

We were interrupted by the crack of a bat through the headphones we'd taken off. The white flowers scuttled across the lawn. The shortstop fielded the ball, got it to second, and then Val Renault, an unimposing fielder known for his hitting, got the ball out of his hand and to first quickly and accurately enough to complete the double play.

Inning over.

An hour and a half later, the game ended with the Dodgers winning by a run and forcing a seventh game. The six passengers on the gondola erupted at the last out. We high-fived and cheered and headed back to Carson.

Chapter 8

Monica

I was a little wobbly getting off the gondola, but Jonathan put his arm around me and pulled me close as we went back to the bike. We thanked the employees we passed as they got the blimp back into place with ropes and pulleys. If their attitudes were any indication, managing a tire company's blimp was the most gratifying job in the world.

We approached the bike holding hands. "Thank you," I said. "That was probably in my top five dates ever."

"Top *five?*"

"Top four, maybe."

He faced me. "What?"

I shrugged. "It was a compliment."

He pressed his lips between his teeth. Before I could decide if he was suppressing rage or laughter, he ducked and thrust forward, throwing me over his shoulder. I squealed and kicked, bouncing as he ran. He pushed me against the side of the metal shed with a clang, pressing my shoulders to the wall.

"Name your top three. I'll beat them."

"With what?" I asked.

"I'll take you to the fucking moon and have you back in time for bed."

"Oh, Jonathan. The moon? Really?" I rolled my eyes.

He just smiled, all teeth and joy. "You're getting such a spanking tonight."

"Kiss me first," I said. "Maybe you'll get in the top three."

He took my hands and yanked them over my head, then kissed me. Or to be more accurate, he attacked me with his body. He pinned my hands hard and pushed his cock against me, grinding his lips against mine. His tongue filled me without finesse, as if he was fucking my mouth. I pushed myself against him in a rhythm until I groaned. I had to have him. He pushed back against me as if trying to get me, through our clothes, to beg for him.

"Hello," came a voice. Jonathan let my arms go and looked around. It was one of the guys who had wrestled the blimp to the ground. "We're closing up here."

"Thanks," Jonathan said without a hint of embarrassment or shame. He popped my helmet off the bike and handed it to me. A smile spread across his face like an uncontrollable oil spill. I took the helmet with the same grin.

The ride home passed with few words. I just rested against him with my hand under his shirt, feeling his warmth. I didn't stroke or caress him at eighty miles an hour, though the temptation was distracting.

He pulled the bike into my driveway. It was midnight, or close to it, and I was sore all over. "You coming in?" I asked, looping his finger in mine. He yanked me to him.

"We playing? Or am I just throwing you down and fucking you?"

Both options held appeal. Something hot and sweaty before an utter collapse into oblivion would be nice, and I'd be fresh and bright in the morning for work. But when he said "playing," I felt wetness condense between my legs, and a shiver went up my spine. I let my finger drop from his and put my arms to my sides. I wanted to be under his control, under his dominance, under *him*. I wanted to forget myself in him and to forget the shame of wanting it so badly.

"I'd like to play again," I said, then added, "Sir."

"Up to the porch with you then, and wait for me." When I turned around to go, he slapped my ass hard. I gasped and strode up the steps.

Jonathan dismounted and, instead of coming right up the porch, stood on the sidewalk. He looked up at the house, then crossed the street and did the same. He jogged back and came past my chain-link fence. "You're wide open to the street."

"Sir?"

"It means you have to keep your clothes on until we get inside."

My street, partly because of the hill and partly because of the neighborhood, was dead at night. If two people passed between midnight and eight in the morning, it would be a newsworthy event. I had the feeling it didn't matter. He stared at me, calculating. I knew that look. He was constructing the game. He faced the street and me, feet planted on my porch, and said, "Step over here, my little goddess."

I did it, heart pounding with anticipation. My back faced the street.

"Unbutton your jeans."

I popped them.

"Unzip, please."

I did, showing my garter belt and the tops of my new, already-christened lingerie. He stroked my stomach, his finger grazing the top of the lace.

"Touch yourself."

He watched my hand go down my pants. Between the sweet, secret caresses in the blimp, and the bike ride home, I was ready for him. I shuddered when my fingers found my swollen, soaked pussy. I buckled with pleasure, and he held my chin.

"Stand up." He put upward pressure on my chin, forcing my spine straight and my view upward. "How wet are you?"

"Very wet, sir."

"What would you like me to do about it?"

"I want you to fuck me, please."

"Hold up your hand."

I slid my hand out of my pants and held it up. The moisture on my fingers glistened. He kissed the tips of my fingers, then put them in his mouth. I gasped as he slid his tongue over them, sucking everything off. His lips might as well have been on my pussy, and I almost buckled again.

"You're delicious," he said.

"Thank you."

"Now, do you remember your ready position?"

"Yes, sir." I wondered how many more times I could call him *sir* without spontaneously coming.

"And your safeword?"

"Tangerine, sir."

"Go inside, get undressed, and wait for me in ready position. Be in any room you want. I'll find you." A smirk played at his mouth. "You have sixty seconds, and you'd better be ready."

I unlocked my door and entered the house. Where to go? I wanted to participate in the game. Surprise him. Make him earn it. So the bedroom was the first place I dismissed. The bathroom was in no condition. That was out. The living room had a nice soft couch, and I could be ready on the coffee table. That would be kind of cool, but the living room was right at the front door, and where was the fun if he practically tripped on me as he walked in?

I undressed as I walked through the house, dropping my shirt in the hamper and kicking my shoes into a corner. No. I retrieved the shoes.

I turned on hall lights and all the warm, indirect lamps. He preferred that kind of lighting, if his house and office were any indication. I'd yanked my pants off and slipped my shoes back on by the time I heard the screen door creak.

I crouched on the kitchen floor, behind the counter, knees and cheek on the linoleum, my hands between my legs until they touched my ankles. I had a wonderful view of under the counter. Not sexy. I turned my face to the kitchen table. Better.

I heard Jonathan close the front door, then his feet on the living room floor, down the hall, to the bedroom, where I wasn't. His smell permeated the air almost immediately, and I drank it in, waiting, my snatch high, a beacon of arousal.

His footsteps got closer. "The kitchen. Little goddess, you are beautiful." His boots came in my field of vision. "The kitchen," he repeated pensively. The refrigerator door opened and its light soaked the room. "What do you eat?"

"I eat at work. They feed us. And I order food out."

He grumbled. From his angle, I couldn't see him, but I felt the sting of his displeasure nonetheless. He closed the fridge, and the room was again lit by the two hallways on each side. He whistled, and though at first I didn't recognize the tune, it came to me at the chorus. "Under My Skin," the song I'd sung the night he surprised me at Frontage.

I heard some clacking and banging, a drawer opening, and the crumple of plastic bags. My heart seized. Plastic bags? Maybe something had been in them that he was managing? Or maybe he was moving something out of the way? Or filling one?

I simply couldn't see without getting out of position, and though I was overtaken by panic, I wasn't ready to give up on the game yet. But the panic wasn't fun. "Jonathan?"

A pause, then, "Monica?"

"You're not going to put a bag over my head, are you?"

Another pause. He came into my field of vision, looking into my face from six feet above. "Never."

I immediately relaxed. "Thank you, sir."

I realized, from the change in my throat's vibrations, that as much as Jonathan had a dominant voice, I had a submissive one. I used softly articulated hard consonants and breathy, aspirated vowels. I felt silly, suddenly, in such a position on the kitchen floor, ass up in stiletto heels, hands to my ankles, while my fully dressed kinda-boyfriend dicked around with the stuff in my kitchen. I knew the break in mood was my fault, but I couldn't have tolerated another second of being afraid.

His boots came in my field of vision again. They were brown, to match his jacket, and ridiculously sexy with his jeans. "Let's talk about ready position." He kneeled at my side and stroked my back and ass, letting his fingertips graze the crack. "This…" He slapped my ass and I gasped in surprise. "This is not ready position." He spanked me again. My cheek erupted in heat and tingles, which he exacerbated by stroking where he'd hit. "Up." He spanked the lower part, where meat met thigh. I straightened my legs. "More." I thought he would slap me, but he stroked instead, eliciting a groan that turned into a cry when he spanked me hard.

I jerked my hips up, not because I wanted him to stop spanking me, but because I wanted to do it right. My twat was fully in the air over an arched back. My breath heaved. I saw him at the edge of my vision, kneeling beside me in his long-sleeve shirt and suit slacks, his hand on my ass and pulling away for another slap that felt like a leather belt. The air left my lungs, leaving pleasure in the wake of the pain.

"The point of this," he said, "is that you are completely ready for me. I should be able to see your cunt is wet. Got it?"

"Yes, sir."

He ran a finger down my back, to my crack, and to my cleft, circling my clit before going back up again. "If you're crouched, I can't see it."

I couldn't form words.

"I'm sorry, Monica, I didn't hear you." He slapped the backs of my thighs, right at my snatch. It stung, and then pleasure blossomed like a thousand flowers.

"Yes."

He spanked me there again. "Sorry?"

I cried out.

"Shh. Behave."

"Yes," I gasped.

"Yes what?"

I knew that game. If I wanted him to continue, and I did, I knew how to do it. "Just yes."

He slapped me again, landing enough of his hand on my snatch to make me bite back another cry. "Monica, is there something you want?"

"Do it again, please." I don't know how I made words out of gasps, but I did.

He did. And then again, harder, and the sharper the pain, the more exquisite the pleasure. My ass must have been red by the third slap, but my pussy wanted more. He stroked me in between, to accentuate the tingle of pain, then held back his slaps until I thought I'd die with anticipation. When they landed, everything between my legs bloomed to pleasure. I thought I'd be overwhelmed with it, consumed, but he stopped, moved behind me, and took a cheek in each palm. He kissed my ass all over, softly, creating little stings of sore pain with his lips. He spread my cheeks apart while his thumbs stroked the sopping crack between.

"How do you feel, little goddess?"

"Beautiful."

"Good." He grabbed a handful of my hair and gently pulled me to a kneeling position. He came around to face me and got on his knees, a ball of plastic bags in his fist. "Your wrists."

I put them out. The plastic bags had been stretched and knotted together at the handles. When he touched me to tie my hands together, I felt arousal and relief. His touch was sure and gentle, his voice humming an old Sinatra tune that would always make me think of him.

When my wrists were bound, he eased me back, pulled my arms over my head, and looped my plastic binds to a drawer handle. He leaned over me, working the knot. So close, I breathed him in through his shirt. That smell mixed with the scent of getting tied up and fucked became the smell of complete release, of an orchestra connected by the simple movements of a skilled conductor. When he was done, he drew his hands down my arms, to my rib cage, thumbs stroking my nipples, and stretched me out across the floor until my arms were straight.

"Perfect," he said, more to himself than me. He pulled up my knees and spread them until they were to either side of my breasts. He leaned back and looked at his work. I saw his erection straining his pants, and I wanted to reach out and touch it. I was tied, and being stretched out added to the sensation of being exposed.

Jonathan pulled his shirt off, and I wanted to touch him even more. I wanted to run my fingers through his chest hair, to his belly, and follow the line of hair to his cock. When he pulled his pants off, it popped out, that wonderful thing. I hoped he'd stick it in my mouth. I wanted to eat it, take it down my throat with my hands tied to a drawer handle. I wanted to watch him come from below him, to see him throw his head back in surrender.

He picked up something off the counter before kneeling between my legs.

"Goddess, this has been done so many times before, it's almost boring." He held up a can of whipped cream. "You and I are too good for it. But it's two weeks from its expiration date, and we need to talk about the contents of your refrigerator."

"Yes, sir."

"Open up."

I opened my mouth, and he squirted some in. He kissed me before I could swallow. The cream mixed between our tongues and dripped down my chin. Still kissing me, he put the cold can on my nipple, sending shivers of pleasure down my body. He pulled away and kneeled between my legs. He squirted each nipple, topping me like a cake, the can making a *kkkkkkt* sound. He licked it off, then sucked each nipple, biting at the end. I gasped and threw my legs up higher. Pulling himself up, he regarded the can.

"This tip is interesting, actually," he said.

"Only you would find it interesting."

He placed the tip of the dispenser at my sternum, the pointed tooth digging into my skin. "Excuse me?"

"Only you, sir." I tried not to smile and wink. We didn't need to break the mood twice in one session.

The can had a pointed, plastic tip that made the whipped cream come out in a striated tube. When placed against the sensitive skin of the chest and abdomen, and slowly dragged while dispensing product, it created more than a sweet, decorative texture. It scratched, opening up the nerve endings so that when the cold whipped cream hit it, the sensation radiated out. Cold. Soft. More so than just cream on skin. Something multiplied by an order of magnitude. When he followed it with his mouth, the result was delicious for us both. He turned the coldness warm, and with the textured top of his tongue, he made the softness rough.

Jonathan dragged the can below my jeweled navel to the tip of my cleft, his tongue right behind. The anticipation made me gasp, which turned into a little squeal. "Shh, now. Be good," he said softly.

He drew the can, its sharp edge, and his warm, rough tongue inside my thigh. I was a throbbing, swollen hot mess by the time he put the can down and placed the tip of his tongue between my legs. He moved slowly up and down my slit, a tease that left me gasping, thrusting, pulling against the plastic bags binding me.

Bringing his tongue back up my abdomen, he landed on my mouth in a kiss. I opened my mouth for him, tasting the mix of cream and sex on his tongue.

"What do you want?" he asked.

"I want you."

"You have me."

"I want your dick in me," I said.

"When?"

"Please, sir," I breathed, "any time after right now is good."

He smiled and kneeled above me, spreading my legs. He dragged his finger up and down my pussy. My hips hitched, and I flung my knees farther apart, begging for him without a word. With one hand on my kitchen cabinet and another guiding his cock, he slid inside me, pushing in and rocking before pulling out. He closed his eyes and moaned. Seeing him feel pleasure brought my mind and body to the same focus. He thrust inside again, harder that time, and a sound left my lungs even as I tried to remain quiet.

"How do you want it, Monica?"

Could I ask? And how? Wasn't what I wanted exactly what scared me most?

"I want to please you," I whispered, telling the truth but avoiding the real answer. My pussy was almost in charge and doing the talking. As long as I had that last sliver of control, I didn't have to admit anything.

"You please me," he said, moving in and out of me in a slow, forceful rhythm. "How can I please you? Say it. Say what you want."

I was close, on the edge. Stoking a white-hot fire where his dick and my body met, I couldn't decide what to say. He sped up just a little, and the words came out of me unfiltered before I had a chance to be afraid. "Take me," I groaned. "Use me."

It took him one slow thrust to start pounding me, deep and hard. Fast. As though his only goal was to finish. He put a hand on my breast and squeezed it. The backs of my thighs, sore from spanking, ached with each thrust as his skin hit mine. Being under him, trapped, objectified, I lost all fear. With Jonathan, I felt safe. I felt a loss of control so complete, a surrender so honest that it became a luxurious indulgence.

"Jonathan, I'm…" I had no words. He was fucking the air right out of me.

"Go." He could barely get words out himself. "Yes."

"Oh…"

If he'd told me to be quiet, I wouldn't have heard the command over my own cry. The wordless sound, not even defined by a vowel, shot up from the base of my spine and out my mouth. I clenched around him, twisting. He held me straight, still beating me with his cock, as I came in a series of explosions that felt like the pounding of a drum hit hard, repeatedly, until it was hot with friction and resistance.

His name left my lips over and over. *Jonathan, Jonathan, Jonathan.*

He slowed down and fell back into a rhythm. He hadn't come yet, and I wanted him to. I wanted to own his orgasm the way he'd owned mine.

"Sir," I said. He put his face close to mine. "Use me for your pleasure. Please. Have me." God, what had I become? Such a whore that when he smiled at the thought of whatever he intended, I felt a surge of delight at pleasing him.

He kissed me, then reached up to the counter and retrieved a steak knife. I was still out of breath when he cut me from the drawer handle. My hands, however, were still tied together. He looked at me with a devilish grin when he stood up.

"On your knees, little goddess." I couldn't with my hands tied, at least not fast enough. He pulled me up by the bicep. My pussy throbbed, and when I got to a kneeling position, I felt warm fluid drip down my leg. Standing before me, his pussy-slick cock in front of my eyes, was my master. He was the ache between my legs, the desire in my belly, the tingle on my skin, the very embodiment of my gratification.

I felt his hand on the back of my head, grabbing a handful of hair and pushing my face forward. I opened my mouth, and he shifted, guiding his wet dick in me. I tasted the sharpness of my snatch on him. Slowly, the length of him went down my throat, and he groaned, tilting his head back in that same position of surrender he had the first time my lips touched his cock. I breathed and took him again, slowly, my tongue coursing him. He jerked out a little, then shoved himself back in, all the way, until my nose touched his stomach. His full, hard shaft filled my mouth. I groaned, vibrating his head.

"Look at me."

I cast my eyes upward. His face was slack with arousal. I leaned back, still looking at him, letting his cock slip from my mouth.

"I own you," he said. He grabbed the back of my head harder, pulling the hair painfully, and pushed back in. His eyes closed a little, and a long breath escaped his lips. "Ah. That's right. I. Own. You."

We watched each other as his thrusts got shorter and faster. I had to breathe through my nose and concentrate on not losing him, not looking away, opening up for him totally as he fucked my mouth.

"Monica," he whispered. His eyes dropped lower and he whispered again, "Monica, Monica, I'm coming, baby. Take it. Ah."

I took him deeper, letting him come right down my throat, the base of his cock pulsing on my lower lip.

"Fuck," he whispered like a prayer, bending in supplication and release. His eyes closed, and after a final hitch in his breath, he pulled out, the last of his erection slick with spit and sex.

"How you doing, sir?" I was smirking. He'd tied my hands and forced the rhythm, but his orgasm was mine. He reached for the steak knife again, and I held my hands up. Slashing my binding, he bent down to take me in his arms. He lifted me, and I wrapped my legs around him, resting my head on his shoulder. He carried me out of the kitchen as if I was a child.

Chapter 9

Jonathan

I don't know how a man can feel ripped apart and whole at the same time.

Under her covers, on my side, and facing her wasn't close enough. I twisted my legs in hers, touched her face while she talked, and held her hand on the mattress.

When I'd carried her out of the kitchen, she'd been sticky all down her front. Her braid was a big knot. Her ass cheeks were pink and sore. Her throat was coated in my orgasm.

I took her straight to the bathroom so we could shower. We soaped, and kissed, and laughed, but she was wiped out. Her eyes drooped, and her hands worked over her body lazily. When we'd finished, I put a towel around her and brushed her hair. She insisted on a braid, so I put a loose one down her back, just to get it over with, and carried her to bed.

"I'm sorry about breaking the mood with the plastic bags," she whispered.

I stroked her cheek. "It's fine. I don't want to asphyxiate you, Monica. That's way past my threshold."

"I was scared."

"I know. And I don't want you to be scared, either."

"I should have put that on the list."

"We'll make a new list." I touched her forehead and drew my fingers down, forcing her eyes closed.

"You're my king, Jonathan." She'd opened her eyes, but they looked heavy. I kissed them over and over, eyelids, cheek, nose, lips, eyelids again, forcing them closed over and over. When her eyes stayed closed, I knew she was asleep, and I could rest.

But I didn't. I replayed the night in my head while looking out her window. Dogs barked. A police siren faded into range, then out. She hummed a little in her sleep, then stopped. She'd thought I was going to choke her. She'd thought I was going to put a plastic bag over her head until her body seized up. For thrills.

Obviously, she didn't trust me yet. It would take time and patience. I hadn't given either to a woman since Jessica because I gave her too much. My relationship with Monica could only go one place. Me, exposed to her, raw at the edges, breaking down at a shareholder meeting. Crying like—

I couldn't let myself finish that thought.

In the dead of night, when everyone else slept, was when it happened. I'd never been much of a sleeper, maxing out at four hours a night by the time I'd finished adolescence. Having business in Asia helped. I could make calls and send emails. Taking a lot of women to bed helped with the voices a little, but the dead-of-night hours were still spent alone. Then it took over.

It was my father's voice. The voice told me that the things I had done wrong were irreversible. My mistakes were yokes I could either break under or become strong enough to pull, but they could not be shaken. Marrying Jessica, which I had convinced myself was the only *right* thing I'd done, sat front and center. I'd screwed it up by trying to get her to fit into my sexual fantasies. If I'd stayed silent, just done things her way, I could have been happy. In the dead of night, the regret of putting my desires above love split me, gutted me, dragged me into despair. Come morning, the voice slumbered. The torment played on an infinite loop until I dreaded the sun's dip below the skyline.

The voice was quiet that night, just a hum of warning. I could be that man again very easily. It was no harder than tripping on a bump in the sidewalk or cutting myself shaving, a slip in concentration long enough to lose control. I could fall off the tightrope to either side if I blinked at the wrong time.

I forced my eyes closed and listened to Monica's breaths. Eventually, I fell asleep.

Chapter 10

Monica

I woke up at 5:16 a.m., sore everywhere. My feet hurt from the stilettos. My knees from kneeling on the kitchen floor. My pussy from getting fucked hard, twice. My ass from the spanking. My tits from the biting and pulling. I wanted Jonathan again. I had about an inch of my body, somewhere, that wasn't throbbing and sore. He needed to find it and fuck it.

I heard his voice from far away, and I realized he wasn't next to me. He was on the side patio, facing the driveway and talking on the phone. After using the bathroom and getting into a robe and slippers, I joined him outside.

He sat at the little table I'd found on the corner of Echo Park Ave and Montana. His elbow was on the glass as he wrote something in a notebook and tapped something else into his phone.

"Good morning," I said.

He reached for me, pulling me into his lap. "Good morning." I flinched when my butt touched the hard surface of his knee. "Sorry," he said when he saw me lower myself slowly. "I mean, I'm not."

"Me neither." I leaned into the pain and sat on his leg.

"I have to go to Washington in a few days. I could be gone a week. A congressman from Arkansas doesn't want me building hotels overseas. I have an appointment to kiss his ass."

He wasn't just telling me he had to split. He was apologizing. I kissed him long and hard, running my fingers through his hair. "I knew you traveled a lot even before I met you."

"Will you keep yourself busy without me?" he asked.

"In all the most boring ways."

He slipped his hand between my legs and stroked inside my thigh. "What will you do?"

"I'll call you at night," I whispered.

"What else?" His fingertips touched my snatch just a little, like a threat of more.

"I'll text you every time I think of you. So, all the time." I opened my legs for him.

"Uh huh."

"I'll go to work."

"Yes." He breathed on my neck, his finger so close to finding me sore, wet, and ready.

"I have to work on the B.C. Mod piece. We're really behind."

His hand stopped dead. "When I'm away?"

I cringed a little inside. Shit. "You're away a lot. Should I stop working?"

"Maybe I should take you with me everywhere."

I stood and threw myself into the other chair. "You think I'm going to run off and fuck someone else as soon as your back is turned? What kind of person do you think I am?"

He put his elbow on the arm of his chair and rubbed his eyes. I had an inner, boiling-hot rage cooled only by remembering what his wife did. He needed reassurance, not defensiveness. Even if he didn't and couldn't love me, thinking he didn't have feelings or carry baggage was immature.

He said, "I trust you. I don't trust *him*."

I leaned forward and softened my voice. "It could be huge for me. Kevin is very important—"

"I don't want to hear that name."

"How are we supposed to talk about it? I mean, you trust me, but you don't trust him. Do you think he'll rape me?" I crossed my legs.

He took a long pause, looking at me. I would have bet two weeks' tips he was deciding whether or not to say something, or reveal a piece of information, but he looked away and tapped his notebook. "Do you think his Eclipse piece said anything about how he'll treat you?"

"He's Kevin Wainwright. He starts with the obvious emotions, then gets cold, then flushes what he can't use down the toilet. So that piece? I never saw the documentation, but my guess is someone just bought a pile of drawings of a dark-haired woman getting the shit beat out of her."

"How is he starting this piece with you? What's the early documentation look like?"

His eyes didn't waver from mine, so he must have seen my reaction. My ears got hot and my arms tensed, because Kevin's studio had been filled with raunchy sex drawings. Was that what he intended to work on with me? Were we talking about love or sex or the intersection of both? Had I been naïve and foolish?

"You can't get in the way of my work, Jonathan."

"He wants to hurt you, Monica."

"He doesn't know how."

"You're wrong. Very, very wrong."

I crossed my arms to match my legs. "Is there something you want to tell me?"

He swallowed, watching me. I watched him back. The tension made my heart pound, my palms sweat. My neck broke out in goose bumps, but I would not waver.

"I do have something to tell you," he said.

"Okay."

"When I say I own you, it's just a manner of speaking. It doesn't mean you don't have your own life, or you're a possession I can throw away when I'm bored. It means I am directly responsible for your well-being. If I sense a threat to your health or happiness, I will step in to protect you, even if you don't want me to."

Those words, so cold and practical, without a flowery phrase or hyperbole, made my lower lip quiver and a swelling, wet pressure collect in my eyes. Fuck.

"You can't keep me from working," I said, breathing hard, trying to forget the tears threatening to drop. "You have my word. I'm yours. You are the only man I want. I know what happened to you before—"

"Monica, you're not hearing me—"

"I am hearing you. You think Kevin wants to hurt me, and I'm telling you he can only hurt me if I give him my body, which I won't do."

He leaned forward as though he wanted to touch me, but wouldn't. "You said yourself he gets raw, then he gets cold, and then he does the piece. Maybe you're the piece."

I watched my hands fidget. "I can't stop my career for maybes." My eyes went back to him. "When I say you're a king, you are. You rule the world. You have everything. You can do whatever you want. I'm nobody. I have nothing to call my own. I could die tomorrow, and I'd be forgotten in a year. Like Gabby. If I don't record her music, it'll disappear, and if I let you stop me from doing whatever I have to do to make work, I'll disappear too."

I was crying full bore, with little sniffles and big, wet tears. He reached for his pocket, and I knew he would get out one of his expensive hankies. I hated that it was the second time I'd cried in front of him. I didn't make crying a habit. I hated it. I found no release in it, just sore eyes and shame. I grabbed his hand before it could leave his pocket. "Don't let my stupid crying get in the way of what you want to say."

"I wanted to say 'blow.'"

"No need." I cleared my throat, tilted my head, and pinched the corners of my eyes. Then I smiled a customer service smile. "See? All done."

He took my wrists and pulled me to him, gathered me up in his lap, and put my arms around his neck. "You think I'd forget you so easily?" he said, his face so close I could see the flecks of blue in his green eyes.

"L.A. is full of pretty girls. You'd find another one." He started to say something, some petty, pithy reassurance that would make me feel even more insignificant. I put my fingers on his lips before he could get a word out and whispered, "Shh. Behave."

He smiled under my hand, then kissed it. "We're all forgotten. Every one of us. Even artists and rich men. Eventually."

"My voice could survive."

"But with what meaning? This moment, here? On this little patio? This makes us who we are, and in a week, it's going to be a few pieces of memory. In a year... it's gone, and everything's changed."

"Are you a nihilist, Jonathan?" I stroked the hair on his cheeks as I teased him with my tone.

"I believe in plenty. You, for one. Your loyalty to your friend. The way you took care of her and still take care of her." He kissed my lips and kept his face so close to mine I felt his breath. "Will you let me take care of you?"

"To an extent."

"I want to get someone in to put food in your fridge."

"No."

"Your deadbolt is broken. That day when I said the door was unlocked, it wasn't. I opened the doorknob lock with a credit card. The deadbolt wasn't even set right."

"I'll fix it."

"I'll get someone in." His fingers found their way between my legs again, stroking inside my thighs.

"Jonathan, I put the first one in. I can do it again."

"Oh, is that why it works so well?" I pursed my lips. He pulled my hand off his cheek and held it. "I'm not questioning your competence, but I don't think you're defining yourself by your ability to set in a deadbolt. Or are you going to become L.A.'s first singing locksmith?"

I rested my head on his shoulder. "Fine. You have someone lock me up tight."

"On all the doors." His fingertips found a place between my legs where moisture gathered in response to his touch and his breath.

I sighed. "If it'll make you happy."

"It would keep unhappiness at bay." He dragged his finger up my pussy and across my clit. My breath hitched from the soreness and pleasure. "Open your legs for me."

"Another go?" I murmured.

"Yes."

We shifted so my back was to him. He released himself with the clink of a belt buckle and the purr of a zipper. I put my hands on the table as he reached around and pulled my legs farther apart.

"All the way," he said. "I want you to feel me." He stretched me apart to the point of pain, then pulled off my robe. Again, I found myself nude against his clothed body, exposed, vulnerable to him. His dick rolled past my ass and found the source of my wetness. I put my weight on it and groaned with how deep he went, how the soreness stung, and how the skin of my snatch felt abused and loved.

Our hands met between our legs, feeling where we were coupled, taking turns touching my clit, stroking his shaft when it was exposed and feeling it enter me. I rubbed his balls under his clothes. Our hands went wild, fingers kneading, palms rubbing. He ran his damp hand up my belly and held my breast, twisting the nipple between two fingers. I was crazy with him, a circle of hunger and desire. He pulled me toward him until the back of my head was on his shoulder, and he whispered in my ear, "You are mine, goddess."

I groaned. Close, wrapped in a web of hands and wetness and throbbing shaft moving inside me.

"Mine," he said, pressing my hand to where were coupled, his sliding dick against my wet flesh. "This is us together. I own it. This body is my plaything. Your ache is mine. Your orgasm is mine. Your hunger is mine. Your dirty thoughts are mine."

"I'm going to come."

"Say it."

I was so close, but I wanted to say it before I exploded. I turned so my lips were close to his ear. "I'm yours. My pleasure is yours. My wet pussy is yours. You own me, Jonathan. You are the master of my fuck."

"Jesus, you are something else."

He thrust his hips forward. I sat up and matched him thrust for thrust. He moved my hand between my legs, my palm rubbing his dick and my clit at the same time. It was beautiful, soaking, earthy, celestial, electric. I slammed myself on him, driving him deep as I groaned, grinding my orgasm against the base of his cock, bending my body forward, winding like a spring, and unwinding with a shout.

A few gentle rocks, and I felt his hands tighten on my hips, grabbing flesh and digging in. He'd done it. He'd found the place I wasn't sore and bruised it, moving me up and down against him with decreasing gentleness.

He groaned, and with a final thrust forward, he yanked my hips down, coming inside me while whispering, "Monica, Monica, Monica."

Chapter 11

Jonathan

I had a sinking uneasiness. It wasn't necessarily about leaving her for D.C. It was about how often I left and stayed gone. I trusted her intentions, but I didn't trust her ability to make wise decisions. She'd basically admitted Kevin had vengeful thoughts about her, and dismissed them as part of his artistic process.

I wondered if she'd been bitten by a shithouse rat. If she expected Darren to protect her, she was sorely out of her league. He was a mother hen. He'd tuck her into bed and feed her soup if she got sick, but if that guy started doing the revolting shit I saw in those drawings, Darren was as good as useless.

I didn't feel much more useful.

Mostly because as soon as I hit the 101 and got too far away from her to turn back, I started planning the next time I'd see her. Nothing between visits occupied my mind. I already wanted to taste her again, feel her legs wrapped around my waist, and hear her sighs. I wanted to take action. Do something. Make some gesture that would bring her closer. Some sort of act that would bind her to me, even when I was away.

I felt greedy thinking about how much I missed her. I wanted more. More time. More sex. More laughing. I wondered if each of my sisters would like her. How each would react. Five out of seven would love her, and that thought warmed me. The warmth, instead of providing comfort, grew to a painful burn. I'd let my mind wander. I'd let something happen since last night when I kissed her eyelids. She was mine to protect and care for, a responsibility I relished.

Chapter 12

Monica

Jonathan had left only hours ago, and I'd gone right back to bed. A rumble in the driveway woke me at eight a.m. It sounded like a farting tuba being played in a closet. I peeked out the window. A Ford pickup as long as a bus pulled into my driveway, blocking my car.

I threw on last night's clothes and ran out to the porch. He was obviously in the wrong driveway. He was right at my door when I opened it. Six four. A solid wall of muscle with a face to match and blonde hair that looked as if it had already done a full day's work.

"Dr. Thorensen is next door," I said.

"I'm here for the Faulkner residence?"

I looked at his polo. The logo on the breast said The Foundation Guys, and the name DAVE was embroidered above it. Jonathan said he had guys.

"I wasn't expecting you so soon," I said.

"Yeah, well, it's been slow lately. Anyway, coming to check it out. Get kinda like a bead on the situation?"

"Yeah, well, I gotta get to work. Do you need me?"

"Nope, just your crawlspace. You got a dog or something? Gonna bite me?"

"No, but I'll bite you if I'm late to work. I have to get the Honda out."

He laughed and ran to the truck, and I shut myself behind closed doors to get ready. When I got out of the shower, I heard scuffling from Gabby's room. Tiptoeing to the doorway, I found Darren stacking and restacking piles of *Hollywood Reporters*.

"Mon," he said, indicating the towel wrapped around me, "I'm still a man, okay?"

"You could knock."

"I could if I wanted to sit on your porch for half an hour."

"Seriously. I have a boyfriend, and you could walk in on God-knows what."

"Ah, right. Stay kinky, Monica. Stay kinky," he said, smiling. I whipped off the towel wrapped around my head and snapped it at him. "New trick?"

I whipped it again, and he grabbed it. I couldn't get it back because I needed to keep the other towel on myself with my free hand.

"Can you get dressed, please?" Darren threw the towel back.

I ran into my room and heard him through the wall as I wiggled into jeans and a shirt. When I got back to Gabby's room, he was sorting through manila envelopes absently, as if deciding what to do with the whole stack rather than whether or not to keep any individual file.

"What's happening with the work crews?" he asked.

"My foundation's slipping, or actually, *has slipped*."

"No shit. How you paying to fix that?"

When I didn't answer, he waved his hand, looking as if he was holding back a torrent of recriminations.

"Can we be done fighting?" I said.

"What fighting? Who's fighting? The thing in the parking lot?"

"Yes."

"I thought that was foreplay." Though his words were a joke, his voice took a serious timbre.

I felt a shudder that turned to heat on my cheeks. I didn't want him to know. I didn't want anyone to know. He must have imagined me tied up and gagged, like the girl suspended over the bar with wet underpants and come dripping out of her mouth. Would he avoid making eye contact with me? Would I always think he thought less of me?

I changed the subject, indicating the piles of papers and envelopes. "We should just throw it all out or keep it all. Going through it is just going to make you sad."

"She spent so much time on this stuff. It feels wrong to just trash it."

"It doesn't feel wrong," I said. "It feels too easy. And like a fast train to regret."

"Cheap. Like everything would feel cheap."

"It's not the same as throwing *her* away." I sorted through stacks, not really thinking. Some envelopes were thicker than others. Some had trees and webs of relationships penciled on them. Some were so thin they couldn't have been more than an idea. "I miss her. I think about her all the time. I should have called her when the location changed. I shouldn't have made that scratch cut without her. I'm sorry, Darren. I'm so sorry. I feel like I took your sister from you." I couldn't look at him, just the never-ending pile of envelopes left behind as her legacy.

"It wasn't your fault, Monica. It was a stupid accident."

"No, it wasn't. Stop defending me. She committed suicide because she was getting cut out. You know it, and I know it."

"No, you *don't*," he said with a pointed finger and raised voice. "You have two possible scenarios, and you believe the one that makes you responsible? Sorry, no. You want to get beat up during sex, that's fine, but this emotional masochism is bullshit."

"She committed suicide whether I take responsibility or not," I yelled back.

"No. She. Didn't." Darren ground his teeth. If I took responsibility, he'd have to as well. For not babysitting, for not watching more closely, for not counting her meds. It could go on and on in ever-expanding circles of self-blame.

"Fine," I said. "It was a freak accident. I'm still sorry."

"Me too."

Agreeing on everything and nothing, we looked through the envelopes as if we were doing more than touching what she'd touched so we could commune with our memories.

"I can take it all back to my place," he said. "Clear out this room. You need a new roommate."

I hadn't given that a moment's thought. I'd paid bills like a robot. Since they always came out of my checking account anyway, it didn't feel like anything had changed. But that account wouldn't make it another month without help.

I realized I didn't want the room cleaned. I didn't want anyone else living there. No one else was family. I didn't want a stitch removed until I was good and ready, which I wasn't yet. "How much are you paying for that place around the corner?"

"Not too much. Why? You want to move in?"

"Live here. With me."

"Here? In this room?"

"You can have my room. Or the living room. I can clean out the garage."

It seemed like the most sensible thing in the world. We would stay together, which I wanted so much a knife of anxiety went through my chest.

He sorted through files as if he didn't want to look at me. "What would your new boyfriend say?"

"I don't care."

"Ask first."

"I don't have to ask permission to live my life, Darren."

"It's not permission. It's courtesy. Seriously." He glanced at me. "You and I were intimate, in case you forgot. Guys have a problem with stuff like that. Trust me. I'd like to move in, but not at the expense of whatever you have with him. Not that I understand it."

"Fine." I held my hand out, realizing too late my wrists were black and blue from straining against plastic bags tied to my kitchen cabinets.

"Jesus, Monica," he whispered.

Before I could even think about it, I hid them behind my back. Stupid. I was the cause of my own shame. "It's not a big deal."

He held out his hands. "Can I see?"

"No."

"Please? I won't give you a hard time." When I didn't move, he said, "Promise."

I put my hands in his. He turned my hands over, assessing the damage. I couldn't look at him. I knew what was on his face and what was in his head. It wouldn't be too far off from the truth. Me, naked on the floor. Knees up. Hands tied, straining. Add whatever darkness lay in Darren's imagination, and I'm getting choked, slapped, fisted… whatever act he decided was too sick to perform, too deranged to even think about, had a shape and a voice and they looked and sounded like me.

"Do we have a problem?" I asked.

He let go of my hands. "It's not a problem for me if it's not for you."

"You sure?"

"Sure? No. But close enough."

I put my arms around his shoulders and held on for dear life. He rocked me back and forth and gave me a big, hard kiss on the cheek. I heard another knock on the door and pulled away to go answer. I checked out the window and saw a rock-solid woman in her fifties carrying a beat-up leather case.

"Hi," I said when I opened the door. "You must be the locksmith."

"Sure am. Benita's the name."

I let her in. "Okay, well, this deadbolt isn't set in right, so if you could fix that."

She fiddled with the lock. "Uh, I was told to replace all the locks with Kleigs."

My face hardened. I couldn't afford Kleigs, naturally, but I'd agreed. "I have three doors. Back, front, and side."

"Done. Checking the windows, too."

Was there any use arguing? She was just doing her job.

"Fine. I'm going to work. You don't need me here, do you?"

"Nope, just your key. I'll leave it and the new ones in a box in the front. Code's 987. All you need to know." She handed me her card, and I saw her eyes widen when she saw my wrists.

I thanked her and ran back to my room. I caught sight of my wrists as I put rings on. That wouldn't work. I looked as though I'd been in a hostage situation. I put bracelets on to cover the bruises. I needed a more solid pair that didn't slide around so much. Whenever I lifted a tray, the bracelets would slip and reveal my weekend's activities.

Which was exactly what happened. I'd been at work thirty minutes when Debbie noticed. She flicked the bracelets, then looked at me when I got back to the service bar.

"How are you doing?" she asked. I knew exactly what she meant.

"Very well, thank you." I was pretty sure I blushed as I put empty glasses in the bus tray. She smiled at me then disappeared downstairs.

I serviced some tables, threw snide comments back and forth with Robert, and wore a ridiculous smile that was probably the exact opposite of the customer service smile I usually used. Debbie caught me on a bathroom run and handed me a black velvet bag with a drawstring.

"Put these on." She took off as if she had more important things to do than explain.

When I got to the bathroom, I opened the bag. Inside were two bracelets that were more like metal cuffs in hammered silver. Two inches wide, with red stones set into them, they looked heavy but weren't. When I put them on, they stayed put as I moved my arm.

"Well, there's a hint I can take," I said to Debbie when I saw her.

"I can't have customers thinking we tie you up in the basement."

"Thank you."

"Are you happy?" She indicated the bracelets, but I knew she meant the bruises underneath them. "This is good for you?"

Debbie knew Jonathan, and her voice often told me she was some sort of dominant. I knew she knew, if not the details, the broad strokes. "Inappropriate" was too mild a word to describe talking to her about my relationship with Jonathan.

"When I'm in the middle of it, it's very comfortable. But if I think of it any other time, I start to feel like I should be ashamed. As a woman. I'm sorry I'm..." I'd gone too far.

"Don't be sorry. You are what you are. You don't have to apologize for it to me or anyone. Especially yourself. And not feminism either. It'll get along fine with you doing what you want in private. Now, get to the floor."

"Okay." I ran back out to do my job.

When I got home that afternoon, the street was crowded with parked cars, and the foundation guy was still in my drive. I was stuck. I found a spot down the block and walked up the hill, wishing I'd worn sneakers. I crossed the street to my house next to a green minivan. I lived on a small block and knew most of the cars, but sometimes the odd car parked nearby when the lot at the coffee shop got too crowded. The minivan shouldn't have raised an eyebrow or a hackle. I looked at it anyway. Just a glance. I saw a glass circle enclosed in a larger black one tucked behind the driver-side window, near the side mirror. Must be a trick of the evening light. Why would a camera lens be pointed at my front door?

I peered into the car. A cord went to the eye of the camera, which looked like a webcam, and a red light blinked at the bottom of the cable.

That was not okay.

What was he trying to do? Make sure I didn't fuck the foundation guy? Check to see if Kevin came around? I stormed across the street, getting madder with each step. A camera was not protecting my health and happiness. It was creepy, stalker bullshit. I got my new keys out of the lockbox, then I remembered who paid for them.

Fucking great. He would have gotten the keys from Benita. I'd have to call her so she could take things out so I could have another locksmith, who I hired, put in new tumblers. Pain in the ass.

I took the whipped cream out of my fridge.

Asshole.

I couldn't even think straight. I was full on white hot rage from my core to my fingertips as I stomped back across the street and sprayed whipped cream all over the minivan's driver's side window.

Let's see what he saw through that. Motherfucker.

As I crossed back to my house, I texted him.

> —*WTF did you think you were doing*
> *with the stalker bullshit*—

Dave, the foundation guy, stopped me at the sidewalk, wielding a clipboard. "Miss Faulkner? I have an estimate." I took the clipboard. The number was insane. "Your house is falling down the hill. We need to jack it up and shift it. The whole thing. Then it's gotta be bolted. It's a big job."

I scanned the work list, then the line at the bottom for a signature. "I'm not the homeowner. It's my mother's house."

"Oh."

"I assume you can't continue without the homeowner's signature?"

He looked disappointed. The guy needed work, and I didn't want to screw him out of it. I read the estimate again. I couldn't afford the work, but since I found out Dr. Thorensen's house would meet my house on the day of "the big one," not getting it fixed was irresponsible.

"I'll bring this to my mom to sign and let you know."

He brightened. I didn't know if I was lying or not. Maybe my mother would shell out the money to protect her property. I could mail her the permits to sign. Or fax them. Or carrier pigeon. Anything to avoid Castaic.

But as God was my witness, I would not let some guy who couldn't trust me, and who put cameras on me, pay to fix my foundation or change my locks. Oh, fuck no.

My phone rang. Jonathan. I waved to Dave, and he walked to his truck. I answered the phone in a white heat. "I can't do this," I said.

"What happened? What are you talking about?" He was in a crowded place full of voices shouting. In my mind, I saw him pressing his finger to his other ear.

"I do not need to be watched. I don't need you if you can't trust me." He didn't answer. "Say something."

"I just want to make sure you're all right."

"I'm. All. Right." My voice was tight and firm, pure intention in every syllable.

"I didn't think it was that big a deal."

"Fuck? What? You don't think it's that big... Are you from another planet?" I paced my living room as Dave pulled his truck out of my driveway.

"Monica, calm down."

"Calm… What? No! I will not calm down. This is serious. This is a problem. And you know what? I don't have time for it. I don't have time to describe to you proper boundaries outside the bedroom."

"You're out of line."

"Don't you use that voice with me now. *You're* out of line."

"Monica."

"Jonathan."

"I'm coming over there."

"Don't bother."

I hung up.

Chapter 13

Monica

I wanted to run. I wanted to somehow foil his stupid fucking plan to come over and soothe the common sense right out of me. But I had to shower and change to play at Frontage. Rhee and I had agreed to continue on a trial run, and I wanted to be my best, not all screwed up. When I got out of the shower, my phone was ringing. I picked it up without looking, thinking it was Jonathan.

"My doors are locked."

"Okay?"

Fuck, not Jonathan. The caller ID identified the caller as Jerry, the producer I'd done a scratch cut with two weeks earlier.

"Hi, sorry. Thought you were someone else. How's it going?"

"Good, I'm having drinks with Eddie Milpas tonight. He's one of our acquisitions guys. You playing that dinner club?"

"Frontage, yeah."

"You playing the song we cut?"

"I don't usually play my own stuff. I can ask."

"Do it. He's looking for something, and I think you have it."

My heart raced. "Thanks. I'll see you tonight."

"Great. Keep the doors locked."

I hung up. It had been twenty minutes since Jonathan called. I stuffed my crap in a bag and ran out with my hair still wet.

Chapter 14

Jonathan

"Lil." I knocked on the window. "Forget Sheila. Take me to Echo Park."

"Yes, sir."

Turning around was no small feat. She had to crawl off the exit of the 134, crawl back on, and sit in rush hour traffic. Dinner with my favorite sister and attendant children was officially cancelled.

When I got to Monica's house, she and her car were gone. I stood on the porch calculating my next move. She'd said something about a gig at Frontage, and I was tempted to go over there. I saw Dave pulling up the hill in his dually.

"Hey, Jon. The lady of the house home? I had a few more permits to pull."

"Nope. What happened today?"

He leaned out his window and offered me a fry from a McDonald's bag, which I refused. "What do you mean?"

"Did you say something about watching her?"

"No, man, I was watching, not telling."

"When I said to keep an eye on her, it was a casual keeping an eye. Because she knows, and she's pissed."

"Sorry. I didn't say anything. She did tag up that car with whipped cream. Don't know what that was about." He craned his neck to see the other side of the street. "Right there."

I followed his gaze to a green minivan. I got a sinking feeling as I walked toward it. The whipped cream wasn't just whipped cream. It was the kind from a can, and Monica was sending me a message.

I used my hankie to wipe the whipped cream away and saw a camera behind the glass.

Ah. She thought I did that. The thought had crossed my mind, but I did have boundaries.

And then the other question: who did it? Who wanted her watched?

I said good-bye to Dave and crawled back into the Bentley. "Lil, take me home." I needed my car, and Lil had been driving all day. Monica would be trapped behind that piano. I could still make it.

Chapter 15

Monica

"One song," I said to Rhee. "The rest can be the same as we've always done."

She chewed the inside of her lip, glancing around the room. It was already getting crowded. "What's it sound like?"

"Like a woman on the piano," I said. "Here are the lyrics."

Asking permission to sing my own songs wasn't something I would have accepted a month ago, but so much had happened, and I depended on the job at Frontage to keep Gabby's memory alive.

The lyrics made me nervous, but I had to do it, just once. If I didn't take opportunities when they presented themselves, they'd dry up.

"Little hardcore, sugar," Rhee said. "Collar? Licking the floor?"

"It's metaphorical."

"I figured that."

Of course she did. What woman would have to lay that out for a man literally?

"It's important to me," I said. "Someone's coming to hear it. A producer and a record exec. And the composition, Gabby wrote it. I laid the lyrics over after…"

"Okay, okay." She handed back the sheet. "You're fine. Have fun. You deserve it."

"Thanks, Rhee." I dashed back to the dressing room. I'd played for Rhee earlier in the week to prove I could manage lyrics and music at the same time. I was only halfway into "Under My Skin" when she stopped me and told me I was fine to go back on my old schedule. I was happy for the distraction, but the feeling that Eugene Testarossa had been right, and Gabby had been redundant, nagged at the back of my mind. Some little guilt-inducing voice insisted that by playing her part, I was driving her deeper into the grave.

The dressing room was like a second home anymore, but it was lonely and my anger at Jonathan wasn't good company. I put on my makeup and hummed my new song. When it was time to go into the dining room, I looked at myself in the mirror and said, "I hope you get carpal tunnel and a frog jumps down your throat."

It wasn't the same, but it was the best I had.

Chapter 16

Jonathan

Nothing moved. The Jag was caught between a bus and a silver SUV. I should have brought the bike. I could have gone between the lanes and been there already. Even though I knew she wasn't going anywhere, I wanted to see Monica right away. Had to. First, she was angry with me, and that fact bored a hole right through me. The more I thought about it, the more I wanted to rush to her. Second, the surveillance equipment across the street just turned the dial up on my concern. That equipment wasn't a joke. Someone was watching her. I didn't know why, or who, but I could buy those answers with money and time. One, I had plenty of. The other, I'd have to manufacture.

"Margie," I said when my oldest sister picked up her phone. She was fifteen years my senior and had been more of an aunt to me. Her law firm had a huge criminal litigation division and billed thousands of hours keeping celebrities from going to jail.

"Jonny, you never call anymore."

"Because I don't have any problems."

"But tonight? You have a problem?"

"Are you sitting?" Western Avenue opened up just as I had to turn down Santa Monica Boulevard. Too bad all the money in the world wouldn't buy me a flying fucking car.

"Sure, I'm sitting."

"There's a woman."

"You just gave me a migraine. That poor girl. What did you do to her?"

I'd squirmed when she litigated my divorce and I had to tell her it was about sex; what kind of sex and how I'd been rebuffed. She needed details and received them only after I'd drunk half a bottle of scotch.

"It's not that," I said. "She and I, we're good. It's something else."

"Where does one find a woman who likes—"

"Enough." I knew all the wisecracks already. "I'm not in the mood, Margie. I found a camera outside her place. Temporary surveillance inside a car. I need her house swept for more. I think you might know someone who could do it."

"Do you have access?"

"No, and irony of ironies, I just had new locks put in."

"You're not doing that controlling thing again, are you, Jonny?"

"Just round people up and I'll get you access. Okay?"

"*She* might like it when you're bossy—"

I hung up. My sisters knowing I had a kinky streak wasn't easy. Another thing I could thank Jessica for.

I got Hank on the phone at the next red light.

"Jaydee."

"Did you burn those drawings?"

"Not yet."

"Can you pack them up and have them to my Wilshire office tomorrow morning?" I asked.

"You want them packed to archiving standards?"

"No. Put them in an envelope. No more. I'll let you know how to proceed." I hung up.

I was sure it was Kevin. He'd been at the funeral and could have planted cameras then. Video of Monica entering and exiting the house would be perfect for an installation, especially with her music over it. Another homage to a breakup. He knew her well enough to know that once he presented her with the footage in the completed work, she'd buckle and let it happen for the sake of art and her career. Or he'd neglect to mention it until the show was installed. She'd be even less likely to gripe since her name would be on the thing already. A humiliating stab in the back. If there were cameras inside the house, I would have to kill him.

I felt as if every cell in my body needed to be near Monica. To protect her from whoever watched her and to soothe her anger at me. I just had to brave the traffic and the ridiculous synchronization of the lights on Santa Monica Boulevard.

Chapter 17

Monica

With Gabby gone and the promotional machine at a standstill, the room's body count went back to normal. It was the same-sized crowd as the first night we'd played: just tables and a few people waiting at the bar. Any buzz we'd had about our shows died with Gabby. Basically, I was starting from scratch, which was fine. I didn't think I could take much more than that without her to lean on.

The table by the warm speaker had a RESERVED sign. Jerry and Eddie were meant to sit there, if they came at all. I said hello to some lovely couples by the front and asked if they had any requests, which I'd play if I knew. A group of frat boys had heard about me and come for dinner. They were half drunk already, and their appetizers hadn't even arrived, so I didn't linger. I made a last visual sweep around the room and cast my eyes to Rhee. She was leading two women to a table in the corner. I recognized both of them. One was Jonathan's sister Deirdre. One was his ex-wife.

My skin burst into tingles and my throat closed. I couldn't feel my fingertips. Then I remembered I was playing that song. Jonathan's song. I hadn't shown it to him or told him about it yet. Jessica would hear it. And she would know.

She would *know*.

I wasn't ashamed of what I was doing with Jonathan, but letting her hear my fears as if I'd whispered them in her ear was sickeningly intimate. A cold trickle of regret ran down my back. I should never have made the thing, never written it down, never set it to Gabby's music. Though I wasn't hiding it from Jonathan, at the very least, I should have shown it to him before playing it publicly. I hadn't even thought of that.

I sat down at the piano and touched the keys. No, I'd skip it. Play something else. Jerry wasn't there, so no one would be the wiser. Rhee didn't really care. I started playing. Yes, I'd hide behind Irving Berlin, then Cole

Porter. I'd stay safe. I'd still paint them the colors of Jonathan. I'd still feed them his lust, his touch, his voice. But Jessica would never hear it because I was protected by dead men's lyrics.

I was coming off "Someone to Watch Over Me," the middle of my set, when I saw Jerry with two men at the bar. He tipped his glass to me. They weren't sitting at the table. Stopping by, maybe? Well, shit. I'd have to play it.

With the lights in my face, blinding me to half the room, Jessica didn't loom as large. After warming up with the standards I knew so well and hiding behind that shiny, black baby grand, I didn't feel as vulnerable. I could play that song.

I could do it. I could belt it out. Fuck her. Fuck her to Sunday. Fuck her with the lights on. Fuck her fuck her fuck her. It was my room. My song. My audience. My rules.

Rule number one? Fuck her.

I hit the keys, owning them, and I launched into Jonathan's song as though he was naked and I was jumping him.

We wove words under Popsicle trees,
The ceiling open to the sky,
And you want to own me
With your fatal grace and charmed words.
All I own is a handful of stars
Tethered to a bag of marbles that turns

Oh, her ears would burn off at the mention of Popsicle trees and a ceiling open to the stars but guess what?

Fuck her.

My questions and fears were pregnant with heated longing, a desire for encouraging answers, begging for appeasement. My list of acceptable and unacceptable behaviors became a list of exciting possibilities.

Will you call me whore?
Destroy me,
Make me lick the floor,
Twist me in knots,
Turn me into an animal?
Will I be a vessel for you?

Slice open our lying box
Through a low doorway for our

77

Shoulds and oughts.
Choose the things I don't need,
No careless moments, no mystery.
And you need nothing.
My backward bend doesn't feed.

And just to call to her, just because she'd hurt me, and just because I could, I changed the last chorus on the fly, turning questions into statements.

I will own you.
Tie you.
I will collar you
Hurt you,
Hold you, and take you.
You will be a vessel for me.

For all my inner ferocity, the song had to complement the rest of the set, so I didn't scream or wail. I didn't hit the top of my range, but the ragged emotion was there as I hit the last note at low, dinnertime volume. A whisper even. I moved right into "Stormy Weather." The lights blacked out for half a second. Jerry and his buddies were leaving, blocking the spots. I felt a core of relief. I didn't think I could deal with managing them and Jessica.

I finished my set, thanked my audience, looked humbled for the applause, and strode back to the dressing room with my chin up. I didn't start shaking until I got the door closed and locked. My breath became ragged and my eyes filled. Jesus, fuck, what was she doing there? With Deirdre? Who was going for gold in the family Olympics, for fuck's sake? God damn it. Which lie was incoming? Which bomb would she drop? I would stay in the dressing room. I'd tell Rhee I was too upset about Gabby to do the good-byes, and I'd stay in there until the bar closed.

That actually seemed like a viable plan, but when I scrolled through my contacts so I could text Rhee an apology, I slid past Debbie's number. Her words came back to me as if whispered in my ear.

Be a woman of grace.

Yeah.

Maybe it was time to grow up. Maybe if I knew I wasn't doing anything wrong and if I stood by my right to be with any man I liked, I didn't have a reason to hide in a filthy dressing room.

I texted Rhee.

—I'm a little upset about Gabby—

She got right back with a bloop.

—Can I do anything?—

> *—If you could bring back two Jameson's?*
> *One shot and one on the rocks for my*
> *nerves? And I'll be out right after—*

—Sure sugar—

I straightened my dress, wiped mascara from under my eyes, and reapplied my lipstick. A waitress came. I cracked the door to thank her for the drinks and remove them from her tray.

Once the door closed, I knocked back the shot. The other one was my prop. I looked in the mirror and tried out my customer service smile. Awesome. I was just smashing. And fuck her.

I went out to do my job. I entered the room and said a few hellos, smiling and graciously accepting compliments. Deirdre was at the bar. Jessica was alone at the table, half paying attention to her phone and half pretending she didn't see me.

I went to the bar and squeezed next to Deirdre. "Hi, I think we've met," I said.

She was more polite than before and nodded, a noncommittal smile playing at her lips. "Yeah. Nice singing." She tucked a strand of tight curls behind her ear. They bounced right out.

"Thanks. I, uh, I don't want to launch into this and be rude, but I couldn't help but notice you came with someone?"

"Yeah. She's family. She wanted to see you. I knew where you were, so…" She ended with a shrug.

"She's borderline malevolent."

"She's my brother's wife."

"Not anymore."

"You have a lot to learn." She tried to put the hair behind her ear again, but it sprang in front of her eyes.

I took a deep breath. She was one of seven, and I was alienating her. "I'm sorry. I just don't understand."

She considered me deeply. There was something about her, some sadness, a touch of melancholy. She had a deep spring of sorrow. I saw it in her eyes and the way she fought a losing battle with the strand of hair that wouldn't tuck behind her ear. "Like I said. Family. A man is meant to marry one woman. One life, one wife."

I wondered for a second if Deirdre lived in the twenty-first century, then I saw her crucifix necklace. I got it then. She was saving Jonathan's soul by serving Jessica.

"All right," I said. "I'll go say hello. You walking over there?"

"In a minute." She smiled at me. I couldn't read it. Besides the spring of sadness, I couldn't read Deirdre at all.

Jessica pretended to see me for the first time when I was halfway to her. Quelling a tidal wave of hatred that would surely overcome even the power of my customer service smile, I sat at the edge of her booth. We were equals. I wouldn't stand over her as if I was her waitress.

"Nice to see you again," I lied.

"Same here," she lied back. "You play beautifully."

"Thank you."

"And your voice is heavenly. You're an artist."

I put my elbows on the table and fondled my glass of whiskey. "Is there something you want? Being here? Because I do believe in the odd coincidence, but not this one." I was all smiles. If Rhee saw me, she'd assume I was making friends with a customer.

Jessica looked down at her own drink, a half empty clearish-brownish thing with soda and lime. "You played a song in the middle I didn't recognize. I mean, let me correct myself. I did recognize it. I asked myself many of the same questions."

"Were you as honest with yourself as you were with me?"

A smirk played at her lips. "I deserve that."

I could have pounced, but I didn't. She wasn't there to get beat up. She wasn't there to apologize, and she certainly didn't come to see me sing. She came to get Jonathan back. As far as I was concerned, I was pissed as hell at him, but I hadn't decided I was finished with him. So I stayed silent, waiting for her to explain. She didn't move a muscle unnecessarily. Her face gave away nothing. She didn't twitch or fondle a glass like I did, and she didn't have a customer service smile. She had an expression that went deeper. It was more practiced, more ingrained. She had the grace Debbie tried to instill in me. In spades.

"There will come a day when you want to talk to someone." She reached into her bag and took out a card. "Someone who knows more about who you're involved with. If you can forgive the little joke I played on you, you can contact me. We can talk."

She slid the card to me. It was a plain, matte, white business card with her name, number, and an address in the industrial part of Culver City.

It was so wildly classy I resented her all over again. I slipped it into the pocket of my dress. "If I have something to ask, I can just go to Jonathan, don't you think?"

She sipped her drink. "Has he told you about Rachel?"

"Yes."

"Everything?"

"I can't prove a negative. Neither can you. And if you think I'm repeating what he told me so that you can cross-check it... well, that says more about you than it does about me, doesn't it?"

"Your hostility does the same." I felt slapped, and I shouldn't have. She barely moved a muscle or changed her expression, adding to my feelings of inadequacy. "There are a lot of moving parts here, and if I may be honest, you're out of your depth."

I rolled my glass between my palms, cooling them, thinking of Jonathan's porch on our first night together and how he'd used his glass and the ice in it. The shot had loosened me, reducing my stress and inhibitions. I'd walked minefields like Jessica's before. Unfortunately, I always forgot my map. "So what you're telling me is you want to help me stay away from your ex-husband, whose heart you broke? No, I don't think so."

"It's not that simple."

"Oh, yes, it is."

"Things have been put in motion. I wanted to warn you away, so you don't get hurt."

I didn't like threats, especially vague ones. They implied the person making the threat didn't respect me enough to explicate, and that was guaranteed to twist my knickers in a knot. I tried to keep my game face on. "I'd understand if you just wanted him back, but you want something else."

"Right now, I'm trying to get you out of harm's way. I'll be happy to explain but not here."

Oh, that was a sneaky trick. I wouldn't touch it. Wouldn't believe it. Why would she have my best interests at heart? I thrust myself forward. She didn't balk. "He has one dick, and it can be inside one woman at a time. Nothing you say will stop me getting peeled off the ceiling every time he puts that astonishing cock in me. If you miss it badly, if you imagine it when your new man's on top of you, if you think about it when you're alone with your hands under the sheets, I understand completely. He's a monster fuck, Mrs. Drazen, and you're going to have to go through me to get him back."

Through the slight smile spread over her face, she practically whispered, "You're a class act." I tried not to react. I tried to be implacable and cold, and I knew, as sure as it never snows in Los Angeles, that I failed. My face was lemon Jell-O held up by toothpicks. Jessica pushed her glass away and stood. "I'm sure your refinement will keep the astonishing gentleman coming back for more."

Lemon Jell-O turned to cherry, and if there was a deeper shade of red to turn, I had no idea what flavor it was. She looked over my head and smiled. "Jon, how are you?"

His voice came from over my shoulder like a warm sweater, fresh from the dryer on a cold night. "Fine, Jessica."

My plan had been to rail at him, to throw rage his way. To let him know he couldn't have me watched. I had boundaries even if he didn't, and I didn't like being stalked. But when he put his hand on the back of my neck as if he owned me, I was awash in gratitude. It was the best possible comeback to Jessica's jab about my lack of refinement, and I didn't have to say a word.

Jessica said, "I was just having a word with Monica about her song. It made me think of you. Deirdre, honey, you all right?"

Deirdre had entered the circle, still tucking her stubborn red curl behind her ear. "Yeah." She turned to Jonathan and punched his arm. "Hey, man."

"I hope you're getting a lift home, Dee. Monica and I are leaving." He looked at his ex-wife. "Jess, I don't know what you were doing here, but I'm dispensing with all the niceties and saying good-bye." He squeezed my neck and looked down at me. "You ready?"

"My stuff's in the dressing room."

"Let's go, then." He held out his hand and I took it, sliding from the booth as he helped me up.

I walked to the back without saying good-bye, pulling him along. I didn't start shaking until we were both behind the dressing room door. Before I could even flick on the light, he pushed me against the wall, his mouth on mine, pressing my head to the plaster.

"Jonathan," I gasped. Didn't I want to yell at him? Wasn't I mad about something? I knew I had things to say.

He kissed my neck and stroked my breast through my dress. "The camera. Not mine. I asked Dave to keep an eye on you is all." He pressed his club of a cock against me.

Fuck it. Fuck explanations. Fuck boundaries. Whatever he said was good enough for me if it let him take me right then.

With both hands under my skirt, he kneaded my ass as he kissed me. His finger looped in the crotch of my fancy Bordelle panties and yanked them. I pulled one leg out, and he draped it over his hip, opening me to him. He taunted my nipple through my dress, drawing his thumbnail against it before putting his whole hand over my breast.

I undid his pants and released him. He put one hand on my chest, leaning into me, and he used the other to guide himself in me, which he did with a hard, fast thrust.

Eyelids half-mast with pleasure, he thrust again, even harder. I squeaked when his dick hit the end of me. He put my other leg over his hip so I was wrapped around him. He leveraged me against the wall with his body, a fulcrum where we were joined, the base of all that held us together.

I put my hands on his face, and he took them off, holding them down.

"You ready, goddess?"

"Take me."

He grunted as he pushed hard, getting so deep it hurt. Without a moment's hesitation, he pounded me again, forcing me against the wall as if he wanted to punch through it. Again and again he took me, hard and fast, pushing into a tingling warmth, forcing pleasure to current through me, the base of his cock slamming my clit over and over.

"Look at me," he demanded in a husky voice. I did, though my hair was falling into my eyes. My breath was timed to his thrusts. "You talk to me, do you understand?"

"Yes, sir." I could barely understand myself.

"Never shut me out."

"Never. Oh, God. Jonathan. My king."

"Don't come, Monica." He slowed down, angling himself differently so I felt him inside me, deep, hard, deliberate. "Don't let your emotions get the best of you. Talk. To. Me." He thrust with every word, sending me into a place where verbalization was nearly impossible.

"Yes."

"What do you want to say?" he asked.

"Let me come?"

"No. What else?" He slammed into me and ground against me, pushing all the way in, his face by mine, his scent of leather and earth and clean laundry overtaking me. "Why did you shut me out?"

"I'm scared. You scare me."

He cupped my cheek. "Why?"

The room wasn't well lit, but I saw the green in his eyes where the lights from the parking lot cut through the window blinds. "You can hurt me, Jonathan. You can do damage."

He stroked my bottom lip with his thumb. "Your honesty is beautiful." He pulled out and pushed into me again, jamming himself against my wide-open sex.

"Again, please," I begged.

He thrust into me again. And again, until I thought I'd explode from the crotch out in a spray of screams. My breath got raspy and hard, my chest hurt with the effort to move air through my body when I wanted to stop breathing completely. He put his hand over my mouth and took me fast and hard. I came, crying out into his palm. He put his chest to mine, his cheek against my face, and with a long groan, he filled me, jerking and rocking. I felt his warm breath on my neck, his hand sliding down my sweat-coated face, whispering my name. We leaned against each other for a minute, breathing together, until he kissed my cheek.

"You're staying with me tonight, at least," he said softly.

"Why?"

He kissed my mouth again and said, "Your house and your car need to be swept for cameras. I can't let you go back there until it's clean."

"What if whoever put that there was really after you? How do you know your house isn't full of cameras?"

"It's getting checked right now."

We kissed as he pulled out of me. He let my legs down. I was still short of breath, still sensitive between my thighs. My lips hurt where his late-day scruff had rubbed me, and my spine ached from being pushed into a brick wall. As usual, I felt as if I'd been beaten near death with a fuckstick.

Jonathan kneeled before me and helped me get my lacy underpants back on, kissing a trail up my leg. When he'd straightened my dress, he kissed me.

"We have to talk," I said.

"About Jessica. What did she say?"

"About that, and—"

There was a loud knock on the door. The handle jiggled. "Monica," Rhee called, "you in there?"

"Yes."

"Bernie's here." Bernie was the guy who played after me.

"Out in a second."

I hoisted my bag. Jonathan ran his fingers through his hair and took it from me. We got outside into the crisp, autumn night. The valet went for Jonathan's car. Mine was parked on the street. He walked me to it, our fingers linked. "People are waiting at your house to sweep it for cameras and mikes."

"This is so weird."

He held my chin when we stopped by my car. "It's probably nothing. We need to go there so you can let them in." He put his arms around my waist. "You, darling, will gather clothes and things. Then I shall bring you back to my bed, and I will have you again. And maybe again."

"We have to have an unpleasant conversation."

"Do you believe I'm not spying on you?"

"Yes."

"Did you fuck someone else?"

"God, no!"

"Are you leaving me because I interrupted your work?"

"No."

"Are you leaving me at all?"

"No, Jonathan, really—"

"Then I fail to see the urgency. Let's take care of business and let unpleasantness take care of itself."

Chapter 18

Jonathan

I didn't want to hear a word about what my ex-wife said. I didn't want to navigate her labyrinth of lies and half-truths, and I didn't want to explain anything to Monica while my mind was on Kevin and the cameras. We needed to hand off keys, pack her for the night, and get her into my bed. Then I would explain or fuck away whatever Jessica told her. Jessica was going to the mat. I couldn't deal with her shit for another minute. Her worst nightmare was seeing me happy, apparently, because I hadn't seen her as much in the past half year as I'd seen her in the past month.

I got to Echo Park first and parked across the street from Monica's house. The green minivan was gone, replaced by a black van. Margie's guys. I walked up to her chain-link gate. A man greeted me. Late twenties. Suit and tie. Pinkie ring. My eyes adjusted and I saw two others shaking the bushes.

"Jonathan Drazen?" he said, holding out his hand.

"The same." I shook it.

"Name's Will Santon. You look exactly like Margie."

"Tell her she looks younger."

He smiled at me. "This place yours?"

"Girlfriend."

"We found a wireless minicam on the porch. Not the best, but good enough. Middle-class work."

The porch. What had we done on the porch? Anything? My mind was a blank. I was blinded by the lights of a little black Honda tearing up the hill and into the driveway.

"Don't tell her," I said. "Let me take care of it."

Monica got out, all legs and hair, looking like a force of nature, a wild animal entitled to her own sovereignty. Her sexuality wasn't coy or cute. She wasn't saucy; she was feral. Her very presence on the earth stirred me.

"Hi," she said, smiling.

Santon smiled back at her. "Miss, is this your house?"

"I live here."

"I'm Will Santon. I'm a licensed private investigator in the state of California." He showed her an ID card. She looked at it, back at him, and back down to the card. "I've been hired by the law firm of Bode, Drazen, and Weinstein to check your house for surveillance devices. Do I have your permission to enter?"

She glanced at me. I nodded.

"Yes." She flicked her keys and headed in. We followed her, a line of four suits. The other two fanned out, glancing at everything, as Santon gave Monica papers to sign. I stood behind her and prayed that whoever watched her did so only from the outside. If they got inside, I would have the strong urge to burn the place down.

Finished with Santon, Monica turned to me and whispered, "I'm uncomfortable."

I kissed her forehead. "Go get your toothbrush and whatever, and we'll get out of here."

Chapter 19
Monica

I found a bag in the closet and threw it on the bed. My drawers were a mess. My closet was even worse. I took whatever I touched first and threw it on top of the bag. I needed work clothes and after-work clothes. Shoes. Underwear. Lacy Jonathan shit seemed absurd. Would his rule still stand? Garter belts and stockings felt frivolous and ridiculous with men in my house looking for cameras and microphones.

I threw both options on the bag. From the bathroom, I got makeup, a hairbrush, ties for braids, and my toothbrush. I was sure I was forgetting something, but I wanted out of there. I'd buy whatever else I needed.

I stuffed everything in the bag and picked it up. It had covered something: a manila envelope labeled *Jonathan S Drazen III* in Sharpie. One of Gabby's files. Darren must have found it and left it for me. I picked it up. There was enough inside to give it some heft, but it wasn't as big as the envelopes she'd created for people in the music industry. Twenty pages, tops. Probably a bunch of friends highlighted in orange and family in yellow. Jessica in pink. The corners were curled and the color faded. I almost slipped it in the bag. But no, I wouldn't bring it to his house. That was crazy.

"How you coming?" Jonathan leaned in the doorway, his jacket falling on his shoulders in a perfect expression of some kind of victory over gravity. Over everything. If owning a doorway just by standing in it was possible, or beating the shit out of a space by existing within it, he did. His concern over what was happening in my house had a physical presence. It emanated from him in a dense aura of worry, making him seem bigger, more present, more powerful. I was suffocating under the weight of it.

I glanced down at the envelope. His name faced down. "Thirty seconds or less," I said. He didn't move, making me nervous. "Shoo. Girl stuff."

He slipped out of the doorway, and I breathed again. I slipped the envelope into my top drawer, slung the bag over my shoulder, and walked out of my room with my head down.

Chapter 20
Monica

Telling him about my conversation with Jessica, and the song, weighed heavily on me. I couldn't think about much else. I couldn't do it in a neutral space. I couldn't just tell him and walk out. It was late. My house was overrun.

Jonathan put his hand on my thigh as his other hand rested on the steering wheel. "They're going to be out of there by tonight."

"Yeah. It's a small house. Yours took how long?"

"Couple of hours."

I looked out the window. I still felt invaded. "If there's nothing there, you're in trouble for making a big deal about it."

"We'll work out a suitable punishment." He didn't look as though he expected to be punished, though. He looked as though he was placating me. I didn't care for it. I would have given anything for it to be yesterday again.

We waited as the gate opened. It seemed to take forever, rumbling and clacking in a way I didn't remember it doing before. When Jonathan took my hand and looked at me, he seemed tired. Gorgeous and powerful as always, but wrung out.

"I don't want you to worry," he said.

I squeezed his hand. "I'm fine."

"But I want you to think about who might have done this."

"Something tells me you have an idea."

He didn't say, but I knew he thought it was Kevin. The fact that Kevin had nothing to gain from watching me notwithstanding, anything evil in my life, and stalking me was truly evil, could only be one person's responsibility. Career going poorly? Kevin. Art show hits a snag? Kevin. Bad day at work? Kevin. Camera trained on my front porch? Kevin.

When we got inside, he dropped my bag and put his arms around me. I rested my head on his shoulder. We rocked together, entwined, fitting together like puzzle pieces. He kissed my cheek, my jaw. A tingle of heat pooled between my legs. I looked up, giving him access to my neck. He was going to take me again, and it would be slow and sweet and generous. His hands worked up my back, and I put my fingers in his hair as he kissed my shoulder.

My body screamed for him. Just once. Before telling him anything about Frontage. Just a little bit of comfort. Just to be enveloped inside him. I didn't need a fuck. I needed to make love, and the way he touched me showed me he understood.

"Jonathan."

"Monica."

"Wait."

"No."

"Please."

"You're mine."

"Tangerine."

He stopped and stood back, looking me in the eye. His hair was mussed, and his eyes hooded with heat. "Okay, little goddess. What is it?"

"I have to tell you things. I can't put it off anymore."

"All right. Let's get some fresh air." He took my hand and walked me out to the backyard.

We sat on the outdoor couch, in the near dark, which I appreciated. I didn't want a bright light shining on our conversation. His hands stayed on me, stroking my palm, my thigh, soothing me.

"So, you saw Jessica there tonight," I said. "I don't have to tell you that part."

"Yes."

"And you saw us talking."

"Yes."

"She gave me her card and offered to tell me everything about you." His expression didn't change. "I said 'no, thank you, if I need to know about Jonathan, I'll ask him.'"

He squeezed my hand. "You're perfect."

"Well, maybe not. She asked if you told me about Rachel, and I said yes. She asked if you told me all of it, and I kind of went off on her."

"Really?"

"I told her I didn't know what she wanted, but she couldn't have you back because you were too good in bed."

He laughed good and hard, throwing his head back and showing the night sky his face. His laughter filled the huge yard, and even I smiled a little, because really, what man could be upset at that? I wanted to end the conversation right there. If I crawled into his lap, he'd put his arms around me, take me upstairs, and we'd make love so sweetly. Just the thought of it made my arms tingle.

"I haven't gotten to the really uncomfortable stuff yet."

He wiped the tears from his eyes and leaned back, smiling, totally relaxed, his arm draped over the back of the couch. "Go ahead, then."

"You really are good in bed, you know."

"Thank you. It takes two."

"Right. Okay. There's a song." I said the last sentence as if I'd jumped off a cliff. *There's a song.* Three words, and I was committed to finishing. I stared into my lap. I couldn't look at him. "Jessica heard it." I cleared my throat. "I wrote it after you called me submissive and before I gave you the list." I glanced at him. His smile was gone. "I recorded it as a scratch cut, which is something passed around the industry as a sample. I hadn't written a song in a while, and it was all I had. So, it came out good. One of the acquisitions guys heard it and wanted to hear me sing it. They came tonight."

"What was his name? The acquisitions guy?"

"Eddie something." Jonathan's eyes closed slowly, and his mouth shut tight. "What?" I asked.

"Let's hear it."

"Hear what?"

"The fucking song."

My heart beat so hard my ribs were going to break. My lungs quivered, filled, and seemed to empty only part way. I didn't have an instrument to hide behind or a piece of paper with my requirements for him to read. I just had two minutes of pure, raw, fucking vulnerability in his backyard while he pondered not only what he thought of the song, but me, what he felt about me, what his ex-wife heard, and what *she* thought.

"It doesn't have a title yet."

"The song, Monica." His voice was like a brick, blunt and hard, without nuance. He waited. I didn't know what he was thinking, but I realized the more time I took to start, the more crap would run through his head, and maybe that wasn't a good thing.

I sang it in my soft, jazzy voice. I didn't look at him because I didn't want to see his reaction. I just wanted to get through it. I started to crack in the last bridge, where I asked if I'd do the things to him he did to me, because the questions weren't about sex anymore. The song revealed too much. Fuck. I hated music right then, as I sang the last line. I wished I'd never heard a note.

His face was in his hands, and his elbows were on his knees. "What were you thinking?"

"About you."

He looked up. "When you *recorded* it? What the fuck were you thinking?"

I couldn't answer. I had been thinking about myself. That it could be an opportunity. That it was a good song, and once it was a song, it was mine, no matter what it was about.

Even in the dark, his face frightened me. I'd seen that expression before. On my father, just before he threw something or tore apart the living room drapes.

"I'm sorry," I whispered.

"I'm glad you're sorry. But what are you sorry for? Exactly? Are you sorry you had to tell me or sorry you were so selfish in the first place? Because it's not about you. It's about *us*, and we're not a big secret. Unless we split tomorrow, that song is about me and it will follow me wherever I go. Fuck, Monica, I know you're ambitious. I don't expect any less. What I didn't expect was that you'd do something so stupidly self-centered."

Even though we were outside, I felt as if a box closed in around me. If he'd been wrong or if I had a leg to stand on, the box might not have felt as though it was filling with water and I was three seconds from drowning. But I had done wrong. I didn't realize it when I first recorded the song, but I knew it when I played it in front of Jessica. I'd chosen my ambition over my respect for him, and there was no denying it.

His expression was impassive, walled off. The box filled further, and I felt not only trapped, but alone and scared. If he said another word, I would lose my shit.

"Okay, I get it," I said before walking back into the house.

Chapter 21

Jonathan

When the screen door slammed behind her, I kicked over the glass-topped coffee table. It shattered. I considered doing more violence to the furniture, but I wasn't angry at the furniture. I was angry at myself. I had no business feeling what I felt for Monica. I had no business getting involved in a kinky, emotionally charged relationship with an unpracticed submissive. Stupid. This, I'd earned.

When I'd held Jessica's hands down during sex, she told everyone I wanted to rape her. One slap on the ass, and I was an abuser. It hurt badly enough when she called me those things to my face. When she did it behind my back, it was worse. Later, I realized she'd had a rough time with men before me. I should have been more understanding, but it wasn't like I didn't have my own shit.

When Monica sang her song in the husky voice of a fallen angel, I knew her intentions were pure. I also knew the results would suck. Enough of our social circle hated me already. Who knew what or whom her performance would affect. My business? My family? The possible repercussions came in flaming scenes of scorn and derision. Lost deals. Uncomfortable dinners, come-ons from the wrong women, bruised ribs from jocular elbows of men thinking Monica was my whore, or worse, available to share.

Jessica had added humiliation to my confusion by confiding in our whole social circle and enough of my family to make Easter dinner a nightmare. I never dug out of it, and the song could just bury me further in a reputation I didn't earn and didn't want. I didn't want an entire lifestyle of bondage. I didn't want the clubs or the costumes. I wanted to be normal, except when I wasn't. Yet again, I'd be branded.

I paced around the pool. Monica had to go. She and her song and her god damn artistic aspirations had to get cut out before I got infected. I had to do it quickly and move on. I had to ignore any and all pleas for forgiveness. I had to forget my feelings, how she wrapped herself around me, how she'd charmed me and disarmed me. I needed to shock her out of my system.

I stopped, and like a siren's call, the pool invited me. I kicked off my shoes and dove in. The water was cold and heavy, and my clothes only made me sink lower. I swam to the surface, and the effort brought me back to my head. The panic and worry came back, but a lower grade. The usual stuff, not the all-consuming stuff.

I navigated to the edge of the pool. I was afraid to get out because I would freeze my ass off, but mostly, I was afraid to deal with the woman on the porch, if she was even still there. I leaned my cheek on my forearm and said, "Monica, Monica, you were perfect."

I was sad to lose her, but I couldn't be seen with her if she was singing that song, and she'd made clear I wasn't to interrupt her work. I knew my little string of sadness would grow into a ball of yarn. I knew how much I wanted her, and why, and how. After knowing her only six weeks, I'd miss her.

My phone rang. It had been on the glass table I'd smashed and apparently survived. I pulled myself out of the pool and dripped my way over to it, my pant legs sticking.

It was Will Santon.

"Hi, Will."

"We found five, with mikes, all over the house. They were on wireless, and they've been disconnected. Probably after she sprayed the car outside."

"We'll need you to work on finding out who did this." I wasn't supposed to care anymore, but I found myself talking as if I did.

"Any ideas?"

"She's working with an artist, Kevin Wainwright. They have a history."

"We're on it," Santon said.

"Send my sister the bill."

"You got it."

I was about to hang up. "Santon?"

"Yeah?"

"Any in the kitchen?"

"Nope."

"Thanks," I said softly and hung up. My relief dripped off me with the cold water. None in the kitchen. What did we do in the bedroom? I'd kissed her eyelids. Not optimum, certainly. Definitely a problem to be solved, because the fact they'd gotten inside at all was bad news, but nothing kinky got on video. At least if my private life was all the buzz, her dignity might be saved.

I don't know how long I stood there holding my phone, but when my teeth chattered, I went inside.

No cameras in the kitchen. Monica's imagination had saved me a shard of embarrassment. Meanwhile, she was having a huge crisis, and I threw a temper tantrum over something she apologized for. I had been ready to abandon her when she needed me to protect her because she wasn't perfect. And why? Because I was worried about what people thought.

They didn't know what I knew. They didn't know what it was to be completely in control of a woman's body, her pleasure, her thoughts, her emotions. They didn't craft moments the way a sculptor molds clay, tapping her consciousness during the day to create anticipation for the night, pushing her, crafting our climaxes not just as a pleasurable endpoint, but as a carefully timed, deliberate *act*. The culmination of my intention was what was most gratifying, and I couldn't give up control any more than Monica could give up music.

I had tried it with other women and failed or come up short. But not Monica. It wasn't just what she allowed and how she obeyed; it was the ways she didn't. Her moments of spontaneity came not in response to a weakness on my part, but the openings for surprise that I left her. Like the kitchen. The last place I expected to find her might have been the only safe place in the house.

What we made together was greater than what I would have created myself. Monica was my perfect canvas. The rest would have to fall into place. She was mine. What we had was mine. I'd earned it.

Fuck the rest.

Chapter 22

Monica

The blanket I'd wrapped around myself smelled of the old Jonathan. Sage. Fog. Jessica had chosen it for him, but I buried my face in it anyway. I stared at the open gate. A cab was on its way. If he didn't show up before the cab, I would just fold myself back into the world and never see him again. It couldn't be any harder than what I'd done before.

I smelled him before I heard him. The leather-and-sawdust Jonathan. I looked back inside and saw him standing behind the chair closest to the door. His hair was wet, but his clothes were dry. He wore his trademarked mask of implacable amusement.

"You waited."

"Cab's coming."

He sat in the chair. "I'm sorry I went off on you."

"It's fine."

"I feel like I should explain."

"Look, you got mad. I know why," I said.

"No, you don't." He leaned back in the chair and crossed an ankle over his knee. "When I married Jessica, I was a nice vanilla guy. We had plenty of sex, and we thought we were just fine. We were. Except I always had this dark place because of what happened with Rachel. I was so young, and not ready. And my father... well, I couldn't look at him. I still can't. I never told anyone. No one knew about it, except Jessica. Her knowing made me happy, and being happy, well, I started getting ideas about how good it would feel to fuck her just a little harder. Hold her hands down. Tell her when to come. Slap her ass." He paused, as if remembering some specific incident. "It didn't go over well. I didn't know how to stop, and she didn't know how to shut up. All her friends were convinced I got off on beating her up. They told their husbands, and before you know it—"

"No one's talking to you at the Eclipse show."

"Right. And I lost her. When you get divorced, you don't just give up the person, you give up all the dreams you had with that person. Those are harder to let go of." He uncrossed his ankle and put his elbows on his knees. "Now I'm with someone else, and she's beautiful with me. But she sings this song, and everyone will hear it and think I'm trying to rape and abuse her. It all came back."

"I can't tell you how sorry I am."

"You should cancel that cab."

"I really want to go home."

"You're not going home tonight. They found cameras."

"Oh, God." My chest felt as if a spike went through it. That was my house. It had always been my house. I felt myself breaking down and I had to grind my teeth to keep together.

"It's clean now. And there were none in the kitchen."

I laughed with relief. The episode on the kitchen floor was the first thing I'd worried about and the one thing I tried not to consider as a possibility.

"We need to find out who did it. And now I really want to have you watched."

I shook my head. "I'll stay with Darren."

"That's not a long-term solution."

I got annoyed. He'd taken the conversation and made it his own. "Jonathan, stop it. Long-term solutions are my problem."

"How's that?"

I took a deep breath. I knew what I wanted to say, but after finding out about my house, and his story, I didn't know if I had the strength. I curled deeper in the blanket. "I'm sorry, Jonathan. What I did with the song was wrong. I'll do what damage control I can. I'll record something else and get it to Jerry. I can't make Jessica unhear it, but it's not like she didn't know about your preferences."

"I know Eddie from Carnival Records, by the way. You met him at the Loft Club. Buddy from—"

"Penn. Right. I'm sorry. I can't make him unhear it either. Maybe he'll think you're hot shit now?"

He shrugged and swung his legs over the chair's arm. He seemed really relaxed for a guy who looked about to belt me twenty minutes ago.

"I was careless with your feelings," I continued. "I should have run it

CD REISS

by you first. Because it's your life, and you may not want your kinky shit all over. I mean, it *is* all over, but you don't need your lover confirming it. I thought about it, and I don't want that shit all over either. I could play it off as metaphor, but your rep means I can't. Then we become the couple no one can talk to because we make them giggle."

He laughed a bitter little laugh, as if he knew exactly what I was talking about. He did. I was just repeating history for him. I'd be the second woman to leave him because he was dominant. Before he came outside, I'd consoled myself with the fact that he didn't love me and we hadn't known each other that long. That seemed untrue, though. I was going to hurt him, and I was powerless to stop it.

"So," I continued, "that's when I realized if I'm going to be with you, I can't talk to anyone. I have to keep a whole part of my life locked up tight or people will look at me. I'm the submissive here. I'm the sucker getting her ass spanked. I'm the one walking around with bruises on her wrists. You're the master, and I'm under you. I mean, what the fuck am I doing? Do I not care about my life and my career? How am I supposed to get a leg up in a meeting when the guy on the other side of the desk is imagining me with a ball gag? How can I be seen as a musician who can deliver in front of a crowd if they think I'm a man's slave?"

The cab pulled into the driveway in a flash of headlights.

"I'll send him back." Jonathan swung his legs straight.

I unwrapped myself from the blanket and stood. "No, I'm going. What we have is not what I want. It's too much. I've never met a man like you, and god willing, I never will again because I don't think I could take it. I already can't imagine myself with anyone else."

He looked at me. "You're not leaving, Monica." He took my hands. His were cold, and the temptation to warm them between mine was unbearable.

I said, "I wanted you to know, before I go, that I love you. I thought I didn't want to love anyone again, and maybe I didn't. I mean, look what it comes with, right? The more I fell in love with you, the harder it got to leave you. It's the hardest thing I've ever done."

When he stood, he seemed taller, closer, more solid. "You're not going."

"I am."

"No. Don't you see how perfect we are? What you're breaking isn't some little, meaningless coupling. We aren't some casual fuck, and we never were. Not from the first night. Not from the first time I laid eyes on you. You were

98

built for me. I denied it as long as I could, but we were meant to be together. You are the sea under my sky. We're bound at the horizon."

"Please don't make this worse." My voice cracked. I sniffled. God. Damn. Those fucking tears.

He stood and put his arms around me, engulfing me. How he fit. How his touch felt perfect on me. How I wanted him as he kissed my cheek and neck and breathed my name. "Don't go," he said softly. "I want you, little goddess. Always. Please. Tell me what you want. Tell me what I have to do."

The cab driver honked.

"Let me go, Jonathan."

"No."

I pushed him away with all the force I had, and still he held me. "Let me *go*."

He squeezed me harder. "We're not finished."

I wanted to fall into him, to acquiesce completely. Giving in to his embrace and his touch, letting him take me upstairs would have been so easy. That night would have been beautiful and tender, but what about the next day, and the next week, and the next month?

When I pushed him away again, he released me. I stepped back, almost falling. He held his hand out to help me, but I avoided him.

"Good-bye. I'm sorry," I said.

"Don't be sorry." He stood straight, his chin proud and his shoulders relaxed. "This isn't over."

I wanted to tell him I loved him again, but it would have done more harm than good. I ran down the steps. The cab was about to leave without me, but I grabbed the door handle and opened it. The driver stopped, and I got in.

With one last glance back, I saw Jonathan backlit on that magnificent porch, standing as if he had complete control of the situation, every inch a king.

burn.

The Submission Series
Book Five

Chapter 1

Monica

The newspaper was open to a seemingly random page toward the back, but when it caught my eye, I had to examine it further. Discreetly. Because studying such a thing would draw attention from the man I sat across from. The girl in the paper was naked, on her back, with her legs thrown over her head. The light cast the seam between her legs in shadow. Her hands were tucked behind her back, and she was gagged with black cloth. She looked uncomfortable. She looked unhappy. Worse, the picture's appeal was in her miserable expression and the gleeful yet benign expressions of the men watching her.

Only when I heard metal tapping against porcelain did I return my attention to the man across the table or, at the very least, to the ring clicking against his coffee cup. He picked up a business card he'd let drop next to the creamer.

I was ambivalent about the pinkie ring.

On the one hand, it ate at my trust. Who could have confidence in a man who wore one? On the other hand, its oddness was intriguing. Will Santon's fingers slipped down his business card, pivoted it, rested it on the coffee shop table, and slid down its long side again. The fingers were thick and well-formed I imagined them sliding inside me two at a time, the ring resting against my asshole as the thumb teased my clit. I found the thought as unarousing as the woman in the paper. What normally would have sparked my desire, sparked exactly nothing. My mind was on sex all the time, but my body had taken a powder. I couldn't feel a damn thing between my legs no matter how hard I thought about fucking.

"I promise you," he said. "Your place is clean."

"I believe that you believe that." I twisted my teacup in its saucer. The pink roses were worn, and the saucer didn't match. All the décor in the café was found, thrift-shopped, or rescued.

"I've been doing this a long time," he said.

How long could he have been doing it, though? He was thirty-five, tops, without a grey speck in his dark hair or his two-day-old black scruff. His eyes, grey as a rainy day, looked as though they'd seen their share of nastiness. His gaze did not waver, but I knew his peripheral vision was as clear as my narrow field. His jacket fit perfectly, but it was the open shirt collar, the haircut around the ears, and the comfortable shoes that told me who he was.

"You're military," I said.

"Marines."

"Something ending in 'ops,' I bet." He didn't answer. "My dad was killed in Saudi escorting a second-rate prince to some mosque."

"I'm sorry to hear that."

"You have kids, Mr. Santon?"

"Daughter. She's four."

And no wedding ring, I noticed. "Would you let your daughter go into that house?"

His gaze slipped to his empty cup. Black coffee. He'd finished his black coffee in a single swig when it was burning hot. "I got a call from your boyfriend—"

"Ex."

"Ex-boyfriend."

"Ex-lover."

"He asked me to reassure you. I'm reassuring you."

"You know what would reassure me?"

"For us to sweep it again?" His head was cocked as if he thought that would be an acceptable answer.

"Find out who it was."

"We're working on it."

"I believe you are. And I'm sure he paid you a lot of money to come here and tell me my house was clean and you were working on it. But I'll be reassured when I know who did it, not when Jonathan Drazen says it's time to be reassured. Thanks for trying."

"He also asked me to see if you looked okay, how you sounded. He said when you're upset, it's in your voice."

I swallowed, feeling scrutinized in a way I hadn't a second earlier. My chin went up a notch, and my shoulders straightened. I couldn't help it. "I'm sure you're not supposed to tell me that."

"Do you know what I'm going to say to him?"

"No, and I don't care," I said, caring a great deal.

"You're terrified."

"I'm fine."

"I've heard terrified women. Some were scared for a moment when bad shit was happening, and others got beaten down by a daily, low-grade fear." He arched an eyebrow, as if asking me which one I thought I was.

I stood. "You can tell him whatever you like, but if you tell him I'm anything but perfectly all right, he's going to worry, and that's going to make more work for you."

"I don't need the extra work."

"Then you know what to say."

Will stood and handed me the card he'd been fingering. "If you want the place swept again, call me, and I'll have it done." When I took the card, his pinky overshot its destination and brushed mine. Though the touch surprised me, it did not rouse any feelings between my legs.

Chapter 2

Monica

The desire to be touched, to connect, to find commonality between myself and someone else overwhelmed my common sense. It wasn't just anyone I wanted to touch. It was him.

Though I was alone by choice, I was desperately hurt. I carried around an ache in my chest and a cloying desire on my skin. I missed Jonathan. I missed his sharp tongue and his strong arms. Yes, I missed his dick and all our play, but it was the loss of his stare, the warmth of his attention, and the emotional safety of his sphere of influence that made me feel unmoored.

Did I look scared? I leaned into Darren's bathroom mirror. I looked the same to me. I could call him. I could see him just one time. Maybe I would. I put my mascara down and looked at my phone.

It was 8:59 in the morning. In one minute, my phone would bloop with some short, pithy message from Jonathan. He sent me a text at nine every morning on the dot. I never texted him back, and I never told him to stop. I had two weeks' worth of pings from him, making sure that at least once a day, I thought of him. It was controlling in such a precise and unemotional way that on day four, when I realized what he was doing, I tapped him a livid response. But I never sent it. I thought of him so much more often than once a day anyway.

—*Bring an umbrella. It's going to rain*—

I scrolled back. He had reports from DC:

—*It is truly awful here*—

—*Another lunch meeting. Bullshit on
    the menu*—

—*You belong with me*—

And when he got home.

 —Debbie said you aren't living in the house?
  Will Santon is going to call you—

—Sea and sky—

I'd replaced my beautiful platinum diamond navel ring with the fake one I'd bought when I got the piercing. I returned Jonathan's through Yvonne, who had spent a lunch warning me about connections between BDSM and abuse, and had left it in his office when no one was looking. The next morning, his nine a.m. text read:

 —I'll hold this for you—

He was so confident I would come back, and all he had to do was wait. It made me crazy. I wrote songs about how crazy he made me, scrawled on the backs of napkins or on my forearm while I raced down the freeway. I wrote verses about his eyes and choruses on his voice. I wanted to exorcise him through music, but I feared I was doing nothing more than keeping the burn in my belly alive.

Chapter 3

Monica

The restaurant seemed specifically designed to attract entertainment industry types, like an oddly shaped orchid meant for the attentions of a specific insect. It was packed at lunch with agents and executives in suits feeling up writers and artists for their commerciality and ass-fuckability.

I hummed to myself in the bathroom as I looked in the mirror for something to fix. I was fine: two loose braids, a black dress, big stinking shoes, mascara. I'd even filed my nails. I was there to meet Eddie Milpas, and I looked better than fine. I looked fantastic.

When I walked back into the restaurant, he was being seated. I gave him my sterling silver customer service smile and sat when the waiter moved my chair. The window by our table overlooked the marina. On that windy November day, the boats swayed as if they were on a keyboard, playing scales.

"It's nice to see you again," he said. "I ordered appetizers. The calamari is fantastic."

"That's great."

Eddie said, "So, I wanted to talk about what we're looking for and what you have for us." I nodded. "Jerry brought me your scratch cut a week ago, and I didn't listen to it until the night before I saw you at Frontage. And when I did, I couldn't believe you pulled it off. That song is a hit, Miss Faulkner. Not to be crass, but it has money written all over it."

My smile went from customer service to nervous and uncontrollable. "I'm happy you like it."

"I may need you to rerecord it with the right production value added."

"I have another song I'd like to do."

"We, meaning me and Harry Enrich, the president of Carnival, we really want that one."

Two glasses of white wine came. He looked at me over his glass as

I took a sip. He had nice marble green eyes and brown hair. I may have taken a second look at him ages ago, before Jonathan, but for now, I was stuck. Temporarily, I reminded myself. Other men would appear, or none. Didn't matter.

I placed my glass on the tablecloth, letting it make a wet crescent in the fabric. "Actually, that song's no longer available."

"Did you sell it?"

"No. It's just unavailable."

He tapped the edge of his glass. "This have to do with the person you were writing about?"

Eddie had seen me with Jonathan at the club. And Jonathan was aware that Eddie had heard the song. So it wasn't as general a question as it seemed.

I wasn't concerned with the existence or performance of the song. It could be played off as a metaphor or a story. Once my past with Jonathan, and his reputation, came into play, the song became about me and what I did in the bedroom. That meant that under Eddie's gaze, at a meeting about my career, I felt naked and vulnerable. I felt his eyes slipping the dress off my body and his inexpert hands experimenting with pain.

"Look," he said, "the BDSM thing is really hot right now, and we're looking to capitalize. We're going all in with the marketing. You'll be an icon. Tall, beautiful woman in black leather, belting that thing out. We have more kinky songs ready to go, but no performer with real experience who can pull it off. I mean, the whole thing will fall apart on the Today Show if our singer uses the wrong phrase, right?"

The intensity of his imagination squeezed my lungs, forcing out the air. Everything I feared was happening, right then, and I hadn't prepared myself for anxiety so strong that every coherent thought ran from my mind like brown specks running from a kicked anthill.

"The song isn't available," was all I could say.

He smiled with his perfect teeth and twinkling eyes. "You'll figure it out. When you do, I'm pretty sure we can sign you." He slipped the menus from the side of the table and handed me one. "You should try the yellowtail. It comes with artichokes that will knock your socks off."

He opened his menu and pretended to look at it, but I knew he was wondering what I looked like on my knees, bound and gagged, legs spread, cunt wet and waiting for him. I pushed the image from my mind and just ordered the yellowtail.

As if feeling my discomfort, Eddie changed the subject. We talked about my plans for my musical future. I made up a bunch of stuff. Making plans was impossible when I had to take every opportunity that presented itself. Except this one. I had to turn this boat around. I had to go from Bondage Girl to something else, but I didn't know what, and I didn't know how. He seemed damned determined to stay on uptrending sexual fetishes as my brand. The more I engaged him on it, the more he'd expect me to say yes and the more I'd convince myself I was nothing more than a bound, spread-eagled fucktoy in his mind.

I didn't want him to know I'd broken it off with Jonathan. I was unprotected without him, sexually available and emotionally vulnerable. Before Eddie had a chance to offer coffee, I used my job as an excuse to get the hell out of there.

I went through my shift at the Stock confused, panicked, and anxious. I put on my customer service smile, made witty repartee when necessary, and delivered drinks as if I had twinkles in my toes, but I felt the rock in my chest go from still and heavy to vibrating. Not in a good way. In a painful way. The hum was the sound of regret. I had a chance at a career move, and I was going to lose it because it was the wrong one. Because I wasn't the audience's fucktoy any more than I was Jonathan's. I'd walked away from him to protect my nonexistent career, and it had careened out of control.

At the end of my shift, I flipped through my tickets, closed out my money, and handed the open tables to Mandy.

"Real bitch on five," I said. "Watch the salt in her cucumber cosmos. She has a 'condition,' and her untimely death is going to become your fault. Henrietta Sevion is by the pool. She's on the phone, so just bring her wine and smile. Renaldo Rodriguez is on the corner with a fucking entourage of blondes. I have no advice."

Mandy cracked her gum one last time and gently spit it into a napkin. "You're grumpy."

Robert, who seemed to hear everything no matter who he was serving at the bar, said, "Needs a drink." He nodded to me. "Want something before you go?"

"No, thanks." His offer was tempting, but it was nine o'clock, and I still had work to do. "Where's Debbie?"

"Office." Robert flipped a bottle as a prelude to wiping it down. "Can you tell her to hurry on the schedule? I have an audition this week."

"Nope. She hates when we nag about it, so I'm not going to do it for you. I'm asking her for time off, and then I'm going home."

Mandy poured the mixers for the drinks on her tray. "Oh yeah? Going somewhere for Thanksgiving?"

"Vancouver the week after."

"Ah that thing you're doing with both your ex-boyfriends? Which you don't think is weird?"

"It's not weird unless you make it weird. The piece, you should see it. It's going to make me famous." I wagged my finger at her. The piece *had* to make me famous. I could be Art Girl instead of Bondage Girl. I could do abstraction. The Vancouver piece gave me a gem of hope in the seven acres of shit I'd slogged through with Eddie. Mandy rolled her eyes and went to serve Renaldo Rodriguez and his blonde entourage.

I'd just gotten a passport. It had just come in the mail, meaning Kevin and Darren had had to go to the B.C. Mod without me to take meetings and do the setup. Letting my passport expire was a stupid oversight on my part, and I promised I wouldn't let it happen again. I would be fully present for every step from then on.

I went into the guts of the hotel to the liquor room, where Debbie's unobtrusive little office sat. When I got to her door, I heard two voices: hers and one male, talking seriously. I knocked. Usually Sam was in there with her, as if she owned the hotel and he worked for her, not the other way around.

"Come in," called Debbie.

I opened the door and saw Debbie first, leaning on the window ledge. Then I had the wind knocked out of me.

Jonathan sat in her leather chair in his work clothes. Blue suit, striped shirt, red cufflinks. He looked at me like the first time, when I felt as if he was drinking me through the straw of his gaze. But back then, though I'd been celibate, I had something for his eyes to drink: a piqued sexuality and availability in my heart that I didn't realize existed until he'd awakened it. When I saw him in Debbie's office, I felt emotionally dehydrated and sexually bloodless.

"I'll come back later," I said and spun on my heel before I heard the answer.

He caught me in the liquor room, by a stack of boxes piled eight feet high. "Monica." His voice was so gentle I couldn't ignore it. I turned. "Hey. How are you?"

"I'm fine." My voice sounded out of tune and ill-played. He looked perfect, well rested and fed, as though my absence had had no effect on him at all.

"You look good." He stood three feet away. Why could I feel the heat from his body? How was his gaze so physical on me?

"Thanks. You too." He wasn't moving away. Just standing. I couldn't even look at him. "I get your texts," I said.

"I know," he whispered and raised his hand, his fingertip touching my sleeve. "You can go in to talk to Debbie. I'll wait out here. You're at work. I don't want you to be uncomfortable."

My laugh was a gunshot on a yesterday's bloody battlefield, so short and awkward that I cast my gaze up to see if he'd noticed. His eyes, tourmaline with blue flecks I'd see if I got close enough, had that bemused look, as though nothing happened in his purview that he hadn't predicted, and the hurt I'd caused myself was simply something I had to get control over.

Until that look, I hadn't wondered, or even thought about, who he was fucking now. But with his heat on me and under the pressure of his presence, I had to ask myself if he breathed her name at the height of his pleasure, if he touched her with all the violence and tenderness he'd touched me with.

"Thanks," I said. "I'll be out in a minute."

Debbie had moved behind her desk. She'd been looking older lately. I'd been led to believe her real age was thirty-eight, but that was never discussed. "Sit," she said.

I stood. I didn't need to stay long. I didn't want to keep Jonathan waiting outside. The thought of him existing on the other side of the wall was painful.

"I need these days off." I handed her a slip of paper. She checked it against the calendar on her desk.

"This should be fine." She looked back up at me. "How are you doing?"

"All right."

"Really?"

"Yes."

She leaned back in her chair and indicated the leather chair where Jonathan had been sitting. Anyone who hadn't been attuned to his lingering smell might have missed it. "You took it seriously, didn't you?"

I sucked my lower lip between my teeth and nodded.

"I told you not to," Debbie said.

"Yeah, I kinda forgot."

"Understandable. Just keep it together on the floor. Yes?"

"I'll be a woman of grace."

Debbie looked at the schedule again. "Thursday, Doreen needs to leave at ten. Can you do half a shift?"

"That's Thanksgiving."

"Do you have plans?"

I shrugged. "I can be here."

She scribbled my name in the schedule and dismissed me.

When I went back out into the liquor room, Jonathan was gone. I didn't know whether to be relieved or sad.

Chapter 4

Jonathan

I don't know what I must have looked like to her. She looked more feral, hungry, and proud than she ever had. On edge, too. I knew if I touched her, she'd calm down. If I put my lips on her face, her breathing would slow. If I put my body close to hers, she'd stop twitching.

But I had to wait. She had to come to me. And she would.

Even as we stood outside arm's distance of each other, I felt the space between us mold into something perfectly matched. I'd thought she was on edge, but the fact was, I hadn't felt right since she rode away in that cab. Two weeks had stretched out into an endless horizon. I was on a path getting smaller in the distance, but always staying the same in reality. She chose to walk away, and she would have to choose to come back. I was a patient man. I could wait, but I didn't have to like it.

"What are you going to do with her?" Debbie asked after I let Monica leave without seeing me again.

"Wait like a good boy."

"How long?"

"I don't know. Why?"

"Because you're here, talking to me about bulk-ordering liquor and borrowing staff, when you have a bar manager to liaison with me." She waved her hand dismissively. "Go run your empire."

I threw myself into the leather chair. "What if the bar manager at K is a douchebag?"

"You're saving me from a douchebag? Have we met?"

"In fact—"

"Did I not help you get through that nightmare with your ex-wife?"

"You were a godsend."

"So stop bullshitting me. You come during her shifts and stay with Sam and me in the back, or you come after her shifts to drink at the bar. How long are you going to wait?"

"You want an exact date?"

"I want an event. Something that has to happen."

"Fine. When I meet someone as close to perfect as she is."

"Better start looking, my friend. She's already moved on."

"What does that mean?" I leaned forward. I felt myself getting pissed as the bottom dropped out of my chest.

"It means if there's not someone else already, there will be soon. I can see it when she talks to customers."

Debbie was always right about people. Usually, that was beneficial. Today, it was a problem. Today, I wanted to hurt someone, starting with myself. I left before Sam even got there. I could drink at home.

My phone rang as I turned onto my street. Margie.

"What?"

"Good evening to you too, little brother."

"What can I do for you, Margie?"

"You have Will Santon's team flying to Vancouver to watch Kevin Wainwright?"

Before I left the Stock, I'd called Will to let him know Monica's travel dates. I had his team following Kevin, to make sure Monica was safe from him, as well as tracking the money behind the cameras in her house. He said he was close to finding out where they came from, as if I didn't already know.

"Yes?"

"Has it occurred to you I might need to use him?"

"To do what? Have some movie producer followed to his mistress's house?"

"What's the difference?"

"The difference is a few million everyone involved can afford, and someone I care about getting hurt. Physically and irrevocably hurt." I was yelling. That wasn't going to get me anywhere.

"You know, Jonny, I don't mind you getting paranoid and crazy, but you're doing it on my dime."

"You're an attorney. You're protected. If I get caught stalking, I fry. I'll write you a check if you can't afford to feed the kids this week."

"Now you're getting nasty."

"Margie, sweetheart, please."

"I gotta pull him, Jonny. I'm sorry."

"Fine. Thanks for letting me know." I hung up.

Things were not going well. My patience with Monica was wearing thin. I hadn't considered her casting around for a new lover so soon. The thought of it made my fingers go cold. Will's inability to trace the cameras before he got pulled, a mere week before Monica was going to Vancouver with that sicko, pushed me out of rational thought and into a place of frozen rage. The situation was getting more slippery than I could manage.

Then I saw Jessica's Mercedes SUV in my driveway, and I thought I might break something. Aling Mira must have let her in before retiring for the night with Danilo.

My ex-wife sat on the back patio sipping coffee from a silver pot that had been on our wedding registry. I hated that thing. I thought about packing up all the shit of ours I hated and giving it to charity.

"Jess," I said, "how are you?"

She put her hand on my shoulder and kissed my cheek. Just one cheek, not a double air kiss. Somehow, that seemed more intimate.

"I'm fine." She wore perfectly fitting blue jeans, cowboy boots, a white shirt, and a bandana around her neck. I used to find her country girl airs charming. She was raised deep in Beverly Hills, where tourists got lost looking for Olympic Boulevard. "I came to talk about something. I thought you'd be here this time of night, but well, I guess not. And my appointments keep getting pushed."

I sat down. "If you came here to fight, Jess, I don't have the time."

"No. Of course not. I, uh… There were guys doing renovations to my studio? New plumbing? And I was confused."

"There's lead in those pipes—"

"I was just worried you were getting it ready to sell it."

"I'll let you make an offer if it comes to that."

"I can't, Jon. You know that."

"You didn't sell the trees?"

"I did. I got two million each for them, and the documentation was bought by the museum. But they cost a fortune. Keeping a dead thing alive takes a lot of engineering."

I nodded. Jessica's problem had always been that the cost and ambition of her work didn't quite jibe with what she could ask for it. She didn't have Kevin Wainwright's way of turning something that didn't exist into money.

Art, for her, wasn't about money, or professionalism, or business. Art was about art. I used to love the purity of her vision.

"You could make smaller things," I said. "And more of them. Just an idea."

She looked away. She didn't know what I was talking about. She said, "Remember when you first took me in *that* way? Right there, by the shed. You pulled my hair back and bent me over the wet bar. Then you yanked my pants down and hit me."

"I slapped your ass. Yes, I remember. I didn't exactly know what I was doing at that point."

"I was offended."

"You were scandalized." I was surprised to find myself smiling. Only in hindsight did how outraged she'd been seem funny. At the time, I was guilt-ridden and devastated over her reaction. "I believe you called me a pig and moved to a guest room on the other side of the house."

"And you—"

"I jerked off. Do you have a point here? We've covered this."

Her tone got hard, as if she feared I'd interrupt again. "You persisted, and I never considered your way. I never gave it a chance. Even when I was trying to reconcile, I still wouldn't try things your way. I don't think I was fair to you." She smoothed a nonexistent crease in her jeans. It was the only crack in her poise.

"This because Erik left?"

She shook her head. "He's back, sort of. We're talking, but I can't stop thinking about you… and kissing you again. You always knew how to kiss."

I leaned back. Was she really going there? Was she really going to offer me my married life back with a little kink thrown in? Did she honestly think I'd take her back? I should have kicked her out right then, but something else was in play. Some other motivation I had to tease out.

"And you're saying you want to try it my way?"

"I want to." She looked me with those big sapphire disks, wheaten lashes blinking. She was so beautiful. Angelic, even. "We'd need to set some boundaries beforehand."

Boundaries. The whole act was about tightly controlled boundaries, and she presented them as if they'd be concessions by me toward her. It was bullshit. The whole conversation. Her whole sudden pursuit of me. She was hiding something, and if she stayed tightly wrapped up, prim and proper, she'd never reveal it.

"No," I said. "My way. Right now. Then you tell me if you can take it."

She bit her lip. I didn't know what to hope for, but the longer she waited, the clearer my plan became.

"Okay," she said softly.

I didn't move. Not a blink or a hair. "That's 'okay, sir.'"

"Doesn't that seem a little silly?"

"You want to do this or not?"

"Yes, sir." A nervous smile played on her lips. Part of me would have loved to wipe it off with my dick. The rest of me didn't want to touch her.

"Stand up."

She stood, leaning on one foot and jutting her hip out, hands on her waist. All attitude. It would take some poor soul ages to train the woman.

"Unbutton your shirt."

She stuck her tongue in her cheek and swung her narrow hips, unbuttoning as though she was in a strip show.

"Stop trying to look saucy. This is a functional matter and not for your pleasure."

Oh, the look on her face. I don't think I could have forgotten it. When she told every mutual friend we had that I wanted to beat her and take away her right to say no, when she told them I had rape fantasies and that I hated women, she'd had no idea. The damage I could have done, but wouldn't have, wasn't to her body.

She unbuttoned her shirt completely and started to take it off.

"Stop."

I could have told her how I wanted her to stand, how I wanted her to look, where her hands belonged, but it would have been a waste of my time. I got behind her and untied the bandana on her neck.

"This is what it is," I whispered in her ear. "This is the kind of sex you're agreeing to."

As I slipped off the bandana, I considered binding her at the elbows like I'd done with Monica the night she got her voice back. But Monica could handle it. Even though I told Jessica I was going to show her what she was agreeing to, in all its pain and messiness, I had no intention of doing so. It would probably damage her psyche forever. Then she'd call the cops. Mostly, I really didn't want to put my dick anywhere near her. I did, however, want to figure out what she wanted.

"Put your hands behind your back."

She turned her head when she "obeyed." Jesus Christ. Two commands and she'd exasperated the hell out of me. I never would have felt an ounce of control with her.

"Face forward, Jess."

I didn't tie her at the elbows. The wrists would have to do. I moved around to face her. Her open shirt showed off her white cotton bra and flat stomach. Her shoulders drooped. I couldn't have tied her hands more comfortably, yet she looked awkward. "How does that feel?"

"Okay so far," she said. "A little weird."

"What's weird?"

"Jon, seriously? What's *not* weird? I'm standing here with my shirt open and my hands tied behind my back."

"Is your cunt wet?"

"Do you have to be vulgar?"

I stood close enough for her to feel me whisper. "Yes. It's about communication. It's about saying what you want and don't want, clearly, and sometimes with a filthy mouth. So let me get you on board with what you just agreed to." I kicked her legs open. I righted her when she almost fell, but the annoyance on her face made me want to drop her. "The answer to my question is, 'No, sir. I'm not wet. This sucks.' I'll tell you I don't care how much this sucks for you. Then I'll prove it.

"I'll undo your jeans. I'll pull them down to the middle of your thighs so it's hard to walk. You'll be uncomfortable, and that will please me. Then I'll get behind you, and I'll grab a handful of your hair at the back of your head and bend you over that table. I'll take off my belt, loop it once, and slap it across those sweet white cheeks until you're pink as a rose and your face is covered with tears. I'll stop when I can stick two fingers in your cunt and feel how sopping wet you are. Then I'll fuck you until you beg me to let you come, which I may or may not let you do. That going to work for you?"

The color had drained from her face.

"Didn't think so," I said, stepping away.

"Do it," she whispered.

"Jess, really."

"Do it! Start with the hair. Or the pants. Whatever."

"No."

"Do it!" she said.

"Stop, Jess."

"Are you a fucking *man*? Or do you just beg and cry for what you can't have? Is that how you get off?"

I threw her over the table. She fell onto it, bending at the waist with a grunt, ass out and arms bound by her own scarf. God, how many times I wanted to hear her grunt, to cut through the thick layers of refinement and find a woman past careful words. The woman I met so many years ago, before she'd built her walls.

I stuck my knee between her thighs and yanked the hair at the base of her neck. Her mouth hung open, and her chest heaved. She wasn't aroused, that I could tell, and I didn't care.

"Choose a safeword, Jessica."

"Do we need—?"

"Question me again, and I'm fucking your ass so hard you won't be able to sit."

I almost heard her teeth grinding. "Declan," she said.

"Interesting choice. Avoid it all and tell me what you really want, coming here. I'll stop for either the safeword or that, but nothing else until I'm satisfied."

I undid my belt after turning her head so she could watch me snap it out of the loops. I put her cheek to the glass. Out of the corner of my eye, I caught sight of a sharp triangle of white porcelain by the chair leg. One of the broken plates had missed the broom the morning after I made Monica recite "Invictus."

"No yelling, Jess." I shifted to her side, still holding her hair and my belt. "No crying. Do you understand?"

"Yes," she whispered so softly she was barely audible.

I hit the edge of the table with a *smack* of my belt. She jumped at the sound.

"Yes, what?"

"God, Jon—" I hit her ass. The belt landed with a satisfying *thwack*. She stiffened and ground her teeth. "It hurts. You're hitting me."

"You asked for it, Jess." I pulled her hair in my fist. "And that's, 'It hurts, *sir*.'" I laid into her ass again, and she yanked her head, making a sound like a bad brake shoe. "Now tell me what you want."

"I want you."

"Bullshit." I whacked her again. That was three. Too many. And I wasn't holding back much. They had to hurt. "This started a month ago. You chased Erik away. Why?"

"You."

I pulled back my arm, yanking her hair. She screamed.

"Fuck, Jess. Stop lying!"

I pulled her hair and looked in her face. Her cheeks were wet with streams of mascara-colored tears. Her lower lip quivered. I had been a white-hot ball of anger. If I had been thinking, I would have stopped. A dom should never, ever have an ounce of anger in his heart when spanking a sub. That wasn't fun. That wasn't all right. But between losing Will's services and Debbie's advice about Monica, I wasn't functioning. I was a panting, heaving mess looking into my ex-wife's tear-filled eyes.

"You used to have such a tender heart," she said through her sobs. "Do you remember when I miscarried? You took me to the hospital, and you were joking the whole way? Trying to make me laugh. But when we got there, you were crying. And you fell asleep in the chair next to me with your head on the bed."

"What do you *want*, Jessica?"

"I want to go home."

I pulled her up and untied her. She was miserable from the experience, and so was I. She wasn't ready for something that hard, even if she'd had any proclivity in that direction, and I wasn't sexually stirred in the least.

"Go take Erik back. He's good for you." I handed her back her bandana. "You know the way out."

I didn't look back when I went through the house, bolted up the stairs, and closed my bedroom door.

My god, three strokes. That was stupid.

Chapter 5

Monica

Working with Kevin and Darren had been intense, and I was grateful for the distraction from my beaten wreckage of a love life. We fought. We drank. We made music and art. I brought my pain to the table, using it to color and nuance a work of art that was basically about heartbreak, loss, and grief.

When we'd had breakthroughs, I couldn't have been more content. And then, one day, we realized we'd done it. Though plenty of it could use a tweak or ten, the piece was generally finished and not a minute too soon.

Standing in the center of the draft room, listening to my viola playing Kevin's lullaby, forty some odd tracks of my voice in wordless harmony, over Darren's techno thumping, I laughed. I felt drunk, melancholy, miserable, high, blissed. For two weeks, I'd cried every night and put on a customer service smile every day, but when I worked with the guys, I was myself.

When the thing was finished and photographed, we lounged around on a circle of couches in Kevin's backyard and drank cheap beer out of the bottle. Darren and Kevin had gotten wrapped tighter than the old amp cords at the bottom of a duffel. They called each other when they weren't working. As far as I knew, Kevin was still into women, and Darren was at least marginally involved with Adam, but I often felt like a third wheel to a marriage of kindred souls.

Kevin made broad intellectual pronouncements. Darren shot him down. Kevin pulled reasoning from the rubble. Darren told him he was full of shit. Over and over. By the time we'd documented every track, sound, and scrap of material in the piece, the two of them had become white noise.

I hadn't gotten over seeing Jonathan looking so hale the other day. So polite. "I don't want you to be uncomfortable." Asshole. But my meeting with Eddie had hardened my resolve. I never, ever wanted people looking at me like that in a meeting, and the only way to change it was to lose the song and Jonathan. I had to do what I'd been trying to do for two years: focus on my career.

"Earth to Planet Mon," said Darren, waving his beer around.

"Yeah." I barely snapped out of it.

"Happy Thanksgiving."

"National Orphan Feelbad Day," I said. We clinked bottles and drank.

"Did you get a flight to BC?" Darren asked.

"Yeah," I replied. Darren and Adam were going a day early to hang out in Vancouver. "Same plane as Kev."

"And your passport?" Kevin pushed his longish black hair back for a second, lowered his hand, and it flopped below his eyes again.

"Done. Do you need me here for the breakdown and pack up tomorrow?"

"No way," Kevin said, worrying the label on his beer bottle. "Pros do that. They'll have it boxed by noon and at the B.C. Mod in a week. We just show up to put it all together and look pretty for the preview exhibit. Black tie. All rich guys. Just like you like them."

"Fuck off."

"Agreed." Darren stood and took a last swig from his beer. "I gotta blow."

"So to speak," I shot back.

"Hilarious. See you on the couch."

"You're joking," Kevin said. "You're still sleeping on this asshole's couch?"

"If it happened to you, you'd feel uncomfortable and violated too."

"The P.I. said the cameras were gone."

"But I don't know who put them there. Once I know, I'll go back."

"And how are you going to know?" Kevin asked. "I mean, you dumped the guy who hired the P.I."

They couldn't see my face go fire-engine red in the dark, which was just as well. They knew I'd split with Jonathan but not why. Kevin had a point, and Darren and I had gone over it all a hundred times. I should have told my mother to sell the place. Just pull it from under me. It wasn't like I'd ever call it home again.

"On that note—" Darren tossed his bottle in the recycling. "This city's bouncing with parties in honor of National Day After Thanksgiving Day, and I'm being dragged to the gay half of them."

"Hey, wait!" Kevin said. "You guys have to sign the copyright papers." He ran inside, and he came back out again as if they'd been right by the door. After setting a stack of papers on the crapped out old bar he'd salvaged from an empty lot, he handed Darren a pen. "Right here."

"Dude, you got me signing papers by candlelight." Darren put his face nose-close to the page, and Kevin laughed. Darren signed. I got up and did the same. I felt as though we were sealing a deal, probably because I was half tipsy, and the outdoor space, candlelit and cool, added a coat of profundity to the proceeding.

"To us—" Kevin held his beer aloft. "The Nameless Threesome." We clicked bottles to our collaborative name. We were a cooperative, the future of creation, the new trend in authorship. Collaborators. Teams. Kevin had seen the trend and made sure he was a part of it. Kevin was a visionary, even to the detriment of his own ego.

It had been fun. More fun than I'd anticipated, and for the first time in weeks, I didn't feel anxious and alone.

When Darren left, Kevin held up his bottle. "Another?"

"I have to be at work at nine-thirty."

He handed me another anyway. "This is a small show, but it was a good idea. I'm glad we did this."

"Yeah. It was good. And I've never been that far north."

"You're smart, Monica, and you get it. You get what it is to make art. I've been meaning to say something to you."

"You're not going to get maudlin on me, are you?" I leaned my elbows on the bar behind me, bottle dangling from one hand. The beer was going to my head.

"I was wrong. The way I treated you. Calling you Tweety Bird. Marginalizing you. I denied the world your beauty, and it was wrong to you and the world." He stroked my cheek with his thumb. I was slow to react, and if I was being honest with myself, the human contact felt nice. He leaned in, his nose close to my cheek, and I caught his malt and chocolate smell. "You were right to leave."

"Kevin, I—"

He put his full lips to mine, and my body responded by twisting. He held me. His tongue tasted of beer. I pushed him away.

"I can't."

"Why?" His face found my neck. I recoiled, hating that I was so hungry to be touched, but only by one person.

"I'm in love with someone. It wouldn't be fair to you."

He clamped both sides of my face. "I'll live with it."

When he went to kiss me again, I scrunched up my eyes and lips, shaking my head. He held me fast. I did not like it. The sweetness of being touched was gone, replaced by a feeling of violation, like control of my body was being taken from me. I panicked.

"Kevin, no!"

"Do you need a safeword?"

"*What?*" When I tried to pull away, he clamped his arms around me and shoved his knee between my legs, spreading them.

"Monica," he said with effort as I wiggled. "Calm down. What's the—"

I bit his shoulder, hard. He screamed, and when he pulled away, my teeth still had him. Skin broke. Blood soaked through his shirt. Faster than an insult, I felt a hard impact on my face, and I lost my bearings from the slap.

He wore an expression both shocked and ferocious. I swung a full bottle of beer at it. The bottle didn't break, but it hit his temple with a *thok*. I lost my grip, and inertia pulled the bottle out of my hand and onto the ground. It landed at my feet in a sunburst of suds.

Kevin was crouched, holding his bleeding head. I didn't know whether to help him or run away. I was shocked into inaction until he came at me. Then I ran.

I ran into the studio, through the kitchen and his workroom, past the installation in its finished form, down the hall, and out the door. When I got to the front, where my car was parked, the metal front door didn't slam right away. He was right behind me, his gorgeous face smeared with blood.

"Kevin. Stop!"

He didn't stop. He grabbed my arm and threw me against my Honda.

Fuck.

My keys were in the studio.

I swung. He ducked. I had my opening. I ran down the block and didn't stop until I heard music.

Chapter 6

Monica

Like any self-respecting Angelino, I kept my phone in my pocket. The party I'd randomly entered, for the sake of being around people, was hopping with kegs and disorganized bottles on a paper-covered table. Art covered the warehouse walls, some of the silkscreens tilted from encounters with drunken partiers.

I called work when I found a quiet corner.

"Hi, Debbie? I can't make it tonight. Something happened."

"What's 'something'?"

"It's personal."

"If you're screwing my girls over, I get to know why."

I didn't want to go through the whole thing. I'd already shown my manager enough unprofessional behavior. "I left my car keys behind a locked door. I'm trying to get my roommate on the phone, but he's not picking up. I don't think he'll get here in time to get me to work."

She sighed and covered the phone to talk to one of the staff. "Where are you? I'll send Robert."

Shit. I could feel my face throbbing where Kevin had hit me. I couldn't go to work like that. "No, Debbie. I'm sorry. I didn't tell the whole thing. I was in a fight. I'm not presentable."

"Stop arguing and text me where you are." She hung up.

My face was throbbing with the bump of the music. The warehouse space had been co-opted for the night by German Benefactors, an artist's cooperative just starting to make waves. The place was huge, and packed, and smelling of piss where it was dark. Though two outstanding DJs had been hired, no one had thought to bring in a Porta Potty.

So I was forced out into the light, clutching some reddish drink, putting the cold plastic up to my face, avoiding people I knew.

Which didn't work. Ute Graden, a struggling actress of German descent with naturally white hair, found me sitting on a cinderblock wall by the street, watching my phone and the road for Robert. She and her four friends milled around, sipping, laughing, and talking about their work and dreams. They were part of my crowd. My world, and I felt so out of it.

Ute and I made small talk about our careers, where I mentioned nothing about a song I had to pull from Carnival because I'd promised my ex-lover I would.

"What happened to your face?" she asked.

"Fell on some bad sidewalk. Fucking Frogtown's falling apart."

"Looks nasty."

"Hurts, too. Hey, what ever happened with that indie film you were doing? About the prostitute with the kids?"

"Ran out of money, like, midway through. I'm 'on call' but… oh hel*lo*."

She was looking over my shoulder. I followed her gaze, and once a crowd of boys in turned caps and low-slung skinny jeans passed, I saw Jonathan across the street, waiting for cars to pass.

"Oh, fucking fuckery," I said.

"Yeah. Head to toe. That's a man."

"If nothing else." *God damn you, Debbie. You are such a yenta.* What was her deal? Was she my boss or my mother? I was going to have to have an honest, respectful, non-job-losing conversation with her.

As he strode across the street, I saw what Ute saw. He had on simple trousers and a sweater with a leather jacket. In contrast to the rest of the men at the party, who spent hours looking as though they didn't care what they wore, Jonathan looked neat and put together, as if he cared. He was tall and lean and straight, with his hair brushed back off his forehead. He owned the world and everything in it. The difficulty of staying away from him was past his looks, past any single physical attribute. He fell into a new, undefined category of "right."

I set my back straighter and tilted my chin up. I thought Debbie would send Robert, but instead I'd have to pretend I was fine and my face wasn't pounding.

"He's coming over here," said Ute, brushing her hair flat.

"He's my ride," I said.

Her eyebrows arched.

I paused. Jonathan liked blondes, if his wife was any indication. Ute was beautiful. She'd do well with him.

I thought about adding a short explanation. Maybe 'I'm in love with him, but I left him' or 'he was my lover, boyfriend, master, king...' None of it worked, and by the time I came up with 'we were together for a while,' he was upon us.

"Hey," he said, and that voice went right into my gut and ripped stuff out.

I stood up. "Jonathan, this is my friend, Ute." She had on a smile that wrapped around her face like a gag.

"Hi." He looked at Ute briefly, then back to me. "What happened?"

"I fell. What are you doing here? Is Debbie being a yenta?"

"I happened to be at the bar, and she couldn't spare anyone."

"On Thanksgiving? You don't have sisters to invite you to dinner?"

"Dinner ended at eight, and the kids went to bed. Where did you fall?"

"On my face." I hadn't seen a mirror yet, but his expression worried me. Was I going to the Vancouver opening with a big stinker on my cheek?

He turned to Ute. "It was nice meeting you." Nothing about his voice was nice. He put his hand on my back, between the shoulder blades, and guided me toward the street. It was a possessive gesture, and he had no business making it. When we were far enough away from the party, I shrugged off his hand.

"Sorry, Jonathan. I wish she hadn't sent you."

"Why?"

"You know why."

"Tell me about your face now. And the truth this time."

The party had street spillage, sending pockets of people onto the sidewalk and neighboring lots. The light industrial district thrived on those parties, but Jonathan and I were constantly getting bumped and shifted by gaggles of half-drunk hipsters.

"Can you just take me home?" I smelled his leather jacket, his cologne, the Jameson on his breath. He stood inches from me. If I just leaned forward, I could kiss him.

"Where's your car?" he asked.

"Kevin's."

"What happened?" His voice was tight as a bowstring, and his posture matched.

I felt the pressure of a big fat cry push out my lower lip, squeeze tears from my eyes, and steal breath from my lungs. "I hate it that I break up with you twice, and both times you show up in a crisis and I get upset."

"What happened?"

"I fell." My voice cracked mid-sob.

"You look like you fell on someone's fist."

"It was actually more of a really hard slap, but you should see him. He looks really bad."

Jonathan blinked. Slowly. "What happened?"

I didn't answer. He put his hands on my shoulders and, as if by force of will, removed all anger and judgment from his expression. It only made me cry harder.

"Fuck you."

"What happened?"

"He wanted..." I broke down. How could I tell Jonathan that I missed being touched by a man, by *him*, so I let something happen I should have stopped? Or why I was blaming myself when I hadn't done anything? "He kissed me, and I bit him. Then he hit me. I hit him with a bottle and ran, and my car and keys are at his place. And you're not supposed to be here witnessing this, so I do not feel guilty at all."

I tried to read his expression, but it was hard to see through my tears. He slipped one of those freaking hankies out of his pocket, and I snapped it away before he could tell me to blow.

"It's my fault," I said.

"Really?"

"Yeah. You said not to be alone with him, and I should have listened. You said he wanted to hurt me, and here I am. Now I don't know how I'm supposed to go to Vancouver with him."

"Where was Darren while you were getting beat up?"

"Parties. It's the biggest night of the year."

He put his arms around me, and I fell into him, putting my cheek to his shoulder, my face to his neck. He felt right. So right. So warm and gentle. That was the touch I'd wanted when I let Kevin near me. I'd gotten it so wrong. I felt a tightening on my ass, then a tickle. He'd slipped my phone from my pocket.

"What are you doing?" I grabbed for the phone, but he held it high, tapping and dragging until a map appeared. He'd found Kevin's address.

He handed me the phone. "Stay here with your friends for a minute. I'm going to get your car."

"Jonathan, just take me home. Don't get in a fight."

"A fight?" His voice was tense with control. "You think I'm going to take him behind the gym and punch him? Do I look like an adolescent?"

"No, but—"

"Stop." He put his hands on my face and got close enough to kiss. "You're mine, and I will defend you. But this isn't a movie. You don't destroy someone with a fight. And Monica, I know you walked away from me, but I am going to destroy him nonetheless."

He kissed my forehead and walked toward the studio.

Chapter 7

Jonathan

I couldn't say exactly how much of the situation could have been avoided if Margie hadn't pulled Will's team, but at the very least, I would have gotten a call when Monica ran out. If I hadn't been at the Stock, she'd probably be begging the bus driver for a free ride back to her hill or crossing Elysian Park to get home. Somalia was safer.

She had to come back to me. Soon. He'd had his lips on her, and I burned from the inside out. I didn't want to get upset about it in front of her. Her lips were mine. Her face was mine. I'd let her go, secure in the knowledge that she'd come back to me. But in the interim, anything could happen with either of us. Though I knew the difference between what was fake and what was real, I couldn't guarantee she made the distinction.

And also, her body was mine, regardless. Mine to kiss. Mine to fuck.

Mine to hit?

The contrast wasn't lost on me. I'd spanked her ass pink with the intention of a harder, rawer fuck. And she wanted it, begged for it. He hit her in anger, on her face, and hard. But what was the difference? When and how did she become a punching bag for the men she was involved with?

Wainwright was two blocks away. I saw her car in the front lot before I saw the building. The poor street lighting left dozens of dark corners and blind turns, but it made it very easy to see that the front door was ajar. Music came from it, a stringed instrument over a hip-hop percussion line that seemed a little bit off. It was disconcerting, all raw nerves and tension.

I pushed open the door and slipped into a narrow hall with doors on either side. Music came from the big room at the end. A voice, layered over and over, with that single stringed instrument and hard percussion. Something was off about it, but it was definitely Monica. I saw her bag half falling off a table in the big room. I grabbed it, and when I turned, I saw the piece.

It stood complete. The sections had been labeled for transport, and the wood packing boxes stood next to it. Like the coal mine, it was a freestanding room with an inside and outside.

It was cut in two by a foot-wide horizontal wound around the circumference. Shingles covered the walls, and the windows, framed in the Craftsman style and broken where the wound intersected them, were painted in gold and silver. Curious, I went inside.

From the inside, the open jaw of wood and plaster in the horizontal cut looked more evil, more hazardous. Detritus spilled everywhere. Broken cinderblocks. Gum-stuck urbanite. Grassrooted clods of parkway. All of it was anonymous, generic, unwanted, ripped out, found but not rescued. On the walls was a huge screen print of an open wound. It could have been any body part, from some ravaging knife fight or a ten-hour surgery; that didn't matter. It was three hundred sixty degrees around, and grotesque. On the other corner was an insect with a mandible and antennae that went around the walls.

Then the music made sense. Monica's voice, her words layered so many times that their syllables and meanings were lost. The strings sounded a little off key and the bass riff was half a millisecond off time, then gradually more, until the core was a disconcerting cacophony that fell back into the correct beat, looping into a false sense of a more permanent rightness. Each corner of the piece accentuated a different vocal layer, and each speaker had a different tone.

"It's good," I said. I knew he was within earshot. "Music's the same inside and out. But you hear it differently."

"Reality's the same inside and outside the relationship." He stood in the doorway, which was too tall for the room. Two people could leave at the same time, but only if one was on top of the other. "Before and after, life sucks. What are you doing here?" The left side of his face was cut and bloody. He held a red-soaked bag of ice to it.

"She did a good job on you," I said. "You deserve worse."

"Come on, man. She's a cocktease."

"Not with me."

"Fine, dude, whatever. What do you want?"

I walked past him and stopped. "Came to get the car. You let her walk out into a dark street alone. I don't know what comes over men like you."

"You know what? Fuck you. You're just another rich guy with ownership issues. Pussy like that's never owned."

I pushed him against the doorframe. The bag of ice dropped, breaking and spreading cubes and shards all over the floor. "You don't—"

He pushed me back. We were evenly matched, physically, so when I pushed him back, we ended up in a lock in a doorway designed for one person, straining against each other, unmoving for our red faces and effort.

I slipped my foot behind his ankle and yanked his leg from under him. We fell, with me on top. I got my knee in his sternum while he was still disoriented. I got lucky. I kept my head. In that millisecond, I looked at that piece of shit and thought, *One hard hit to the face, and I have him.* Then the voice of reason chimed in. I wouldn't have him. Knocking him senseless would do nothing but give him a headache in the morning. Worse, I'd lose Monica's respect. She expected better of me, and we were too precarious for me to do something temperamental and stupid.

I had to remove him from her life peacefully and permanently.

"Listen to me," I said, out of breath and knowing my upper hand wouldn't last. "I'm going with her to Vancouver. We will both act like gentlemen. You will not speak about her like that to me or anyone else. Do you understand?"

"You don't know her," he choked out.

I dug my knee in his chest. He swiped at me, catching my cheek. "Do you understand or not?" I asked.

"Fuck you."

I stood up. "I'll take that as a yes."

Chapter 8

Monica

I made sure I was facing the block Jonathan had walked down. He was taking too long. I knew Ute's crowd by sight, name, or both, and under normal circumstances, I would have had a fine time listening to their Hollywood war stories. Broken commitments. Rich executives demanding endless hours of free work. All of the tales laced with hope hope hope.

I didn't mention my meeting with Eddie, or his insinuation that if I'd just release a single song about being a submissive under the beautiful Mr. Drazen, I'd have a deal. A real deal, with a real record label. I just smiled and accepted condolences about Gabby. I talked briefly about the B.C. Mod show as if it was some little project that may or may not actually lead to something. I kept it vague and kept Kevin out of it.

A pressure on my shoulder made me jump. I was still edgy from wrestling with Kevin, but when I turned, it was Jonathan. He had a scratch on his right cheek.

"He's left-handed," I said, pointing at the scratch on his cheek. "You said you wouldn't get physical."

"What are you...?" He touched his face and came back with blood. "Thorn bush. It's dark over there." He held out my bag. "I parked your car around the corner. I'll have Lil drop it to you tomorrow."

"Why can't I just take it?"

"Because I'm driving you home."

"No, Jonathan—"

"I want to talk to you."

He looked as though he had to tell me something, and since he'd just gotten back from Kevin's, I was pretty sure I needed to hear it. I said goodbye to everyone with Los Angeles hugs, promising calls and get-togethers that I wanted from the bottom of my heart, but I would never make happen.

He walked me down the block, saying nothing until we got to the Jag. He opened the passenger door for me. I leaned on the car, not ready to commit to letting him drive me home.

"Get in."

I crossed my arms. "What happened at the studio?"

"I saw the piece."

"And?"

"You know it's phenomenal. You don't need me to tell you that. Now get in."

"I don't need to be pushed around twice in one night."

He leaned on the car, one hand on each side of me. "I need to get off this street with its four hundred drunk kids going back and forth from a party." He wasn't touching me. Not even our clothes were touching, but I felt him in a push of desire. I wanted him. My lips, my cunt, even my throbbing face wanted him. When he spoke again, his voice went from his mouth to my heart, lighting it on fire. "I need to speak to you privately."

"I don't want to speak. I want to go home and look in a mirror."

"You bruise easily. Okay? Now get in the car."

My hand went to my face. The skin was numb, with pain underneath it. "It must be awful."

He took my hand and kissed my cheek. It hurt and gave me incredible pleasure at the same time. When he moved his lips from my cheek to my neck, the hurt disappeared and the pleasure increased. "It's not," he whispered.

"Is this a ploy to get me in the car?"

He looked in my eyes, then he kissed my lips, parting them with his tongue. He paused only to say, "Yes."

I gave in to him, his arms resting on either side of my head and closing out the rest of the world. Only in that kiss did I realize how bad the last weeks had been, how much I'd missed him. Not just his physical attention, but his words and gestures, his protection and devotion.

He dragged his lips along my jawline and said, "What do you want, Monica?"

"I want you."

"You want me what?"

"To take me to bed."

"I'm not a toy." He said it while kissing my ear and touching my throat, his erection firm on my belly. He used his most tender voice. "You can't throw me away, then reel me back whenever you feel like fucking."

"Then stop touching me whenever I throw in a line."

He pulled away slowly. "You're right." His eyes scanned mine, and his expression changed, as if he'd realized something. I didn't know if I liked it.

A part of me wanted to reel him back in. It was the part of me that loved him in the first place, naturally. That part wanted to rub against him. That part had watched him walk across the street like a stranger, with all the heated possibilities that implied.

But my brain said "no." My mind was the repository of memory, and in that repository sat Eddie Milpas's suggestion that I become Bondage Girl for the masses, the symbol of their unspoken, unwanted desires. I could sing like a frog, and it wouldn't matter as long as I wore a rich man's collar.

"Let's talk in the car," I said, "but I'm taking myself home."

He paused, and I wanted to fall into his eyes, so close, so piercing. I slipped from under him and into the car.

He shut my door and walked around the front. I was so disappointed in myself. I had left him for good reason. I left him for the same reasons I left Kevin: my life, my career, my work. So how did I end up in the front seat of his car, about to talk about things I didn't want to talk about? How would I handle being in close quarters with him when all he had to do was touch me and I'd fall to pieces? I was weak, and I knew it. That was why I'd left Kevin so sharply. That was why I was celibate for so long. If being in control of my pussy wasn't an option, at least I could control who I saw and under what circumstances.

As weak as Kevin had made me, and as much as that weakness had made me run from him, it was nothing compared to what Jonathan did to me.

He got in the driver's side, and I closed my eyes. I didn't want to see him or the way the light hit his cheekbones or the taut skin of his jaw. If I could just close off my nose and ears, I'd get out of the car intact.

"Monica," he said, "are you all right?"

"It's been a long night."

"You can't go with him."

"Fuck you, it's my career."

"The masochism's not supposed to leave the bedroom."

"Go to hell." I went for the door handle. He reached across me and grabbed my wrist.

"You're not hearing me. You don't belong near him. It burns a hole

136

in me."

I was entitled to see whomever I wanted for whatever reason I wanted. Jonathan and I were broken up. But I felt guilty for leaving him, and my guilt spoke. "Who was she? In DC? You going to tell me you don't have someone to fuck in every port of call? Tell me about her, and we'll call it even."

He leaned back, letting my wrist go. "Are you serious?"

I shouldn't have asked, because his look wasn't one of denial, but "How dare you ask?" The way he said it, I was sure he'd done some fucking in the past two weeks, and it immobilized my heart. When I was a kid, a hole the size of a fist opened up in the middle of our street. Three inches of asphalt dropped into a deep nothingness. It got bigger and bigger, falling into itself until Teddy Ramirez's Toyota got stuck.

My chest had that sinkhole in it. It just fell in on itself, creating a bigger opening into nothingness and sucking the breath out of me. No. That was not good. That was the very definition of awful. I shifted and went for the door. He reached across me again and blocked the handle. "You can't run away every time something gets difficult."

"Jonathan, please, I can't bear the thought of you with someone else." His body was so close to mine, so real. The son of a bitch. Built so right for me, and how many others?

"Wait. You think there was someone else?" he asked.

I bit my lip. I didn't know what I thought anymore.

"Monica. There's. No. One. Else." He let the handle go and stared at me for a second. "There's only you. You think I'm stupid? You think I can create what we have with another woman? I know the world. I know the people in it. Us? What we have isn't something we made. It's something that existed before we even met."

The sinkhole in my chest reversed itself, like film run backward, from broken to whole. "I'm sorry. I shouldn't have asked. It wasn't my business."

"Why did you walk away from me if you still care?" he asked.

"I'm human. It's a terminal condition." I wanted him to kiss me. I wanted his lips, his hands, his tongue, but I couldn't, not when there were so many sensible reasons not to. "I took a meeting with Eddie Milpas. He wants to make me a star, which I'd laugh at coming from anyone else. But it's not funny because he has the power to do it. He wants to put Carnival's muscle behind me. If he does, I'll have everything I ever wanted."

"Monica, that's—"

"He wants the song," I said. Jonathan leaned back, against the door, a rueful smile at his lips. "He's not getting it. I keep my promises, and to be honest, I wish I never wrote that thing. But that's not the rub. He has plenty of songs with kinky lyrics that'll sound great from a girl all dolled up in leather and chains. BDSM is hot right now, apparently, and I'm 'in the know,' so I can pull it off."

I paused, because the image exploded in my mind. "Fuck! I spend a few weeks with you and I'm Bondage Girl. What the fuck am I supposed to do now? Do you know how hard I've worked? Do you know what I've put into this, and to sit across from this guy, and he tells me… wait for it… he tells me that I'm perfect because I'll *know what I'm talking about*? Who am I? What the *fuck*?" I slammed the dashboard. "And Kevin, do you know why he forced himself on me? Because *he thought I liked it that way*. God damn it. Jonathan, what if those cameras were in my house because someone wanted to blackmail *you*? And I'm getting caught in that net now. This is not what I want.

"I want to sing. I want to make music. I alienated my mother, I sacrificed a hundred other careers, I lost my best friend over it, I practice and work all the time. It's all I think about. It's all I want. But I'm trapped in this kinky thing with you right when all the work could be paying off. This sucks. My career could break any minute. These should be the best days of my life, and I wish I was dead."

I had to stop or I was going to cry, which I didn't want. Crying would derail my whole point. I didn't look at Jonathan because I didn't care what he felt or thought. I didn't want to see his beautiful face because he'd turn me into mush. I looked at my hands in my lap, then out the window at the party.

"I'm sorry," he said.

"I don't blame you. You didn't intend to ruin my life. But I'd really like for it to not get any worse, if that's okay."

We sat in silence. I considered saying goodbye and opening the door, but I couldn't. I considered running before he could catch me, but I couldn't do that either. Instead, I faced him. He rubbed his chin absently and stared into the middle distance.

And then my mouth opened and words came out. "The worst part is, I miss you."

He didn't react, but I did. I turned into stone. Jesus, what was I saying? He was the last thing I needed. He was trouble. Six feet two inches of life-damaging trouble in a sweet, tempting motherfucking devil of a package.

He turned to me, as if having decided something. "You and Darren take my plane up to Vancouver. Let me put you up in a hotel."

"No."

"Would you stop making me crazy?"

"You're not hearing me."

"I'm hearing a lot of pain from all quarters. It's going to get worse if you don't let me protect you. When you get back safe, we talk."

"There's nothing to talk about."

"Oh, goddess." He brushed my cheek with the backs of his fingers.

"Don't call me that."

"We have so much to talk about."

I closed my eyes. His touch felt like a boat on still water, leaving ripples in its wake. When would I stop craving him? "I don't want my life ruined."

"Neither do I. But this…" He brushed his hands over my face, bringing my skin to life. "This, I want. I've never wanted anything so badly. I feel your hands on your phone when you read my texts. I go to the Stock after your shifts just to stand where you've stood. I fall asleep on the pillow you used when you were in my bed. I need to share whatever piece of the world you're in. Tell me you don't feel the same."

"You know how I feel," I croaked.

"We can't go backward. You and I are going to figure out how to make this work."

His confidence should have made me hopeful, but it only filled me with dread.

"I want to go home now. Please."

He walked me to my car. When he handed me my keys, dangling them from his fingertips, I had the desire to do what I did when we'd met, what Will Santon had done: overshoot my grasp for a touch. Just a little. But then Jonathan spoke.

"Until we talk, and you get your head on straight, I'm not touching you. You were right. We get reeled in, you and I. We touch and we feel good, and then we land in bed and we forget the basics."

"Talking's not going to fix this."

"Neither is fucking."

I snapped the keys from him. "We can fix us, but we're not going to fix the world, Jonathan."

"The world is full of assholes." He opened the driver's door for me and closed it when I was safely in.

I lowered the window. "When I met you, I thought you were an asshole." He smiled. "You did not."

"I did. A gorgeous asshole."

His laugh came from deep in his chest. He bit his lip and reached out to cup my cheek but fell half an inch short. "I was an asshole for making you another conquest." He put his hand in his pocket, and I missed the potential in that almost-touch. "Get out of here, goddess. Get some rest."

When I got back to Echo Park, Darren was out. My face was a little swollen. I made myself an ice pack and went to the couch. I lay there with the TV muted, remembering him. The kiss we shared. His touch, the heat. I slid my hand under my cotton panties, shuddering in anticipation. I wanted to come. I wanted to want to come. I wanted to fall into my filthiest imagination and wrap myself in sexual desire.

But when I touched my opening, I found it unprepared for attention. A little fiddling got me nowhere, and I felt as though I was trying to get music from an instrument I'd never heard of. I pulled my hand away and went into an uneasy sleep.

Chapter 9

Jonathan

I'd walked her to the car with few words, but not because I had nothing to say. I had plenty to say. In the time it had taken for her to forgive me for destroying her career, I'd thrown a dozen mental balls in the air, and if I spoke, I would have dropped them.

I didn't have compassion for her situation. I had a raw empathy that made me want to hold her and whisper lies of comfort. But it wasn't going to be all right. Things weren't going to go back to normal. The only one way the whole thing would blow over was if she lived a life of obscurity. The recognition and success she'd earned and deserved promised to exacerbate her situation. There was absolutely no chance of people unknowing what they knew, and there was even less chance she'd drop her ambitions to protect her privacy.

If I let her go, the most likely scenario was that she'd swear off men until another dominant appeared. Then she'd fall right back into her submissive role with him.

That was not acceptable.

I had calls to Asia until well into the night. In the morning, after what felt like thirty minutes of sleep, I had Kristin find out when Eddie Milpas would be at the Loft Club. I needed to feel him out. I didn't want to take action based only on Monica's exploding imagination.

Chapter 10

Monica

I woke at half past eight and stared at Darren's popcorn stucco ceiling. The vertical blinds cast stripes across it, and only when my eyes hurt from looking at their odd symmetry did I get up.

I had an email from Kevin. I was tempted to delete it without reading it, but I was curious. I read on my phone while bleary-eyed and in the bathroom.

> *Dear Monica,*
>
> *You're not going to pick up my calls. I know you.*
>
> *I feel like such a fuckup. I don't care. I'll put it all in writing.*
>
> *I never knew what I did wrong. I should have damned my pride and waited on your porch until you told me why you left me. Really why. Not because of Tuesday nights. That could only be a symptom of some other disease.*
>
> *I didn't know what I was doing making the coal mine piece. I just did it, and it took a year. I wasn't going to invite you. I thought if you saw it, you'd be pissed, but you'd know how I felt. I figured it was the equivalent of me waiting on your porch, but twenty months later.*
>
> *Everyone said you were single, but you weren't, were you? When I saw you go in there with another man, I wanted to eat my face off. And then you were in the garden crying on his shoulder. I can only imagine it was over the piece.*
>
> *Remember how we read Blake sometimes? I thought of this one—*
>
> > I told my love, I told my love,
> > I told her all my heart,
> > Trembling, cold, in ghastly fears—
> > Ah, she doth depart.
>
> *I went a little crazy. I knew I wanted to do cooperative work before Eclipse, and you were the first person I thought of. I was just going to mention it to you later. After we talked. But the crazy took over.*

We did good work together. You wouldn't talk about what happened with us, even though it was all over the piece. I heard about your new boyfriend and the kind of shit you were into. I thought maybe that was what you needed from me and you couldn't say.

Wasn't that easy, was it?

Last night, after you left, I was pissed. And hurt. And I said a lot of shit to that dickhead about you I shouldn't have. I'm sure he repeated it to you. In the moment, I meant it because my face was busted. But now I'm too embarrassed to wait on your porch. Once we get back from Vancouver, I will.

—Kev.

I sat on the bowl and read it again. Then the Blake poem. Then the letter in full.

I was a heartless bitch, hiding behind silence and self-righteous indignation that stayed unchallenged. I thought I was taking control of my life, but I'd left a mess behind me. How many people had I done that to? My mother? She never failed to hurl some innocent-sounding cruelty at me, but I'd cut her off and call it independence.

Everything hurt. I'd woken up with no more than a dark spot under my eye, but it weighed down half my face. My back felt twisted and weak, aching as if I'd lifted a piano up the stairs. I didn't know what to do about my pain, or even if anything needed doing.

My phone blooped at nine a.m. exactly.

—How's the eye?—

I'd never answered a nine a.m. text, but after the night before, and Kevin's email, I thought I ought to.

—You should see the other guy—

There was a longer pause than usual. I imagined him reading my text, so surprised I answered he had to take a second to organize himself.

—I feel your hands on the phone—

I caressed the little plastic and metal box like a lover, feeling a warmth and tingle between my legs that had been missing the night before.

—I have to go to work. Lunch shift—

—I know—

Asshole. Gorgeous asshole.

Chapter 11

Jonathan

"I really could have used you guys last night," I said, blaming Will for something that wasn't his fault. Margie, the money source, had moved his whole team onto a divorce case with triangulations from Flintridge, to Santa Monica, to Monterey Park, and back. I could have deduced who was splitting up if I cared.

Santon seemed unperturbed by what had happened to Monica. We sat at a table at the Loft Club. Santon didn't seem impressed by the club at all. A mark in his favor.

He slid his hand over his glass in a way that looked like a threat. "I can't get into the house, so even if one of my guys was there, I make no guarantee it wouldn't have gone down that way."

"Do you have anything on this guy? Or are my hands tied?"

"We found some warrants in Idaho. He led an anti-war protest outside Boise city hall and got picked up for inciting a riot. He dropped out of sight a month after he did his thirty days and no one up there actually gave a shit when he showed up down here. Parole officer my guy talked to never thought of him as a criminal. Then we found two open. One battery charge. A DUI. Different parole officers."

I scanned the club. Larry poured drinks. Guys in suits laughed at the bar. I expected Eddie soon, and I wanted to be done with Santon before he arrived.

"The cameras?" I asked. "Anything?"

"We got taken off before we found out how it was done and who ordered the job. We did track the serial numbers, though. Followed the money."

He paused, and I rotated my hand at the wrist for him to continue. He didn't. The guy was unflappable.

"Well? Where did it come from?"

"You."

I snorted a laugh and drank the last mouthful of whiskey. "Fucking fantastic. Was it out of Ibiza?"

"Canary Islands. Someone's got their fingers in your pie."

"Apparently." I held out my hand. "I appreciate you coming here to finish this off."

Santon took it, and we shook. "Call me in a couple of weeks when things free up."

"Will do."

He left, and I went down to the locker room, chewing on what the fuck was happening with the Canary Island trust. Kevin certainly didn't have the right kind of mind or connections. It was possible I was underestimating him. It was also possible I had latched onto him because I despised him.

The club's huge lot had a driving range, tennis courts, batting cages, and a fake pitcher's mound and home plate. The owner had owned a major league team or two, and he kept baseball in the club even if the facilities weren't used much. Eddie and I used it more than any other two members. I'd set up the time with him to feel him out about Monica. Maybe I could convince him to try another marketing angle, any other angle, because I knew what he wanted to do was putting her through hell.

I rubbed the ball, scraping the fake pitcher's mound under my cleat. Eddie stood in the batter's box. Such a cocky fuck. Guy hit .209 in his best season.

"Come on, Drazen!"

I waved him off, getting ready for my pitch. Eddie's stance was as comical as it had been at Penn. "Eddie! You constipated?"

"What?"

"You're standing there with your ass out."

"Fuck you."

"No, fuck *you*." I threw. He hit it to the left field, smacking a target marked SINGLE before it puckered the nylon mesh. A minor miracle. I caught a glimpse of the speed clock to my right. Sixty-five. My shit was rusty. Or I was distracted.

After his success connecting bat to ball the first time, Eddie was back in the box, looking triumphant.

I took another ball from the bucket. "I heard you met with Monica Faulkner."

"She's a hot number." Eddie whipped the bat around before getting into constipation position. "You buy her song or you're just keeping her from singing it?"

I fingered the ball. "Why?"

"We want it, and she's not giving it up."

"It's her song."

"It's all about collaring and floor licking. Got you written all over it." He pointed the bat at me. "I want it. It's money. I think you're keeping her from releasing it."

I threw a strike. Seventy-five, but my elbow had snapped a little from the exertion. I wasn't pulling from the shoulder. "You're giving me a lot of credit."

"You're the master."

I hated it. I hated knowing the undertone of what he meant, because someone like Eddie trivialized something I took seriously.

"Doesn't work like that, douchebag," I called out.

I threw another strike, well inside the zone. Clocked at seventy-seven, but it didn't jerk my elbow.

"Then help me understand 'the point.'"

"The point is you can't trick her out like a whore and put her on stage."

"Come on, man. Give the world a taste of what you got."

When I threw the next pitch, he connected. Hard. I stuck my glove in front of me and caught it before it hit me in the nuts.

"Sorry, O'Drassen." He used my great-grandfather's name from the old country when he wanted to tease me. It had bothered me in college, and he'd latched on to it. I was setting up the next pitch when Eddie stepped out of the box. "Seriously, I want her. *We* want her. She's got that thing. You know the thing. The thing I can sell. Every man in the room will want to fuck her."

"What?" I had it coming. I'd been the joker, the storyteller, the adventurer. I'd been the guy making cracks about who I fucked, and where, and how many times, over beers. Meanwhile, I'd defended Jessica from every unkind word hurled behind her back. Why should anyone think I gave a shit? "She won't fuck you, Ed."

"Why not? I'm a record executive," he joked.

Despite the fact that he was kidding, the images came to mind like a neighbor I avoided. Her eyes half-closed. Eddie on top of her, pushing one of her legs up as he pumped into her, and her saying his name when she came. Over and over. Then the images came faster. Her laughing with him. Bending over for him. Holding his hand. Looking up at him with love, a smile spread across her face while he thought of using her and dumping her.

I shook it off. I was being an adolescent. "Get in the goddamn box."

"All right. Sorry, man. I didn't know she meant something to you."

When I felt the ice in my chest and my mind went completely and utterly clear, I should have known. I'd spent a long time getting my temper under control, and I knew it well. My temper wasn't a fire burning out in a confused jumble of thoughts; it was a frozen lucidity, a clarity of intention, whose sole purpose was to harm. I'd learned the warning signs, but on the mound, I fooled myself into thinking I was concentrating on the strike zone.

I threw a fastball, straight and hard. I coiled the power from my hips, up my back, and to my shoulder, pivoting my arm like a catapult. The ball landed right where I aimed: between Ed's ear and eye.

He didn't just fall. He spun around from the impact and landed on his back.

Fuck. I glanced at the speed clock. 91. That's about what it had felt like as it left my fingers. I ran up to Eddie and kneeled beside him. He was unconscious.

God damn, what the fuck *was on your mind?*

Nothing. That was the problem.

A crowd rushed over just as Eddie opened his eyes. I got him to his feet. A pretty doctor had been at the pool, and she took a look at him. He was well enough to flirt with her. It was too late to have a gentlemanly conversation about Monica and her place in the musical lexicon, of course. I could hardly say, "Listen, Ed, take the BDSM shit down a notch, and she'll sign with you."

I had to go to Plan B.

Chapter 12

Monica

I almost didn't answer Kevin. Three days passed in a heat of songwriting and waitressing. When I realized I'd let the time pass, I thought that maybe I was doing the same thing I'd always done: turn my back on someone until it was too late to go back.

> *Kev,*
>
> *I want you to know I got this, but I don't know how to answer it right now. See you on the plane.*
> *Mon*

The day before I left for Vancouver, I stood at my locker, shoving my work shoes in and stepping into my street shoes, when Jonathan appeared like a shiny new penny.

"Your eye healed up nice."

I jumped. "Jesus, stop that. I thought you were leaving me alone until I got back."

He leaned on the locker bank, crossing his ankles. "Take my plane. Seriously."

"You came here to convince me to take a private jet to my art opening? Talk about a nice problem to have." I slammed the locker shut and locked it. He smiled at me, then for half a beat, too quickly for anyone to notice, he dropped his eyes and drank me in. I felt as though he was stroking me from toes to shoulders, and a tingle went through me.

"Great, I'll make sure it's ready."

"I didn't say I'd take it."

I brushed past him. Not because I wanted to make a threatening gesture, but because my desire to be near him made the hallway too narrow. He walked beside me as if he belonged there. As if I'd agreed to a discussion about our relationship before the appointed time, which I hadn't.

"So, what's keeping you going to LAX in traffic and getting on a coach flight with three hundred other people?"

The employee exit spit out into the parking lot, which was crowded with staff arriving, leaving, and greeting each other with laughs and short conversations.

I had to walk close to him or talk loud enough to be heard by everyone. "Look, I'll have the conversation if you think it will change something, but if I start accepting favors and gifts beforehand, it's tainted."

I approached my Honda with my key out, but as I went for it, he put his hand on the car, covering the seam between the door and the roof. That hand was right in front of me, with its spray of copper hair and fingers shaped to please. All I could think about was it running over my body, flat first, then curving to my shape. It would stop to hold and grab the parts it found, tightening on my skin, bruising me with badges of agonizing pleasure.

He said into my ear, "I admire your nobility, but the conversation's already tainted by a few dozen orgasms."

He still wasn't touching me, and he pulled his face away enough so I'd have to do just a little more than lean into him to steal a kiss. I craved the warmth of his breath and his touch. God, his touch. His body was arched and I stood straight, though the desire to fit into him like a spoon in a drawer was an almost chemical impulse.

Kiss me kiss me kiss me...

But he stood still. "You don't want to be on a flight with Kevin Wainwright any more than I want you on it."

I could have mentioned Kevin's email as proof that our encounter was a misunderstanding, but I wouldn't be an excuse-maker for a guy who didn't understand the word "no." He'd ended up with a bleeding shoulder and bashed-in face for the trouble, but that was hardly the point.

"We've done everything wrong," I said. "Me, mostly. So I'm not going to walk into a conversation with you all sexed up from your money."

His smile spread, and his eyes closed a little. He bowed his head as if he didn't want me to see his amusement, but I saw his shoulders shake a little with laughter.

"The things you say," he said when he finally picked up his head.

"The things you *do*," I replied. "Can I get in, please? I have to pack."

He took his hand off the door. "You should wear that thing you wore to the Eclipse show. I know you won't let me buy you something new."

"Forget that, Drazen."

"The shoes at least." He stepped backward twice, and I couldn't help but give him the same type of look he'd given me earlier. I drank him in. His neck, his shoulders, the dark blue suit covering the body I imagined. The chest pressed against mine. The arms stretched over me, holding my hands down. The hips thrusting into me cruelly. He took another step back, and I felt as though I was being pulled forward.

Stunning creature. I wondered if, like he said, God had made him for me as much as I'd been made for him. Of course, God then spitefully created a world where we couldn't be together without being puppets of other people's imaginations.

Chapter 13

Monica

I stood on my front porch, shaking. I looked only at my keys as they slid into the lock and only at the knob as I turned it. My gaze zoomed no wider than the door as it opened. I hated acting like a toddler playing peek-a-boo, believing if I couldn't see Mommy, she couldn't see me.

The house already smelled musty. I put my head down and walked to my room. I shut out my peripheral vision because I couldn't be sure there weren't eyes in the corners. I focused on my feet as they traversed my living room rug. My kitchen floor. The wood floor of the hall.

My room.

I threw the duffel on my bed.

The closet. The dress, still in a dry cleaning bag.

The shoes, clumped on the floor.

The bathroom. My fancy makeup.

The dresser.

The top drawer.

I only had the Bordelle underwear left.

Under a manila envelope.

The bed.

The duffel bag.

The objects pushed inside.

Shoes. Dress. Underwear. Makeup. Envelope.

The zipper.

My feet on the floors. The rug.

The porch.

The door.

The key.

Click.

My breath.

Exhaled.

Chapter 14

Monica

I dried my hair with the bathroom door open. When Darren's screen door opened, I jumped. He was on his way to Canada with Adam, and I wasn't expecting anyone. I half hoped it was Jonathan but knew it wasn't. Peeking out to the living room, I saw Darren shuffle in. I pulled a dress out of the hamper and wiggled into it so I could get to him quickly.

"What the hell are you doing here?" I asked.

He shrugged. "Men."

"Men? What's that mean?"

He grabbed a beer from the fridge and cracked it. "I mean, how the fuck do you deal with us?"

"You're cute and you have these nice dangling bits. So?"

"So, well. Adam."

"I've met him."

He rubbed the label on his bottle. "Really nice guy. Really."

"Really. So? Why aren't you at the airport?"

"I kind of freaked out on him."

I threw myself on the couch and patted the seat next to me. "Go on."

He plopped onto the chair. Somehow, the couch had become my territory. "As we were loading up a cart, I just… I don't know. There was this reflective metal panel in the wall, and I was standing next to him. I saw us in the metal panel. Foggy, but it was us. He was looking at his phone, and I was looking at the panel thinking, 'Oh fuck. This is what other people see. Is this who I am? Did I decide this? And when?' I care about him. I love being with him, but when do I start calling myself bisexual, or gay, or… who the fuck am I, Monica?"

I had plenty of platitudes. I had advice I couldn't even pretend to take myself about just being who you are and letting the world see what they wanted, but uttering those words without hurtful irony would have been obscene. "I don't think any of us know ourselves."

He rubbed his lips together, a gesture I remembered from our early days. Darren was trying not to cry. It was painful to watch.

"I've been trying not to worry about it," he said. "I've been trying to figure out if I care whether people think less of me or not, and honestly, I don't think it's that. I mean, fuck, I'm a drummer. I'm always the one standing in the back. It's just... I feel like I never had the chance to work it out and say, 'All right. This is what I'll be to the world.' I got all wrapped up in him, especially after Gabby. Am I gay without him? Or am I back to who I was? Because I never thought about it before him, so now I'm taking on this whole identity without ever deciding on it. Am I making any sense?"

"Yeah." My throat was dry. "Did you leave him at the airport? Did he get on the plane?"

"No. He followed me to the parking lot. I mean, the poor guy was so baffled. He's asking me if there's someone else, or if I'm upset about Gabs and that's causing the freakout."

"The thing about a freakout is you don't know why you're freaking out," I said, opening the fridge. "How do you feel about him?"

"I don't know."

"Ah." I cracked a beer for myself.

"I do know how I feel about missing that flight."

"How?"

"Fifteen hundred in the hole. Non-returnable flight. Whole new last-minute ticket. I have seven hundred in the bank and two maxed out credit cards. I could take the car, but even if I start driving now, I'll miss the show."

I swallowed my beer, thought for a second, and said, "I think I have a solution to that part of the dilemma."

Chapter 15

Monica

Darren had taken some convincing. He was obviously uncomfortable with using Jonathan's money, but he needed it. He was swayed when I assured him it would be just him and me. Jonathan wasn't coming, and I wouldn't let the plane ride color my decision to stay with him or not.

We took the bus to Santa Monica Airport to avoid parking fees. I'd explained as much of the situation to Jonathan as I thought appropriate. I left out Darren's freakout and replaced it with "he missed his flight." Jonathan didn't seem smug about winning the Great Private Jet Battle, only irritated that I insisted on taking the bus.

"It's just a waste of time," he said. I heard him tapping computer keys. Multitasking again.

"I have nothing else to do. And I like the bus. It reminds me of when I was a kid."

"Were you this worried about tainting conversations when you were a kid?"

"My spankings weren't undertaken so willingly back then."

He sighed and let it go.

Darren and I sat with our bags between our feet. He got up for women with children twice during the hour-and-a-quarter-long ride. By the time we got to Sepulveda, the crowd had thinned, and he and I had stopped the seat flip.

"Did you tell Kevin you wouldn't be on the flight?" he asked.

"Texted him."

"He told me his side of what happened the other night."

I shook my head. "I bet he did."

"Really, Monica, I've been meaning to tell you. I think you should give Kevin another chance."

I twisted around to look at him. "Are you serious? Is your mind totally poisoned?"

"He's not the same."

"No, he's worse. Let me ask you something: Were you the one who told him about me and Jonathan? Maybe you mentioned the bruises on my wrists?"

Darren pursed his lips and looked down. "He had an idea already. Geraldine Stark spent a couple of nights with Drazen and came back with some stories. To Kev, it was like a lightning bolt."

Geraldine fucking Stark. Of course. The artist who put the trompe l'oeil on the side of Kevin's building had to have been with Jonathan. She told Kevin, probably post-coital, and then Kevin went ahead and told Darren. Together, they'd strategized how to get us back together.

"It bothers me that we worked together so many hours at a stretch to make this thing, and the whole time, you and Kevin are planning a reconciliation I don't want."

"What do you want?"

"Right now? To be left alone by anyone with a dick. You're all trouble. I want to never again hear who Jonathan fucked before I met him. Even if it was the first lady or Brad Pitt, I don't want to know."

"Why not?" His tone was confrontational, as if he was daring me to give him the truth.

"You know God damn well everything about this *hurts*. So stop being a prick." I turned toward the window, shutting out further argument. We traveled in the fold of time between day and night, when headlights got turned on and the streetlights went from dead cold to humming half light.

"Did you open the envelope I left?" he asked.

"No, did you?"

"No. Is it still in the house?"

I turned away from the window to reengage our conversation. "I left it at your place."

"Not even curious?"

"It's probably a family tree."

"Then why not open it?"

"I haven't had time." I could see, from his expression, he didn't believe me. "I need to talk to him. And I need it to be clean. About us. No external shit. If there's nothing in there, it's nothing. If it's external shit, then it's not fair for me to know it."

His eyes locked onto mine, and I felt naked. "You want him back."

"I don't know what I want."

"Fuck. You want him." He shook his head in a way that indicated nothing less than disappointment and shame.

"What? Is that a problem for you?"

"I should have driven up."

"Are we back on the whore thing?"

"Don't hit me again!" He covered his cheeks with his hands. "Please. My manhood couldn't take it."

Despite the fact that I wanted to belt him, or yell at him, or even shut down and go ice cold, I laughed.

He smiled and said, "Can you tell me, do you think this is you liking to get tied up? Or are you doing it because he likes it?"

The woman in the seat in front of us turned her head a little, and I shot her a look. She had a baby on her lap and a hemp sling over her shoulders.

"Both," I said, looking straight at her because fuck her. I was ashamed and horrified, and that made me feel hostile. She turned away. "It's his reputation I don't like. And everyone knowing. That's coloring the type of attention I'm getting from the industry.

"I want to reassure you. I want to tell you this is who I am, and this is me now and forever, and I'm so happy I discovered this side of myself. But I don't know. Everything about it is wrapped up in him. I can't imagine letting anyone else touch me like that, which is not what you want to hear. I know that. You think it's a power thing, and sure, it is. Would it be with anyone else? If I met the right vanilla guy, would I go vanilla?" I shrugged and put up my palms. "It could go either way. I'd have to be in the situation to find out."

"Well, I like him because of the way he treats you. But I don't, because of the way he treats you. And I think you're missing out with Kevin. He loves you."

"Oh, please give me a break."

"Deal with it." He squeezed my hand but looked away. "This is our stop. Let's get out of here." He waved to the baby in front of us. The mother held the child tighter.

Chapter 16

Jonathan

As soon as Will confirmed he couldn't send anyone to Vancouver, I knew I was going. I'd sleep even less than usual if I didn't. I arranged a revised manifest, made my calls, packed, and met them on the plane already set to leave that night.

My hope had been that she'd take the plane, I'd slip on with her, and we'd have three solid hours to sort ourselves out. Her fears about what other people thought were well-founded but meaningless. They'd think what they would. She needed to know that what we had was bigger than them and that any concerns she had about being dumped were unfounded. Sexually, she and I needed hard limits. Our discussion had to include how much control she actually exerted when we were alone. I'd gone too far with her without properly setting limits and explaining kinks she had no experience with. In my delight over her, I'd been irresponsible.

I still wasn't sure how to convince her without touching her. But I felt as though she was slipping away, and I couldn't let that happen.

I'd gone through immigration and carried my own bags. Security was non-existent. It was my own plane after all, and everyone at the airport knew me. I told them not to hassle my two passengers, and they joked about my habit of bringing women on planes and sending them back without me. I looked forward to the jokes changing. The prospect of keeping Monica was more exciting than bedding a hundred women. I rejected the offer of a ride to the plane. My legs worked, and I didn't want to announce myself so loudly.

Monica and Darren had gotten through immigration in record time, apparently, and they were already stepping up into the cabin. They were inside and out of sight before I reached the stairs. My pilots, Jacques and Petra, had been married seven years and still held hands as they waited for me.

"Jacques," I said.

"Jon. We're scheduled to wait for you. Two days," Jacques said.

Petra chimed in. "We might have to bounce back for a doctor's appointment."

"Well, I think you're going to have to come back and do a pickup anyway. I'll text you the names for the manifest when I have them." I looked them both over. They seemed nervous. "Something you want to tell me?"

Petra smirked.

"No," Jacques said. "Come on. We have a schedule to keep."

I stepped onto the plane behind the pilots.

Chapter 17

Monica

The plane was probably the nicest thing I'd ever seen. The pilots had pointed us up the little stairs embedded in the dropped-down door and into a cabin with ten cushy leather seats. Two seat banks faced each other around a gleaming lacquer table. The wood matched the liquor cabinet and the galley, which was cleaner than my kitchen had ever been.

Darren threw himself into a seat, and I sat next to him. We had work to do. We'd detected a flaw in the sound for the show. It wasn't much, but the music was meant to be loud, and the little click in one of the forty-some tracks would seriously ruin the experience. I freed my phone and headphones to start.

I smelled Jonathan. Then I saw him standing over the table. I felt like a kid caught eating her lunch before the bell.

"I had a feeling you'd show up," Darren said.

Jonathan slipped in across from us. "And you didn't bring me flowers or chocolates or anything?"

I slid toward the window, watching Darren smile as he said, "I didn't want you to get the wrong idea."

"Or Monica to get the wrong idea," Jonathan said. He looked at me with that irrepressible smile. It was nice that he was smiling and nice that Darren was remembering that part of him liked the guy, but I had a mixed bag of feelings.

"This is the second time you've shown up where you weren't supposed to be," I said.

"It's my plane."

"You know what I mean."

"I do. I am going to the opening and the viewing the night before because I love art and because I'm on the finance committee at the B.C.

Modern. Now, I have work to do." He put his laptop on the table and glanced at each of us expectantly. Despite the six other seats, that table was the only laptop-convenient surface. Bastard.

Darren followed suit, his Mac out in a flash. He glanced between Jonathan and me as if one of us would suddenly go into heat.

"I need to check the loops," Darren said to me, all business. "There was a weird clicking. Then I'm mixing down again." Darren handed me the clunky pro headphones he'd brought and looked at Jonathan. "She has a perfect ear."

"Indeed."

I put on headphones and watched Darren's computer screen, listening for a flaw that might be part of the hardware or a tiny blip on track thirty-two of forty.

The plane took off. The tiny thing felt shaky, unsure, too fast. My stomach fell between my feet, but I tried to keep a straight face, even when I gripped Darren's forearm. We had to start the loop again when the laptop slid across the table. There was no one there to tell us to put our stuff away, and it didn't seem to be a requirement anyway. Jonathan pretended to work, but I knew he was watching me.

I glued my eyes to Darren's screen when the plane evened out and I could swallow again. I'd heard the music for the B.C. Mod piece a hundred times, but in only a few minutes, I was listening with my whole brain for a click that may or may not have been there. I watched the wavy lines flow across the screen like heartbeats until my phone buzzed and lit up. A text. From the guy sitting across from me.

—*Is it hot in here? Or are you just gogeous?*—

He was looking at me over his computer screen, lips curled in a smile.

—*That's so unpoetic. Even for you*—

—*Shall I compare thee to a summer's day?*—

—*In Los Angeles? Yuck. Is there a shower in this tin can?*—

He leaned back, a smile creeping across his face. He ignored his computer in favor of the phone. The cold, electronic blue lit his face while the soft light from above warmed his brow and hair.

"Mon?" I barely heard Darren through my headphones. "Did you hear the click?"

"Uh, no. Can you run the loop again?"

—I feel your hands on the phone—

My heart skipped a beat. Or stopped. Or did the thing where I felt its presence in my chest.

—How, exactly?—

—As if they were on my body—

—We have a no touching rule in effect—

—Only until you commit yourself to me—

I knew where this was going, and I wanted it, dangerous as it was.

—What if I don't commit myself?—

—You will—

—Then what?—

—Then I'm going to take those touchy little hands and tie them to your knees—

—No kissing first?—

—No—

—Not even your cock?—

He pursed his lips and looked at me. His hands slid over the glass. Fuck that, he was not taking control of this conversation. I put my elbows on the table, leaning over it toward him.

—What if I crawled at your feet, kneeled before you, looking up at you as you pulled out that piece of meat between your legs—

He glanced at Darren, who sat in the dark, eyes glued to his computer screen and unaware of our bloops and dings. Then Jonathan leaned forward, mirroring my position on the table, as he texted.

—When I'm done tying your hands, I'm going to bend you over and press your cheek

to the mattress. Then tie your ankles to
the bed's legs, holding them spread for me
as you stand—

> *—What if I kissed the tip of your*
> *cock? And you took me at the back of*
> *my head while you rubbed it along my*
> *closed lips, and I opened them—*

Our forearms rested on the table, lateral, not touching, as we watched each other and our little glowing screens. Our phones dinged and blooped and buzzed rapid fire, like electronic jumping beans.

—I'm going to put my thumb on your clit, then
move it up to your asshole until it's wet—

> *— In one move, you put your*
> *whole shaft down my throat—*

—I'll lean my wet thumb on your asshole
until it yields to me—

> *—I flatten my tongue on the base of*
> *you as you pull out of my mouth—*

—My thumb will enter you and you'll groan and
strain against your ties—

> *—I look up at you and open my*
> *mouth for you to fuck it again—*

—I'll kneel and lick your cunt until you
beg for me to fuck you—

> *—You tighten your grip on the*
> *hair at the back of my head—*

—I won't—

> *—and press your cock into me until*
> *my tongue touches your balls—*

—I'll spank you until you can't do
more than sob—

> *—Cruelly, you fuck my mouth and*

I love it because it pleases you—

—When you least expect it I will enter you and
fuck you. Hard. Two strokes, then pull out
and rub my wet dick all over—

—Spit drips down my chin and onto my chest—

—Your asshole will be fresh and wet and ready
for me to slide into it. You will scream—

—oh—

—Then you will moan—

"I heard it," I said, pulling off my headphones. "The click."

"Me too," said Darren. "Okay, all I have to do is—"

"Slide over, I have to get out." I bumped him, and when he didn't move fast enough because he was wound around the equipment, I stood on the back of his seat and climbed over him.

The bathroom was probably nicer than anything I'd ever seen, and I didn't care. I didn't have to pee. I slapped open the door and Jonathan was right behind me, closing it behind us. I put my arms around him.

"Behind your back," he growled and laced my hands behind me. My back was against some kind of counter, I felt more than saw cabinets, a toilet to my left, and a tile floor. Mostly, I saw Jonathan. His hands were on the cabinets, his face an inch from mine.

"Touch me, Jonathan. Please."

"Commit yourself to me."

"Oh, God. Don't—"

"Commit. Yourself. To. Me." He said it softly and firmly, half whisper, half scream.

"I'm yours. Touch me."

"You don't even know what you're promising."

"Yes, I—"

"I cannot watch you walk away again. If you commit yourself, you're mine. You will set your limits, and I will honor them. You will be exclusive to me. You will submit yourself to me sexually. Completely."

"Yes."

"People will know."

I thought I would have agreed to do anything for him, but that stopped me dead in my tracks. "Why can't we be discreet?"

"I want everything. I want to take you out. I want us to be tied without worrying about who sees us, and I don't want men looking at you like you're single."

"Fine, then Carnival's going to put me on stage in a collar."

He raised an eyebrow as if he found that interesting, not repulsive. "You crossed that off your list."

"Figurative collar. If everyone knows already, I might as well let them have their way and put one on me. But it won't be your collar; it'll be theirs."

"Tell them that's not acceptable."

"I'm not in a position to negotiate."

He bent his knees a little to get his face level with mine. "You don't know the power you have."

My hands were still behind my back, but my shoulders sagged. I was uncomfortably aroused, and though I was happy my pussy remembered sex fondly enough to moisten, the sweet physical desire was in opposition to the shitstink in my heart. "I just want us to be secret for a while."

"No secrets."

"Oh, you know what? Mister No-Secrets-Sir. Mister Your-Honesty-Is-Beautiful. Tell me about when you were sixteen. Westonwood Acres?"

If I'd held out any hope of him putting his hands on me, I'd dashed my chances pretty cleanly. He removed his hands from the cabinets and leaned against the opposite wall. I flushed red.

"It was Gabby," I said. "You didn't know her deal. She wanted to know everything about everyone she thought could help her. People with money or connections or both. Westonwood Acres came into my hands the day of her funeral."

"Those records were sealed."

"Everything was blacked out but the institution, your name, and the date."

He scanned my face, his eyes flicking back and forth, then he cast them downward. "I took a handful of pills. The Adderall was mine. The Oxycontin and the rest were my mother's. I don't even remember all of them."

"Why?" I reached for his hand, but he pulled it back, still obeying the rules. Damn him.

"Do I have to talk about this in the bathroom of a Gulfstream?"

"Commit, Jonathan."

"Are you sure you never considered law school?"

I could have cracked a joke, denied it, or even demanded an answer, but he was stalling. I wouldn't give him something to answer with another stall. I folded my arms.

As if understanding the gesture, his mouth curled in a wistful smirk. "Now you know why I ran to you when your friend killed herself."

"I thought it was because you cared about me."

"That too. Believe me, that too."

"What was so bad you'd try to take your own life?"

He nodded and slipped down the wall until his feet were wedged against the opposite counter. He put his hands in his pockets. "Remember Rachel?"

"I'll never forget that story." I slid down as well, leaning my feet on the opposite wall, a mirror of his posture.

"It wasn't just the once, her and I," he said. "It was a thing. I was infatuated, and she was fucked up. It was intense. All encompassing. My father wasn't in the picture then, but we snuck around. Tough to do when you're fifteen, but enough money makes it easier. I got my license and a car as soon as legally possible." He smiled as if some uncomfortable, yet pleasant memory flooded his mind. Then he shook his head. "Anyway, drunk driver. Meaningless loss. Devastation. A family I couldn't lean on or they'd know the truth. Et cetera, et cetera."

"I don't think you can 'et cetera' any of that."

His laugh was short and humorless. "No. I shouldn't." He hooked his thumbs in his pockets. "I have a big family. I know, we're loaded, so it's not like we all lived in a one-bedroom apartment, but someone was always around. It wasn't until she died that I realized I was surrounded by seven sisters and two parents and all these friends, and I was alone. Very, very alone. My dad said, 'Oh, son, by the way, I took care of her family, so don't worry.' Like that was all it was about for him. Or not. Maybe he was hurt and didn't want to show me because he was in denial? Or she really didn't mean shit to him, which disgusted me, because I knew it was true."

"Your dad sounds like a charming guy."

"You have no idea just how charming he is." He looked at his feet, then continued. "I felt like I came from shit, and that was what I was. Rachel, for what it was worth, understood the dynamic. She made me feel less isolated. And when she died, I felt worthless and alone. A handful of pills seemed like the best way to take care of it."

We watched each other for a second before I said, "I want to hold you."

"Commit yourself to me."

"Yes."

"Will you be okay with people looking at you, knowing you're submissive to me?"

I swallowed. I wasn't ready. I didn't think I'd ever be.

"From your face, I can see that's a no," he said.

A buzzing noise came from the speakers, shocking me straight and alert. Jacques's voice came soon after.

"Mister Drazen and passengers. Please buckle in. We're landing in a few minutes."

Jonathan snapped open the door and let me go out first. He pressed himself to the doorframe as I passed so our bodies did not touch.

Chapter 18

Monica

We piled into the limo, exhausted. Nighttime in Vancouver looked much like nighttime anywhere else. Though I was excited to be outside the U.S. for the second time in my life, my body, mind, and heart had been through too much in the last six hours.

"We're at the Travel Lodge," Darren said. "I assume you're not staying there."

"Neither are you," Jonathan said.

"Jonathan," I grumbled.

"I own a hotel practically on top of the museum. Don't be stupid. Staying in Richmond's going to waste time and money. Separate rooms, in case you're concerned."

"I'm not," I said.

"Thank you. That'll be great," Darren said.

I wanted to kick him. Why was it okay for him to accept an expensive hotel room, but whenever I accepted a gift, I was whoring myself? I tried to give him a look, but he just dicked with his phone. Then he smirked a little and glanced over at me. Then I realized that in his mind, by accepting it himself, he was saving me from doing so. Thus, I was no whore.

Men.

"Boxes arrived this afternoon," he said.

"Have you heard from Kev?" I assumed he wasn't invited to Hotel Fancypants, and he'd need to know where we were.

"Nope."

"I'll arrange food sent up to your rooms, and an early wake-up call," Jonathan said. "When's the earliest you can get in for set up?"

"Seven," I said. "It's gotta be done in time for the preview at four."

"It's tight," Darren said.

"And we have zero experience doing this kind of thing, so Kevin needs a wake-up call, too." I kicked Darren. "That's you."

I noticed Jonathan's silence, but I didn't look over. I didn't want to see his reaction.

Hotel C looked like all of Jonathan's hotels—a sleek, modern building no one would mistake for home. The long front drive had a marble fountain, and the entire hotel seemed to be made of glass and steel. Staff descended upon us immediately with Mister Drazen this and Ma'am and Sir that. Darren stayed outside to manage the equipment unloading. We got through the door and entered a lobby done in black and brown, wood and matte surfaces, with a cement floor and warehouse ceilings. A woman with her brown hair in a French twist and a black leather skirt handed Jonathan a clipboard. She looked lovely despite the fact that it was after ten p.m.

"Mister Drazen, happy to see you back."

"Thanks, Marsha. Can you call Kristin for tomorrow's meetings please? There were some changes."

"Of course."

"Should we go check in?" I asked Jonathan, who was signing a bunch of papers.

"Done already."

"Must be nice."

"I admit it," he said as he handed the clipboard back to Marsha with a smile. "It is. Where's Darren?"

"Getting the processor and mixer out. His life is those computers."

"Are you and I having a drink before bed?"

A drink. I'd agree to anything after a drink. I'd beg for anything, even without it, and he'd deny me just to make a point. "I'm wiped out."

"Come on, then. Marsha will sort Darren out."

I looked back at my friend and found him talking to Marsha earnestly while indicating equipment. My guess was he wanted to take it up himself and sleep on top of it, and she wanted to put it in with hotel security. That argument could go on indefinitely.

A man appeared behind Jonathan. "Mister Drazen?"

"Anthony."

"Can I help you with anything? Take you up to your room? Get you a table at the bar?"

Jonathan turned to me and asked, "Do you need something to eat?"

I didn't answer right away. I don't know what my expression said, but something about it caused Jonathan to turn to Anthony and say, "We'll let you know."

"Very good, sir." He spun on his heel and walked away.

"What is it, Monica?"

"I have a problem."

"Say it."

"I know I'm tired and hungry, and I have a lot to do tomorrow. But I can't play this game with you. I'm not good at it. I want you. I want to be naked with you right now. The fact that I'm this close to you and I can smell you, feel you, hear you... Fuck, I'm going crazy."

"It's entirely reciprocated."

"You don't look like you're going nuts."

"Self-control. That's all it is."

"I can't sit across a table from you. I barely made it through the plane ride. The past few weeks have been dead for me. My body shut off. Then you came along. I want it shut off again because I'll agree to anything right now."

He leaned into me, not touching, his hands in his pockets. "I'll only let you commit to me if you mean it. I won't let you make a mistake, because I won't tolerate you walking away again."

I leaned toward him a little. I felt the warmth of his breath, and his open jacket brushed my shoulder. "That first time we met, in your office, I threatened you with a lawsuit."

"You floored me."

"You handed me Sam's card. I brushed your finger with mine."

"Yes."

"I wish I hadn't done it," I said. "I wish I'd just walked out."

"It was too late way before that."

"I need to go to my room alone. And I need to not know where you are."

He smiled. "I'm right next door to you."

"I just told you not to tell me."

He chuckled and shrugged.

Darren came up to us, a valet rolling the hardcase behind him.

"I have some things to do here," Jonathan said. "I'll have Anthony show you to your rooms."

With that, he strode off to meet Marsha by the counter.

"Handsome guy, I'll admit," Darren said as we watched Jonathan move across the floor as if he owned the joint. "And not half the asshole."

"But Kevin's better?"

Darren shrugged. "Kevin's my friend at this point. And so are you. So for me, it seems natural."

"Not to me."

"I'm getting that."

Chapter 19

Monica

The room wasn't a room. It was one of two suites on the top floor. I saw the skyline through the floor-to-ceiling windows in every direction. The décor matched the lobby's—matte blacks and dark matte woods with textured grains stained for contrast. I traversed the corners and expanses of the living area and bedroom, every step further proof that I was alone. The black leather couch was too big. Seating for six. Closet space for a family or clothes horse.

Something was missing. After the second time I circumnavigated the rooms, I realized that I didn't feel as though I was being watched. I hadn't realized the feeling stayed with me when I locked my door behind me, but in its absence, I grasped that it had.

I tried to call Kevin and got no answer. We were on international roaming. He'd probably shut off his phone. We needed him. He'd taken us on to energize the creative process, but the practicalities of an installation were beyond me. If he got held up too long, Darren and I would be in a world of shit.

I pulled my jacket off, and the sleeve went inside out. The poly-satin undersleeve's seam had split ages ago, but the loose threads and edges were invisible when I wore it, so I kept the thing, promising to fix it someday. Were our relationships jackets we wore? Everyone was a manageable, condensed, digestible thing on the outside with a gaping wound on the inside. Then when we pulled ourselves out, they prolapsed, like a jacket sleeve, and exposed the raw, broken places we never got around to fixing?

I looked at the jacket a little too long. I was so fucking horny and pink, it was painful. Jonathan was right. We could fuck ourselves blue, but until we figured out how to be together, we were only using each other's bodies for mutual immolation.

His room was likely behind the thick wooden door with the big lock. It sat next to the empty china cabinet that would probably be filled if I called the concierge and announced I was entertaining. If Jonathan wasn't in his room already, he would be soon enough. He had to make a show of sleeping. I touched the door, trying to feel him on the other side. I lay my cheek against it. How I wanted him. If only he wasn't carrying the baggage of Bondage Girl: the looks, the smart comments, the self-defeating turning of my own brain.

What if I rejected him completely, again? Like an addiction, the bodily ache needed to be broken first, then the habit. If I made it through this trip, I might get home ready to take on something new. Maybe date? Maybe meet someone nice? Like any addict, I couldn't see a world outside the drug. But I knew there was one.

I stepped away from the door and got ready for bed in a haze. I hung up the dress and got out my work clothes for the next day. I'd done all right. My voice was an instrument for the piece. I'd recorded cleanly and done good work. I just needed to finish the job. Tomorrow. I had to focus on that.

I got into bed naked, feeling the brush of cool, hotel sheets on my skin, and immediately Jonathan was back on my mind. The drug. Putting his hands on me. Stroking my back, my ass, my thighs. He cupped my breasts, caressing them, then pinched and twisted the nipples until pleasure turned into a sharp bullet of pain. My hand followed the path my mind created for him, and I looked forward to release and rest. Arching my back into the imagined warmth of him, I spread my legs, giving my fingertips a place to land. I slipped them between my folds, pretending they were his, imitating the tenderness he showed right before the roughness took over.

I rolled over onto my stomach and slipped my fingers over my clit. I wasn't ready. How could that be? I couldn't go to bed frustrated. I wouldn't be able to sleep. My mind needed to talk some sense into my body, but apparently, they weren't on speaking terms. I put my ass up and felt a little tingle that might have been something or nothing, but I didn't touch myself. I just imagined myself in his ready position, waiting, unsure of what he'd do next. But it was too comfortable.

I slipped down to the floor.

The carpet was grey wool, rough to the touch. It dug into my knees and palms as I crawled, naked, into the living area. My arms and legs kept a midtempo rhythm, head bowed in submission to someone who wasn't in the room. Everything was taller. I was lower than the table, the couch, the chairs. My body's reaction was almost immediate. Fluids collected between my legs, lubricating them against each other.

What a repulsive creature I was, unable to find arousal without crawling on the floor. Even my self-loathing turned me on so intensely I had to stop crawling for a second to shudder at the power of it.

I was alone. I was safe. No one was watching. I could allow myself to feel it, to do it, to be however I wanted. I got to the door between my suite and his. On my hands and knees, I put my lips to it, thinking his name over and over, tasting the flat flavor of wood and dried lacquer, finding his sawdust scent inside it.

Doubts came, but I washed them away in the knowledge that no one had to know. Only a locked door kept the company of my submission. My sexual abdication. The resignation of responsibility and control.

When I moved my lips from the door, I saw myself in the window, a translucent reflection of a lone, naked woman crawling to her master's door. I fell to the carpet, put my cheek on the rough wool, and watched my reflection as I turned my back to the door, hoisted my ass up, and slid my hands between my ankles.

I was ready for him, but he wasn't coming.

I spread my knees and slipped my hand from my ankles to between my legs. I gasped, then as I pushed through the layer of thick slickness to stroke myself, I groaned.

"Jonathan," I whispered so softly I barely even heard myself, "my king."

Knowing him, knowing how he played and how he fucked, I touched myself ever so gently, around the opening, over the tip of the clit. I placed my fingers at the tip and pressed my hips into them slightly, then back, anticipation and hunger in every move. Two sides of myself warred. The side that wanted to just rub an orgasm out of myself, and the side that wanted to lie there with my cheek to the floor and milk it for every second of pleasure. I wanted the milking side to win. So I stroked my clit with a single fingertip three times, then once hard, then three times lightly, then stuck two fingers in my soaking pussy.

Repeat.

I heard sounds on the other side of the door. A shuffle. A light clicking on. A drawer opening. A voice speaking a foreign language as if it was on the phone.

173

Right there. He was right there on the other side of the door.

I pressed my finger against my clit and drew it down, hard. It hurt, just a little, then exploded into pleasure so deep I had to lift my cheek off the floor. I rubbed it again. I'd jumped four stages of desire right into orgasm close. My thighs warmed. My folds shuddered when I touched them, and my back straightened. My face came off the floor, and I kneeled, legs spread, fingers between my legs and rubbing in a circle. A ball of heat wound tight around itself in my pelvis. I crouched, pressing the heel of my hand against my clit, and then bent my back. I drew my wrist, then my forearm, along my wet slit until my fingertips reached my lower back. The constant, single direction of pressure broke the coil of pleasure, and when I straightened, bringing forearm, wrist, and hand back over my clit, I exhaled in a clenched groan. I did it again until my forehead was on the floor, and I pulled back, my forearm now a slick instrument. My ass and pussy clenched repeatedly as I tried not to cry out loudly enough to be heard by the king on the other side of the door.

Chapter 20

Jonathan

Sometimes, talking to people in Asia was enough to make me want to do bodily harm to myself or others. I shouldn't have let that phrase enter my mind after what I'd revealed to Monica in the bathroom of the Gulfstream.

Sunshine and lollipops. I thought the words so hard I almost said them in Korean as I explained to my VP of operations that the vision for Hotel M in Seoul was exactly the same as the ones in Los Angeles, Vancouver, New York, and Chicago. The spirit of the thing was what mattered. Getting the exact same designer for Seoul as we had in New York was less important than getting the same *type* of designer.

I hung up, then looked at a calendar as if I could deny the truth.

I had to go to Asia tomorrow afternoon at the latest.

Fuck.

I wanted her so badly, and it took all my concentration not to take her too soon. I couldn't lose focus. Too much was going on. But there I was, getting Jacques on the line and telling Aling Mira to pack. I had no choice. Putting business first was a habit I couldn't break.

That was two weeks right out of the gate. Two weeks outside L.A. Outside her sphere. I didn't want to go away. I was so close with her. So close to getting her commitment, her heart, her promise, then some shit across an ocean threatened to explode into a fuckstorm of red lacquer shrapnel. I dropped my laptop and phone on the table. My jacket went over the chair. My tie got yanked off as if it had offended me personally. Shoes, kicked. Cufflinks, tossed.

I hadn't intended to tell her about the suicide attempt. I didn't like talking about it, and I didn't like her knowing, but the minutes in the bathroom between deciding to tell her and actually doing it were more intimate than anything we'd experienced. She'd peeled off my skin and seen the isolation inside. She couldn't turn away from me now. Couldn't.

The door between our suites opened with a keycard, and I had it. It was mine, after all. The wood was warm to the touch, and smooth. Dry. The moldings were curved by the most perfectly even paint job money could buy. Running my finger along the seam, I imagined the little bit of air seeping through was shared between us. We were conjoined by the molecules, the scents they carried, the temperature, from her lungs to mine and back again.

I peeled off my shirt in the dining room. I didn't want to look at an empty bed, and I wanted to be close to the door for reasons that didn't have words my mind could define. I didn't want to waste the air, or something equally absurd and impossible to accept.

Wearing nothing but my briefs in a hotel dining room, next to an empty china cabinet, I put both my hands flat on the door, stroking it downward. I didn't know what was coming over me, but that door became her body, and I wanted to touch it. Needed to.

Then, through the door, I heard it. Her voice. Singing.

Chapter 21

Monica

My forearm had been covered in sex fluid, and I stank of the flight and fast food. After collapsing on the hotel floor, ashamed, exhilarated, and sexually satisfied until Jonathan worked his way into my sphere again, I needed a shower.

The bathroom was black with white fixtures, and I was alone. The four showerheads were powerful, and the water was scalding hot. The frosted, glass-walled shower stall was as big as a walk-in closet. I scrubbed with over-perfumed hotel soap, and as I rinsed, I started singing a song I'd started the day before in a pencil-dulling heat. I'd memorized the words even as I wrote them. As I leaned against the glass tiles, I worked out the bridge, over and over. I felt like I had it, and it had been sticking in my craw since yesterday.

> *I'm scared all the time*
> *And I need all the time*
> *I'm scared all the time*
> *And I need all the time*

I heard a click behind me, and a chemical infusion of fear made every vein in my body pulse. A man. In my shower. Uninvited. I screamed, or tried to, but because I'd forgotten to breathe, it came out a croak.

"Shhh," Jonathan said. He wore nothing but boxer briefs that showed the glory of his erection.

"You fucking fuck."

"Please." He put his hands up in a gesture meant to show me he wasn't going to touch me.

"What on earth would compel you?"

"You." He leaned forward, and I stepped against the wall. His forearms pressed against the wall on either side of my head, and he got inches from my face. Water fell on his dry hair, running dark paths to his face. It dropped off his nose, his brow, his chin. "You. Goddess."

Suddenly, the sexual satisfaction I'd achieved on my knees with the whole length of my arm was inadequate. "Take me."

"Commit yourself to me. Be mine for all the world."

"I already told you yes."

"Make me believe it." His eyes closed, slowly, as if he didn't want to see my face. He was wet, his body a waterfall. The rushes of water accentuated every curve and angle of him.

"How?"

"What was that song? I couldn't hear all of it."

"I wrote it yesterday."

He opened his eyes. "Would you sing it for me?"

His body still didn't touch mine. I felt his breath on my shoulder and the presence of his erection, and I wanted it as much as I'd ever wanted anything. He wasn't going to touch me. Not a finger. He was going to breathe on me and whisper in my ear, naked in the shower, until I burst.

"Please," he said.

A part of me wanted to tell him to fuck off, but another part wanted to be close to him so badly that a song seemed as, if not more, intimate than sex. "Are you ready?" I whispered.

"Yes."

I took a deep breath and sang for him, my voice low, much the way I sang him my song of fears in his backyard. This time, I sang without shame or contrition.

> *Craven runs*
> *Crave stays*
> *Craven runs*
> *Crave stays*
> *A cold, dark stain on a hot sidewalk*
> *From a water balloon thrown*
> *Craven freezes*
> *Crave ducks*
> *And writes the sound of nothing in crimson chalk*
> *Craven stays*
> *Crave runs*
> *Craven stays*

Crave runs
Puzzle pieces in an open box
Find perfect fit, alone then
Crave touches
Craven sees
Pieces shifted, while five little lenses watch

I sang the bridge a little louder, looking into his jade eyes. I wanted to connect with him, to put my feelings into him so he'd understand.

I'm scared all the time
And I need all the time
I'm scared all the time
And I need all the time

I stopped. We said nothing, our voices shushed, and the only sounds in the room were the droplets of water falling on our bodies and the whoosh of the showerheads. His eyes flicked over mine, his expression a mask. I didn't want to hear his thoughts. I didn't want to talk. I wouldn't like what I heard; I knew it.

"That one's not so revealing, I guess." I knocked the handle down to shut off the water.

"More revealing, actually." His lips were at my cheek, but I didn't have the courage to turn and kiss him. "Puzzle pieces. A box full, and only one fits. And you leave me standing on my porch because you're scared."

"I was either going to stay with you because I was scared or leave you for the same reason. At least this way I'm not dragging you into my shit."

He leaned away. The tile pattern was pressed into the flesh of his arms.

"Don't," I whispered, putting my hand on his waist.

He didn't twist away, but he didn't want me to touch him. I sensed it in the way he stiffened, his sharp intake of breath, the way his eyes closed halfway. "The cameras in your house. I know who put them there."

The *plink plonk* of water dropping from the faucets and our bodies echoed like slaps on the tile. "Who?"

"Me." He opened the door with a snap.

"What?"

He stepped out and grabbed a towel, wrapping it over his shoulders. I was still naked and wet, unimpressed by towels or anything else, standing half out of the shower.

"Santon found the serial numbers and followed the money to one of my accounts."

"What does that mean?" I felt wound up, hot, heart pounding like a drum machine.

"It means someone who had access to one of my accounts had them put in. To answer your next question, yes, Jessica had access to that account. Yes, I think it was her, and no, I don't know why."

"Why?" I asked as if I hadn't heard him.

"Still don't know. What I do know is you're not ready to deal with whatever she's going to dish out."

If I had been mentally sober, I wouldn't have been so insulted, but it had been a rough ten minutes. "So basically, you burst in, mostly naked and fully hard, terrifying the hell out of me. You make me sing this heavy song in your ear, and then you tell me your ex-fucking-wife is the one who shit on my house, and for a finale, you call me *weak*?"

"I'm protecting you."

"Bullshit. How about the sadism staying in the bedroom?"

I balled my fists and stared at him, trying to transmit how offended I was. The showerhead dripped three times. *Plink plonk plink.*

He moved so fast I didn't even see it, but I felt it in the shifting of the air. I flinched as though I was about to get hit. His hands grabbed the sides of my face, and his mouth came to mine, his tongue parting my lips forcefully. I opened them once I was over the shock. His tongue touched mine. It may as well have touched my clit, my cunt, my ass, such was the intensity of the feeling. Between the song and the adrenaline rush, the chemicals in my body were set to respond, rushing blood and fluids between my legs. I put my hands on his neck, moving my face against his. He pushed me against the glass of the shower.

I pressed my pelvis against him, grinding against his dick. He felt good. Better than good. He felt right. I wanted him. I wanted his chest against mine. I wanted his hands to grip my ass. My nipples hardened for him, as if drawn millimeters closer by sheer magnetism.

Grabbing my hair as if for leverage, he pulled away. "Monica," he gasped, eyes closed, lips grazing mine.

"Jonathan, please."

"I shouldn't even be in here."

"Yes, you should. It's fine. We'll just do it now. Figure the rest out later.

I'm screaming inside; you have no idea. I don't feel like myself. It's like something in me is sleeping until you show up. When you do, it turns into a wild animal in a matchstick cage."

He pulled away. "You drive me crazy."

I felt him leaving even before his body moved. "Don't make me beg."

"I won't let you." He dropped his hands. "I'm sorry. I just lost control when I heard you singing. But you can't come back to me just because we're naked in the same room. I can't..." He looked at the floor, then back at me. "Jessica's the tip of the iceberg. You being afraid—it hurts in my bones."

"I know," I said, resigned to him walking out of the bathroom without fucking me blind. "I'm the one sleeping on her best friend's couch."

I snapped the robe off the hook. It was warm, white, and plush as hell, yet when I put it on, it offered no comfort.

"Just go," I said. "I can't even look at you."

He paused, looked at the floor, then he spun on his heel and strode out without looking back.

Chapter 22

Monica

Two in the morning.

No word from Kevin.

I heard not a peep from Jonathan's side of the door. I touched it once before bed. At one-thirty, I sat on the floor with my back to it, looking at the ridiculously opulent suite. Everything was done perfectly, and nothing was fixed.

I knew who'd put the cameras in the house. Maybe I could go home, or maybe knowing it was Jessica would make it worse. What the hell was she trying to do? Make a public scandal? If so, why now? Why with an anonymous waitress she'd tried to take into her confidence? Who did it and when was it done?

I wished I hadn't found out. All the questions I'd tried not to ask because they were upsetting came to me in a flood, and I couldn't sleep. I repositioned myself on the floor, pulling cushions from the couch. I was about to open a work of art in a museum, and at early o'clock in the morning, I found myself curled up in front of a locked door, my mind going in circles.

In between those questions and stumbling blocks over my house, I had to ask myself if I wanted that man in my life. Due to my prolific musical output over the past Jonathan-free weeks, I knew he was a work-stoppage waiting to happen. He knew it. That was why he'd walked out in wet underwear rather than take me right on the floor.

I really did wish I hadn't touched him that first time. I wished I hadn't taken that monkey of a bet that night at Frontage. I wished I hadn't met him at the Loft Club after his trip to Korea, and I wished I hadn't forgiven him for kissing Jessica. I had had every opportunity to take control of my life, but I didn't.

I watched the sky go from navy to royal, to cyan, to baby boy blue. I'd entered a fugue state of regret and dissatisfaction but had found no sleep. It wasn't a good day to be tired, but I had to get up and do the work.

Chapter 23

Monica

"Have you heard anything?" Darren asked without a "hello" or "good morning."

"No." I peered over his shoulder at the breakfast buffet. It was ridiculously luxurious. "Nada. I called him, like, seven times." Silver chafing dishes held three different preparations of egg, sweet treats like pancakes and French toast, and breakfast meats all in a row. Or if we preferred our breakfast fresh and had a minute to spare, stations with men in chefs' hats were ready to make us an omelet or waffle. The dishes were pure white and spotless. The flatware was heavier than a clarinet. Everyone who worked there smiled in their crisp whites, and all the guests seemed perfectly comfortable with a white-linen-and-crystal breakfast.

I got a little fruit and a croissant, feeling as though I wasn't taking advantage of what was given, but I had no appetite.

"I called the hotel," Darren continued. "They can't tell me if he checked in or not. It's against some kind of law or rule or whatever." He carried his corn flakes to the table.

I grabbed tea and followed. "We should blow by the hotel."

"Yeah. Then we gotta go to the B.C. Mod and pray we can figure it out."

I shrugged. "You know he's probably there in a designer suit already, chatting up the curator about luminous banalities and cultural fetishism until she lifts her skirt."

"It's a him."

"Kev's not that picky."

"Crabby this morning. Did we fail to get Mister Drazen into bed?"

"He means nothing to me."

Darren cracked a laugh.

"Good morning," came a voice that shouldn't have surprised me at all.

"Speak of the devil," Darren said.

"Good morning," I said as Jonathan sat down. He looked well-rested and fresh as a fucking daisy. Suit pressed. Shoes shined. Hair messed up exactly enough so it looked as though he spent no time on it at all. I figured I looked pale and wrung out, dark circles and all. My body wasn't built for three hours of sleep a night, and certainly not for as little as I'd gotten in front of his motherfucking door.

"How are you guys getting around today?" he asked.

"Don't even think about it," I said.

A waitress brought Jonathan scrambled eggs, potatoes, and fruit. He didn't even have to stand at the buffet for it.

"Please," Darren said around his cereal. "Whatever you're going to offer, I'll accept. She won't take anything from you in front of me. We had this fight—"

"Shut up," I snapped.

Jonathan put sugar in his coffee, smiled at me, and turned back to Darren. "The hotel car is a blue Audi. Your driver's name is Feran. He'll take you to the museum and back, and he'll take you back for the event tonight."

"We have to make a stop," I said. "We haven't gotten in touch with Kevin, and I want to go to the Marriott and see if he's there."

"They won't tell you anything," he said. "Not even his room number. It's the law. Do you want me to find out for you?"

"You own that hotel, too?" I said.

"Yes," Darren cut in. "Can you do that please? See if he checked in? Text me if she's being a bitch."

Jonathan raised an eyebrow at Darren, seemingly offended by the name-calling. Was he seriously being protective against Darren? And this was the same guy who left me in my bathroom, fully unfucked, without looking back? This guy was bristling about me getting called a bitch by a guy who was practically my brother?

"Darren," I said, "it's cunt to you. See-yoo-en-tee."

Jonathan smiled behind his coffee cup.

Darren laughed but didn't repeat the word. "I prefer bitch, but whatever." He threw down his napkin. "I gotta arrange the equipment. When is the driver going to be around?"

"The front desk knows who you are. Have them send him when you're ready."

"This is the only way to fly, isn't it?"

"It is."

Darren kissed me on the cheek and left me with Jonathan, who looked unflustered.

"I couldn't sleep," he said.

"You don't sleep anyway. You nap."

"Three hours I need, and I didn't get them."

I leaned to the right, just to be a little closer to him. "I crashed in front of the door."

He sighed as if he got no satisfaction from the information. "I was lying on the couch not sleeping."

"My guess is it was for the same reason I was on the floor, not sleeping."

He fingered his water glass, and again I couldn't keep my eyes off his hands. His watch had a fat metal band in a blackish silver. Analog. One dial. The simplicity of it, draped on his wrist, brought out the arch of his hand, and I remembered the deep clinking sound it made when he fucked me.

"What are we doing?" he asked.

"You're trying to get me to beg for you back."

"I'm trying to get you to see that your fears are real. If we do this, if you commit yourself to me, you're going to get consumed. I think that's what you're trying to avoid."

"Yeah." I could see it. The cameras in my house were no more than a sign of worse things to come. The uncontrollable publicity that had nothing to do with my music. The implication that any success I had was because of him. The kink. The enemies. But worse, the emotional entanglement. I already felt more than I wanted to. If I actually let myself go, he would truly devour me.

I shook my head. "Can we decide when we get back? My brain's mush right now."

"Would you come to Seoul with me?"

"What? Why?"

"I'm going to have to leave as soon as I get back to L.A., and I can't wait another two weeks for us to figure this out. If I take off, I could lose you. I need to convince you, and I need it to be real. I can't fuck a commitment out of you. That'll be worthless. I have to have your heart, Monica. The real thing. Without fear."

"I can't promise I won't ever be scared."

"Of me." He put his hand over mine. He didn't touch it; he hovered as though he wanted to touch me and was as afraid of the contact as I was. "I don't feel close to anyone, except sometimes you. Sometimes I have moments with you." He took his hand away and put it back on his glass. "I want you, and I need everything from you. First, that you take me the right way. No compromises. No halfway mark."

He didn't equivocate with his gaze or posture. A part of me melted in his direction. How I wanted to yield to him, and how I wanted to run in terror. The tension between those compulsions made words as impossible as movements. I couldn't run away from him or touch him. I couldn't agree to two weeks away from L.A., the logistics of which were no small thing. I had a job and a commitment to Frontage.

"Will you come?" he asked. "I'll be working, but I can make sure you have the time of your life."

His eyes seemed bigger than they ever had. As if he really wanted me to come and would be devastated if I didn't. As if our relationship hinged on a trip to Asia.

"Monica." Darren spoke up from behind me, interrupting a gaze a hundred feet deep and a million years long. "Come on."

"We'll talk later," I said to Jonathan.

"See you tonight." He smiled as if nothing in the world was wrong.

Chapter 24

Monica

Feran, a handsome Middle Eastern guy in a black jacket and pants, was waiting in the navy blue Audi sedan. I didn't know Audis came that big, but the equipment fit in the back, with one of the back seats folded down. I told Darren to sit in the front, and we were off to the museum.

Vancouver was huge in a different way than Los Angeles, more vertical. The towering glass buildings clumped together like schoolchildren lining up for homeroom. The lower architecture was old, with brick brownstones backed by narrow alleys. Parking lots were few and far between. I guessed that posed a problem people were willing to live with because the streets were wall-to-wall humanity, even at eight in the morning.

About a minute passed before both my and Darren's phones dinged.

—He never checked into the Marriott—

"Shit, Darren," I said.

"Yeah, I got it. What could have happened to him?"

"Why are you asking me?" I had an unjustified defensive reaction, as if somehow it was my fault he was M.I.A. because I didn't sleep with him.

"I'm not asking you." Darren twisted to face me. "I'm asking generally. What could have happened? He doesn't *miss* shit like this."

I said what I wouldn't have said if he really had accused me. "It's not because of the other night? Do you think?"

He pulled his phone from his pocket and scrolled around. "Get over yourself. Let me make some calls."

And call he did the whole way to the museum. A virtual glad-hand and polite, warm ends to conversations allowed him to make four calls in fifteen minutes.

We pulled up to the loading dock behind a blond stone building.

Though the museum itself was new, the old warehouse in the center of town was a hundred years old if it was a day, gutted and repurposed to save it from extinction. That was when Darren got through to someone who knew something.

"Geraldine, hey, man," Darren said as we got out and Feran started unloading. "Have you heard from Kevin?"

I ignored the pause because I already expected the call would be a dead end.

But Darren bent his neck to the sky and closed his eyes, mumbling, "Oh fuck." Then he put his arm around my shoulders. That did not bode well. "Did you get him one?" I heard her voice through the phone, with its New Yawk twang and fast talk. "Why didn't you call us? We're sitting here—"

He obviously got cut off. Geraldine's voice came through loudly in a machine gun fire of clipped consonants. "Fine, fine. No, it's okay… We don't blame you. Can you call me if you hear anything?" He hung up soon after. "We're fucked."

"Is he okay?"

"He's alive. He called Geraldine for a lawyer since she has family in Idaho."

"He's in *Idaho*?"

"He got himself on some international watch list. When he was stopped at customs, they found out he had open warrants and shipped him to the state where the crimes were committed. Back home."

"Crimes? Watch list?"

"He was on parole. He skipped when he came to L.A. We've hit the end of my knowledge. "

I was glad he was okay, at least. Not hurt or dead. Not drunk in an alley. And though it was egotistical and narcissistic to even consider it, I was glad he didn't stay away because of what had happened between us.

"We can do it. Right?" I said, taking a box from Darren.

"He has the diagrams."

"Do you remember how it goes together?"

"I want to say yes," he said without confidence.

"Me too. We can do this."

"Yeah."

We were relieved of the boxes of equipment as soon as we got into the guts of the building. Four men in dark blue suits and badges opened the boxes, checked them, checked our ID, and asked a ton of questions.

"Unnamed Threesome. Where's the third?" asked a bald guy who looked as if he was made of lead.

"Late," I auto-lied. "We need to check on the rest of the piece? It was coming through L.A. Special Transport?"

"Do you have the tracking numbers?"

"No."

"Commercial invoice?"

"No."

"Customs transfer certificate?"

"Look," Darren cut in, "the guy with all the paperwork got held up with an immigration mix up. We have the sound equipment and specs for it, but that's it."

"Mister Rivers!" A man in a black turtleneck and wire-framed glasses approached us. He seemed to be in his mid-fifties, with a close-shorn head of grey hair. Darren recognized him. They shook hands.

"Monica, this is—"

"Samuel Kendall, your curator. You must be the lady without the passport."

"I fixed that."

"Obviously." What could have been an insult actually wasn't. He said it with a slight bow of his head and a little play of a smile. "I heard what happened to Kevin. We actually have a problem far more serious."

As if a mask had been removed without him moving a muscle or changing his expression, I saw that Mr. Kendall, under his veneer of jolly intelligence, was livid.

"How serious?" I asked.

"Career-ending serious." He smiled again in that same way. "Please, follow me."

Darren and I walked down a long hall with him. He spoke with his head half-turned, his words echoing against the cinderblocks. "We allocated space for this piece, and a ton of it. We have financiers who expect a full show, and collectors waiting to see a whole piece."

We entered a larger, unfinished space with exposed ductwork and sprinklers. Crates and boxes stood everywhere. Kendall found three crates close to the loading dock and indicated them. Two were eight-feet tall. One was as big as a kitchen table.

Kendall stood by them and smiled, tilting his head. "What the fuck is this?"

Kendall stood by them and smiled, tilting his head. "What the fuck is this?"

Darren picked up a clipboard from the short crate and flipped though the paperwork. I never realized how brave and unflappable he was. At least in situations that didn't involve me or his sister. Or his sexuality. He was as easy to throw as anyone, just not in matters of his career. Bless him, that was the only place I felt as though I had the wrong time signature.

"We're missing four crates." He flipped through the pages. "A page of the commercial invoice is missing."

I inspected the tall crates. They'd all been labeled and numbered to match the assembly instructions. Kevin had reviewed it with me for no other reason than to sate my curiosity.

"They're currently in customs, thank you," said Kendall. "Even if they're released immediately, they won't get here for the preview. Sir and Madame, I cannot express to you the financial impact this will have on the museum if we do not have this piece installed. Allocation of space is eighty percent of our concern, and to have a gallery empty is unacceptable."

"The gallery won't be empty," I said. "We'll have to figure out the sound system, but I think we can get this to work. It won't be a complete piece, and it won't match the catalog, but the space will have something in it."

"If it sells, there will be financial repercussions."

"If it doesn't, it'll be worse," muttered Darren. He looked up from the clipboard. "Can we get these moved?"

"Right away," Kendall replied. "We've gotten a lot of interest in this piece." Darren and I looked at each other as Kendall hailed down a guy with a forklift.

Chapter 25

Monica

My idea was simple. The installation had four walls. Two had been delivered. A bunch of carefully indexed detritus was in the kitchen table-sized box. That was enough for half a piece. If we placed it against a corner of the gallery, we would at least have four walls.

"Two of them will be plain white," Darren said. "The whole meaning of the thing was about the overwhelming nature of emotional vulnerability."

"Think about the overwhelming nature of telling *that guy* his gallery's going to be empty."

We didn't know what we were doing. We'd made something using Kevin's expertise, and though we tried to learn all we could while contributing to the visuals, Darren and I had essentially designed the sound. We placed the speakers, deciding which types to use and where. We conceptualized it, recorded it, mixed it, and made it work. We talked with Kevin about how the sound would work within the scope of the piece, but anything that could be seen was his. He had the last word.

So the assembly design had been up to him, and it concerned us only insofar as the speakers needed a place to be hidden.

The galleries were packed with artists hanging their work, and when they heard about our plight, we found volunteer helping hands and working minds who understood how to put up an installation. The front of the house, with the doorway, and the adjacent wall. The bug inside was a whole, finished asset. The thing didn't look entirely broken. Darren and I decided how to get the sound to work by using the museum's walls, which we decided to leave white. Darren could have drawn something on them, but it wouldn't have matched Kevin's artistry. We placed the glass and broken cinderblock as we remembered it. When it was as good as it was going to get, with the walls stabilized, the top part hovering over the gash, and the layers of my voice filled the room, the artists that had helped us stood back and applauded themselves and us for pulling a rabbit out of a hat.

Though we'd make a success of the show if it killed us, the talk around the galleries was that Kevin's career was jeopardized. Non-delivery of work was such a dead serious infraction that even the craziest artists didn't get away with it. Non-delivery was a loss of space. It was a loss of prestige and face. It was apologies and returned money.

When he got out of whatever hole he was in back home in Idaho, Kevin would have to dig himself out of an even deeper hole in the art world. I didn't envy him. As a matter of fact, I felt very, very sorry for him.

Chapter 26

Monica

We were very close to being late. The piece had gotten up and the music turned on as the caterers finished the buffet and bar. Feran had been at our service the whole time, even shuttling Darren around to pick up a cable he needed to reconfigure the sound. He sped us through the city, around side streets and highways, and got us back to the hotel with seven minutes to spare.

"Dude," Darren said, "thanks."

They shook hands like only men can, and Darren and I ran to our rooms.

The door between our suites was open. I peeked into Jonathan's space and found him in a tuxedo shirt and tie, setting in a cufflink. Clean-shaven, hair neatened for the event, wearing a suit sexier than any lingerie, he silenced my reproaches about the open door just by looking as though he'd stepped out of a magazine.

"You look nice," I said.

"Thank you. I had some things sent from Yaletown," he said. "They're in the closet."

"I brought my Eclipse dress."

"No doubt you did." He tapped his watch. "I'm leaving. But you guys are going to be late if you don't move it."

"I have to close this." I indicated the door.

"Shoo."

As painful as it was to cut him out of my vision, I closed the door. Of course, I had no intention of wearing any dress he had sent from wherever he said they were sent from. I got out my Eclipse dress, which was the most beautiful thing I owned. I loved it. But next to it in the closet hung a wide garment bag designed for multiple hangers. In this case, seven.

I hung the Eclipse dress in the bathroom, behind the door, so the steam would relax it, and ran the shower. As I undressed, I made it a point to not think about the seven dresses. In all likelihood, they didn't go with my shoes. I didn't have the right accessories, and looking at them would only hammer home what I already knew. The dresses had been picked out by someone who didn't know me, didn't know my taste, and obviously shopped with an eye to making that gorgeous man's female interest look like a wet dumpling.

The shower wasn't the right temperature. Not quite too cold. Maybe it was too hot. That was it. I inched the handle a quarter inch toward cold and ran to the closet as though the bag held candy and opened it so fast the zipper screamed.

"God help me," I said. "I am not made of stone."

Seven dresses. Four black. I pushed those to the side. Everyone was going to be wearing black, and time was ticking by. Darren would knock in minutes.

One tonal print. Out.

The last two fell just below the knee. A sparkly, flesh-colored halter with a handkerchief bottom, and a red, low-cut power suit that screamed *don't fuck with me*. That was it. And it went with the shoes.

I showered fast, keeping my hair dry. Quick shave. Soap all over. Dried like lightning and out to the closet.

Right. Red dress.

I pulled my underwear out of the bag, and of course, though I intended to wear my regular cottons, the lace and garter were right there. The set was white with gold hooks and clasps. The suspenders were satin with overlaid lace, and the rings holding the straps were as big as quarters. The front was held together with tiny gold hooks. Fuck it. At least I had an outside chance of getting laid in it.

When I pulled the dress out of the bag, I saw another, smaller bag was attached. I opened it to find a pair of red-soled shoes inside. Oh. Could it be?

Removing the cream halter dress, I found a pair of five-inch stilettos in a matching cream. Fuck, they all had shoes. Which meant I needed another hour. I had to look at every dress in the bag, every pair of shoes, and God help me, two of the black ones had scarves.

There was a knock at the door two rooms away.

"Mon? Come on!" It was Darren.

I ran through the bedroom, the living room, the dining area, and called through the foyer, "One second!"

Red dress.

But when I got to the closet, I realized I didn't want to look like a bitch on fire. I didn't want to be dangerously sexy. I wanted to be sweet and approachable. I slipped on the cream dress. I looked pretty. Like a woman of grace.

Chapter 27

Jonathan

Plan B was on his way to the museum from the airport. Petra had gone to her doctor's appointment and gleefully told me she'd have to stop flying in a few months. I envied Jacques.

I'd left Feran with Monica and Darren, sent someone else for Plan B, and drove myself to the museum. I was much more comfortable at B.C. Mod than at the Eclipse show. My wife held little sway on this side of the border, and my place on the finance committee came not through family connections but a love of art that Lanie Jackson had noticed when I donated some postmodern pieces to the burgeoning museum.

It was a small space and would never be the MoMA or L.A. Mod, but Vancouver didn't need a palace. It needed something intimate, like the city itself.

That night would be a smallish, boozy affair with collectors and fellow curators. It was Monica's moment, and without Kevin around to suck the wind out of her, she could enjoy it. At the entrance, a string quartet played lilting top forty classical with a pianist at a black baby grand. I said some hellos, shook some hands, laughed at a couple of stupid jokes about L.A., and got a whiskey. I eventually found the Unnamed Threesome by following the sound of Monica's voice.

It wasn't the same piece. Though her voice, layered forty times like angels singing, then screaming, then moaning, was perfect, the piece wasn't as good. Adequate. It would do. It wasn't shameful, and it didn't look wrong as much as it looked somehow aborted. I couldn't figure out if the difference was that I'd seen it in its complete state and my eye had been colored, or if it truly did have something truncated about it.

Samuel Kendall approached me, hand out, wearing the same black turtleneck he always wore. "Did you see the Simulcra Brothers piece in the

West Hall?"

"Not yet." I pointed at the truncated house. "Got stopped by the voice."

"What do you think?" he asked.

"I saw it in L.A."

"Ah, so you saw it complete." He ground his teeth. He was not a happy man. "It was good. Amateur mistake." He wagged his finger at me. "Never deal with amateurs."

I swallowed my drink and smiled. "Amateur comes from the Latin agent *amatus*. To love. Never worry about love. Love delivers. It's the incompetent professionals that'll screw you."

Kendall laughed bitterly. "Every freaking time." He looked over my shoulder. "Who is that?" I followed his gaze to Plan B, who had just arrived.

"Harry Enrich, the president of Carnival Records. Great guy. I have some property for him to look at. He's thinking of opening a mini-studio up here."

"Who isn't?"

Harry came my way with his wife, Yasmine, on his arm. He was a small man with wiry hair and cheeks that were never free of late-day shadow. "Jonathan, you've met my wife?"

"Nice to see you again."

"Beautiful plane," she said.

"I'm glad you enjoyed it."

I introduced them to Kendall, and Harry didn't waste a second before asking him, "Who is this?" He pointed at the ceiling. "I know that voice."

"She just walked in," I said, knowing I was smiling.

She'd chosen the cream dress with the tiny sequins. As willful as she was, she proved she was mine with every small, seemingly inconsequential decision. She looked breathtaking, even on Darren's arm, leaning on him as if he were her brother. In my mind, he was. She waved when she saw me and made her way to the bar.

"Don't recognize her," Harry said.

"Monica Faulkner."

It rang a bell. In the tilt of his head and look in his eye, I knew Harry recognized the name. I also knew he didn't know it well enough to be attached to any notion of how she should be signed or branded. That had all been Eddie's idea.

Chapter 28

Monica

I dragged Darren through the lobby and into the galleries without telling him I was looking for Jonathan. I found Jonathan by our piece with three other people, including Kendall of the black turtleneck. The other man looked like Harry Enrich from Carnival, but he couldn't be. Jonathan looked more relaxed and comfortable than he had been at the Eclipse show. More affable, somehow, better in his own skin, if that was even possible.

"I need a drink," I whispered to Darren.

He nodded and pulled me back to the lobby. The string quartet and pianist, two women dressed in long black skirts and three men in tuxedos, played a Mendelssohn quartet I remembered playing a hundred times in high school. Gabby and I had taken a ton of gigs like this through high school and college. Little parties and big events full of wealthy people trying to act wealthy. They paid crap, but we figured we would have been practicing anyway.

"What are you having?" Darren asked, somewhat less comfortable in a suit and tie than Jonathan. He cast his eyes down to his phone.

"Whiskey rocks. Who's texting? Kevin? Is he okay?"

"No." He tapped the bar then shook his head as if a fly had landed on his hair. "No, I mean it's not Kev."

"Okay?"

"Adam has landed."

"Is he coming?"

Darren rubbed his eyes. "I don't know what I want."

"Well, if he's here and he came to see you, you'd better think of something fast. Like a piece of pie or a cookie. You don't want him to waste the trip."

Our drinks came with a flirty glance from the bartender to me. He had arched eyebrows and full lips, reminding me of Kevin.

Christian Rondo, one of the artists who had helped us that afternoon, introduced us to Donna Santonini. Meeting her made me blush because not only was her work unforgettable, it was also pornographic and arousing and high-minded, all at once. I loved her, told her so, and met seven other people in the next ten minutes.

My customer service smile was getting a workout. Everyone thought I was with Darren, and we fell naturally into a brother/sister routine we'd honed since we broke up. The musicians took a break, silencing the background noise. Our klatch of artists didn't notice. We just kept talking about getting shafted, fucked, disrespected, kicked in the ass. Stuff we all had in common.

And Kevin. We talked about the missing status of Kevin Wainwright.

I felt Jonathan's hand on my back. Even through my dress, I knew his touch. His fingertips just grazed me, and I wanted to melt under them.

"That dress makes me want to destroy you," he said in my ear.

I faced him, and I noticed his hand left my back. I felt suddenly cold. "Missed your opportunity last night."

"I'll take you when you're ready and not a minute sooner." He pressed his lips together, looking at me as if he'd swallow me whole once the moment of readiness came. "I have someone here who swears he's heard your voice on some scratch cut one of his acquisitions people brought him."

I looked behind Jonathan and found the guy I thought was Harry Enrich talking to three other people I didn't recognize. "The president of Carnival records?"

"Eddie's boss."

Jonathan and I stood together, looking at each other, no words passing between us. I saw the blue flecks in his eyes and the laugh lines at their corners.

"I could introduce you," he said. "Or you could remind him of the cut he heard." He glanced at the empty piano, then back at me.

"I could prove I'm not Bondage Girl?"

He nodded. "The song can be what you want. Sing it."

"You're releasing it?"

"Yes."

"What if I sang something else?"

"Your call. I'll never hold you back again."

"Jonathan." Leaning into him with my eyes half-closed, I whispered it so softly, I doubted he even heard me.

"Go," he whispered just as softly. "Take what's yours."

He stepped back, and I felt at once totally alone and totally powerful.

Eleven steps to the piano.

I could do the new song. He'd recognize my voice, maybe, but I'd be Monica.

Six steps to the piano.

But if I did "Collared," he'd know who I was right away.

Bondage Girl.

Two steps, and limited time to get the song out before the musicians came off their break.

I slid onto the bench and started with a B-flat scale, then my fingers decided the song for me.

Chapter 29

Monica

The hotel carpet silenced my feet. The sconces lining the hall cast warm light on the wainscoting, and the elevator got smaller in the distance as if it was stepping away from me. I felt as though I was walking down the center aisle of a church after receiving a benediction that actually conferred a blessing.

I touched his door when I walked past it. Just once and exactly in the center. I slid the keycard through the reader. The green light flashed, and I opened my door.

A single lamp lit the living area, and the first thing I checked was the door between our rooms. It was closed. I touched it, pressing my whole hand to the wood, then I knocked. I breathed three times before the door opened.

Jonathan stood there, jacket open, tie undone, shirt open halfway. A glass of whiskey with a single ice cube hung from his fingertips. "How did it go?"

"You left."

"It was your moment." He leaned in the doorframe, but his bare feet were still on his side. "Which song did you pick?"

"I did 'Collared,' but different. Less bondage. More sweet."

He took a sip of whiskey. "And?"

I looked for a negative reaction and saw none. "They demanded another. So I did 'Crave/n.' Went good. Real good. I wish you were there."

"I'm here now."

He was, in all his straight-shouldered, commanding, controlled beauty. Right there in front of me. Close enough for me to smell whiskey and leather.

"I'd like to go to Seoul with you," I said without thinking. Even as it came out of my mouth, I knew it was the right thing. I felt a press of tension flow out of me in a flood from the rightness of it.

Jonathan looked at the floor, and I couldn't see his face. Had he changed his mind? A little tension returned until he picked up his head and looked at me. His smile went wide, and he touched his chest.

"Goddess." He looked as though he wanted to say more but didn't have the words.

"I have to figure out what to do about work. I might lose my job."

"I can smooth it over with Debbie."

"Do *not*." I held up my finger. "It's my responsibility."

"You've made me very happy."

I had a snide response at the ready, but instead I said, "I'm glad." The ice in his glass clinked, and I looked at it wistfully. He held it out. I parted my lips, and he raised the glass to them and tipped a little liquid in, his fingertips at the bottom so they didn't touch my face. The whiskey stung my tongue and burned my throat. Hot and cold swirled in my chest at the same time.

"Thank you," I said. "I should be getting to sleep."

"Of course," he said, stepping backward into his room.

"Not like I'm tired or anything."

"Right."

"But there's this no touching rule, and if I spend another second with you, I'm going to lose my mind and try to take your clothes off. I'm tired of being the one with no self-control around here."

He just looked at me, up and down, a little smirk playing at the corners of his mouth. I knew that look; Jonathan calculating the game, imagining all of its possibilities.

"I'll tell you what," he said. "Your choice. We wait until we get back to L.A. We talk. We agree you never turn your back on me again unless I cheat on you or hurt you, neither of which will happen. We rush off to Korea, and I'll probably have you on the plane or in a car or something. I don't even know. Or the other option, and this is a terrible idea…"

He stopped.

"Go on," I said, a little excitement building between my legs.

"Right now, you agree to never turn your back on me again unless I cheat on you or hurt you."

"And?"

"When this ice cube melts, the no touch rule is rescinded."

I cleared my throat and looked down. My hands were at my sides, fingers twitching as if I was playing a stringed instrument. "Jonathan."

"Monica."

"I can't imagine a situation where I'd turn my back on you again. At least, not for us being who we are. I won't deny it again. I won't pretend it's anything but what it is or that I'm not submissive to you sexually. If you fuck or even kiss someone else, we're through. And if you hurt me or if you're careless with me, I really will walk." I softened my tone and leaned toward him. "Barring that, I'm yours. You own me. You always have."

He stepped into my side of the doorway. He was so close. All I had to do was lean forward, and he'd have to catch me to keep me from falling.

"Here's how it's going to go, then, Monica. Are you ready?"

"Yes."

"When this ice cube melts, I'm going to make love to you so slow, everyone in this hotel is going to know my name. It won't be play. It's going to be dead serious."

"Okay." I peered into his glass. That ice cube looked huge.

"Then it's playtime." As he'd done on our first night, he took his glass and pressed the coldest bottom part to my nipple. He didn't touch me, only the glass did. I hardened through the dress, parting my lips so the *ah* could come out. "I'm going to tie you down and take every part of your body until I'm satisfied. It will hurt, goddess, and you will beg for more."

"Promise?"

"You're not scared?"

"Actually, I'm kind of really turned on."

He drank the rest of the whiskey and lodged the ice cube in his mouth. He put down the glass and leaned toward me. The ice touched my lips, and he dragged it across them, dripping cold water down my chin. I opened my mouth and took the cube, but he didn't let go. Both of our mouths were lodged on that cube, me at six and one and him at five and two. A low groan escaped my throat. I ran my tongue along the bottom of the ice, trying to get it to melt faster. His face was so near, and the cube so cold and big between us, I felt both the closeness and distance acutely.

He yanked his jacket off, taking me with him. I grunted but didn't let go. He undid his cufflinks, tossed them aside, and went for his shirt buttons. I saw the laughter and pleasure in his eyes as I tried to twist my head to watch, but couldn't.

I undid the clasp behind my neck that would release the halter. The bodice dropped, and it was his turn to groan and try to twist his head. My turn to laugh around that god damn hateful ice cube. I unzipped the side of the skirt as he shrugged off his shirt, the yanking pulled our mouths in different directions. Our muffled laughter was a symphony.

Cold water dripped down our chins, and we sucked on that cube, willing it gone. The dress dropped to the carpet, revealing the white lace and satin garter with the big gold rings. He gasped and said something that sounded like it could have been "oh my God." He held his hands over my hips, as if he wanted to caress me, but the ice cube still existed. It was shrinking, but the no touch rule kept him inches above my skin.

His belt clanked when he undid it. His zipper buzzed. He held his head so I couldn't look down, and the cold, amused look in his eyes told me how much he enjoyed my frustration. Bastard. He leaned down to pull off his pants, and I bent with him.

He was naked. I was in garter and heels. The ice cube was half its original size. He pushed forward, still not touching me, until I got the hint and walked backward, connected to him at the mouth. Step by backward step, through the living area and into the bedroom. I backed up to the bed, and he dropped on top of me, hands on the mattress on either side of my head. The ice cube was down to a sliver, and he slid his tongue into my mouth. I gasped, finally feeling a piece of him against a piece of me, even if the ice made him cold. I'd take it. Anything. My skin was hungry for his touch.

I don't know when the ice actually disappeared down my throat, but his mouth on mine became more of a real kiss, more a dance of breaths and movements. I dared to touch his chest. When he didn't pull away, I groaned into his mouth. His skin against my hands, the bumps of his nipples. The ribs at his sides. The hardness of his hips. The line of hair on his belly.

Before I could get my hand between his legs, he shifted down and took my nipple in his mouth, sucking it between his teeth and sending pulsing shivers down my body. I wove my fingers in his hair, pulling him to me.

"Oh, God, Jonathan. Take me. Please."

"Not yet." He moved to the other breast. "Slow. We've waited too long to rush." He slipped a finger under the garter belt, backing away to look at it. "And what you're wearing. It's magnificent."

He leaned back and drew both hands down my thighs over the belts and straps, pressing my legs apart with a gentle push. I opened for him, showing him how wet and ready I was. He kissed between my thighs. Licked. Sucked. I tried to push his head to the center, but he worked the other thigh until I was a pulsing, undulating mess. He looked up at me, pausing, his mouth hidden behind my sex.

"Yes," I whispered. "Please."

He put his tongue on me, and my back arched. He backed off until I calmed, then he licked me again in earnest.

"Fuck!" I shouted, reacting to the gunshot of pleasure in my crotch. He spread me open and lightly ran his tongue over my clit while watching me. His heat ran from my knees to my waist and was about to regroup under his tongue. "I'm going to come unless you stop."

"Come, then," he said. "Won't be your last time tonight." With that, he put his thumb in my cunt and licked my clit in earnest, pressing his second finger on my ass, massaging it without entering it. He was telling me something, and I was listening. He sucked gently on my clit, and a little harder, and a little harder again until he yanked a fast, violent orgasm out of me. I pushed against his mouth, holding the back of his head.

When I was done, he kissed inside my thighs again and worked his way back up to my face.

"Thank you," I said.

"My pleasure." He took my hands and pulled them over my head, pressing down with all his weight. "Open your legs for me."

I did.

"Bend your knees."

I pulled my legs up as far as I could. He looked deeply into my eyes, nose to nose, and slid his cock into me. I was sensitive and wet, and I felt as if a lightning rod had been lodged into my pelvis. All fiery sensation, and slow. He moved as if he was underwater.

"How is that?" he asked.

"Like I'm going to come again. I feel everything. Every inch."

He pushed in, still holding my hands, rocked his hips, then pulled out. He repeated his movements at that pace until a little nugget of frustration built in my belly.

"Faster," I said. "Can you go faster?"

"You mean like this?" He pulled out and pounded me, slamming against me. Five times. I cried out, reaching the next level of pleasure.

Then he stopped, letting my hands go.

"Exactly like that," I said.

"No," he said with a smile. "Can't. Sorry."

"Oh, no. Don't be an asshole."

But his smile told me he had every intention of being an asshole, and worse. The underwater pace continued. I felt like a balloon was opening up inside me, squeezing all pleasure and sensation out, but he just moved on top of me, rocking, kissing my neck, dragging his lips across my cheek, until he gazed into my face.

"I want you to feel me," he said. "I want you to see this side of me, how I feel about you."

I touched his face. "I know."

"Goddess. You're beautiful. Let me be yours." His face lost a little of its control, tightening and loosening at the same time.

"You know I love you," I said.

"Oh, fuck. I'm there."

"Yes."

He increased the pace incrementally, but it was all I needed. The balloon expanded, and I came, pushing my hips forward and taking all of him inside me. My orgasm was slow as the fuck. I felt every second of it as the ball of fire moved from the backs of my knees to the base of my spine, collecting around his cock before it shattered. I kept my hands on his face, feeling the muscles clench as he came. We cried out together, a stream of names and curses and unspellable pulsing vowel sounds. We prayed to whatever god we believed in, because feeling like that meant that there had to be a God, and heaven, and earthly bliss. We rolled onto our sides, still pumping together, emptying the last of our orgasms inside each other.

There was only breathing for a minute after that. He kissed my fingers when I put them near his mouth. I'd wanted him for weeks, yearned for his touch even when he was miles away. Having had him, I could only say I wanted him again.

"I hope you don't think you're rolling over and going to sleep," I said.

"I have promises to keep this evening."

"Ah, the owning me."

"Every part of you."

"When do we start?"

"Give me a minute to change from vanilla guy to kinky guy."

I rolled on my back and laughed. Vanilla? Jonathan? The thought. He turned and stroked my chest, fingers reaching for a nipple. He fondled it hard, then pinched until it hurt. I gasped, and he twisted it until my face contorted and I breathed through my teeth. Then he let it go. I groaned as the blood rushed back.

"God help me," I said.

"Go run a bath, goddess."

I faced him. "Yes, sir."

The bathroom had been merely functional up until then, and the tub had been of no use to me. Though I'd appreciated its size, the curves of white porcelain should be used for sitting and soaking for hours. It had a control panel with buttons for the temperature and the chrome water jets. I ran it hot, because that was how I liked it. Steam rose and fogged up the mirrors. The hotel had provided some scented tubes. I considered each one and decided on the least flowery.

I took off the garter, dropping it on the floor in a pile of white lace and satin.

"It smells like a bordello in here," Jonathan said from the doorway.

"Do you hate it? I can start over."

"No. I like it. I want you relaxed."

I stood by the tub as it filled, the swirl of arousal between my legs matching his more visible excitement. I didn't feel relaxed, necessarily. I felt as if I was tiptoeing on the head of a pin.

"Get in," he said.

I complied. He turned the faucets off before following.

"Now," he said, putting his arms around me and pushing me against the wall of the tub. "Put your elbows here." He placed them on the marble shelf outside the tub, where one might put candles or soap if one wasn't busy giving up control of one's body. He moved his hands over my breasts, my stomach, and my thighs. He parted them until my knees were above the water, resting my feet on the ledges at each side of the tub. My hips floated, leaving my pelvis just below the surface.

Jonathan stroked between my legs, letting his thumbs course the length of my cleft and onto my clit. Then his hands moved over my sides to my breasts again, stroking my nipples with his thumbs, and back down. He repeated his movements up and down my body until I groaned.

He pressed his middle finger to my ass. "Don't clench. Easy. Relax."

I tried to think accepting thoughts as he stroked me again and slid his thumb in my pussy. I let out an *ah*. He hooked a finger in my asshole. I didn't tighten, keeping myself as loose as I could.

"How does that feel?" he asked.

"Good."

He thrust two fingers in before I'd even finished the word. I cried out. It was good. Very good. He drew them out then thrust them back.

"You're ready, and you're mine." He took out his fingers. "Flip."

His pressure on my body told me what to do. I put my hands on the ledge, and my knees on the benches. My ass and sex hitched up, my nipples touching the cold edge of the tub. The sting of his hand slapping my ass caught me by surprise, and I yipped.

"Shh. Don't make me gag you."

"Yes, sir."

I felt his mouth on my cheeks, kissing across them. Then his tongue worked its magic on my pussy, my clit. Everything tingled. He put his tongue on my asshole, and I thought I would die of pleasure.

"You're clenching." He picked up a hotel bottle of something I couldn't identify, because I dared not look around.

I felt something liquid on my back. His hand spread it over me, between my cheeks, lubricating me. When he slid two fingers in my behind that time, I didn't clench because the feeling was much different. I was aroused everywhere, and it became a wordless harmony, a counterpoint note, its existence completing the sensations in my clit.

"Better," he said. "You're doing well."

"Thank you."

He pulled his fingers out and pushed my ass down a little. I felt his dick at my crack, and his thumb dug into one ass cheek, opening me to him.

"Stay relaxed."

"Okay."

"I mean it. I have you. You don't have to worry about anything."

"I trust you." I meant it, and as if sensing my sincerity, he put the head of his cock on my ring muscle as I tried very, very hard not to reject it.

He pushed forward. I tried not to scream as the head went in. I held my voice behind my teeth, letting the rumble fill up and fall down my throat.

"Easy. Easy."

"Okay," I squeaked.

"You're in control for now. Move however you need to. Whatever pace is good. Just stay relaxed. Focus on me. Trust me." He reached around and stroked my front from neck to clit and back again. I couldn't move for fear of the pain. "Breathe. Breathe, then move."

I didn't think I'd be able to move again. He put his hands all over me, relaxing me, reminding me he was there. I thought compliant thoughts. I accepted his calm, his patience, his trust, and moved into the pain a little. I was better lubed than I realized, and he slid farther in. It didn't hurt more, which calmed me. I pushed toward him again, and he went in.

His hands stopped massaging and pressed open my cheeks. "How are you feeling?"

"It doesn't hurt as much as it did."

"In a minute, it won't hurt at all. It's going to be the complete opposite." His voice contained nothing but surety and confidence, and that made me feel safe enough to push into him again. He tensed so that he slid all the way in. He pulled out slowly, coating my ass in unexpected pleasure.

"Ah, that's good, goddess. Very good."

I pushed him back in, and I felt full, open, vulnerable, and cared for all at once. But I did not feel pain. It had gone away and been replaced by something wholly new. A harmony. The note was different, but the song was the same.

As if sensing that, Jonathan took control, pulling his cock from my ass and pushing it back in again. He waited.

"Do it," I said. "Sir. Please. Fuck me in the ass."

"Your filthy mouth," he growled. "I love it."

He slapped my ass and took complete control, thrusting against me, holding my cheeks open so he could get all the way in. I grunted. The feeling of being stretched past my limit was overwhelming, as powerful as relinquishing myself to his pace. The water splashed around us, still hot, still soapy. We leaned into it until only my ass was over the surface. He reached under the water, to my pussy, and hooked two fingers in me, using the grip as leverage. The heel of his hand rubbed my clit every time he pounded my ass.

"You've got it, Monica."

"Sir, may I come?"

"No."

"Oh, God."

"Don't you dare." He grunted it, no help as his hand kept at my pussy. I tried to think of the feeling on my asshole, the pulling and stretching. The raw sensation and the pleasure of the friction. The feeling of being full with him.

"Soon," he groaned.

I did scales on the marble, pressing the correct fingers to the counter for each note. I crossed over in my head and went back down the scale, choosing a B-flat because it always gave me trouble. Anything not to come.

"Please," I cried, "sir, god please."

"Three more."

He took me three more times and barked a "yes." I came with him, feeling my asshole pulse and clench around his cock. He filled me, and I felt him throb, emptying himself in a long, powerful groan.

Still in me, he put his arms around me and held me tight. He pulled me up until he sat on the ledge, and I was on his lap with his dick lodged in my ass. We panted together for a moment before he shifted and slipped out of me. My asshole felt uncomfortable, as if his cock was still hard and huge in me.

"Ah, that feels weird."

"It's still open. Give it a minute."

He held me still, moving my hair off my shoulder, kissing the back of my neck, while gradually I went back to normal. Sore. Fucked in ways I'd never been fucked before, but normal. Functional.

"You didn't tie me down," I said.

"You seemed too tense. I decided on the tub instead."

I twisted to face him. "You're a good listener."

"Thank you. Now, back to bed, no?"

"Yes," I said. "Yes to everything."

Chapter 30

Jonathan

I slept five hours.

When I woke, she was tangled in me. I lay there another forty-five minutes, just pressing my nose to her scalp and filling my head with her scent of canned peaches. As of that very minute, my job was to keep her. Make her happy. I slipped out from under her and packed my things for a trip home, then to Seoul, with her.

I ordered breakfast, and by the time it came, her eyes were open.

"Good morning," I said.

She put the pillow over her head and turned onto her side. I slowly pulled the sheets off her, revealing her perfect body. I slid my hand between her legs. It was a compulsion. Rolling her on her back, I pulled her legs apart. She grunted under the pillow.

"I didn't hear you," I said.

"I didn't brush my teeth yet."

"I won't kiss you, then." My fingers found her cunt. I rubbed the moist skin in the center, and she groaned.

"You look so clean and together," she said.

"How's your ass feel?"

"Fucked."

I slapped inside her thigh. The sound was hard and final. "Wider."

She looked at me as she obeyed, spreading her legs as commanded. I didn't have a game plan. I just wanted to see her. I bent to put my face between her legs and licked her lightly. She tasted of sweat, sex, and a little of my orgasm. She whispered my name, and I picked up my head.

"Take a shower, goddess. Breakfast is here. And no touching." I gave her clit a cruel flick that made her yelp and made me smile.

She kissed me quickly before trundling off to the shower. I caught her wrist and pulled her to me, kissing her as hard and deep as she deserved.

Chapter 31

Monica

Darren wasn't coming back to L.A. with us. His return ticket was good, and he and Adam decided to head back together. I assumed my faux-brother was going home as entangled as I was.

Jonathan and I decided to leave the hotel late. Breakfast had been picked over as if attacked by a murder of crows. We sat together on the couch. Jonathan was under me, bare feet up on the cushions, and my back was to his bare chest. I still wore the robe I'd left the shower in. I had a hotel notepad on my lap, and he stroked my shoulder to the collar while kissing the back of my neck.

"If I gagged you," Jonathan said, "I'd do it in such a way that you could still say your safeword."

"Okay, so we'll put it as a yes?" I wrote down *gag*.

"If you want. There are aspects that aren't interesting to me."

"Then why's it on the list?"

"I'll try anything you want to."

"I don't understand. I'm crossing off things left and right."

"I don't get to cross off soft limits. Hard limits, like sharing, yes. But anything that's not disgusting to me, I do it if you want to. That's my job."

I tapped the eraser on the pad. "What other aspects of gagging are you talking about? Besides that I can't talk right."

"We can do it if you want."

"No, it was just something that wasn't horrific."

He paused to run his fingertip over my shoulder. "There's an element of humiliation. Not that you can't talk at all, but you're reduced to grunts. With a ball gag, it's more pronounced, and you add drooling. It reduces the sub to her most primal, animalistic self. She relinquishes control over her voice and her spit."

It was my turn to pause. "Have you used a ball gag on someone?"

"Yes. It's not my favorite thing. I prefer when your silence and submission are a choice. And the humiliation makes me uncomfortable."

I bit my lip. "But cloth doesn't sound too bad."

"Put it on the maybe list."

I flipped pages until I found the maybe list and put *gag with cloth* at the bottom of the page. Jonathan looked at his watch. "We've been at this two hours."

I craned my neck to look at the clock. "Wow."

"You're very thorough. But we can continue this on the plane." He said it as if he was ready to go, but his hand slipped under my robe.

"Jonathan, what are you doing?"

"Adding something to the list." He undid the robe's belt. "Spread your legs. If I told you this in words, you'd say no. I want to show it to you."

"What is it?"

"Knees up. Open all the way. You have to trust me." His fingers reached between my legs, finding my cleft wet from the sex talk and stolen kisses. Gathering moisture from my hole, he ran his fingers to my clit, two fingers circling it.

"This goes on the yes list." I arched my back.

His hand came off me and back down with a solid *slap*. I cried out at the deep sting of pain, gasping. But like a firework shooting into the sky with a hard streak, the explosion afterward lit up the sky.

"Do it again," I groaned. He did, and again the pain was followed by its sister, pleasure. I'd slid all the way down and was fully supine, head in his lap.

"So this goes on the yes list?"

"Yes. Again, please."

"You're insatiable." He cupped my chin and kissed me. "Later. We have to go."

"Jonathan?" I closed my legs and shifted to look him in the eyes.

"Monica."

"Did you have anything to do with Kevin getting arrested?"

"I'm sorry?"

"He's traveled before, so it was weird he suddenly got on a watch list. And then for him to get picked up now? Those warrants have been out forever."

"It had to happen sometime."

"Yeah," I said. "But did you have anything to do with it happening *now*?"

He stroked my bottom lip pensively. "No."

Chapter 32

Jonathan

I gave Jacques and Petra the cockpit-door-closed order, which they were more than used to, and I had Monica twice on the plane. The first time, I had her in a seat like a normal person. The next time, on the galley counter because I could.

We didn't get much further on the list, but we'd made such good progress already that I wasn't concerned about it. Her commitment opened her up to communication about what we were doing in a way that hadn't existed before. She was thoughtful and full of questions. Part of me wished we'd done it sooner, and another part was glad it had taken time.

I let her have the window as we circled Los Angeles over the miasma of smog. She leaned against me. I had my arm around her and pulled her as close as the seat belts allowed, putting my nose in her hair.

"Last night," I said, "I told you I loved your filthy mouth."

She turned to me. "Yes?"

"I lied."

"Really? Should I say 'have intercourse with me' when I want it?"

"No. God no. What I meant was, I love your filthy mouth. And I love your mouth when it sings and jokes. I love your body, and everything it does to me. I love when you come, when you squirm under me, begging for it. I love your hands, and your eyes. I love your honor and integrity. I love your loyalty, your intelligence. I love your honesty, even when it hurts me. I've fallen in love with you, Monica. I didn't think it would happen to me again, but it did. Thank you."

She stared at me, big brown eyes wide, mouth parted just a little. I didn't think I'd scared her but shocked her. If I'd used three words to say the same thing, I might not have faced the same silence, but those three words would have been inadequate.

"You're welcome," she said.

I laughed.

The intercom buzzed as Santa Monica Airport came into sight. "Sir?" came Jacques's voice. "Can you come up front?"

I kissed those parted lips and unbuckled. "Give me a sec."

"Way to kill a moment, Drazen."

I kissed her again, half standing. She put her hands on my neck so I couldn't get away and kept them there until I took her wrists and pulled them down. I walked backward to the cockpit door and opened it.

"Yes, Jacques?"

He pulled off his headphones. "Sir, I just got a call. The LAPD is waiting on the runway."

Chapter 33

Monica

When he got back, his contented expression had changed to something more pensive and tense. He sat and buckled without looking at me. When I took his hand, he clasped back as if making a perfunctory gesture.

"What?" I asked.

He didn't answer.

"Jonathan. Don't shut me out."

He held my hand tight as the plane dropped down to land. "I get sued all the time. It's not even anything. I have lots of things people want. So they come after me." He looked at me finally. "I'm used to it, and I've learned to manage it. So I'm not worried about anything. But you… I'm worried about what you'll think."

"Remember the part of the trip where I committed myself to you?"

He sighed, looking resigned in a way I'd never seen. "I have no idea what this is about. But the LAPD is on the tarmac, waiting for me."

I didn't realize my mouth was hanging open until I had to close it to speak. "Why?"

"I don't know. But I want you to stay on the plane until I'm gone or until I come and get you. I'll have Lil make sure you get home. Pack. I'll call you. We may be off to Korea later than planned, but make sure you're ready."

"No."

He raised an eyebrow. "Is there a good reason you need to exit the plane immediately?"

"I want to be with you."

"Sweet, but no." He must have seen my determined look. He added, "Please."

I sat back as the wheels touched down. We held hands as the plane taxied to the gate. Two black and whites waited, lights flashing. I didn't like it. I knew plenty about cops. I knew how they stood and how they walked. Sonny Rodriguez had been shot gangland style on my corner. On the other end of my block was a narrow strip called "Ghost Alley" because of all the murders there. Those days were done in the neighborhood, but the cops, the questions, and the tension lived and breathed in my mind.

The Santa Ana winds whipped around the plane and bent every palm tree in sight. The windsock on top of the control tower was held still and erect.

Jacques came back, not his usual polite self, and opened the door with the steps behind it. It fell with a scrape to the concrete. Jonathan stood up, and with a look back to me and a raised finger indicating I should stay put, he walked out.

I unbuckled and went to the other side of the plane, pressing my face to the window. There was talk, and four officers surrounded him, which didn't happen unless some sort of violence was involved. Weird. Unless there was a great donut shop by the airport and two extras needed an excuse to come.

My view was obscured by the wing, but it looked as if they were handcuffing Jonathan.

No.

Sorry, but no.

I don't know what I expected to do, but I ran out as he was led to the car by the stocky cop on his left. I didn't call out or demand anything because another cop stepped between us with her hands out.

"Stop. Are you Monica Faulkner?" she asked.

"Yes."

I held up my hands to show they were empty and craned my neck to see around her. I heard the stocky cop's voice uttering the words of the Miranda Act. Jonathan asked something, seeming so together and calm, a picture of control. The Santa Ana winds brought two words of the cop's answer.

Domestic violence.

Jonathan glanced at me and smiled before the cop helped him into the back seat of the cruiser.

resist.

The Submission Series
Book Six

Chapter 1

Monica

At 11:23 a.m., I turned past the historic fig trees. The gate opened. I pulled the Honda in and parked next to the Jag. I checked my face in the mirror and went up to the porch. I dropped my bag and knocked. Waited. As I was about to knock again, the gate clattered closed. The button for the gate was just behind the front door, so he must have been there. I had no idea how long he'd make me stand outside. Patience was always a part of his game.

The door opened. His hair was brushed back and clean, his face shaved. He wore a tan polo that was tight in the arms, accentuating his hard, smooth biceps. His jeans hung on his hips as though they were made for him. And the motherfucker had the nerve to wear a belt.

"You're a sight for sore eyes," he said. His eyes, however, didn't look sore at all. He looked as if nothing ever touched him. I had no idea how he did that.

"Are you okay?" I asked. "I was worried."

"I'm fine. It's going to be fine."

I had been waiting to hear that before I dealt with the other issue that had kept me from eating and sleeping for two days. "Then, what the fuck?"

"What the fuck, what?"

I crossed my arms. "What. The. Fuck. Jonathan."

He put his fingertips on my jaw and slid them to the side of my neck. I sighed at his caress. His thumb brushed my cheek, his pinkie tickling the sensitive part of my throat. I involuntarily tilted my head into him.

"Your safe word?" he said.

"Tange-fucking-rine. Now explain—"

He grabbed the hair at the back of my head and yanked me to my knees. I lost my breath, the motion was so sharp and hard. I was kneeling in a second, and he flipped his pants open in a few swift moves. His dick was rigid and straight at my lips, glistening with a drop of liquid.

I had told him about that fantasy the night I gave him the list that became a song. He said he wouldn't fulfill it until I trusted him. I closed my mouth tight.

"Open," he commanded.

I turned my eyes to him, his cock in the foreground of my vision. His face bent toward me. He slapped his dick against my lips, twisting my hair. I opened my lips to tell him to fuck himself, but I was unprepared for the ferocity with which he jammed his cock down my throat. I choked, gagged.

He didn't stop. He grabbed my hair with his other hand and pivoted me, controlling me, owning me. I felt as if he wanted me off balance and uncomfortable, held up not by my knees, but by the knots of hair in his fists that shifted my head where his cock wanted. I opened my mouth and throat and let him take me. I made noises there were no letters for. Spit ran down my chin, and when I looked up at him, he gazed back with fierce intensity. He took his dick out of my mouth.

"You fucked her," I said.

"No, I didn't."

"You lie."

He pushed me into the house. "Hands and knees."

I fell, but I scooted myself to standing. I backed away. My breath rasped from the facefuck I'd just endured. "Say it. You and Jessica."

"I didn't do anything."

"You. Lie."

He pushed me against the wall, hard. I pushed him away.

"Pick your skirt up" he said.

"Admit it."

"Pick your skirt up, Monica."

"Admit it."

He took my shoulders and twisted me to face the wall, inches from a Mondrian. We had agreed to all of it, more or less, at the hotel in Vancouver. Hours of making that boundary list on the couch, and one scenario we embraced was that sometimes I'd fight him, and I'd use the safe word if shit got too intense or painful Right then, I wanted to fuck him as much as I wanted to resist. I'd longed for him for two days, hovering somewhere between rage and panic.

He yanked up my skirt, pushing me against the wall with his other hand.

"What am I admitting?"

"The cops said you hit Jessica with a belt and fucked her."

"They lied to get you to talk."

"Fuck. You." He moved my panties aside, jammed his fingers in my cunt, and flicked my clit with his pinkie. "First chance you get, you cheat." I moaned.

"You're so fucking wet, Monica." He pulled my hair until my neck was twisted so I could face him. "You wouldn't be if you believed that."

"They didn't pick you up for nothing."

"What if I did fuck her? You left me."

The thought made me so angry I flung my arm back and hit him in the face. He threw me over the sideboard, bumping a little bronze sculpture of stacked squares and knocking over a picture of his sisters. His dick pressed against my ass, hard, hot, and ready. One of my shoes fell off.

"They said they had audio," I cried, face wet with tears. "They have pictures of her ass. It's welted. You did it. Just say it."

"It." He pulled my panties down to mid-thigh.

"You fucked her."

"I showed her what she was asking for." He slid his cock in me as if he had an engraved invitation, fucking me as though he owned me.

"God, Jonathan," I cried, tears forming. "Why? Why don't I mean anything to you?" I didn't say "no" or "stop" because even though we had a safe word, I knew him. If I told him to stop, he would, and the pounding I was getting was the pounding I wanted.

He slapped against me with every word. "I. Didn't. Touch. Her."

"Liar." I swung back, trying to hit him. My reward was having my arm twisted behind my back so I couldn't move it.

"What did you tell them, Monica? You told them I spanked you, too."

"I said it was consensual. I don't lie."

"Good for you." He let my arm go but pressed my face to the tabletop so hard I couldn't move. He changed his angle and fucked hard and slow for a few strokes, pushing me down. The lacquer bit my nostrils. Pleasure was overtaking me, overwhelming my better sense.

That was what I wanted, wasn't it? I wanted to get fucked, but I didn't want to want it. I wanted his cock, and I wanted it hard, without the responsibility of asking for explanations. He pulled my hair again, yanking my head to the side so I could see him.

"I want to see you come," he said.

"Go fuck yourself," I replied breathlessly.

"Put your hand on your cunt."

I twisted, resisting the order, and he used the torque to drag one leg out of my panties. He put that leg over his shoulder while the other stayed on the tabletop. My other shoe fell with a clop. I lay on my side while he stood, shifting to straddle the leg that wasn't over his shoulder.

"Now." He put his thumb in his mouth and made a wet, sucking pop as he pulled it out. He pressed it to my clit.

"Oh, God."

He pounded me hard. The photo bounced off the sideboard and crashed to the floor.

"I said I want to see you come," he gasped, taking my pussy with his dick.

"Fuck. I hate you, fucker." I swung at him with my free hand, but he caught it before I struck him. He pinned it to my ankle with his strong fingers. "I hate you." It sounded like a plea.

"Well," he said, a word for each stroke, "I. Love. You."

He kissed my cheek, and everything in me tightened around him as his cruel thumb pressed, twisted, rubbed my clit. He grunted against my cheek. He pinched the fleshy nub, pushing and pulling in opposite directions. I came like a gunshot, a crack of a scream exploding from my throat. I begged him to stop, but he kept rubbing, and I kept coming until my cries must have sounded far more like pain than pleasure. Jonathan pulled his face from mine, circling his hips as he groaned a long *mmm* sound.

He was coming, and I loved him. Fucker.

Chapter 2

The cops had taken my information and made sure Lil picked me up. They asked me nothing besides my most basic information and let me know I had to make myself available for questioning the next day. They came to my house in the morning, gently asking the most painful questions, breaking my heart with every word.

I'd cleaned every corner of my house except Gabby's room. I stayed up all night, eyes glued to the television and internet. Whatever was happening with Jonathan, it had been either unworthy of media attention or kept under a dark, wet blanket.

I had called Geraldine Stark to thank her for letting us know about Kevin. She should have told us right away, before Darren had to call randomly, but she treated the whole thing like squeaky gossip. I made excuses and hung up. I called Darren. He was with Adam and couldn't talk. I didn't tell him about Jonathan. It would have taken forever to explain that I knew nothing.

I could not have imagined more tortuous days between watching him get into the squad car and getting his text.

—Where are you?—

I'd grasped the phone, letting half the tension in my body drop out of me and onto the kitchen floor.

—Home—

I was frozen in place, looking at the ellipsis at the bottom of the screen that meant he was typing. The shelves from my fridge were dripping soap, forgotten in the sink.

—Can you play?—

Initially, my biggest fear had been that I was somehow responsible for the accusation of domestic violence. That someone had heard about us, or seen my bruises at the Eclipse show. Or that maybe Kevin had gotten a word in edgewise at the border. Because who else had he been with? Who else had he hurt?

—Fuck you—

—Be here at 11:23, exactly—

But then the police had gently questioned me. No cold room. No good cop, bad cop. Two female officers spoke in a soft voices and told me they'd protect me from the man I loved and the sex I craved. They told me Jessica had come to them for an order of protection with photos proving he'd abused her during sex. Her reputation as someone who wanted nothing to do with Jonathan's kinky side indicated she'd been the unwilling victim of abuse and possibly rape.

I had gotten through the interview by using my customer service smile, but inside, I boiled.

—You missed the fuck you part—

—No, I saw it—

At 11:22 a.m., I had sat outside his gate in my car, waiting for the time on my phone to flip. I didn't know what the exactness of the time was about. I felt as if he was trapping me, taking a slice of control and connection in a situation where he felt he had none.

I didn't believe he'd raped her, because I knew him. I didn't believe he'd struck her without consent for the same reason. I was livid because during the time we'd been separated, he'd been so broken up about me he fucked around with, who else? Jessica.

At the same time, for two days, I had missed him. I worried about him. I didn't sleep enough. I went to dinner with friends but barely ate. I checked my phone so often, Yvonne had snapped it off the table and pocketed it. When he finally did text, I felt relief, and rage, and at the sight of the word *play,* I felt rushing need between my legs that only he could release.

After he took full control of my resistant body, yanking an orgasm out of me, he picked me up and got me standing. I touched the hem of my skirt, but he moved my hands away.

"What now, Jonathan?" I was emotionally frustrated, sexually satisfied, and physically exhausted.

"Let me," he said, kneeling in front of me. He held out the empty leg of my panties, and I stepped into them.

"You hurt me. And you cheated."

"Hurting you isn't my fault. It's Jessica's. And the second isn't true." He slid my panties back up my legs, running his fingers under them to get them in the right place.

"It doesn't matter that we broke up," I said.

"Yes, it would, if I'd done anything." He pulled down my skirt, caressing my ass, my thighs, and my knees as if they were precious. "She came here the day I saw you at the Stock. Debbie said you'd moved on, and I was upset."

"She said that? It wasn't true."

He looked up at me, his hands on the backs of my thighs. "I know. Debbie's a yenta. I should have known. But Jessica was here, and she goaded me. That's not an excuse, but it's what happened. She said she wanted to do it kinky just once, and even after I explained exactly what that meant, she pushed all my buttons."

"So you fucked her."

"No! Jesus, Monica." He cupped my ass as if to make me understand. "I had her unbutton her shirt, and she still wanted it. So I bent her over the table and gave her three whacks with my belt. I'm not proud of it. But everyone's clothes were on."

"Do you understand how unlikely that story sounds?"

"Yes. But you're the only one, Monica. The only one."

"I don't forgive you."

But I did, and we both knew it. I looked down at him, with his tourmaline eyes and copper hair, and believed him despite my better judgment. I forgave him despite my misgivings. I loved him just because I did. My heart wasn't sensible or guarded enough. Not by a sight. I was a walking raw nerve ending of emotion, as if the years I'd spent away from men and sex had made me more emotional, more vulnerable, more foolish. I ran my fingers through his hair, feeling like the victim of a crime of consent.

"Can you stay with me a few hours?" he asked.

"Let me clean up, then I'll let you know."

Chapter 3

He was on the back patio, sock feet on the table, phone pressed to his ear. I watched him, thinking about how much had changed since the last time I watched him on that chaise, talking to Jessica on the phone. I'd left without saying goodbye. How long ago was that? A little over two months? Leaving without saying goodbye again would be unforgivable.

I slid the door, the change in pressure making a clack. He looked up, and when he saw me, he waved me outside. He'd hung up by the time I reached him.

"My lawyer slash sister," he said, holding out his hand. I took it but sat in the chair, swinging my legs over the arm.

"That sounds awkward."

He laughed. "You have no idea. And don't get too comfortable, because she wants to meet you."

"When?"

"Now."

"It's Saturday."

"Lawyers don't get weekends. She has no kids or husband, so she works."

I sighed. I wanted to spend the next hours soothing myself with his body, trying to rub away feeling manipulated and used. My disappointment must have been evident, because Jonathan pulled me up, wrapping his arms around me.

"I owe you. I know," he said.

"Fine."

Lil drove. Apparently, we were headed out to Beverly Hills. Traffic was pretty terrible, even for a weekend. Jonathan and I sat in the back seat. I had a leg hitched on the seat so I could face him. He leaned in my direction but faced forward.

"Are you going to wait for your sister to debrief me? And which one is this?"

"This is Margie. She's the oldest. She's very straightforward. I think you'll like her."

"And she's going to tell me everything in legalese, because you won't say a word about getting picked up at the airport and put into a police car while smiling like your Mirandas were a big joke."

"I was smiling for your benefit." He took my hand, weaving our fingers together. "I didn't want you to worry."

"I'm worried. Very worried. I was sick to my stomach until the cops came and told me what happened."

"Which was false."

"Then I was worried about you and mad at the same time. So, fail. And stop avoiding."

He leaned his head back and looked out the window.

"Is it bad?" I asked.

"We don't know. We've got radio silence from my ex-wife." He sat up and faced me. "The prosecutor's going to want to talk to you."

"I'll tell them the same thing I told the cops."

"I don't want you to think lying's going to protect me."

We just stared at each other for a few seconds, maybe more. It felt like forever and not long enough before I had to break it. He put his fingertips to my cheek, brushing his thumb on my lower lip. His hands were magical, igniting a fire, touching a fuse that ran to the core between my legs by way of my heart.

"I know you have lying in you," I said.

"My lies are all white."

"Flake white."

"The brightest, most guilt-free of the whites."

"And the one so toxic it's illegal."

A smile curled one side of his mouth. "I'm not lying about Jessica or about anything that matters."

"Who decides what matters?"

His hand slid off my throat and down my chest, resting on my sternum. "You matter. We matter. I haven't touched another woman since I had you at the Loft Club. Monica, it's you. Being with you is all I can think about. It's all I want. We are bound. I can't be unfaithful to you any more than the sky can be unfaithful to the sea."

"Nice words."

"Your nipples are hard." He brushed them with the backs of his fingers.

"Your body won't deny what your mind fights."

"If I decide to believe you, understand I know there are things you've lied about."

"Such as?" He drew a nail over my nipple, the fabric like Teflon, letting it slide across. My lips parted.

"I don't believe Kevin got picked up just because," I said.

He pinched my nipple hard, giving a little twist. My back arched.

"Who cares?" he whispered.

"I do. About the truth."

He put his hand under my skirt. I was a little sore from the hate fuck in his living room, but my wet lips fluttered under his touch.

"Open your legs."

I did, and he hitched up my dress until it gathered just under my breasts. He placed my heels on the seat until my underwear was the only thing between me and his eyes.

"The truth, Monica," he said, putting his thumb lightly on my clit, using my juices to slide over the skin. "The truth is that I love you. The rest is unnecessary complication."

"I disagree." But I was lost. It didn't matter if I agreed or not. I wanted some part of his body to rub against me. He flicked my engorged clit, and my breath hitched with the pain and pleasure.

"You won't." He took a small box from his pocket, opened it, and plucked my diamond navel bar from its velvet bed. He kissed between my legs, over my underwear, breathing on my clit to make it warm and receptive. His lips traveled to my naked navel, which he kissed gently. "You belong to me. That means I take care of you. Your body and your heart." He slid the navel bar through the piercing. "That means I'm committed to your happiness. And it means there is no other woman." He slid the smaller diamond cap on top, sealing the gem to me. "I don't share. And you don't have to either. You have to trust me."

"I can't."

"It's a choice. Make it." He slid to his knees before me and slipped his fingers under my panties. I lifted my butt, and he pulled them off. His tongue ran from my knee to my thigh. When his tongue found my folds, I thought I'd burst.

"Oh…" I put my fingers in his hair.

He looked up and said, "Hands under your ass."

I sat on them.

"Keep these legs open."

The commands turned me on, sending another wave of pleasure through me. By the time his tongue found my clit, I was non-verbal. He licked so gently, flicking it, then circling my hole, making sure every inch of me was on high alert. A little suck, a flick with his fingers. Sweet, exquisite torture. He slid those flicking fingers in me, then sucked my clit again.

"May I come, sir?" I asked in a breath.

"Maybe," he whispered. "Keep these legs spread for me." He ran his tongue over my clit again.

"Oh, God."

He slid his thumb in my cunt, and when he drew it out, he traced the line up and down me. Another flick made me bite back a scream.

"Let me come, sir."

"Say please."

"Please, I'm begging. Please."

"Are you mine?" he asked.

"I'm yours. You own me. My cunt is yours. Please let me come."

"Am I yours?"

"I own your sorry ass and everything it's attached to, please. Please."

He licked my clit again, sucked it through his teeth, and made my ass lift off the seat. He got three fingers in my cunt and hooked them, pushing into the rough spot inside me. His name left my lips over and over, and I tried to keep my legs open when they just wanted to clench around him. His tongue and teeth worked me until a tidal wave of pleasure broke through, sending shocks of fire through me. His fingers inside me did something else, blinding me with a different note, a severe release that felt sharp as a razor, strong as a sledgehammer.

I pushed into him, holding myself up on the hands he'd commanded under my ass. I hissed his name through my teeth so Lil wouldn't hear through the glass. My orgasm abated, fading like the end of a song. His tongue's ministrations slowed. My hips twitched around him.

I ran my fingers through his hair as he kissed the inside of my thighs. "Jonathan?"

"Monica."

"One day this will stop working."

"But not today."

Chapter 4

We went into the elevator with a man in a grey suit, putting our backs to the wall and watching the floors light up above us. Jonathan's hand hooked mine and clutched it.

He was holding my hand in an elevator. Like a normal person. I looked at him, and he turned to me.

"What?" he asked.

"Nothing."

Grey Suit got out, and the doors slid shut.

"Margie litigated my divorce," Jonathan said, still facing the doors.

"Okay?"

"We had a lot of talk about irreconcilable differences over sex. How it was had, et cetera. There were gag orders that were broken. No pun intended."

"Okay."

"My sister may look at you in that way you were afraid of. She's still curious about the whole thing."

"That's awkward."

"You have no idea."

My face hurt from holding back a nervous smile. "If she's curious, you should send Debbie at her with a riding crop."

He glanced at me, and I knew he was trying to hold back nervous laughter as much as I was. The elevator dinged, and the doors slid open. "Madame Silk would have her crawling on the floor in a second."

"I knew it!" I exclaimed.

He put his arm around me, and we walked into the hall. He opened glass doors for me. Two receptionists sat behind a stark white counter topped with red blooms. The older seemed to know him and picked up the phone when she saw him. He still had his arm around me.

"Did Madame Silk ever get her crop on you?" I whispered.

"We discussed it and decided against."

"How thoughtful and sensible of you."

He pulled me to him. "It was much, much more complex than that."

"Mister Drazen?" the receptionist called. "Come this way." We followed her past the desk and into the belly of the office. He held my hand the whole way.

Margie was almost as tall as I was, and she shook my hand like a man. She did not size me up, nor did she give me the impression she had an ounce of curiosity about what I did in bed with her brother. Either Jonathan was wrong and she didn't give a shit, or she was as in control as he was. Her sage pencil skirt and tapered jacket were tailored to exist without being noticed as anything but part of a God-created whole. I knew her age, and she wore it well. She had the alertness of a child, yet her comportment was so graceful and self-aware, she was more adult than I thought I'd ever feel.

We sat across from her desk like recalcitrant schoolchildren, facing huge windows that looked over the city. We shared small talk, a few lines about their family I didn't understand, a word or two about traffic on the 405, and a couple of innocent questions about waitressing and music.

Then Margaret Drazen put her elbows on the desk and indicated her brother while speaking to me. "So what did this one tell you?"

"He lied. As usual." I glanced at Jonathan. He leaned into the arm of his chair and rubbed his upper lip as if he was trying to hide his mouth. I knew he was biting back a smile.

"Which lie was it this time?" Margie asked me.

"The one where they both had their clothes on and there was no touching."

"This the same scene where he hit his ex-wife with a belt?"

"That one."

Margie leaned back. She looked as if she was going to fall out the window and get poured over Los Angeles. "This is so fucking fascinating. See, he tells me this story, and I'm thinking assault and battery. You hear the exact same story and think infidelity."

Jonathan broke in. "You're going off the rails, Margie."

"But, Jonny…"

"We talked about this," he said, his posture still relaxed.

"It's very simple," I said, my voice clipped and brusque. "His belt is for holding up his pants, binding me, and hurting me. His body, any part of it, is to give *me* pleasure and pain. If he gives any other woman either of those things with his body or any clothing accessory, it's cheating." I turned to him. "The fact that we were officially broken up notwithstanding."

"You said she wouldn't want to talk about it," Margie said to Jonathan.

"Apparently I was misinformed."

"You two need to talk more."

"Sorry if you're an hour behind the curve."

Margie put up her hand. "Okay, that was fun, let's move on." She turned back to me. "First. Let me tell you about the great state of California. We're a preferred arrest state. Any domestic violence accusation with some merit warrants an arrest."

"Define merit," I said.

"You're sharp. Merit means she had a recording of the incident on her phone and pictures of a reddened ass consistent with getting hit hard with a belt. Since she provided all of this to the police, the prosecutor decides how to proceed. But with the multimedia presentation available to him and the years of rumors, if he didn't arrest Jonathan for felony battery, he'd lose his job. Even if she drops the charges or recants, the prosecution still has to continue."

"Felony battery?" I said softly.

"They're required to arrest as a felony," Margie said. "The DA can bump it down to misdemeanor, but if the Ice Queen remains trenchant, a reduction's unlikely."

I couldn't look at Jonathan. It sounded so dire, and yet, what he'd done to her wasn't a fraction of what he'd done with me. "I don't understand how this will lead to getting her husband back."

"Ex-husband," Jonathan grumbled.

"Agreed," Margie said, "especially not with the mandatory order of protection."

"This is very simple." Jonathan twisted his whole body to face me. "My ex-wife doesn't want me back. At the time, I didn't know what she wanted, and I was trying to get it out of her. You don't have to like the way I did it, and if you want me to apologize again, I will."

"You can stick your apology."

"I'll be sure to do that. You and I were broken up, but I knew you were coming back." His face flashed with that cocky confidence then changed to something more sincere. "But what I wanted to tell you was that at the time, I didn't know what she wanted. Margie and I figured it out last night."

"She wants you, Jonathan," I said.

"No. She wants money. She's had trouble maintaining her lifestyle and her art at the same time. I set up a trust for her to pull from whenever she wants. It's a few million a year and I don't notice it, but that's what she uses to finance her work. We were set to renew the terms after ten years, and I cut her off."

Margie broke in. "It's a revocable trust. He can do what he wants unless he's declared incompetent. Then it automatically flips to an irrevocable trust. The terms will be reinstated. It's a stopgap against hospitalizations, drug addictions, that sort of thing."

Jonathan broke in. "She's using my kink to call my sanity into question. She pushed me into spanking her and tape recorded it to show how out of control I am."

They paused their tag-team routine, and I glanced from one to the other. Margie leaned forward with her elbows on the desk; Jonathan with his ankle crossed over his knee, leaning over the arm of the chair toward me.

"The cameras?" I said. "She was trying to get something to show you were crazy? How would it be admissible?"

"It's all back room deals," Margie said. "We think she might have counted on a little shame from you to corroborate, as well as my brother's desire to protect you. Kinky shit on tape could have served a hundred purposes."

"Fuck her."

"That's the spirit."

He took my hand. "She came to me only because the cameras were a bust."

I squeezed his hand. "I've met her. I'll tell you one thing. She'd drop everything to have you back."

"I'm spoken for."

"Regardless. She always manages to get you to do things, doesn't she?"

Silence built between us as we held hands and searched each other's faces. I examined his for understanding that what he did was wrong, and I think he searched mine for forgiveness.

Margie cleared her throat.

He and I didn't move.

"Monica," she said. "I want to tell you why you're here."

"To verify that he's telling the truth?" I said without moving my eyes from him.

"No. I need to tell you what to expect."

I moved my gaze from him to Margie and leaned back in my chair. He didn't let my hand go. She took that as her cue to continue.

"She's probably going to contact you and ask you to verify that he hits you. Just know anything you say will be twisted. She has to prove that what he's doing is impairing his ability to function. Barring that, since she's after his money, she'll threaten to go public and blackmail him."

Jonathan squeezed my hand, and I turned to him. "If I spend even thirty days in jail, we go back to the old terms of the trust and she can drain it."

"Arraignment's next week," Margie said.

I felt as if I was being played, as if those two had worked out a routine and delivered it. I couldn't tell if I was being lied to or just manipulated, but I didn't believe Jonathan gave a rat's ass about a few million a year. Something else was at stake that they weren't talking about, and I needed to shake things up.

"I think I should go see her," I said.

The air went out of the room.

"No," Jonathan said.

"I'm sorry?" Margie seemed keen for an explanation.

"Absolutely not." Jonathan's tone was definite and dominant.

"I wasn't asking permission," I replied without my submissive voice.

"Let's hear it," Margie said. "She might have something."

"The only way you're going to get an angle on what she intends is if I see her. If she makes an offer, I can take her up on it and go see her to get dirt on you. I'll tell her I'm pissed at you because you spanked her. We'll have tea and talk about what an asshole you are. I come back here and report everything."

"No."

"Are you going to the Collector's Board thing?" Margie asked Jonathan before turning to me. "She'll be there. It can be a casual conversation."

Jonathan's tone was clipped, as if he didn't even want to talk about it. "It's all Jessica's people, and they're going to be snickering about this arrest. I won't subject Monica to them, and I'm not going without her. So. Done."

"What is it?" I asked Margie. "It sounds like a great idea."

"Fifty of the city's biggest art collectors drinking and spending money," Margie said. "I went with him last year. It was like high school without the acne."

"And Jessica will be there?" I asked.

"Four artists for every collector." Margie smirked. "You never met a bigger bunch of whores in your life."

Jonathan was right, I *did* like her. "I want to go."

Jonathan stood up. "Margie, as usual, a fucking pleasure." He looked at me and held out his hand. "Let's go."

Margie pushed her chair back and stood. We were done. I got up without taking his hand.

Chapter 5

Monica

I didn't speak until the elevator doors closed. "You know I'm right."

He was on me in a second, his tongue prying my mouth open, his hands on my face, his hard cock against my hip. I had much to say, but none of it seemed important. I was helpless. A ring of fire built between my legs at his touch, portents of pleasure pushing me forward. He hitched my leg up and did a slow grind against me.

"Jonathan. I should do it. I mean it." My words came in gasps.

"No."

"I can help you."

He smacked the red button on the control panel, and the elevator came to a halt. A bell rang in a constant clatter, but he didn't pull away. He pulled my skirt up and hooked his finger in the crotch of my panties, sliding his finger along my wet folds.

A voice came over the intercom. "What's your emergency?" It sounded automated, as if there really wasn't someone on the other end.

He turned to the panel and said something in a language I didn't understand, then put his lips on mine as if it was our last kiss.

"Can you repeat that?" asked the voice robotically.

He repeated it and undid his pants, pulling out his gorgeous cock.

"I'll have someone there in ten minutes."

"Cameras."

"It's Saturday. No one's at the desk. Whole system's probably shut down."

He fell into me, pushing me into the wall, a hand pulling the crotch of my panties away as the fingertips dug into my ass. I hitched my leg on his hips. He guided himself into me and thrust hard, shocking the breath right out of me. Bringing my other leg around him, he thrust again. And again.

"Oh, fuck," I said.

"Fuck is right." He twisted my nipple through my shirt. The exquisite pain was a direct line between my legs, making me spread them wider. My left shoe fell off. He buried his face in my neck. "You are not to see her, goddess."

"Jesus. I can't think."

"Don't think." He pushed his belly on my clit, and a thousand fireworks went off between my thighs. "Just do what I ask." He rotated his hips, rubbing me sideways, then forward. He looked me in the eye, and let his hand creep up my face. He slipped a finger in my mouth. I tried to suck on it, but I couldn't keep my lips closed; I was gasping so hard. He pulled it out, dragging saliva across my cheek.

"I'm coming," I said.

"You're coming, what?"

"Sir."

He didn't withhold. He pummeled me, driving forward until I cried out through clenched teeth, pressing my legs around him, praying to a God I didn't even believe in. Jonathan's prayer was right behind mine, and he grunted it into the spot where my ear met my neck. His purposeful thrusts slowed into jerks, leaving nothing but hot breath on me. Our chests rose and fell in time, and our mouths found each other in a gentle, satisfied kiss.

The alarm suddenly seemed louder and more annoying, and the elevator cold and hard. Only Jonathan's face, as it took up the whole of my vision, was soft and inviting. He pulled himself from me and gently lowered my legs. As I straightened my skirt, he pressed the alarm button. Blissful silence followed, and the elevator jerked down.

I had about thirty seconds to say what I wanted to say, and I was not eager to do it. "I'm going. She's wanted to tell me something for a month, and it's time I heard it."

He pressed his lips together. "No."

"You have to trust me. I committed to you. That means something."

"I get it. You don't need to prove it to me."

"I'm not trying to prove anything to you. I don't have to. I dedicated myself to you. I gave my body to you. That doesn't mean I'm suddenly more compliant."

Chapter 6

Jonathan

I put Monica in the Bentley so Lil could take her to work. I refused to hear another word about her seeing Jessica, but I should have acted more laid back. Such rigidity would only make her want to see my ex-wife that much more. Yet I couldn't even pretend I would talk about it later. I had to let Monica think it was about money, but the truth was that Jessica knew too much. "Just paying her off" might have seemed cheap in the short run, but in the long run, it did nothing to protect me. I had to find a better way to manage the problem, and I needed to buy time with compliance.

My lunch with Eddie Milpas was three blocks away. I called my sister and walked.

"So?" I said.

"She's not your type," Margie said. "She has dark hair and a brain."

"Thank you. I didn't need your approval."

"Neither did she. Which I like. I always expected your next one would be on her hands and knees, licking a doormat. That's not what you got. You got someone bigger than your grip. So, good luck with that."

"If they put her up on the stand, I'm worried."

"You shouldn't be. She looked me right in the eye when she made her claim on the contents of your closet. If the truth is something you need to use, she'll tell it. But I wouldn't count on her to lie," Margie said.

"Monica? No. I'd never ask her to. She's..." I stopped myself, wanting to use words like *clean* and *pure*. They sounded ridiculous. "She's honorable."

"God help you, then."

"I don't want her talking to Jessica."

"What did you want me to do about that?" Margie asked as if bored, but I could tell she knew what I was going to ask.

"I want Will Santon's team back."

"You want to follow her. After she just got over surveillance equipment in her house. You're a paragon of sensitivity. Really."

I stopped outside Karen M's. I saw Eddie at a window seat. No small thing. A year ago, they would have seated him by the bathrooms. "Do *you* want her talking to Jessica? Because that woman's going to lie. She's going to turn a sexless spanking into a grudge fuck, and then I'm going to be the one licking a doormat."

Margie sighed. "I gotta tell you, little brother, on the rare occasions you feel something, you go deep."

"And with respect to that, I'd appreciate your indulgence."

"Take Santon. But on a personal note..."

"Yeah?"

"Don't get caught. In case you haven't noticed, you're on thin ice already."

We hung up. Sheila was my favorite sister, but Margie was always a voice of sanity when things got chaotic.

I sat across from Eddie. The window looked over a line of tall bamboo meant to block the sight of Wilshire Boulevard traffic. Eddie looked at the menu, then at me, then back at the menu, as if he didn't know exactly what was on it.

"Nice tie," I said as an opener.

"Thanks." His tone was clipped and quiet. I knew the guy. He was a percolating case of verbal diarrhea unless he was pissed off.

"I hear they've changed to locally grown tomatoes," I said, "so avoid the caprese."

"I heard the same."

"There's a shitstain on your cuff," I said. He glanced at me, then away. "Are we dating, Ed? Did I just fuck your best friend or get you the wrong birthday gift or something?"

Eddie, reengaged in the conversation, leaned on the window, spreading his arm over the table so he could fuss with a matchbook. "My boss gets back from a trip Friday. Some last minute thing to look at property up north, and he saw the girl I've been pushing. But according to him, I've been doing it wrong. My whole marketing strategy? Wrong. So *he's* managing her. *He's* signing her. Personally. Harry Enrich hasn't personally managed talent in fifteen years."

"She'll be happy to hear it."

"She shouldn't be. It's not all skinny ties and burning CDs any more.

He hasn't caught up to MySpace falling apart. She'll be on his learning curve when he doesn't even know he has one. That leather corset's gonna start looking real comfy."

The waiter came. We ordered quickly. That had apparently been bothering him, and I needed to clear it up. He was burned. The collection of talent was his job, and a singular voice had been pulled from under him. In a city full of hopeful musicians, voices like Monica's were impossible to come by. Needles in haystacks. Finding another voice he could use could take him a year or a lifetime.

"Ed, listen. I don't want any hard feelings. But it wasn't happening your way. I could have gotten Randy from Vintage Records up there just as easy."

"Randy Rothstein? Please."

"But I kept it at Carnival out of respect for you."

He laughed. I admit I smiled as well. The notion was ridiculous. He was up a creek and had a right to be angry. I had the right to not care.

"You went over my head less than a week after you beaned me," he said. "I had a headache for a day and a half."

"I apologized."

Eddie pushed his drink aside as if it was an actual obstacle. "Listen, asshole. If you had a problem with me signing your girlfriend, you could have told me."

"So you could what? Tell me to go fuck myself? She wasn't signing with you anyway. Not all decked out in leather and chains."

"You don't know that."

"Ed. She was walking. Who's going to know it better than me? I saved your ass and hers. Now you can all make money together."

"I got nothing. Enrich can have her. Without a marketing angle, she can sing like a mermaid and it wouldn't matter."

"Mermaids don't sing. You're thinking of sirens."

He shook his head and smirked. "You need to go out and find me another girl who likes to get tied up."

"I have one for you." I lowered my voice and leaned in. "Nice voice, but she comes with an angle. Might not be as hot as what you had in mind, but it's like a slot and a tab. She's got something already going."

"I swear to god. Where do you find the time?"

"She's an artist," I said. "Think Laurie Anderson but drop dead gorgeous. Plays everything. She can play the spoons and bring you to tears.

Has the chops for installation and performance work, knows the art scene."

"Not as commercial," he said.

"It's what I have."

"You got a name?"

The waiter came with lunch, and I wrote the name on a napkin.

Chapter 7

Monica

I headed down Echo Park Avenue on foot, phone to my ear.

"Are you in the house?" I asked as I pushed the gate open.

"Just got dressed," Darren said.

"I'm on my way. No, wait, I'm on your patio. Are you alone?"

He opened the door in jeans and his red Music Store polo. "Yes. How was the trip home?"

"I really, really like that plane." I pocketed my phone.

He stepped aside, and I entered. My stuff was all over the living room, neatly piled, but the room still looked as if someone had been crashing on his couch without paying rent.

"Did the police question you?" he asked.

I was a little taken aback, and it must have been all over my face. "How did you know?"

"It's all over the society pages. And the *LA Times*, you know… It's news if it's about rich people beating their wives."

"She's not his wife, and he didn't beat her." I defended him and his word, knowing that the truth and Jonathan had a passing, convenient acquaintance.

"Not in the conventional sense." He placed his laptop on the kitchen bar and spun it so I could see the screen. Then he set about making coffee as if he didn't want to look at my reaction.

The Celebrity section. A section I ignored because Gabby had always read, assimilated, and digested the entire thing every morning, distilling it for me over breakfast. I was grateful I wasn't in the habit of looking at it because the day after Jonathan was arrested at Santa Monica airport, a picture of him and his *ex*-wife appeared in Rumors Bureau column. It was the only mention of his arrest anywhere in the news, and it was short, with little but a wedding picture of two people happy to commit to each other. The burning jealousy that bubbled from my gut left an awful taste on the back of my tongue. He was mine. I owned him. Those pictures were lies.

"Monica?" Darren watched me as he filled the pot with water.

"What?"

"Are you okay?"

"It barely says anything. Arrested at the airport on domestic abuse charges brought by his ex-wife. History of kinky activity. Wife declines comment because she's 'too upset,' Oh, and I'm an unidentified female passenger. His little trick fuck whore. Remind me never to look at the internet again." I pushed the laptop away and turned to my pile of crap. I could have stalled and pretended to rummage through my stuff, but I knew exactly where that manila envelope was. I ran my hands over it, the aged edges, the curled flap.

"That what I think it is?" Darren asked.

"Yeah. Did you open it?"

"It's long and involved, so I just put it back." He looked at me over the edge of his coffee cup.

"Great. Long and involved." I slid out the contents. Eight and a half by eleven printed pages, stapled. About twenty pages, pure text. Double-spaced with wide margins. Markings all over it in red pencil. Lines. Scribblings. Hash marks. Slashes. Across the top: *Lloyd Willman/Evert Toth, ed.*

"It looks like someone's term paper."

He looked over my shoulder. "I think the ed. means *editor*. My first assumption was that it was a newspaper article."

"Fan-freaking-tastic."

"And unpublished, looks like. Or it wouldn't look like something someone handed in for eleventh grade finals. My sister was a scary girl. I think digging dirt on people was more fun for her than actually trying to get them to sign her."

"When do you have to leave?" I asked.

"Fifteen minutes."

I threw myself on the couch. I flipped through. All words and marks. I looked up at Darren, who was wiping down the counter. I cleared my throat.

He didn't look up when he said, "You're stalling."

"Why would I stall?"

"You tell me."

I had a hundred answers.

Because I know half-truths and pieces of a story.

Because I'm committed to a man who is still a mystery to me.
Because I love him, and I will stand by him, no matter what the papers say.
Because Jonathan lies.
So I didn't answer but tilted my head down and read.

Chapter 8

The star of the article was the rain.

There had been a winter of storms. I was nine. Dad was away, as usual. Christmas sucked because we were broke and the crawlspace flooded. Pebbles from the driveway of what became the Montessori school came in on a tide of floodwater, pecking the north side of the house for hours.

I hadn't done the math before. Why would I? Why would I remind myself that I was in third grade when he was busy having sex and falling in love? But that was the year I learned multiplication and long division and the year Jonathan lost Rachel.

The story wasn't much different than I'd imagined. A party had started out as a family affair for Sheila Drazen, and it became wilder and more drug-infused once the adults left and the kids arrived. The police found a bong containing chartreuse absinthe, the remnants of White Widow bud, and sixteen-year-old Jonathan S. Drazen III's DNA.

What happened after was the stuff of police procedurals, but according to witnesses, Jonathan argued with his girlfriend, Rachel Demarest. She grabbed his keys and ran into the rain. Everyone assumed she was keeping his fucked-up ass from driving. The next morning, Jonathan was found passed out on the muddy front lawn of a house a quarter mile off, and his waterlogged car was found on the beach three miles south with no girlfriend in it. A day and a half later, he was committed to Westonwood after an almost successful suicide attempt. It wasn't a half-hearted cry for help; he did almost die of heart failure.

Three months in Westonwood. The place was known for its lockdown: no phone, no radio. Nothing. A prison for the rich and disturbed.

But while he was away, his world was not quiet. What had happened during the rains had rippled outward in those months, and the Drazens had deflected and shrouded all of it.

Rachel's body wasn't found, and her death dissolved an already troubled family. The police had been to the Demarest house for over a dozen domestic disturbances over six years. Neighbors told stories of sexual abuse by her biological father, and near constant yelling and fighting after her stepdad moved in. Rachel had found solace in her classmate Theresa, who opened the Drazen home to her for study.

In the months before the accident, according to Rachel's mother, Rachel started coming home with gifts. Pearl earrings. Gold bracelet. A new laptop. She became closed and distant. When police questioned Mrs. Demarest about the gifts, she threw around accusations. She didn't believe her daughter had had an accident. She wanted the matter looked into because Rachel had been intonating that the Drazen family wasn't all they were cracked up to be. She called the *LA Times*, who interviewed her and dismissed her as a crackpot, and the *LA Voice*, which seemed to be the paper the article was written for.

Suddenly, she didn't want to talk to anyone. She called everything off and became non-responsive to further investigation. No interviews, and only the required police depositions, which she attended with a very expensive lawyer.

The Demarests had been paid off, that much was clear, and the article ended right there, mid-sentence.

"What the fuck?" I said. "Even this thing is half a fucking story."

Darren stepped into his shoe. "What's it say?"

"His girlfriend from sixteen years ago died under suspicious circumstances, and the family paid off anyone associated with it. Or got them fired. For all I know, the rest of the article is about who they killed."

"You gonna tell him?"

I slid the papers back in the envelope. "How can I? I don't know if any of this is true. It could be someone's idea of a short story. He's got enough shit going on without me coming to him with this… this… I don't even know what this is."

"Gabby's causing trouble from the grave." He shrugged on his jacket. "I like that."

"You would. Can I use your computer? I want to look up some of this."

"Yeah. Not that I care, but will you be here when I get back? You look like you got your walking shoes on."

"I'm going home today." I glanced at my pile of crap, wondering if I could make it on one trip.

"I'm thinking about Gabby's room."

"Move in."

"Did you ask?"

I rolled my eyes. "Fine. I'll ask daddy if it's ok if a boy lives with me."

I thought that was hilarious. Darren didn't.

Chapter 9

The all-knowing internet revealed a big fat goose egg, but I was never much of a researcher. I did find Evert Toth, who had a masthead listing as managing editor of *elLAy Rag*, a local left-wing free paper picked up in coffee shops all over the city. Though one might assume such a paper was trash from front to porn-filled back, it wasn't. Some of the biggest exposes, blown whistles, and no-bullshit journalism happened inside. I called the paper, got routed all over the place, and finally ended up on voice mail. I left a message.

I walked home, phone in hand, unwilling to put it in my pocket. I had something else to do. Someone else to call.

I was many things. I was submissive. I was masochistic. I was trusting. I was a sexual slave. But obedient?

Not as much.

I rooted around my bag and found a matte white card. I stopped at the corner because if I waited until I got home, I might change my mind. I dialed the number. The voice that came over was silky smooth, betraying nothing, giving nothing.

Hello, you've reached the workshop of Jessica Carnes. Please leave a message after the tone, and I'll get back to you as soon as possible. If you are a curator calling to schedule a studio visit, please press five.

I choked a little. I knew what I wanted. I wanted to probe her plans. I wanted to represent myself as her friend and ally to bring back information to Jonathan, but I suddenly felt highly unqualified to protect him.

I almost hung up, but her caller ID would reveal who I was, and if I hung up, I'd look weak and manipulative. She wouldn't trust me. She'd use me. I needed her to respect me if I wanted her to attempt to partner with me.

"Hi, Jessica. This is Monica Faulkner. I'd like to take you up on your offer to talk if it's still on the table. Thanks."

I hung up before I could say something stupid or laugh nervously.

Fuck.

What did I just do?

Chapter 10

The Stock was busy. Super busy. Wall-of-drunk busy. Ass-pinched-turn-around-and-I-can't-tell-who-did-it busy, especially considering rain threatened on the horizon. I put on a happy face, but my preoccupation reduced the power of my customer-service smile. I couldn't check my phone while I was working, and I needed to know if Jessica had called me back. I wanted to see Jonathan's texts, because I was sure there was at least one.

I barely had time for a break, but I ran to the bathroom. On the way out, I saw Debbie.

"I'm going at midnight," she said. "Robert's handling the tips."

My disappointment must have shown on my face. Not about Robert managing the tips. The system for their division was fool-proof, which was good since Robert needed a system with exactly that name.

"What?" she asked.

"I wanted to talk to you after the shift."

She looked at her watch. "You have four minutes."

"I don't want to say it so fast I offend you and lose my job."

"So don't."

I'd rehearsed it a billion times, but there was no neutral way to ask. "You told me I shouldn't have taken Jonathan seriously, and you told him I'd moved on."

"Yes."

"Why?"

"I don't understand the question. He's not usually serious. It looked to me like you'd moved on." She shrugged as if everything had been on the up and up.

I started to feel like maybe it had been, and I was the one who had the problem. "I'm sorry to be blunt, but it gave me the impression, well… that it was…" I stopped. How had I painted myself into such a corner?

Debbie just waited for me to get myself out. She didn't say a word or look impatient.

"Why do you want us together?" I asked. I managed to not use the word *manipulative*.

"You think I'm motivated by something other than friendship?"

"I don't pretend to know." Another wait. I felt as if I could hear the seconds go by.

Debbie didn't look at her watch, and there was no clock in the hall, but when she straightened a fraction and said, "Time's up," I knew she was right to within the second.

Break over. Time to get back on the floor. The second half of my shift passed painfully but quickly. Every douchebag with a Hugo Boss suit or Audi keys made me want to scream. The intensity must have served me well, because my tips were more than I'd ever seen. I started to think about putting some cash away in my dwindling savings account or buying myself more pretty things to wear under my dresses.

I was snapping my locker closed when Robert came up, a little self-important swagger in his gait.

"Someone's here for you."

I didn't want to smile, but I did. Jonathan had come, obviously. "I'll be right up."

He turned and walked off, calling behind him, "She's by the bar."

"Ok, thanks."

She?

Chapter 11

I went upstairs with less anticipation, less heightened awareness than I would have if I thought I was meeting Jonathan. It was probably Yvonne or some random friend who was passing by and wanted to hit an after-hours.

Seeing a bar after closing, with the lights on and the music off, is much like seeing a beautiful woman without makeup. All the parts are there but made unappealing. Glasses thunk against bus trays, squeaky-wheeled press buckets make their way across the floor behind the slap and swoosh of grey-fringed mops. The staff laughs at each other's jokes, which are invariably on customers. Guests lingered, mostly in earnest conversations about the next destination for drinking or fucking. Some clung by their fingernails, as if a change of venue would break a spell.

In the case of the Stock, the city had darkened beneath us as much as it ever would, and the sky was a burnt orange with reflected light. It was one fifteen in the morning. I had a pocket full of cash. Maybe I'd go the hell out and talk to people. Maybe I'd cling to a venue until four a.m. to avoid sleeping in my house for the first time in weeks.

But I wasn't going out. I wasn't getting drunk, and I wasn't reacquainting myself with anyone. Only one woman was at the bar. It was Jessica, and she was not alone. Jonathan stood over her, and they were arguing fiercely. They looked like a married couple on the verge of a blowout, talking over each other, tense hands in front of them. I didn't want to approach them. But something else took over.

She wasn't supposed to talk to him. She wasn't supposed to be in fifty feet of him. He was mine. I had a reaction that could only be described as biological. Rage filled my blood from some angry gland until my fingertips clenched and my teeth ground together.

Jonathan looked up. As soon as he saw me, he came my way like a torpedo.

"What the fuck?" I said.

He gripped my shoulder and spun me around. "Walk."

"No." He pushed me toward the back room. I shrugged him off. "I want to talk to her. That's why she's here." He took my bicep and yanked me off the floor. "Get off me."

He didn't listen. He pulled me through the halls, past the few coworkers left, along the concrete floors of the back hallways. His face was stern and blank, a fixed mask of intention. He pushed me into the break room, locked the door, and drew shades over the window to the hall. When he finally faced me again, I pushed him away.

"Don't you *ever* do anything like that again," I said.

He pressed me against the wall and put his face to mine in a punishing kiss. I gave in to the heat, the urgency of his mouth on mine, his tongue demanding response, his hands still pushing my shoulders. I groaned into him, my voice a breath I had no choice but to take.

"I told you not to meet with her," he said, face near enough to kiss me again.

"You're not the boss of me."

"Oh no?"

"Dragging me away from a conversation, trying to isolate me, you're giving her quite a case."

"Pick up your skirt."

"Using sex to control me…"

"Show me your cunt, Monica."

I felt a pool of arousal below my waist at the command. Though Jonathan didn't hold my arms, his grip on my shoulders made skidding my hands over my skirt uncomfortable and awkward. I pinched the fabric and bent my wrists, hiking up the skirt one inch, then two. I got a fistful of cotton and yanked. The whole thing rode up as our eyes met, our breath mingling.

"So, what? You going to fuck me now?"

"I am."

"You think that's going to stop me?"

He put a hand at my throat, fingertips at the base of my jaw, forcing me to look at the ceiling. The restriction and posture sent a tidal wave of desire between my legs. I wanted to wrap them around him and take him inside me.

"I've never punished you, goddess. But I will."

"Go on. I'm not scared of you."

He looped his fingers in my panties and drove his fingers along my wet cleft. I gasped and moaned when he thrust two fingers in me. When he pulled them out, I felt their loss. I wanted to be filled with him, despite the fact that he was pissing me off, or because of it. Pressing his torso to mine and keeping his hand on my jaw, he put his wet fingers in my mouth.

"This mouth is mine," he said. "It doesn't talk unless I tell it to."

The taste of my sex filled my mouth as he drove his fingers down my throat. I sucked them clean to please him, to please myself. The sensations caused by his forcefulness were overpowering.

He took his hand off my throat and ran it along my belly, to my thighs, inside them. He found the crotch of my panties and pulled them off. Then, without a pause, he pushed me onto the lunch table. The metal legs scraped the linoleum as he slid me back and bent my legs so my sopping pussy lay before him.

"You're not fucking my decision out of me."

Standing between my legs, he unbuckled his belt. "Don't make me gag you."

I held up my middle finger. He smiled as if he couldn't help it then grabbed my hand and held it down, hard. His thumb dug into my wrist, and I knew my expression broadcast pain. My legs tightened and closed, but he pushed them apart.

"I'm going to fuck you, and you're going to shut the hell up for the fucking duration." He drove into me without an ounce more warning. He fucked me as if he owned me, my body bent, powerless, exposed.

He told me to take it, but he was the one who was doing the taking. He held the meat of my thighs, spreading my legs. The pain of his hands digging into my skin, his banging cock, him standing over me in dominion. I'd never look at those humming fluorescent lights without feeling a buzz in my cunt again.

I got up on my elbows, and he pushed me back down. "Don't move unless I tell you to."

"I'm going to—"

"You are not."

I *was* going to come. A tsunami of pleasure rushed over the horizon, rising waters pooled at my feet, ankles, knees. I had another half a minute to complete oblivion. But his eyes shut and he grunted, then moaned, pushing into me slowly. He was coming, motherfucker, and he'd never just come because he couldn't help it. Outside the first time he fucked me without a condom, he never lost control. Jonathan's orgasms always had a purpose.

Taking his hands off my thighs, he leaned in. "Give me a number between one and ten."

"Two."

"Forget that, then. Between five and ten."

"Seven."

"That's how many times you're coming before sunrise. But you have to come home with me."

"You son of a bitch. We're playing orgasm games again?" I asked.

"You're being a poor sport."

I got up on my elbows, feeling done with that conversation already. "Tomorrow's my day off, and I want to work on some songs."

"I have a piano."

"All my staff pads are at home. All my notes. Forget it."

He picked me up gently by my biceps, but his fingertips sent bolts of not-so-sexy pain through them. He must have seen me flinch. "Are you all right?"

"I'm fine."

"I'll come to your place. Let me drive. Please. Give me a couple of hours to do nothing but make you squirm." He tugged at my skirt, and I hoisted myself up so he could get it back in place.

I put my arms over his shoulders and kissed him. I couldn't help it. I had absolutely no choice. His lips sat so close to mine, and they were so responsive. His tongue ignited the smoldering fire between my legs. I wrapped my legs around him, letting his mouth take mine.

"My place until sunrise," I said as he kissed my jaw, then my neck. "Then you get the hell out so I can get to work."

"To write," he whispered.

"Yes."

"You promise?"

I pulled away. "I might also go to the bathroom once or twice. Do I need to fill out a form or call you first?"

A smile drew across his lips. A joke was incoming, but there was a click as the door was unlocked from the outside. Jonathan got his dick back in his pants before the cleaning crew swung the door open.

Chapter 12

"Saying I don't know what I'm dealing with is plain insulting."

We were on the matte black rocket, which I loved because I had my arms around him, inside his jacket, and I could feel the angles and bumps of his body. I'd tucked my skirt around my thighs to his satisfaction so I wouldn't expose my pantie-less glory to Los Angeles. Once that was settled, he'd put my helmet on me as if to cut off any further discussion. Talking to him when he was a disembodied voice was hard. I didn't want to wait until we got to my house to talk to him because we'd be in a private place and he'd try to shut me up with sex again. It would work, for the hundredth time.

"I'm not insulting you. I'm telling the truth. Jessica can teach Machiavelli a few things," he said through the speaker in my helmet.

"I need to see your face."

"You'll see plenty."

"Stop the bike."

We were on Sunset, by the Junction, the one neighborhood where people gathered on the street, walking from bar, to restaurant, to bar, to home.

"We'll be to your house in eight minutes."

"Now."

He stopped at a light and pulled off his helmet. His hair spiked and curled with the disruption, and when he turned to me, incredulity was in his eyes. I couldn't hear what he said, and I folded my arms. I meant what I said, no matter his unheard response.

He held the corner of the helmet to his lips, and his voice came through my helmet. "You don't get to give orders."

I pulled off my helmet. I could only imagine what it did to my hair, but I was past giving a shit. I put the helmet on the seat and slid off the bike.

"Monica."

"Jonathan."

The light changed. Horns shrieked. Curses cut the night. Jonathan and

I stared at each other as our lane slowly sifted around us.

"What's the problem?" he asked, paying the flipped birds around us no mind.

"I want to talk, and I want to do it somewhere you can't fuck me."

"You think dragging me into a coffee shop is going to stop me from fucking you? Shit, if I want you in the middle of this intersection, I'll take you."

He would, too. But also, he wouldn't.

I stepped away from the bike. A dented Acura came to a screeching halt inches from me.

"Fuck!" Jonathan shouted, swinging his leg over the seat as if he was about to cradle my broken body in his arms.

The Acura's driver cried obscenities. Something about me being a stupid fucking bitch. Blah blah. I'd been called worse on a random Tuesday night at the bar. I flipped him off without even looking, walking backward, drawing Jonathan out of the street.

But what I considered a meaningless gesture, the driver considered a call to arms. He leaned so far out of the car I had no idea how his foot stayed on the brake. "Get your big flapping twat outta the street, you bitch whore!"

Jonathan put the kickstand down on the bike, which I didn't understand. Why on earth would he park it in the middle of the street? The light had turned red again, but obviously that was temporary. The guy in the Acura flung some more curses my way. Apparently, he didn't see the guy with the stone-cold expression heading for him. If he did, he might have stopped calling me a fucking skank and started getting into a defensive posture.

Shit.

I darted in front of Jonathan, but he was moving so fast, I had almost no time to get between them. My ass pressed against the door of the car, and Jonathan was nearly there. I held up my hand. "Stop."

"Get out of the way."

"Hey, bitchface!" said the guy behind me.

"Get the bike, please," I said to Jonathan.

"Get out of the way."

"Are you a fucking adolescent? You're going to get into a fight on Sunset Boulevard? What the fuck? Please, bend me over in the intersection instead."

"You people are fucking crazy!" said the driver the second before the light changed. Despite the fact that I was practically leaning on his car, he took off.

More honking as Jonathan and I stared each other down in the middle of the street. More cursing as his bike sat in the middle of the center lane. We had to yell to be heard over the noise.

"Why can't I meet with Jessica?" I demanded. "Why is it so important to you?"

"You're asking me *here?*"

"If you can fuck me in the intersection, I can ask questions." He grabbed my arm. I shook it off.

"You don't know her! This is a game, and you don't know the rules. If she gave you her number, it's because whatever she's trying to do to me, she's going to use you for."

"So you're protecting yourself," I said.

"And you."

"I don't need protecting," I yelled. A delivery truck missed me by inches as it tried to make the light. The wind shear thrust me forward a few inches.

"Goddess," he said, pulling me to him for safety, "you are a shitload of trouble."

"You sorry you wanted a commitment?" Cars whipped around us at the green, horns screaming again.

"No. You've turned my existence into a life."

An SUV swerved, but we held our gaze. "I'm about to turn it into your death."

As if daring L.A. drivers to hit a couple in the middle of the street on a Saturday night, he leaned over and kissed me. I kissed him back. It's not every day you get to flip off a whole city.

Chapter 13

Monica

I didn't tell Jonathan my phone had started buzzing while we were in the street. As I dismounted in my driveway, I glanced at it.

Jessica.

As if sensing something was amiss, Jonathan took hold of my wrist. He saw the screen display his ex-wife's phone number in brilliant backlit blue and white. His eyes flicked up to mine, the phone lighting his face from beneath, as the phone purred in my hand like a kitten. His lips tightened.

"What?" I asked.

"You know what."

"I'm not convinced I'm a tool for your destruction. I might be a tool for your salvation. Have you thought of that?"

"What if she told you I fucked her?"

"Did you?"

"No."

"Then what's the problem?"

"You'll believe her. And even if you don't, a part of you will always wonder. She'll alienate us from each other," he said.

"I'm insulted by the notion that I'm going to be used to hurt you. I'm not so weak-willed. Not with her or you. I'm going to see her. I'm going to let her think she's using me, and I'm going to find out what she wants. I'm going to let her think I'm on her side."

He gritted his teeth. "This is not a woman you take on a fishing expedition."

"You may not love her any more, but you respect her. Which is more than I can say for how you feel about me." I walked toward my house. I felt him reach for me, but I was too fast. I jangled my keys and approached my door.

Jonathan came up behind me, pressing his front to my back. "I'm sorry." He nuzzled my ear.

"No, you're not." I turned the key.

"I am."

"Good. I'll let you know how it goes."

He reached around and pushed the door open. "My apology doesn't mean I'm letting you go."

"I'm going."

He pushed me in and slammed the door behind him. He reached for my clothes, attacking my mouth with his, lips churning, tongue probing, hands yanking. My hands explored him as well, taking the edges of his clothing and unbuttoning, unzipping, unfolding, exposing whatever piece of skin I could find. He pushed me back into the bedroom, kissing me as he went, stripping my shirt. He thrust me against the doorframe and lifted my bra, exposing my hard nipples. His tongue found them, then his teeth. I held the back of his head as his hand found my other breast and twisted the nipple he wasn't sucking. My fingers ran through his hair, and my legs wrapped around him. I felt his erection, hard and hot, pressing into me as he shifted and dropped me through the doorway. We fell onto my bed.

He pulled his shirt over his head, exposing his tight, lean frame. I reached for his chest, but he held my hands down and kissed my neck then my breasts, biting where curve met plane.

"Oh! Yes."

"Hurt?"

"Yes," I said, my voice husky with lust. "Again."

He did, biting and sucking the skin of my neck and breasts. I thought I'd explode. The pain was alive, coursing through my body, a sensation like pleasure but hard, cruel, heated. He opened my legs while sucking the skin of my shoulder. My pussy was ready for him. He put his head between my legs, kissing me from knee to the curve where thigh met pelvis.

"Ah, yes," I cried.

He slapped inside my thigh, and the sting went right to my pussy. When he leaned in and bit where he'd slapped, gently, then harder, I uttered affirmations. I didn't want him to stop. I wanted to feel it. All of it. His tongue slid over my clit while he bent my legs to my chest, his teeth on my wet cleft. His fingers scratched my skin and landed in my hole, thrusting inside. It felt, raw, passionate, all-consuming.

He sucked my clit, and the pain made bookends for the pleasure, heightening it. Reaching with his other hand, he put three fingers in my mouth, and I felt bound and helpless, like a hooked fish. The pain was my only companion as the flood of pleasure came. I screamed into his fingers, arching my back and ass off the mattress.

He kept me immobile with his teeth, fingers, and tongue, licking and sucking until even the pleasure was pain, and tears streamed down my face. He picked up his face, kissing inside my thighs, my belly, licking the diamond navel ring that came to signify his ownership of me. I breathed heavily, eyes half-closed in post-orgasmic rapture.

"I'm going to be sore all over tomorrow."

He kissed my cheek, pulling one knee back up to my chest, gently pushing my calf until it rested over his shoulder. "You have no idea how sore you're going to be."

I was so wet from his mouth and my own arousal that he slid all the way into me in one stroke.

"Do it." I gasped. "Make me sore. Make it hurt again."

"I can make it hurt. You know your safe word?" He fucked me slowly, knees under him, my leg over his shoulder.

"Small, orange fruit." I felt another orgasm scratching and mewling at the door. It wanted in, but Jonathan had to turn the handle.

"I need you to promise me something," he said.

"Anything."

"You'll let me take care of my business." He fucked me harder, leveraging himself by gripping my bicep.

"Yes."

"You won't interfere." He went deep into a thudding pain inside.

"Yes, sir."

"Say it."

"Sir. I won't interfere. Just do it. Please." He slapped my breast, then grabbed it painfully before he slapped it again. "Yes!" I cried.

He continued, hurting me just enough to heighten sensitivity, hitting me with exuberance as I cried *yes, yes* so he wouldn't stop. He hit my breasts, my ass, my inner thighs without humiliation or punishment. Only joy. He did it because I liked it, and he liked it. Together, we were red-faced, near laughing, sometimes screaming, twisting, begging, fucking deep and hard, shamelessly gratifying each other's most secret needs.

And when the thunderclouds gathered, coalescing into a solid wall of sensation, blocking out the sun and sky, I had his name on my lips. Pain and pleasure became indistinguishable, and I shut down into a clenching ball of *now*. His face was close to mine. I was twisted in a knot from the pressure he put on my knees and elbows and exposed sensitivities. I caught the last of his orgasm as my sky cleared and I could see the firmament again. He dropped his head in the crook of my neck and bit. The pain brought me back to myself, like a wakeup call from a dead sleep.

When his mouth slackened and his groans stopped, I said, "Ouch."

"Sorry."

I turned my head toward him and laughed at the absurdity of it. He caught on and laughed with me, holding my head close as we kissed, smiling. I untwisted myself and lay flat, joints and muscles loosened. I knew I'd suffer tomorrow from our fucking, as well as the promise I had no intention of keeping.

Chapter 14

Jonathan

I ordered breakfast from the diner around the corner, and when the delivery guy rang the doorbell, I was on the patio setting out plates. I heard the bathroom door shut. She was awake.

What Monica didn't know, and what helped me sleep, was that her house had been swept twice for cameras while she'd spent weeks crashing on her friend's couch. The place was clean, so I felt fine about giving her the roughest fuck I'd given anyone in my life. Even with Sharon, who'd suffered getting shit beaten out of her to the point of an emotional breakdown, I'd been more careful. She was breakable. Others had done a good job of proving that.

Monica, on the other hand, was made of tough stuff. That toughness was showing in her insistence on seeing my ex-wife. I had a gut feeling that by seeing Jessica on her terms and her turf, Monica would be walking into more than she could handle. She thought they would have a conversation, but it would be a game. The end result would be us separated by my ex-wife's casual half-truths and outright lies.

The idea that I could keep tabs on Monica until the whole thing went away looked more and more impossible. I couldn't suddenly restrict her. She was used to being her own woman. She had to work, and she had to play music. I couldn't put a team of people on her when she'd just gotten over the cameras in the house. I had to make her not *want* to see Jessica, and the only way to do that was to make the trouble she was causing seem unimportant. It was a good strategy, and I was failing at it.

She came out as I finished putting out her tea. She wore a long-sleeved, black turtleneck and skinny jeans. She walked stiffly, but her smile was loose and relaxed.

"Good morning," I said.

"The king sets the table."

"He's hungry." I put my hands at her neck and kissed her. Her lips tightened. I pulled back and saw what had made her flinch—a tiny smear of reddish-grey where my fingertip had touched her jaw. Stroking her collar away, I saw that her neck was covered in bite marks and bruises. "Jesus Christ."

She refolded the collar until her neck was covered. "I didn't know whether to show you or not."

"Up." I tugged at the hem of her sweater. She bit her lip. "Come on."

"The last time I looked like this, you felt too bad about it to fuck me."

I pulled up the shirt. She lifted her arms, her face contorted in pain. I pulled the sweater off completely, and she tucked her head so the collar would expand around her. She stood before me, naked from the waist up, looking as though she'd been beaten in a back alley. The curves under her breasts were deep red where blood vessels had broken under my teeth, and the mounds themselves were bruised. The bend of her neck had the same beaten mottle. Her biceps were blackened in fingertip shapes. I touched them lightly, drawing my fingers down to the striated ligature marks on her elbows.

"Your knees?"

"Yeah," she said. "Matching marks on those. You tied me really tight."

"You said it felt okay."

"It did."

"Your thighs? Your ass?"

"I'm fine." She put her hand on my face, but I didn't want to be comforted. I unbuttoned her pants.

"Come on," I said. "Let me see."

She slid her pants down, pain on her face. She'd have to put them back on and that would hurt, but it was too late to undo the order. I kneeled, sliding the jeans over her legs. Her thighs were a mess, and her knees did indeed have matching marks from when I'd tied the joints together with an extension cord.

"Don't be sorry," she said, stroking my hair as I kissed her bruised legs.

"I am."

"I said not to be."

"I don't take orders."

"You should try it. It's amazing."

From my kneeling position, I eased her into a chair and spread her legs, kissing the devastation inside them. I didn't have a mother's healing kiss on a scratched knee, but I had no other way to show her the pain in my heart at seeing her hurt and knowing that I'd done it and I'd do it again and again.

"You only came six times last night," I said. "I promised seven."

"I couldn't take another."

I probed her folds with my tongue. "Take it now."

"I need my tea," she groaned, running her fingers through my hair. I didn't touch her with anything but my mouth. My hands had done enough damage. Though pain had been welcome a few hours earlier, the aftermath would be straight pain, without the accompaniment of pleasure. I wove my arms around her until her hands found mine, and I clasped them as my mouth worked in service to her. Gently. Without urgency. Her sweet, sore cunt tasted coppery, like raw flesh but got wet and responsive, her clit filling into a hard, slick pebble under me.

She groaned as I worked her with my tongue and lips, teeth tucked safely away. I looked up at the broken skin of her chest, making eye contact as her lips whispered my name, and I prayed to whatever deity would listen to please, please not take her away. She arched, clenched, gasped like the beautiful kitten she was. When I leaned up to her, fresh cunt on my lips, my phone dinged.

"You gonna get that?" she asked.

"When I'm done kissing you." I put my hands on the arms of her chair and slowly put my lips on hers. I wanted an unrushed moment of forgiveness and gentleness.

"Can you make love to me?" she asked.

"No."

"Why not?" She drew her legs around me. I knew it hurt.

"I'm flattered, but I'm simply not attracted to you."

She had her hand on my erection before I could back away. "Really?" She smiled, kissing me, stroking me.

"That? That's nothing. Something I left in my pocket." She could stroke my dick all day, but there was no way I was taking her in the condition she was in.

"Please? I'll beg."

"Tempting offer. But I'm hungry." I pulled away. As I went to sit down for breakfast, my phone dinged again, then rang.

"You'd better check it," Monica said, pulling her sweater back over her head. "Could be a towering inferno at Hotel K and you didn't know about it because you were eating eggs."

I checked. Margie. And it was Sunday. I looked at Monica then pocketed the phone.

"Jonathan, I see your face. Take the call, would you?" She stepped into her jeans gingerly, eyes like chocolate coins, looking at me as if I was being serious over nothing.

"Save me some," I said as I started to step away from the table.

"You got enough for an infield and everyone in the dugout."

I slipped my phone out of my pocket and walked down the stairs to the driveway. With one look back at my goddess buttoning her pants, I answered the phone. "Margie. Working on the Lord's day?"

"Your problems never rest, Jonny. Your beautiful and talented ex-wife wants a meeting."

"Today?" I climbed up to Monica's front porch, noticing the cracked, slipping foundation still hadn't gotten fixed.

"Tuesday. And in other bad news, are you sitting?"

"Out with it." I sat on the porch swing. It creaked.

Margie took a deep sigh of a breath, which she never did, because she was utterly unflappable.

"Come on. Speak. I'm sitting."

"It's Rachel."

My brain stopped functioning.

"Jonny?"

"Can you be more specific?"

"Why did you move her a month ago?"

I heard Monica getting plates and silverware together. If I could hear her, she could hear me unless I was careful. Even if I remained cryptic, Monica had enough intellectual curiosity to connect the dots into the shape of a web of lies.

"I moved her to protect someone."

"Monica? Or yourself?"

"Yes. I'm a selfish prick. I have someone I don't want to lose, and I needed to protect that. If I left her where she was, Jessica could have shown Monica where she was. I needed to maintain a little plausible deniability."

I had panicked very badly when Debbie called six weeks ago and said Jessica had shown up at the Stock and said something so upsetting to Monica that she was visibly shaken. I'd been convinced Jessica insinuated things about Rachel. Because everyone in the world who had cared about her, and there were painfully few, thought she was dead.

She wasn't. Not quite.

Jessica knew everything. At our engagement party, I'd been hypnotized as a party joke and remembered what the whiskey had blacked out. Rachel had survived the crash. She didn't walk away. But on the night of the Christmas rains, she'd been pulled out of the ocean with a part of her brain intact. Jessica had helped me find Rachel and helped me move her. She'd helped me fail in finding her family. Mother dead. Father disappeared. Her stepfather had never been worthy of her. Jessica, by my side, had reminded me to man up and take responsibility for my part in her condition.

"Okay, I know you did your best," Margie said, her tone promising bad news. "But people in vegetative states don't travel well. I just got word from the new facility that she has pneumonia."

"She's had it before."

"She's dying, little brother. I'm sorry."

Chapter 15

Monica

Jonathan left me with a lot of breakfast.

He'd come back without any color in his face, looking as if he was miles away. With no chance in hell of talking him into a good-bye screw, I walked him out.

"I'm going to be gone for a few days," he said. "I'm sorry."

"We talked about this. You travel. It's fine."

He stood half on the porch, half on the steps when he turned back to me. "You promised you wouldn't see my ex-wife."

That was a hard comment to answer. If I told him I had every intention of seeing Jessica, he'd worry needlessly. If I said otherwise, I'd be lying. "Jonathan, honestly, promises made while I'm in a submissive posture shouldn't count."

He paused, looking at our clasped hands. "Probably not."

Even though it hurt to lift my arms, I put my palms on his cheeks. He did not look well. His skin was cold. There really must have been a towering inferno at Hotel K.

"I have a meeting with her on Tuesday," he said. "Can you wait until after that?"

"I don't see why not."

My sneaky non-promise must have been completely transparent to him. There was a pretty good chance the only time I'd get to see her was when he was out of town and unable to use his dick to lure me away. He knew it. I knew it. Pretending otherwise was absurd. Yet we did. Somehow, he was willing to take the chance and walk down the steps to his bike after a deep, soulful goodbye kiss that let me know he was still my master and king.

I cleaned up breakfast and dressed to rehearse. I had a lot to say about pain and its relationship to desire, glory, satisfaction. Maybe I had too much to say, because I wrote a seven-page ramble of a song with three alternating choruses and verses up the wazoo. I still felt as though I hadn't scratched the surface.

My body ached. I was tired. I felt isolated. Jonathan's touch stayed on me in the soreness between my legs, the rawness of my lips, the sharp bite of pain when I moved my arms. I pulled my collar up over my face to see if his smell lingered. It did, if only slightly, and I kept the collar up even though it increased the heat of my longing with every breath.

A couple of days. How could I last that long? How would I think about anything else? And what would happen on the next two-week trip? Did he think I would agree to come with him every time?

When I realized I'd been staring at the piano keys for twelve minutes, I shut off the metronome and crawled into bed. Our scents lingered on the sheets like the twin deities, pain and pleasure, lulling me to sleep with thoughts of their harmonized perfection.

Chapter 16

Monica

I woke when the sky was melting from light to dark, and the nest of crickets outside my window started screaming their mating call. Every living thing was trying to fuck, except me. My aches took on a new level of sharpness after a decent rest, and the smell of sex exhausted me. I stripped the bed.

I'd brought piles of clothes back from Darren's. I hadn't done laundry in his building unless it was absolutely necessary, but I was home now. The sheets needed doing, and the towels, and my clothes, obviously. The Bordelle underthings I hand-washed lovingly, caressing them the way he did.

I passed Gabby's closed door a dozen times. That part of the house was as much mine as it ever was, but I still couldn't go in without Darren. I still braided my hair for her. I still kept what little music she'd written to integrate into my mine, to save her name and her legacy.

The battery on my phone had died, so I plugged it in and went about cleaning my bathrooms, mopping the kitchen floor, doing all the things I'd neglected while I was away. In my mind, the metronome ticked in four-four time. A song was bubbling up, and my verbal mind waited patiently while my non-verbal brain processed the point and purpose of it.

I was on the porch shaking the dust out of the couch throws when the phone blooped. It must be Jonathan saying something that would make me smile. I ran to it.

—*are you there?*—

—*Yes*—

—*I feel your hands on the phone*—

—*I miss you already. Can we have a call*—

—*Can't. Just checking in. I feel good*

knowing you're there, and mine—

The subtext was he felt good knowing I was there and doing what he told me. Which meant, no Jessica. He either thought very little of me believing I was obedient, or a lot believing I'd get the right message from so few words. Or maybe I should just take it at face value.

Bored, I checked my email from the phone. I hadn't set up digital roaming while out of the country, and then the phone died, and the fact was, email wasn't my thing. Most of my social interactions were local and done with a phone call or text.

But that couldn't be said for everyone. I'd given Harry Enrich my information after the B.C. Mod show, and shockingly, he'd used it, sending me a personal note early Friday.

> *Ms. Faulkner,*
>
> *It was a pleasure to hear your work tonight. I understand Eddie Milpas has been working to sign you on with us. Why don't you come by our offices Tuesday to discuss further?*
>
> *Best,*
>
> *Harry*
>
> *PS – Do you have representation?*

Eddie had been working to sign me? Sounded like he was trying to put a collar on my neck and shackle me to a display case, but who was I to question?

My phone rang while it was still in my hand. I didn't usually answer numbers I didn't recognize, but the green button was a reflex, and I put the phone to my ear. "Hello?"

"Hello." The voice was female and tight as a drum. Pleasant, but not effusive. Welcoming, but not warm. "This is Jessica Carnes. Am I speaking with Monica?"

"Yes." I sat on the piano bench, willing myself not to shake. All of Jonathan's warnings and the events of my two prior meetings with Jessica blew out my nerves. I had to remind myself to channel him, his utter dedication to self-management no matter his feelings.

"How are you?" she asked.

I had no answer prepared. No story to tell to get what I wanted. "I'm fine. You?"

"Very well, thank you," she said. I didn't think I had another nicety left in me, and she saved me from having to come up with another. "You left me a message?"

Oh, she was going to make me ask. She wasn't giving me an inch or admitting she had made first contact at Frontage. She wasn't going to admit she'd shown up at my job at whatever o'clock in the morning. "I thought I'd take you up on that offer to meet."

"Things have gotten a little more complicated since we spoke last."

"Yes... I... I guess you're right. I thought you came to see me last night. Never mind."

After saying that, I felt a sense of relief. I was avoiding immediate repercussions from seeing Jessica, and it wasn't even my fault. Coward. Yes, that was the craven woman. I wasn't her any more. But I couldn't push Jessica. If she wanted to wiggle out she would, no matter what.

"If you feel differently at some point, I would like to meet. We can do it under your terms and talk about whatever you like," I said.

"Why the change of heart?"

"Things got more complicated, like you said. I feel like I can't see the whole picture." That was probably too specific and would leave me little room to flip my story around if I needed, but that was it. I said it, and it was very close to the truth.

"Can you get to Venice in the morning?"

"Yes." A lump rose in my throat. I was doing it. I was going directly against Jonathan's wishes. I had to remind myself that I wasn't trying to hurt him. I was trying to help him.

"I'll text you the address."

"Okay. Thanks." I had nothing else to say, so I hung up.

I'd started an evil thing and had to go through with it because I wouldn't stand by and watch him get run over. Maybe I was going out on a limb, and maybe I'd make it worse, but how could I sit still while someone was trying to hurt him?

"Fuck," I whispered. My car was at the Stock.

Chapter 17

Monica

A black Corvette pulled up in front of the house, taking the downhill nice and slow. Robert cared about his ride the way most people cared about living things. I skipped down the porch and met him at the curb.

"Thanks," I said, getting in. I was more or less on the way from the valley, but it was still an inconvenience for him.

"Fucking hill, man." He put the car in gear and inched downward.

"When I was a kid, I rode my bike down it, no hands."

"Bet you did." He paused briefly. "So, car's at work, huh?"

"Yeah."

"You went home with the guy from Hotel K? Sam and Debbie's friend?"

"You got a problem with it?"

"Naw, man. Just curious what his deal is."

I didn't know what he meant, and I didn't want to know what he meant, either. I just wanted to get my car. I didn't want to hear about anything Robert might have seen or heard. Nothing. Not a word.

We sat in silence down Temple, to Hill, around the block a few times or ten until we stopped at a light a block from the hotel. It was the same light Jonathan had stopped at when he met me after work and told me he'd always love his ex-wife.

"What did you *think* his deal was?" I asked.

Robert snapped out of some sort of reverie. "Huh? Who?"

"Jonathan, the guy from Hotel K?"

"Shit, I don't know. He was there that time you couldn't talk, then gone, then... coupla weeks, he was in the corner yacking with Debbie and Sam all the time. But not when you were there. Shows up last night, you're there. I dunno. Just asking."

"Asking what?"

"Is it serious or what?"

"Yes. It's serious," I said.

"All right. Thanks for letting a guy know."

The light changed, and I laughed to myself.

"What?" He turned into the lot.

"I thought you were going to tell me that you saw him with other women."

He looked at me and smiled, turning into the employee level. "Guys don't rat on other guys."

"Robert! Don't even—"

"But there was nothing to rat. Seriously. Stop with the girl style. It don't suit you." He pulled in next to my little black Honda.

"Fine. I wouldn't have believed you anyway." I blooped my car and got out.

Robert cut the engine and pulled his small black duffel from the back. "You think I'd lie?" He slung the duffel over his muscular shoulder. "I'm not saying I woulda minded getting with you for a night, but I wouldn't lie to do it."

"I don't think you'd lie," I said, getting in my car. "I think you could misunderstand."

"That's where you're wrong."

"Oh really?"

"Yeah. If I saw him with someone, and it was something, I'd know."

I looked him up and down. "You know what? I believe you." I turned the ignition. Nothing happened. Just one click. "Uh oh. Do you have time to give me a jump?"

"Turn it again."

I did. One click, then nothing.

"It's your starter." He walked to the front of the car and knocked on the hood. "Pop it."

I did. He lifted the hood and chocked it up with the metal brace.

"Should I turn it again?"

"Yeah."

I did. Same. I got out and stood next to Robert as he shone his phone's light at the engine, analyzing the mass of wires, compartments, and hoses. I knew what most of it was but not how to fix it.

"All right. If you got a bad starter, I can bang it while you kick it over. Sometimes that kinda gets it going. But you need a new one, probably."

"Shit."

"Yeah, except… It should be right there. Just back of the battery and down, past these wires that serve the electricity. But there's bolt holes. No starter."

"What do you mean?"

He looked more closely then got under the car. I leaned down, amazed at how he would just crawl under a chassis out of curiosity.

"Do you want a proper flashlight?" I asked. "I think I have one in the trunk."

"Nope. I'm telling you. There's no fucking starter on this car. It got jacked."

"My *starter*? Are they expensive?"

"Three hundred. Two? Look, I know it's weird but…" He shrugged.

"Oh my God," I said, realizing who would do the surgery required to remove a starter from a twelve-year-old Japanese car. "Fucking Jonathan. Son of a goddamn bitch."

He'd stranded me. I couldn't get out to Venice without a car. A cab would cost a fortune, and if a bus that far out of town even existed, it would take hours one way. I couldn't get the car fixed in time for a meeting in Culver City in the morning. That was why he'd left so easily. He walked away accepting that I had no intention of keeping any promise I made while my legs were spread. I should have known better.

"I gotta get to work," said Robert. "You wanna call a tow?"

"Nope. I'll figure it out."

"How you getting home?"

"I'm not. I'm going to go upstairs and get a whiskey. Then I'm going out. If I can't drive, I can drink."

"Debbie's gonna make you pay for it."

"Fine. I'm not too broke for a little alcohol." I took out my phone when we got to the back hall and scrolled to Jessica's last text. I didn't want to talk to her. The ice in her voice put me on edge. I had no idea how I would handle our conversation tomorrow.

"You can get some guy at the bar to buy you a few," Robert said, stopping by the lockers.

"No way."

—Sorry. Can't make it out to Venice
tomorrow. Maybe somewhere more east?—

"Why not? It's just a drink."

"It's cheating."

"Girls are crazy. I'm tellin' you, if I were a girl and I had a nice pair, I'd never pay for a drink."

—My studio in Culver City, then?—

I loved how she managed to keep it on her turf. If I asked her for an Echo Park location, she'd probably manage to find a place she rented, owned, or regularly patronized.

"If you were a girl with a nice pair," I said, "you'd be the one all the guys wanted to fuck but hated. You'd have a string of one-night or one-week stands until the guy saw you letting someone else buy you drinks. Then you'd only attract the guys looking to spend a little money and put their dicks somewhere comfortable. You'd wake up one morning at fifty years old with a pair that wasn't so nice any more, and you'd wish you'd bought your own."

—Great. Thanks for the change.
                                    See you at ten?—

Robert and I walked up together. "You don't know nothing about men. Sure, we might get a drink for a girl like you to get laid. But being seen with you? That's what gets *other* girls. See what I'm sayin'?"

"No. I'm still buying my own drinks."

"Whatever."

I sat in the corner in the same spot Jonathan had been known to occupy and tried to arrange a car for the next morning. Darren had work the next day, but once he found out what I was doing, he refused to let me drop him off in the morning and borrow his car, texting me like he was my fucking therapist:

—You have a way of sabotaging your
    own happiness. I'm opting out—

A guy with glittering dark brown eyes, messy black hair, and a mouth like a movie star leaned on the bar next to me. "What are you drinking?"

"Piss and vinegar." I was busy answering Darren's accusation in a flurry.

"That a new thing?" he asked. "What's in it?"

I pulled my eyes away from my phone for a second. "Piss. Also, vinegar."

He laughed. Ignoring my bludgeon of a hint, he leaned toward me. "Let me get you your next one. I'll piss in it myself."

I slugged the dregs of my whiskey, letting the ice cube linger on my lips. I parted them to touch my tongue to it, reminding me of Jonathan, the master of melting ice. I slid the glass to Mister Eyes and said, "Piss your little heart out."

He looked at the empty glass then back at me. I turned to my phone. I should have known better than to be a total bitch, because in L.A. you never knew who you were speaking to, but I missed Jonathan. I was angry at him and I was trying to avoid lashing out.

—Nice try with the car. I'm not Kevin.
You can't orchestrate my demise—

—Lil can take you anywhere you want to go—

"Someone break your heart today?" Mister Eyes asked.

"No, but really," I said, "it's not personal. I'm sure you're awesome. But there are a hundred girls in here right now who are available. Okay?"

—Except where I want—

—Please wait until I get back. We can talk—

—I am officially done talking—

I slipped my phone into my pocket. When I looked up, Debbie was watching me. That alone was not abnormal, but I felt as if they were Jonathan's eyes watching me talk to a handsome man, and I was suddenly uncomfortable.

I texted around and got some responses. A party in Koreatown. A show in Silver Lake. Nothing appealed. Fuck going out. I walked out to catch one of the cabs that usually waited outside the hotel. If I was seeing Jessica, I'd need a good night's sleep.

Chapter 18

Jonathan

The machines beeped and sighed, blinking like the dashboard on a 747. The room smelled of rubbing alcohol and dying flesh, and in the darkness laid a once beautiful, intelligent woman who had been reduced, by me, to a pile of idly reproducing cells. I'd been driving that night. Drunk. Stoned. Stupid. Then I passively let my family cover it up while I sat in a padded room feeling sorry for myself.

Sixteen years, a dark room, and maybe she would finally get what she'd always wanted. She'd wanted to be free of her family, and by the time Jessica and I had found her, they were dead or missing. She'd wanted to be free of hunger and pain, and she'd gotten just that. But I didn't think this was what she'd had in mind.

I'd gone from her lover to her guardian because no one else cared. She'd been forgotten, and I was the carrier of her memory. The man who broke her became her keeper. When she'd "died," everyone felt sorry for me. Even though I had no memory of what happened, I knew something was wrong. I knew there was a debt to be paid. When Jessica and I found out she was alive and we'd sent a team of smart men and woman to find her, I'd hoped she'd be in some suburban house with two kids and a dog. But the trail had led us to an expensive, secret facility for people who couldn't move. Fuck, how I'd cried and thanked God and the saints for Jessica's shoulder.

A million years before, we'd lain on our backs on the grass of Elysian Park, where my family would never find us. Rachel liked to wonder what it was like to be me. She thought I had not a worry in the world. Yes, my father was a fucking sociopath, but he didn't stick his fingers inside me like hers had, and he didn't scream and hit me and lock me in the house like her stepfather had. Whatever I endured would end when my trust fund spread its legs at twenty-one. For her, the light at the end of the tunnel had not appeared.

"Do you wish for things you can't buy?" she'd asked.

I'd looked over at her. Blades of grass sat in the foreground of my vision, slashing her face, which was turned to me. Her eyes were tobacco brown, wide and light with sun inside them. "You're fascinated with money," I said.

"I think I am." She'd smiled. "It's made you different, you know. You're fearless. It's exciting, kind of. Watching you is like watching someone who's really, truly free."

I'd laughed. I never felt free in my life. "What do you wish for? Besides money."

"You make me sound like a gold digger."

"You are, but you're terrible at it. I think a few more years and you'll be sleeping with the right guy."

She'd flung herself on top of me and pinched my sides. I laughed and rolled her over until I had her pinned.

"Tell me what you wish for, and if it's any part of my body, your wish will come true at the Regency Hotel in forty minutes."

She'd giggled and turned her face to the sunlight. "Free, Jonathan. I wish to be free."

I'd unpinned one of her shoulders to pluck a seeded dandelion out of the grass. "Blow." I held the white puffball in front of her.

She'd blown hard, and the seeds went into my face. We laughed, and blew the rest of the seeds off together, wishing her free from the constraints of her family and her scarcity. They floated away on their sinuous parachutes, like little messengers to God, saying *take me, take me, take me. Set me free.*

Chapter 19

The bus. West on Sunset. South on La Cienega. Hour and a half. A cab ride from my house to Jessica's studio was fifty bucks one way. I wished I could have taken the hundred for a round-trip cab out of Jonathan's ass, but that would have to wait for another day.

I wore three-quarter sleeves and long pants. I wrapped a scarf with a spider web pattern around my neck to cover the bruises. I felt lucky it was getting cold, but I had no idea how I'd hide the roughness of my private life in the summer.

The walk was a quarter mile, but it was cool, and I'd worn comfortable shoes. Jonathan hadn't texted me back the night before, nor had I received a nine a.m. ding. Was he angry? Was he shutting me out because I hadn't fallen for the busted starter trick? Or was the emergency that pulled him away so dire he couldn't answer me? Both concerned me. I had a gnawing anxiety that grew worse with every step toward Jessica's studio.

Up ahead, a big white truck was parked and running outside a light industrial building. The building was painted west-side tasteful—charcoal, with white trim and a chartreuse door—and guys in bunny suits trotted in and out with six-inch diameter hoses. I checked the address, and I was sure I had the right one.

A guy in a polo shirt put orange cones on the sidewalk, stopping me. "Street's closed."

"Is that twelve thirty-eight?"

"Sure is."

"I have an appointment here."

"Not today, you don't. Got a lead and asbestos removal team coming in. It's a hazard, so you're going to have to go around the block if you want to pass."

I pulled out my phone. No message. Crossing the street, I craned my neck around the truck and saw Jessica in the side alley, arguing with a guy holding a clipboard. Her smooth veneer was slipping, just a little. It seemed to be as much of a surprise to her as it was to me.

Of course.

Jonathan.

Well. Didn't that just suck ass.

I started calling him and thought better of it. I texted him and deleted the whole thing. I'd already thrown out one unfounded accusation and gotten no reply. A string of them would do no more than make me look psychotic.

I walked to Washington Boulevard, where I'd at least be able to find a café where I could sit down and blow my cab money. I found a purple building housing a tea shop called Yellow Threat. I got something hot and herbal and sat down on the outdoor patio.

She texted me soon after.

—So sorry. I'll be held up 30 min—

I felt like her co-conspirator at that point. Jessica and me against Jonathan. I was determined to understand the situation so I could help him. His ex-wife, perfectly content with his broken heart until she saw him with me, was hell-bent on destroying him for money and spite. She wanted to meet so she could use me, and Jonathan wanted to prevent that so I didn't hurt myself or him. Both of them underestimated me.

They forgot I was a musician, that I'd gone to a performing arts school and been the victim of manipulation and backstabbing. I'd already opened my case and found my strings cut and my staff notes swapped. I'd already been given the wrong time for auditions. I couldn't come out of that world without learning a thing or two.

*—I'll be at Yellow Threat for an
hour if you want to come by—*

Jessica and I, working against Jonathan to see each other. Ridiculous, yet somehow inevitable.

I checked my watch. I'd definitely lost a writing day. I wasn't happy about it, but there was nothing I could do but warm my hands on my tea. The sidewalk made the block walkable, but it was empty. The light industrial street had been taken over by architects and production companies at the turn of the twenty-first century, and they'd painted everything in bright colors and edgy murals. I noticed one of Geraldine's half a block away. She'd painted the side of the building to look as if I could see through it to the highway, as if she wanted to negate whatever happened inside.

I saw him walking across the crosswalk in a dark suit with a blue shirt open at the collar. His black hair caught the wind, and his eyes scanned every plane and surface.

"Mr. Santon," I said when he reached me, "what a coincidence."

"You believe in those?" He sat down.

"No. I'm assuming my lover sent you to talk me out of seeing his ex-wife?"

"Close. But no. I can't tell you what he hired me to do, except I'm not supposed to be sitting at a table with you."

"You must have put your own cameras in the house. If you know where I've been, I don't know how. I haven't seen you."

"That was off the table, obviously. We're not watching you. We're watching the other one. And you'll never see us, Ms. Faulkner. Any trace of us is gone before we even are."

"Big scary ops guys. My dad always said he could take any of you in a brawl."

"The idea is to avoid the brawl in the first place. Knowing what I know, which is too much, everyone involved wants to avoid a clusterfuck. Except you and Ms. Carnes. So I am going to sit here and enjoy a cup of tea, until night if necessary. If anyone joins you, I'll be right here. Then I am going to drive you home."

I leaned forward, elbows on the table. "How do I shake an ops guy?"

"Guys. Plural." He glanced at a guy on a cell phone halfway down the block. He gestured and spoke loudly to make himself just another piece of furniture. Someone standing quietly with a phone to his ear would attract notice. Then Santon glanced at a black Toyota at the light and waved to the driver with a flick of his wrist. The driver flicked back and drove off when the light changed.

Great. Even if I ran away and jumped in a cab, I'd have to shake the other two. "He needs to trust my loyalty."

"That's between you and him." He twisted around, hailing a waitress. "Personally, I don't give a shit."

The waitress came, and he ordered himself a cup of coffee and a muffin. She flirted with him, a nervous grin crossing her face. He was a nice-looking guy. I'd forgotten to notice.

"What's with the pinkie ring?" I asked when the waitress left.

He held up the simple gold band always present on his pinkie, not an affectation or accessory as I'd assumed. "My wife's."

"She wearing yours?"

"Around her neck, with her dog tags. We swapped when we re-upped. Weren't there four weeks when she took sniper fire half a mile from the Green Zone."

"I'm sorry."

"It was messy. Death always is."

"You understand, I'm just trying to protect him."

"I'm just trying to do my job."

I sipped my tea, and we sat in silence as his coffee was brought. A black Mercedes stopped at the light. A blonde driving. Jessica. The parking lot was around the corner, and her blinker flashed for the turn.

I looked at Santon, and though his eyes appeared to be on the scalding black coffee he was about to swallow in a single gulp, he gazed in the halfway point between the table and the street. Blank sidewalk, but Jessica and I would be in his peripheral vision.

Jessica saw me, and I shook my head. She nodded and turned off her blinker. Will Santon could take me home. Motherfucker.

Chapter 20

I knew Will wasn't gone for good. I had a gig at Frontage that was well-attended, including a table of five guys in agent-gear by the warm speakers. I greeted them, played, and said goodbye with a stinker of a smile, but my heart felt made of lead. Jonathan hadn't called, texted, written. No contact besides Will Santon's unwelcome presence.

Could he be that mad?

Was that *how* he got mad? Falling off the face of the earth? How was I supposed to react?

Irrelevant questions. What I needed to ask myself was how I *wanted* to react. So I called him. It went to voice mail, which I didn't want. There would be no angry, terse, or blustery messages. I texted.

—Are you shutting me out? WTF?—

I had friends who had given men their hearts only to find them turned to ice directly after. Or slept with them after declarations of indefinite amounts of attraction, but the indefinite amounts lasted no more than a week. I wondered if that was what I was dealing with. Had my commitment to him chased him away? Or did he expect my submission to be an abdication of control over my decisions? Was obedience required inside and outside the bedroom? Had I missed that point on the list?

I couldn't have. I never would have allowed it, and neither would he.

I had just gotten home when my phone blooped. I dug around my bag and found it, hoping against hope that it was Jonathan. An outsized level of disappointment flooded me. It was Jessica.

—I'm at Make on Echo Park and Baxter.
I believe you're nearby?—

That presented a problem. It was a block and a half away, but I had to get there. I believed Santon when he said I wasn't being watched, but Jessica was. That meant something or someone would stop us from meeting in that block and a half.

Fuck it.

I looked out the back door. My house was built on a lot that was nearly vertical toward the rear. A retaining wall of cinderblock held the hill at bay, barely. Behind it, untouched chaparral stretched five hundred feet to a walkable dirt alley kids used to get into trouble. The whole stretch was unlandscapable without a bunch of money, which Dr. Thorensen had, apparently. His plot was terraced into vegetable gardens, private spaces, and a little utility area with a shed. My part of the hill, naturally, had fallen to scrub and brush. A hundred-year-old ficus with exposed roots was on the downslope, and wildflowers bloomed in spring. In the first weeks of December, dead thorns twisted around the trees, weeds turned to sticks, and brown was the new black.

I'd have to go through that to get to the path, then get spit out onto Echo Park Avenue. Of course, it wouldn't work. I'd get bitten by a rattlesnake or something. Worse, Santon, who'd probably taken a vow to never sleep again, would be waiting for me on the street.

I dug my old cowboy boots out of the back of the closet, and a pair of jeans I didn't care about. I'd spent the whole day trying to get this done, and I wasn't giving up yet.

My yard needed some love. I hadn't trimmed anything at the end of summer, so the flagstones and garden patches were covered in dead leaves and detritus. I tossed the pink and orange balls back over the fence to the Montessori school and made for Dad's tangerine tree. He'd planted it for me before he and Mom moved away, saying it would feed me if I got hungry. It just kept growing and was high enough to hug the spaghetti of power lines crisscrossing the sky. I used it as leverage to climb the wall onto the overgrown slope.

It was pitch dark back there. The path was no more than a right-of-way between the backs of houses. Echo Park and Silver Lake were full of untended spaces. Staircases built during the Depression, forgotten paths that were never lit or patrolled that were taken over by residents for extra garden space or burial grounds for unwanted cars.

I grabbed saplings and vines to pull myself up the hill. There was garbage everywhere. Just as I was thinking about how I had to get up there in the daytime with a few plastic bags and clean it out, I was pushed into the ficus.

"Where are you going, goddess?" His voice came from behind me.

His breath in my ear, his scent in my nose, the feel of his chest on my back, the way he fit like a puzzle piece... I didn't even want to ask him what the fuck he was doing in the woody part of my backyard.

"You didn't call." I leaned my head back and exposed my throat. He made me forget everything when he unlooped my scarf and put his mouth on my neck, his lips a lightning rod for the electricity to my core.

"I was busy. I'm sorry." His teeth found the place where my neck met my shoulder, and he gifted me a little crush of pain that translated directly to pleasure. I sucked in my breath. He ran his hands down my arms, to my hands.

"Apology rejected. Return to sender."

Knotting his palms to the backs of my hands, he pressed them to the tree trunk.

"Spread your legs," he said in my ear. I wasn't fast enough. He kicked them apart. He was so fucking rough, and the precarious feeling of not knowing what he'd do next sent a gush of moisture between my legs.

How long would Jessica wait? Until tomorrow. Because Jonathan had appeared, and his hands were on my stomach, pushing up my bra. He pressed my bruised places gently while finding the untouched spots and pushing his hands against them until I groaned.

"You want something?" he asked.

"I missed you."

"I missed you, too." His voice softened as if he meant it, and his hands drifted down to my waistband.

"Are you going to fuck me?"

He unbuttoned my jeans and unzipped without answering, pressing his cock against my ass. I ground against him. "God, I want to." He took my right hand from the tree trunk and, still pressing my left to the tree, he slid it down my pants. "But it looks like you're going somewhere?"

"Yes."

"You wet?"

I ran my finger to my hole and felt the sopping, slick mass under it. "Yes."

He removed his hands from mine but curved his body around me, his front to my back, his voice in my ear. "How wet?"

"Fuck-me-now wet."

"Touch your clit. Do it so it feels good."

I rubbed my engorged member with one finger, circling it, pushing myself into him.

"Two fingers," he said, pulling away just a little. "Use two fingers on it, letting the center fall in the crease between them."

I moaned.

"Feel good, goddess?"

"Yes."

"How good?"

"Not as good as you fucking me."

"Good answer. Hook your fingers. Put them in your cunt. Then drag them back out to your clit. Rub with the very tips."

"Oh, Jonathan, please. Please fuck me."

"Don't you like this?" There was something in his voice, some sarcasm. As though this wasn't foreplay, but him making an argument. I stopped and started to pull my hand out of my pants, but he grabbed my bruised elbow, making me flinch. "Don't stop. Make yourself come."

"I don't—"

"Do it."

I couldn't stop. I couldn't demand he explain what the fuck he thought he was doing because when he said *do it*, I wanted to. I wanted to please him, to submit, to *be his*. I was more than a submissive because submission implied a choice. I was his slave.

I rubbed my clit, gathering fluids, juice flooding between my fingers. I let out a high-pitched *ah* then choked it off.

"Let's hear it, Monica."

"Oh, God," I whispered.

He moved to my side, crouching so his breath was on my cheek. I turned to face him, eye to eye, my legs spread, my left hand on the tree, my right hand in my pants. He still didn't touch me, just breathed with me as my lower lip dropped and my lids hooded.

"You like it."

"I like you better." My breaths got shorter and hitched. My cunt was hot under my fingers, twitching, engorged, soaking.

"I bet," he said.

"Take me."

"Come."

"Yes."

The tingle ran from my knees to my waist, and my ass bucked as if Jonathan was still behind me. I cried out loud enough for the neighbors to hear, driving my hips into the tree as if I was fucking it. My chest rose and fell against the white bark, my cheek feeling its rough winter texture as I looked at him, just a shape in the darkness.

"That was okay?" Jonathan asked.

"More, please." I took my hand from my pants.

"You're insatiable." He kissed my wet fingers. "I'm glad you like it, because that's your life if I go to jail. I'm not one of those nice guys who will tell you to date other men. I'm the guy who owns you whether I'm in jail or not."

"Tell me what you think she's going to say."

He leaned on the tree and put my index finger in his mouth, sucking it clean. "Is it so wrong to want to keep you away from the ugliest parts of my life?"

"Yes." The feel of his tongue as he sucked my fingers was arousing me again. I leaned my shoulder against the tree, bracing myself against the drop down the hill with my boot heel.

"It's wrong to want to protect you? To keep you above my shit? A goddess?"

"Yes. It is wrong. It can't last. If you make me into some perfect thing that's separate from your life, we're going to disappoint each other. And that'll be it. We'll be over."

"I don't think so." He finished with my fingers and knotted our hands together.

"Yes, Jonathan, yes. We'll be over. I love you. I love your past, no matter what it was. I love your present, and I want to be your future. But lying will break us. One day you'll wake up and realize I don't really know you, and it'll be too late to bring me close. That'll be it, whether you leave me or not. We'll be over."

"My secrets might be out for public consumption very soon. So let's have *now*, before you run away."

"I want to hear it from you."

"No."

"Then I have to go meet someone." I dropped my hands and grabbed a branch, hoisting myself up the hill.

He put his hands on my biceps and pulled me back. "Don't. Just give me time."

"No."

I said it, twisting a little to face him, and lost my balance. I fell back, my weight on him. He lost his footing, and we tumbled down the hill, all elbows and feet, complete with *oofs* and screams and the sounds of cracking, rustling brush. My world blurred into a spinning, dark vortex before I landed in a heap at the top of the retaining wall. Jonathan fell onto the flagstones in the backyard, his back slamming against the low wall bordering the tangerine tree.

"Oh!" I shouted, scrambling up. "Jonathan!" I jumped the wall and landed by him.

"Are you okay?" he asked, though I was standing and he was prone.

"I'm fine. I've fallen down that hill a hundred times." I pulled him up. He cringed.

"Are you sure?" He picked a twig from my T-shirt, and I brushed his collar. He turned his head and grimaced.

"Could I be any more bruised than I am already?"

He smiled, then I smiled, and we laughed. He put his hands on my cheek, and we kissed through our laughter. He bent his neck and drew a long breath.

"I think you twisted your neck good," I said. "You should have just let me go meet her."

"Never." He kissed me again, keeping his neck straight. I kissed him back, deeply, because I was about to disappoint him.

"Now," I said. "And if not now, tomorrow."

"I'll take you to bed."

"I thought I was too beat up to fuck?"

"I'll make it work."

"Every day between now and when you're ready to talk to me? Your whole plan for dealing with Jessica can't be to keep me in the dark? She's going to get you declared incompetent. This is all right with you?"

He went to put his right arm around my shoulders and stopped himself, groaning.

"What?" I asked.

"Nothing."

"You're hurt."

"I'm fine. It's not that big a hill."

"But you fell on a bunch of pavestones." I put my arm around his waist and helped him to the back door. "And you're not that young any more, you know."

"Oh, you are getting such a spanking for that."

"Not if you can't lift your arm."

"I'll spank you with my dick."

He barely got through the sentence before he started laughing. I joined in because the visual was so close to a pornographic Monty Python skit that we couldn't hold it in our heads without laughing. We were still cracking up when I sat him in a kitchen chair.

"Ow!" he complained between laughs. I kneeled in front of him and unbuttoned his shirt. "Not now, baby. I'm too tired."

I pushed the shirt as far over his shoulders as I could. "Can you get out of this?"

"Are you making a pass at me? Because I'm already taken by a brown-eyed goddess."

"Can you just do it, please? My God, you are a pain in the ass."

He leaned forward, and I helped get his shirt off. The left sleeve was the hardest on him. Even though he smiled through it, his arm was stiff and he moved gingerly. The T-shirt under the button down was easier. I pulled out the good right arm, stretched it over his head, then dropped the whole thing over the stiff left arm. His bicep was swollen and red, and his shoulder blade had a red bump the size of an egg growing on it. He bent his arm.

"Not broken," he said, grimacing.

"But you're going to have some nice bruising from your neck to your elbow. Welcome to my world."

"Mine don't come with the memories."

I kissed him. He put his right hand on my cheek, and I put my arms around him, still treating him tenderly. I opened my eyes while I kissed him because I wanted to see his eyes closed in surrender to me, and I had that blissful sight. Jonathan, enjoying my kiss, in that slight abdication, made my heart flutter. I sighed. Then his eyes opened just a little, as if he wanted to see the same thing, and we smiled.

"Sit still. Let me get some ice." I stepped to the freezer where Gabby and I had kept compresses for fingers and arms that ached after hours of practice.

"Why don't you just take me to bed?" he said as I put compresses on his neck and arm.

"Not a bad idea. Get up."

We walked to the bedroom, and I propped him up on pillows, happy that I'd changed the sheets. His arm was getting stiffer, and by the time I'd set up the compresses, he could barely move it at all.

"Guess who's not driving tonight," I said, holding out my hand. "Give me your keys so I can put your car in the driveway. There's alternate side parking tomorrow."

"I can afford a ticket."

"But if the car blocking the sweeper in the morning is my guest's, Roger across the street and puts all the garbage in *my* front yard. He did it with Darren, like, a hundred times."

He reached into his right pocket and pulled out his key. "You need to move to a better neighborhood."

"I know what you're thinking"—I swiped the key—"and forget it. I'm not a kept woman."

"We'll see about that."

I pocketed the key and went to my bathroom. Stepping onto the toilet, I reached the top of the vanity where I kept bottles of pills hidden from Gabby: painkillers I'd been prescribed for an extracted tooth, muscle relaxants for painful menstruation, and Xanax a friend had given me for a short bout of insomnia. I took them to Jonathan, who was dicking with his phone with his good hand.

"I have painkillers."

"Why? You in pain without me?"

"Let me get you some water."

"Monica"—he looked me with dead seriousness—"no painkillers."

I put the bottle of Oxycontin on the dresser. "How about some Tylenol and a muscle relaxant?"

"Deal."

I took the bottles to the kitchen, and as I poured a glass of water, I considered what I had in front of me, what I wanted to do, and what was keeping me from doing it. As I poured the pills in my hand, I reconsidered then went back to the bedroom. "All right. This is the Tylenol. This is the muscle relaxant. Go."

He popped them in his mouth and swallowed, then drank the water. "You're a good nurse."

I put my knee on the bed and swung myself to a straddling position. "I'm not done nursing you." I undid his pants.

"Oh, really? What nursing school is this?"

I pulled out his dick. It was half hard already, and when I kissed it, it stood at full attention. "I have no clever answer." I licked the length of his shaft with the flat of my tongue.

"Hell is freezing over," he groaned, putting his right hand on my head and running his fingers in my hair. I opened my mouth and let him put pressure on the back of my head, slowly pushing his cock into my mouth, past my tongue, and down my throat. He kept the pressure, and I breathed calmly through my nose, my eyes locked on his. When he eased up, I drew my head back, sucking him on the way out. He sighed, and a look of pure, relaxed pleasure overcame his face. A line of saliva connected my mouth to his cock. I licked my lips.

"You never let me use my hands," I said.

He blinked, as if thinking about all the times his dick was in my mouth, counting off instances and places. "Total oversight on my part."

"You like control."

"Guilty as charged."

"Let me have you," I said. "Give yourself to me."

"Submission's not fun for me."

Hands behind my back, I took him again, all the way down, tasting sharp sweat and a drop of salt as I sucked him on the way out. "Let me please you, sir. Let me give you my best."

"When you put it that way..."

I placed one hand at the base of his cock, and with the other, I cupped his sack. I took him completely, trying to keep submission on my mind and in my attitude as I controlled what he felt. The pace was mine. The intensity was mine. When he put his hands on me, it was with affection, not control, and when he came, filling my throat and closing his eyes, I maintained that attitude of gratitude and abdication, licking him clean.

"Thank you," he whispered.

"How is your arm?" It hung at his side, unused during the whole episode.

"Feels stiff but okay." His eyelids drooped as he watched me. He stroked my hair and cheek, and I kissed his fingers.

I kneeled and pulled him gently from the waist. "If you scoot down, I'll rearrange the compresses."

He did. I put a pillow under his head, elevated the sore arm, put him under the blankets, and drew them up. I shut the light and curled up next to him. Seconds later, his breathing slowed, and I slipped away.

Chapter 21

—I went home—

The content of Jessica's text didn't surprise me. The fact that she'd bothered to send it did. She was desperate for contact.

Jonathan's car was parked right out front. I'd never actually driven a Jaguar, but as soon as I turned the key, I understood the difference between it and my Civic. It was smooth everywhere. The seams didn't rattle. No crumbs were in the corners, as if one simply ate more neatly, or not at all, in such a car. It went from park to drive as if by the power of thought, and the dashboard lights didn't glare or ask me to read them. They existed to be understood in a hueless grey and whispered information urgently. *Half full. Forty thousand RPM. Seventy-five miles per hour.*

What heaven, driving a black Jaguar on PCH at midnight.

I enjoyed the ride so much, I hadn't even thought to turn on the radio, and when a classical station came on, I woke up to the complications of being in Jonathan's car. She had an order of protection. If his car pulled up to Jessica's place, alarms would be raised. Possibly by Jessica, the police, Santon's team—wherever they may be. Whatever the case, once she saw the car, I couldn't pretend we had broken up and I was looking for vengeance. I was going in as the loyal girlfriend, and my leverage would decrease. I passed her house. Lights out. Car in driveway. It was midnight on a Monday, after all. I spun around the corner, wound up all turned around because the streets weren't on a grid, came back to the beach side of the street, over shot the house by two blocks, and parked. I needed all my options, and that meant walking in as if I'd taken a cab.

The modernist house sat on an incline with twisting stairs to the top and desert flowers on the way up. I slipped up the concrete steps quickly and inconspicuously, hoping the crickets and ocean waves covered my footfall. The door was huge, heavy, and red with a knob in the center. The front of the house had small plate windows since they faced the street. The back would be made of glass from floor to twelve-foot ceiling, since it faced the ocean.

I stood on my toes and peeked. Lights were on farther back in the house, and I saw the blue flicker of a TV. The bell was the light-up kind. I put my finger over it and held my breath.

Then I pressed it.

Ring and run! Ring and run!

When I was a kid in the EP, as we called it, we'd ring bells and run away, hiding behind parked cars or a hedge, just for the joy of watching as someone came to the door. No game was more infantile, yet I was tempted to play it.

Ring and run! Ring and run!

She wasn't coming. I had enough time to run away and get back in the car. Take PCH to the 10 to the 110 and get off at Stadium Way. Take a leisurely drive through Solano Canyon in Jonathan's car. Pull the sleek machine into the drive. Crawl back into bed with the love of my life and make him breakfast in the morning like I oughta. Explain I was moving the car and had to take it for a spin. He'd love to hear that. Delight him. That was my job.

Ring and run! Ring and run!

A light flicked somewhere in the house, sending wide bands of dim light across the concrete path. I had a meeting tomorrow with the president of Carnival Records, and my voice would be hoarse and I'd have bags under my eyes. I had to go home and rest. Go immediately. I had a career. I'd worked hard. Jonathan could take care of himself. He was a big boy. Sing. I wanted to sing.

The front light flicked on, and the big knob flicked and twisted. I stepped back. One step.

Run!

The door swung open as I stepped down. She was dressed in slacks and a button-down shirt. She looked as if she'd just walked out of a soap ad. How did Jonathan ever fuck her? Did she sweat? Did she groan? Did a tear of post-orgasmic joy ever drop down her cheek?

"Hello, Monica," she said. "Finally."

"Hello, Jessica."

"Won't you come in?" She stepped out of the way, and I walked into her house.

Chapter 22

The ugliest lamp in the world illuminated the room in warm light. It was gold with a parchment shade and a neck shaped like seven tennis balls stacked on top of one another. Everything else was impeccable. Somehow, though, a mark of impermanence stained the décor. Nothing looked settled or important. The corners were visible. The surfaces were without tchotchke or photo. The art was original but marginal. I had been right about the back wall. The windows stretched corner to corner, exposing a lit up pool and a view that was pure blackness at night, but in the day would be clear to the horizon, where sky met sea.

"Would you like a cup of coffee?" Jessica asked.

"More of a tea person."

Jessica made a *mmm* sound, as if my choice of hot beverage spoke volumes about my worth as a human being. Of course, that was my imagination. Her face betrayed nothing. "I'll have some made. Decaf? It's late."

She'll have some made? Did the staff not get time off? Did they work in shifts? Well, if that was my new life, if those were the entitlements one was to expect, then I was going to be as considerate as possible.

"Caffeinated is fine. Doesn't bother me. And green, if you have it."

"Would you like to sit outside?" She indicated the back.

"Sure."

She opened the sliding door to a patio and flipped a switch. Heating torches went up, lights went on. I nodded and walked out. I sat on a chair, listening to the ocean I knew was there but couldn't see. I had trouble imagining having access to such a patio every night and being at anything but complete peace. Or was that what she feared? That losing the money to maintain the patio, the house, the studio meant she couldn't be at peace? I imagined the level of anxiety I'd face if the things that kept me sane were taken away. My voice. My ears. Even my piano, with its broken pedal, was a rock I held tight when I felt anxious. Jonathan removing that much of her income had thrown her off a cliff, made her panic. Cornered her. Poorly thought out for a man who controlled everything at all times.

Even with the torches, it was chilly. I realized then, too late, that I didn't have my scarf. The crew neck on my tee was relatively tight, but my bruises were visible with even the most minor inspection.

It was darker at the chair across from me. But Jessica was coming. She'd see me move to a darker corner.

I reminded myself to always remember the rules about Jessica, especially rule number one. Fuck her. It wasn't about her. It was about protecting Jonathan from her little rat eyes.

I moved to the dark corner.

"So," Jessica said as she closed the door, cradling a manila envelope.

I looked at her linen slacks and button-down white shirt again. Maybe she'd just gotten back from somewhere, or maybe she and Jonathan were partners in their sleep habits, hanging out until all hours and waking up after what most people would consider a nap. Maybe they used to stay up all night giggling and sharing stories, all dressed to the nines, not a hair out of place.

I had to shake myself out of my thoughts. "I'm sorry to come so late, but it seemed like everything was conspiring against us meeting."

"'Everything' being Jonathan?"

"I don't know."

"Did you ask him?"

"No." Her question had been so direct and her tone so kind, yet condescending that I started to understand why Jonathan didn't want me near her.

An older woman in a black dress came out with a tea tray and left silently. Jessica poured tea into two white cups that were so plain, they must have cost a fortune.

"I understand why you don't want to ask him. He can be intimidating."

I didn't answer. I still didn't know if I was playing rabbit-in-the-woods or qualified-to-kink, so I just poured myself tea. "I'm sorry I was rude to you when I saw you last."

She waved it away. "I understand. I came on too strong. I assumed you were naturally curious."

I consciously, and with great effort, let the insult slide. I'd asked for it, considering I hadn't asked him the details of blocking me from seeing her and I had aggressively avoided Jonathan-bashing at Frontage. "This is a very nice house. The view must be incredible in the daytime."

"It is. You can see all the way to the horizon. It's cooler too, with the breeze coming in."

"Have you lived here long?"

She smiled a little, and I wondered if she could see that I was feeling her out. "Erik and I moved here after I left Jonathan. It was far away from him. That was the best thing about it."

"And Erik? Is he still here? It's a big house to live in alone."

"Moved on." Turning the line of questioning over to her life was obviously not on her agenda because she changed the subject back to me. "So, why the change of heart? You wanted nothing to do with anything I had to say."

It was time to pick what and who I was going to be. "When he got arrested, I got... Well you used the word curious. I felt like there were things I needed to know, and you were trying to tell them to me, but I wouldn't let you."

"And you figured you'd get them out of me so you could go back and tell him?"

I held my breath. I'd failed somehow, because she jumped on my motivations so quickly. I must have looked like a deer in headlights and turned shades of pink, even in the dark corner. "I don't know what I'm going to do." My voice crackled like a piece of paper being thrown in the trash.

"You're going to tell him everything I said. And he'll rebut me. Like my wrist, which I'm sure he denied breaking during sex. And beating me in his backyard. What did he tell you about that? Did he tell you I told everyone he wanted to rape me and hurt me? But he didn't, of course, says *he*? Do you have any other source of information?"

I didn't, but I said nothing.

"My lawyer says you found surveillance devices in your house, and he's saying it was me. Is that what he told you? That I did it?"

"Yes."

"I'm not the one with the sick fantasies. Why would I do that?"

How could I answer? How could I say, "So you could try to prove he was an abuser. To shame him. To get him declared incompetent." I wouldn't tip Jonathan's hand. I gazed down at my palms in my lap and tried to think of some rebuttal that made sense, but I had nothing.

She took my silence as permission to continue, her words measured and careful. "Every piece of information you have comes from him. Let me tell you something. He has control fantasies. If cameras were in your house, you have no farther to look than the man next to you. If a woman says he broke her wrist because he was holding them behind her back during sex, believe her."

"You said you were joking."

"I shouldn't have told you when you were working. That was the joke. It wasn't funny, but I don't lie. Jonathan does. You know that, right? You know he lies."

I took a deep breath. How could I admit that without betraying him? To sit there and say I believed everything he'd ever said would earn me nothing but her laughter. I felt cornered, hateful. Jonathan was right. I shouldn't have come.

"His father ruined my family. Did he tell you that? He killed Daddy. Broke his heart with some sneaky business deal. I didn't know when I met Jonathan. I had been protected. Daddy never even told me he'd lost nearly everything until I introduced them, and by then, it was too late. I loved him, and I fought for him. Just like you're doing. His whole family ruins people." Jessica leaned forward and put her hand over mine. "I know he didn't tell you about Rachel either. What he did to her."

My eyes shot to hers. My breathing picked up. "What?"

"You have bruises on your neck," she said.

I impulsively touched the bend where shoulder and neck met, as if to hide them or make sure they were still there. "What did he do?"

"He killed her."

He killed her. Had I known that, somewhere deep in my gut? Had I been avoiding it? Lying to myself, as I often did? Or were there more lies on top of those?

I felt trapped. Months ago, I'd been flying, my own buzz filling my ears, with a destination in mind but a path not mapped. I had a job and friends and hope. One night, I spilled a drink. I touched a man's hand, and I let him kiss me on the hood of his car. Some time after, I don't know when, I fell into a web of lies and deceit. The harder I struggled, the more trapped I became. But who was the spider? Was it Jonathan? Or Jessica? And how could I get out of their fucking web?

I glanced around, feeling the wetness in my eyes. God, one blink and I'd be a mess. I sniffed and took a napkin from the tray. I saw the manila envelope she'd brought out sitting on the low table. On top of it, face down, sat her phone.

"I'm scared," I said. She squeezed my hand. "He is rough. He..." I trailed off.

"Go on."

"He calls me names, and..." I put my hands to my neck and looked into the distance.

"Does he choke you?"

"He calls me whore. Did he say those things to you?"

"Well, no."

I started to get up "Never mind."

She took my hand and squeezed it, pushing me back down. "It was just different for me. For me it was bitch and slut. Humiliating women is part of his sickness."

I looked away. I needed to keep the pain on my face. I touched my neck again and whispered, very low, "He hurts me."

"I'm sorry," Jessica said, "I can't hear you?"

I looked back at her, finding the tears of a minute ago were still available. I blinked them out, and they dropped like stars.

"Does he choke you, Monica?"

I nodded.

"He does? He chokes you?"

I shook my head. She looked confused. I cleared my throat and eyed my bag. "I think I should go."

"He choked me," she said. "I had bruises just like yours. I thought I was going to die. That's the turn-on for these men. Watching your pain and fear."

"These? Bruises like these?" I said, touching my neck.

"Yes."

"I fell down a hill."

"You don't have to lie to protect him. I've been in your shoes."

I squeezed her hand. Her French manicure was perfect on all of her fingers but the right thumb, which was cracked. "Can I have a glass of water?"

"Sure." She craned her neck to see in the house. "She's gone to bed. God. Couldn't wait another half an hour." She slid the manila envelope from under her phone and handed it to me. "This is for you. There's nothing in there Jonathan doesn't know, and it's everything he won't tell you. I know everything, and that scares him." She patted my head as if I was a terrier.

"Do you want ice?"

"Yes, please."

She squeezed my hand one last time and got up, closing the door behind her.

The temptation to open the envelope was intense, but I had very little time. I hugged it to my chest, unopened, and snatched Jessica's phone. I slipped through the sliding glass doors and out the front. The phone was recording a voice memo. I shut it down as soon as I hit the street. If she tried to chase me, she'd be looking for my car. I still walked behind hedges and in the darkest parts of the street until I got to the Jag. I sped away as fast as the car and common sense allowed.

On the drive home, I considered that I'd done something really stupid. I didn't know which stupid thing I'd done. A string of things had seemed right at the time and could still be right. The phone, which wasn't getting signal and would be untrackable until it was turned on again, frowned at me like a hostage. I could turn it on and quickly put it into airplane mode. I could pop the SIM card. I could hear everything if I really wanted to.

"Fuck off," I said to the black rectangle on the passenger seat. "You're full of shit."

I giggled at my double entendre that recognized the recording of Jonathan's spanking was inside. Then I laughed because my brain emptied of everything but the one thing that mattered. I trusted him. He hadn't earned it and he certainly had pushed my limits, but deep in my heart, I didn't need to hear the recording. I believed him. I always had.

When I realized I was going ninety-five, I pulled over. I rubbed the tears from my eyes, got my breathing to a normal rate, and turned on the overhead light. Once I got back, I wouldn't be able to open the envelope because Jonathan would be there. Whatever was in there needed to be read furtively, in the dark of night, alone. It would be evil and ugly, written with the silk of a spider's web.

Chapter 23

My feet dragged up the steps, boots clopping on the wood. I was fucking tired. I should never stay up late the night before any meeting, but especially not *that* meeting. I was going to crawl under the sheets with Jonathan, curl up next to his beautiful, warm body, and sleep.

Except he was sitting on the porch. He did not look happy.

His jacket was slung over the back of the porch swing. He wore his pants, fastened, his shirt, unbuttoned thrice, and his shoes. The shoes bothered me. He could walk away any second. He held out his hand. I dropped his car keys in it.

"I shouldn't have to tell you," he said, "but don't do that again."

"Do what? Steal the car? Or drug you?"

"See my ex-wife."

"That's the one thing I won't apologize for."

I put the envelope and phone next to him then leaned on the porch railing. He didn't even look at them but kept his eyes on mine and his foot braced on the table in front of him. We regarded each other in silence for a second.

"Have you put the starter back in my car?" I asked.

"Yes."

"I'll get over there later."

"Lil will take you."

"I'll take the bus," I said.

"No, you won't."

"Go to hell, Jonathan."

"*I* should go to hell? I? Me? I should go to hell?"

"Yes, you. You have felony charges against you, and you spend all your time finding ways to keep me from helping you. What was your plan for dealing with her? You gonna just let her blackmail you because you have the money lying around?"

"No, Monica, I had a plan. But I spent all my time making sure you didn't fuck it up."

I sat back on the railing and crossed my arms, locking my feet against the vertical rails so I didn't fall over. "You could have just told me."

"I don't tell people things like that. It's not my way."

I rocked back on my feet. The railing had held for a hundred years and would hold for a hundred more, but Jonathan didn't know that. He stiffened when it looked like I'd fall.

"Did I fuck it up?" I asked.

"No. You just fucked *me* up. I couldn't think. I knew all the things Jessica would say to you, and I thought she would drive you away. Whatever you needed to hear, and I thought the worst, she'd say it. Then this time, you'd be gone for good."

If touching him would have been appropriate, I would have stroked his cheek and kissed his mouth. I would have held his hands, warning them against the late November chill. I would have whispered my love in his ear in the cadence of his laughter. But we had too much of the last two days between us to make any of that meaningful.

"I am very sorry about the sleeping pills," I said. "I didn't think until after that you need your self-control, and I took it away. That was wrong and a breach of trust. I'm sorry." When he didn't answer, I continued. "I may steal your car again, though."

"Take it." He waved his hand as though he was giving me the last bite of dessert. "Can you tell me what she said?"

"Apparently, you killed your first love. She made it out like cold-blooded murder."

The anger drained from his face, replaced by the flatness of fear.

"Don't look like that," I said. "I love you."

"But I did it."

"I know."

We regarded each other for what seemed like a long time.

"That envelope, right there, she gave it to me. It's a draft of an article written for *eLA Rag*. I already have piece of it that Gabby got her hands on, don't ask me how. They suggest that you were driving the car Rachel was in when she drowned. You saved yourself and let her die. Jessica said you're aware that she knows all this."

"I am."

"Can I hear the whole story from your lips, please?"

"No, Monica. No. A thousand times, no."

"All I got from her was the goddamn envelope before I took her phone. So I can go back and—"

"This is *her* phone?" He pointed to the black rectangle on top of the envelope.

"Yes."

He picked it up. "You stole her phone."

"I prefer the term *lifted*," I said. "In any case, if she did 'ask for it' like you said, the raw audio might be on there."

"You *stole her phone*." He cradled in the space between his palms, as if he didn't want too much of it touching his skin. "Did you listen?"

"No. That's all you. Figure it out."

"You don't want to know how far I went with her?"

"You told me how far you went."

"You are so strange, Monica."

"I never made the decision to love you. But I decided to trust you. That was a choice."

He fingered the phone, flipping it over as if contemplating a greater meaning. "If the whole scene is on this phone, its best use may be to go public."

"Whatever you want."

"People will know." He looked at me with meaning, as if trying to impart a few volumes of knowledge.

I knew exactly what he meant. They'd know how we were together. They'd talk, and they'd look at me in a way I didn't want to be seen. "Fuck people and fuck what they know. Do what you have to."

He held out his hand, and I took it, letting him pull me onto his lap. His arms wrapped around me and pulled my legs to one side. I put my fingertips on his cheeks, letting the rough stubble scratch them. I traced his jaw, the angular line, the hardness of it, and his lips, source of so much pleasure, their softness on my fingers as I imagined them between my legs. I shuddered a little and rested my head on his chest, losing myself in his leathery scent. *God, please let me not be confusing love and beauty. Let this be as real as it feels, not some imaginary thing.*

"Why did you want to see her?" he whispered.

"To try to lift her phone. But if I told you that, you'd just say no. And if I failed, you would have thought I was incompetent."

He kissed my forehead, my cheeks. "You're not leaving me?"

"No."

"But you haven't heard everything."

"I don't want a reporter's research. I don't want Jessica's lies. I want it from your mouth. I chose to trust you, and I want you to choose to talk to me."

Chapter 24

Jonathan

I held her silently for a long time, wondering if she could keep her promise to stay with me. I'd become so attached to that woman that her presence, somewhere in the world, comforted me. The connection, once I'd admitted it was there, was palpable, a rope of energy between us. Knowing what she was doing at any given moment was an almost religious experience, specific to her, and almost sexual in its purity. I knew she felt too, but she was a wild card. Her reactions never fit my expectations.

If she was going to leave me because of things I'd done, she would have done it already. The effects of unburdening myself could last indefinitely and affect me the way they'd affected me with Jessica, in well-timed words and the sense that I was trapped by her knowledge. But it didn't matter any more. As of last night, I'd done enough to alienate Monica from me and more to bring her close. The tension between the two had to break.

So I formulated a way to express the narrative. It didn't run in a straight line. It started on a rainy December night, took a left when I was twenty-three, came around the bend a year later, switched gears the previous month, and only began the previous night, with a death.

"Rachel died last night," I said. She pulled away to look me in the eye. Even in the dark, I saw her confusion. "Well, I lied."

I wanted to see her face, so I pulled her up to a straddling position. Her shoulders slouched. I brushed her hair from her shoulders. It was too dark to see her face clearly, but I knew I wouldn't like what I saw.

"I'm sorry. There's more. Do you want me to come clean?" I asked.

She put her hands on my shoulders. "Ok, go ahead."

"Rachel required constant care. The accident left her in a vegetative state. She wasn't even herself anymore, so little of her brain was functioning. She could have lived forever, except that when Jessica first met you at the

306

Stock, the day with the cast on her arm, I panicked. I thought she'd tell you everything. I didn't know why, and mostly, I didn't know why I cared so much, but I knew I did. I needed time to think, so I moved her to another facility. She never fully recovered."

"I'm sorry," Monica said. "Are you sad about it?"

I felt myself smile, because that would be the question Monica would ask, not the thousand others. "Yes, but other things too. It's complicated. I'd assumed she was dead between the accident and when I was about twenty-three. I'd done my share of grieving over it. But I found out she was alive, and Jessica and I found her and moved her."

"Okay, wait—"

"Hold on, Mon—"

"You found her? Who was keeping her?"

"I said hold on, goddess, please."

"Have mercy on me, Jonathan. I thought she was dead until a minute ago. You have no idea what's been going through my head."

"What?"

She put her forehead to my shoulder. "You killed her during sexual asphyxiation and covered it up with the accident."

"You have a very vivid imagination."

"So, that's not what happened?"

"You know that's not my kink. I mean… Jesus, I should have explained this sooner." I pulled her up again and took her face in my hands. She looked very tired. I had no idea how to make this any shorter, but I knew we had to finish it, if she could stay awake for it. "I have to stop and tell you about my father."

"The passive drunk you told me about?"

"One of the many lies I tell about him."

"The one who seduced Rachel first."

"Not a lie. That was the beginning of me learning the truth of who I am. He's a sociopath. Clinical. He has no empathy. He only finds things interesting or not interesting, and hurting people is interesting. Young girls are interesting. Seeing my mother scream during childbirth? Same. My sister Carrie is a psychologist, and once she realized it, realized all the shit he'd done over the years, she moved to Italy. Swear to god. I see that look on your face. It's not genetic."

"I didn't think you were a sociopath."

"No, but I'm a sexual sadist." Saying those words was hard, even though I knew how true they were. As much as Debbie had tried to remove all of my negative connotations from them, I still felt a pang of self-loathing. Monica didn't seem perturbed, probably because it was just us on her porch. I knew that her shame was in how she was seen by strangers, not what we called each other when we were alone. "I thought for a long time that made me like him. That we were the same because I enjoy that look on a woman's face when I squeeze a little too hard, or that I like to make her uncomfortable. I thought it was a part of him inside me."

"And it's not?"

"It is. But even he's capable of doing good things. He was the one who rescued Rachel from the car and put her into a facility."

She leaned back as if stunned. "Why?"

"She was about to blackmail him. She was going to expose that he had been with her when she was sixteen. You don't blackmail J. Declan Drazen. He doesn't appreciate it, let's say."

"Why didn't he just let her die?"

"I don't know. He has a thing about not shitting where you eat, so if he thought she was within his circle, he wouldn't have hurt her. But he was secretive. We found out everything about the accident the hard way. When I went to him about it, he literally laughed. I found out I was driving when some reporter came sniffing around, probably this guy." I tapped the envelope. "I found out she was alive right after that. It was, let's say, overwhelming."

"You felt like a fly caught in a web."

She'd captured that feeling exactly. What she didn't capture was the feeling that if I got free of it, I'd be less human for letting go of the grief and guilt. It was mine. I owned it. If I unburdened myself, what would I become? An animal who stopped caring about the things I'd done? I couldn't allow that. My shame was made me a moral person, even if it crippled me emotionally.

She snapped up the envelope and pressed it to my chest. "You should read this."

"I don't need to."

"It says you were soaked in salt water. Has it occurred to you that *you* rescued her?"

"I dove in, but I was too drunk to rescue anyone," I said. "Probably nearly drowned myself."

"They got your medical records. The skin on your hands was totally fucked up. You were banged to shit. Like you wrestled with the ocean pulling someone out of it."

I remembered that. In my sequestered hospital room, my mother had been at my side, smelling of whiskey, and she claimed ignorance about that and everything. Dad spoke to me after, describing Rachel's death by drowning, the body's absence, the car "she stole" floating into the Pacific with the tide. He'd get me another. Not to worry.

I'd been so shredded about Rachel, I'd paid no mind to my bruises or the skin missing from my hands. I figured that in my blacked-out stupor, I'd fallen. Repeatedly.

Maybe Monica was right. Maybe I hadn't been such a passive player. Or maybe it didn't matter anymore, because Monica's big brown eyes looked at me for answers as if I had any. She looked at me as if she was on a starting block, waiting to win the race to forgiveness. I could tell her anything. I could tell her I'd strangled Rachel and buried the body, and she'd forgive me. God damn. I had done something truly evil in letting the woman love me.

"We ruined her family," I said. "Not that it was worth much."

"You know, I think—"

I didn't let her finish. "Jessica's family, too. My father put hers in his grave. And when I married her, she was cut off. Then she became this *thing* that tries to squeeze me."

"Jonathan, listen—"

"And Kevin. I mean douchebag, yes. I had my chance to hit him on the head with a cinderblock, but that somehow wasn't permanent enough. I needed him wiped off the map of Los Angeles. So I had his warrants checked at the border. I needed his career with you to be over, so I made sure the last page of the commercial invoice was missing."

The look of shock on her face, the feel of her limbs tightening made me want to reassure her at the same time as it strengthened my resolve. "I mean, look at you. You're surprised. You can't believe I'd do something like that, right? You knew it was true, but you can't believe it. Say it."

"I believe it." Her voice was soft and low, as if she was telling herself more than me.

"And you still love me? Because you believe in my innate *goodness*?"

She rolled off my lap and sat next to me, looking into the empty, diagonal street. "You hurt me too, when you did that. With the invoice. Any box could have been held up. I might not have been able to figure it out."

"I didn't care. Don't you get it? I wanted to possess you, and I didn't want Kevin in my way. And you love me, Monica? Do you still love me? Are you that naïve?"

"I still love you."

"You have no idea what you're talking about. Look what I've done to you already. You're stealing things and drugging me. What are you turning into?"

"You're turning into a dick."

"I'm not turning into anything. What I am now, I've always been. I can't believe you can hear this story and sit there as if it's nothing."

"It's not nothing." She pulled her knees up to her chin, a defensive posture if I ever saw one. "Did you want me to judge you?"

"Why wouldn't you? Don't martyr yourself to me."

"Jesus Christ! What is *wrong* with you?"

"Your decency is endearing, but it's already dying." I stood up, my course of action set. I felt that tightness in my chest again but ignored it. "At least with Jessica, she knew what she was getting, and she could handle it. I can't say the same for you."

That hurt her, as it was meant to. The urge to gather her in my arms and say I was sorry was overwhelming. I had a moment where I could have done that, explained it all away, but that would be an act of a cowardice. I refused to allow another woman to be ruined because of me.

"Get out," she said, feet on the swing, curled and tangled at the ankles. "Just go."

"Your car is fixed," I said, scooping Jessica's phone and envelope.

I walked off the porch without looking back. The slap of the car door seemed final. The roar of the engine and backing onto her sheer drop of a street seemed like continued punctuations in an ever long sentence. I rounded the corner, then another, up a hill, until I was at the top of hers again. If I went back around and she was still on the porch, I'd grovel. I'd pour my heart out to her. If I told her I was afraid of corrupting her, exposing her to my family, turning her into an unscrupulous monster, killing her, maybe she'd prove me wrong.

But she was gone. Part of me was glad she was protected from truths that could be used to draw forgiveness and love from her. But the rest of me felt cracked down the middle.

I parked the car at the side of the road by the freeway entrance because the crack had opened into a void, and I was falling into it. I couldn't drive.

I knew I'd done what I had to. I knew I'd been a man. Done it right. Taken responsibility. I vowed that my single life wasn't going to be what it had been before. I wasn't going to bed whoever caught my fancy. I would play it straight. No looking. No dating. No casual fucking.

Because who else did I want? Who else fit so right? Who else could heal me? Who else could I damage as deeply, hurt as fully? Who needed more protection from me?

Right there, in my car, I said good-bye to a piece of myself. I gave up on it because doing so saved Monica from being the third in line for ruination. Saving her was a dark glow at the edge of the void, and that void... My God, that void was endless, lonely, black with loathing, and I clutched the wheel, white-knuckled, as I fell down it.

Chapter 25

Monica

That was bullshit.

That was a guy who felt responsible for his first love dying.

The choice was clear. I could get upset or not. I could disregard everything we'd been through already and write him off, or I could do him the favor he did me when I walked away and be ready for his return.

I opened my text messenger to let him know I was there for him when he came to his senses. I didn't hit send. The send button would deliver an immediate *ding* across the city, and he'd answer it (or not) and then we'd bounce texts (or not) but nothing would be solved. I'd prolong whatever agony he was going through.

I was fully awake, and though my second wind would be short, I had enough in me to give him something with the ghost of a chance of truly comforting him. I wanted to sing him a song. Make him music, and one *ding* wouldn't cut it. He needed more *dings*. A chorus of them. A symphony. His phone needed to light up and make music.

I crawled out of bed and got my metronome. After placing it on the night table and setting it mid-tempo, I broke down a song into the beats of a send button without sending it.

> *I_a*
> *m_h*
> *er*
> *e_und*
> *er_*
> *the*
> *_r*
> *ains*

If each letter became the tap of a beat, time taken, and the send button punctuated each line, assuming the network functioned properly, his phone should ding to the rhythms of my hurt and my steadfast concern. Three/three/two/five/three. Sixteen beats. Four measures. No downbeats or dynamics with a phone ding, but I could play with the timing and give every fourth a dotted quarter for *umph* if I needed it.

I set the metronome and practiced tapping into my phone. I used the enter key instead of the send button. An hour later, I felt like I'd nailed it, and my second wind was wearing down. Now or never. I cracked my knuckles and began.

Chapter 26

Jonathan

Two in the morning. Still raining. I could have called any Asia office and caught them in time for a good balling-out over whatever. God help them if they called me with some crap they could manage themselves.

I wanted her already. Her body under mine. Her voice saying my name. Her all-consuming hunger for life. The first months would be the hardest. I knew that from losing Jessica. How could I compare the blip that was Monica to the ten years I'd spent with my bitch of a wife?

Even if I hadn't believed it at the time, Jessica had run her course. That was the difference. My time with Monica had been cut off at the knees.

I already wanted to know what she was doing. Instead, I went into the shower and tried to scald the thought of her from me. I undressed in the bathroom, leaving my clothes on the floor like a slob.

My phone dinged once, then again. It was in my jacket pocket, draped over the vanity. Fucking Asia. The whole continent should fall into the sea, and by the urgency of the dinging, it sounded as if it was. By the time I got there, it had gone off another ten times, and a rhythm was appearing. The texts were coming furiously. The thing must be broken or stuck.

I finally got it out of my pocket.

The

_sk

*y_*

split

_ap

art

_t

*ears_*

fal

lin

*g_*

*into_*

the

_un

It went on. And on. It was Monica, singing me a song. I sat on the toilet, dripping, staring at my dinging, buzzing phone, and the seeming nonsense streaming across my screen. I could put it together if I concentrated. The effect was hypnotic.

The dinging stopped, then something came in a full sentence.

I_am_here_under_the_rains_the_sky_split_apart_tears_falling_into_the_ unbreakable_sea_I_am_wider_for_the_rain_fixed_under_the_cracked_ sky_waiting_for_you

A fist gripped my chest, tightening when I thought about what to do next. My neck and arms hurt as if the nerves were being squeezed. I broke out in a sweat. Ridiculous. I tried to get control of myself, but it was hard to breathe. I leaned back again. I must have been coming down with something.

I did the only right thing and blocked her number.

Chapter 27

Monica

I didn't hear back.

How long had he waited for me? Two weeks or more? I felt as though that would kill me, but I'd do what I had to, even if it meant I didn't sleep the night before a huge meeting and I felt like hell. I checked my phone constantly. Nothing. I had to remind myself to breathe.

That was why I'd been celibate, to avoid staying up all night before meetings. Of course the meetings had come just as I was getting more drama than I could handle without a therapist.

I am music.

I am music.

I am music.

In a sense, I was a wreck. The night was emotionally devastating. I never heard from him after my song. I believed I'd have him back, eventually, if he didn't find someone else in the meantime, but I was upset. I'd never been dumped, and the powerlessness and vulnerability was physical. My veins felt sucked dry, and my rib cage seemed to have shrunk too small to contain my lungs.

A good cry might release some of my anxiety, and I'd been tempted to let it come, but I didn't want to risk being unable to stop. I put all of my emotions in a box and taped it shut with words.

I'm fine.

I'm fine.

I'm fine.

I couldn't play my viola. Much as I tried to keep the notes strong, the dynamics kept dragging toward sad. I had better luck with the piano, pounding the keys until I was sure the cops would come.

I got control of myself. I didn't know how long it would last, but if I could keep myself together through the meeting with Carnival, I'd be satisfied.

A text came through. I jumped, anxiety flowing out of me in a torrent and sucking back in when I realized it was Darren.

—*Are you guys decent?*—

—*No, but I'm dressed and alone*—

A knock on the door was the response. I opened it to a perfect, clear fall morning, and Darren with his laptop.

He jerked his finger toward my driveway. "He left his car?"

"No, I—" I noticed a note on the porch swing.

Monica:
   Please know I'd arranged for this replacement before last night. Just take it, and we can call it even.
   -Jonathan

I had an old black Civic with more dings than a bell choir rendition of "Deck the Halls," and what sat in my driveway was a pristine white Jaguar roadster. Convertible. Top down.

"Asshole," I said.

"Dr. Thorensen's parking in your driveway again?"

I reached in my mailbox and found a navy blue Harry Winston box tied with a white ribbon.

"You are fucking kidding me," Darren said, plopping into the porch swing.

I opened the box. Inside was a heart-shaped silver key ring and a white car key. "I don't think I am."

"That for the hickeys all over your neck?"

"I should buy *him* a car for these hickeys." I pressed the button. The lights flashed, and a soft *pip* emanated from the car. Darren left his laptop on the swing and stood next to me, looking at the thing over the porch rail. "It's gorgeous. Too bad it's going back."

"What? That car—"

"We broke up."

"Again?"

I sighed. "He feels so right. When we're together, everything is perfect. But his past, it's ugly. It messes him up. I don't know how to get him out of it."

"Probably not your job."

"Yeah." I sat next to him, and he put his arm around me. "I don't know what to do."

Darren didn't say anything but pulled me closer. I felt exhaustion in my bones and a deep pit of sadness in my chest. I wanted to cry so badly, but I couldn't go to my meeting at Carnival puffy eyed and dehydrated. If I accepted Darren's comfort, I didn't stand a chance of keeping my shit together. I stood up.

"Let's go on Mulholland," he said. "Or hit the 405 at, like, noon."

"I have a meeting in Beverly Hills in an hour and a half, and I think I should leave early in case I wreck on the way. I've never driven anything like this before."

"Can I sit in it for ten minutes? Come on, don't hold out on a guy."

Men, even cute, sensitive, bisexual ones, were still men, and cars and guns were somehow hardwired next to sex and food.

"Whoa, Monica!" Dr. Thorensen leaned over the fence, staring at my car. "Take out a HELOC?" He raised an eyebrow at me, smirking. A lock of light brown hair fell in his eyes. He was in his late thirties and looked as though he was in his late twenties. Single. Straight. My friends melted whenever they saw him walk down his driveway.

"Dr. Nordicgod speaks," Darren whispered, obviously not immune to the good doctor's charms.

"It's a loaner," I called out.

"If you're taking it for a spin, I'll come along."

"I can't. I have somewhere to be, then I have to return it."

He whistled. "Sweet ride. Come over and tell me how you liked it. I might take one for a test drive soon."

"Will do."

He waved and went inside.

"Fucking Echo Park," I grumbled, turning to Darren. "What brings you anyway? New car smell wafting around the corner?"

"My wi fi died, and I didn't want to have to get a four-dollar coffee to use the signal at Make."

"All yours."

"I was going to go through Gabby's room." He looked at me as though he expected me to deny him access.

"No problem. And please raid my refrigerator. It's stuffed."

Chapter 28
Jonathan

"Are you taking Monica to the Collector's Board thing?" Margie asked outside the conference room. Her office buzzed with activity, but no one approached her when she was about to go into a meeting.

"Not going."

"Good. I don't want to get dragged. Dee and Emm are going." Dee and Emm was code for Dad and Mom. The worst thing wouldn't have been taking Margie but Monica.

"All the better." I couldn't tell her I'd walked off Monica's porch with no intention of seeing her again. My sister liked her, and I didn't want to disappoint her or explain my failings.

"You sleep at all?" she asked.

"Same as always," I lied. I'd slept about three hours less than usual.

"You need to rest before you open your mouth in front of her lawyers. I can't believe I have to tell you this again." Her annoyance was a show. We needed to appear to be having an animated discussion when Jessica and her lawyers turned the corner. Margie and I had been in the same room since five in the morning when I drove to her house.

The car had smelled like Monica, and the mirrors were set to accommodate the angle of her beautiful neck. She'd put the seat too far forward and left the wheel turned too far to the left. Still, I wished I could lend her the car another hundred times, just not to see Jessica.

My ex-wife turned the corner, lawyers flanking her. Ryan Myers, who had overseen the divorce, was in his fifties, in a brown suit that matched his fake tan. He'd been ready to tell the neighborhood I beat Jessica for kicks. The other guy was in his thirties and wore a grey pinstripe three-button job with a magenta tie. I didn't recognize him. Margie filled in the blanks without me needing to ask.

"Bennet Rinaldo. Litigator. Ass pain."

"Why do they have three people and we have two?"

"Because you're the aggressor, Jonny. You have to walk in here undermanned or you look like a bully."

"She asked for it."

"Say that any louder and you're on your own."

Polite smiles were exchanged between the five of us. We were having an informal meeting, yet no handshakes were exchanged. Margie held out her hand to indicate they should go in first.

The conference room had windows on two sides and a large wooden table in the center. Coffee and fruit had been laid out on the sideboard. Jessica found her place between her lawyers, and Margie and I sat opposite them.

Jessica was beautiful, and exactly what I'd needed when I was with her. She was sharp, and cold, and in control. I never thought I'd need anything else from a woman because I hadn't yet become a man. I'd changed, but she hadn't. She sat in the clear sunlight, hands folded in front of her. For the first time, she awakened not an ounce of longing, anger, or regret in me. I was glad she was out of my house, out of my bed, out of my daily concern. I wasn't even pissed at her anymore. I didn't think she could get me to hit her again because, somewhere in the past weeks, I'd let her go more completely than I'd imagined possible. A relieved smile crawled across my face, and she saw it before I could wipe it away.

"Gentlemen and lady," Margie said, sitting, "good morning. I understand an order of protection has been filed against my client and is waived temporarily because the plaintiff's lawyers are present."

Legal formality and boring. I tried to keep my eyes off my ex-wife, but she looked like a stranger, and that fascinated me. Had I kissed her lips while she slept? Had I stroked her body languidly while the breeze came through our open window? Had I confessed everything to her in a heat of intimacy or brought her to orgasm with loving care and tenderness?

I couldn't attach any feeling to the events I knew had occurred. I was sure they happened. I'd held her hand when her father died and wiped her tears away with my lips. We'd argued about silly things, like everyone, and we'd argued about serious things. I'd panicked when she told everyone about my kink because I thought I'd lose her. I remembered the fear, and when she told me she was leaving, everything that I was afraid of actually happened. I begged, on my knees, I'd begged her to stay. I remembered all of it as if I watched it on television or read about it in the paper, as if it was someone else's story.

There was a sharp pain in my calf that felt suspiciously like Margie's heel.

"Can you answer the question, Mr. Drazen?" said Rinaldo, the litigator, with a shitheel, superior tone that made me want to punch him.

I leaned forward. "You're going to need to rephrase that." I had no idea what the question was, and I needed him to repeat it.

"On November the twenty-fourth, what were your intentions when you met your ex-wife, Jessica Carnes, at your house?"

"My intentions? My intention was to go home and get some work done before a dinner meeting. She was already there."

"You're stating you did not expect her?"

"Yes."

"Can you describe your frame of mind?"

"No."

"Mr. Drazen—"

"I have to agree," Margie said. "You haven't even filed civil charges, and you want to go into discovery? Or was there something else?"

Myers cut in. "There are circumstances under which we can drop civil actions, which would give the state prosecutor little to go on. We can advocate for thirty-days probation and a standing order of protection."

"Describe the circumstances," Margie said.

"All financial channels between Mr. Drazen and Ms. Carnes can be reopened, permanently."

I looked at my gorgeous ex-wife, whose need for money must be deeply shameful to her. She didn't look at me but kept her back straight, her shoulders relaxed, and her eyes on her lawyer.

"No," I said before Margie, and I felt her heel again.

That was apparently exactly what Rinaldo wanted to hear. He opened a folder with full-color photographs that made me want to avert my gaze. My ex-wife's welted behind, three red slashes across it. I had no idea I'd hit her that hard. I had been pissed off, and it was difficult to feel how hard I was swinging through a haze of rage.

"You admit to giving her those?" Rinaldo seemed to be in charge of the uncomfortable questions.

"I do."

"Why?"

"We agreed to it beforehand," I said.

"Are you saying she asked for it?"

"Not in those words."

"And in the month previous, you broke her wrist during sex."

"She fell."

"Yes, I understand that's the story. You left her in the emergency room as well, so you wouldn't be questioned," Rinaldo said.

"I left her because I had a plane to catch and her boyfriend showed up."

"Your current girlfriend was seen last night with bruises. Did she 'ask for it' as well?"

I glanced at Jessica. Her eyes were in her lap. "You must really want this money," I said.

"Your comment has been noted, Mr. Drazen."

"Monica and I fell down a hill last night. I'd laugh about it if I wasn't so banged up myself."

"Bruises at the base of her neck are not consistent with a fall."

Margie clicked her pen to get everyone's attention and spoke in a tone that stopped Rinaldo and Myers in their tracks. "Thank you, Doctor. Unless you can produce photographs of these alleged bruises, I couldn't care less about them."

Rinaldo listened, then smirked. "We can send a forensic photographer to her right now. The State of California doesn't need her to accuse him of anything."

"The State of California cannot compel a woman to use her body as evidence in a prosecution. Do you have anything else?" Margie demanded. "Because I'm seeing precious little."

Myers nodded to Rinaldo, and the young litigator's shit-eating grin returned. "Ms. Carnes's phone turned itself on to record when you threw her against the table." He pressed a button on his phone.

It started with a scream when I pulled her hair. What a convenient starting point. I looked at Jessica again, and her eyes were glued to the phone. I felt her desire to look at me as her screams echoed through the room.

I demanded a safe word. She questioned its necessity, and I said,

"Question me again, and I'm fucking your ass so hard you won't be able to sit."

It sounded bad. Really bad. As if she didn't know what a safe word was or why one was necessary, and I'd interrupted her with a threat.

"It hurts. You're hitting me."

Calculated. So calculated. Somewhere in my mind, I admired her. She would have made a truly impressive partner if she wasn't such a cunt.

The clacking of my belt opening sounded filthy and violent, and my telling her not to yell when I hit her couldn't have sounded more like abuse. Listening to the scene play out was as uncomfortable as it should have been. And it was quite possible a judge would hear it. The recording could fry me.

"Wait," Margie interrupted. "Can you pause that a second?"

Rinaldo paused it, but the violence of the encounter lingered in the room.

"Where did that start again?" Margie asked.

"With a scream." Rinaldo had a wonderful shit-eating grin on his face that would look great once it was wiped off.

"Funny," Margie said. "I heard this one this morning. It starts much earlier." She pressed her own phone. My voice came through.

"Jess, how are you?"

A vanilla conversation progressed into the lead in the pipes of her studio, her hurt for money, our history.

"And you're saying you want to try it my way?"
"I want to. We'd need to set some boundaries beforehand."
"No, my way. Right now. Then you tell me if you can take it."

"Stop," said Jessica. "This is fake."

"No," I said. "It's exactly what happened. I'd swear to it."

"Okay." Jessica's voice, soft and audible.
"That's 'okay, sir.'"
"Doesn't that seem a little silly?"
"You want to do this or not?"
"Yes, sir."
"Stand up."

"I don't want to hear this," Jessica whispered to Myers.

He whispered *shhh* and patted her hand as my voice came through again.

"Stop trying to look saucy. This is a functional matter and not for your pleasure."

The next part was hard to hear, but Margie turned it up.

"This is what it is, this is the kind of sex you're agreeing to."

I commanded her to put her hands behind her back and face forward, then I checked on her, asking if she was all right.

I watched her reaction across the table. Her face flushed, and her jaw set. I hadn't seen her blush since the first time I'd kissed her. The red deepened for the next part, which Margie turned up.

> *"I'll undo your jeans. I'll pull them down to the middle of your thighs so it's hard to walk. You'll be uncomfortable, and that will please me. Then I'll get behind you, and I'll grab a handful of your hair at the back of your head and bend you over that table. I'll take off my belt, loop it once, and slap it across those sweet white cheeks until you're pink as a rose and your face is covered with tears. I'll stop when I can stick two fingers in your cunt and feel how sopping wet you are. Then I'll fuck you until you beg me to let you come, which I may or may not let you do. That going to work for you? Didn't think so."*
>
> *"Do it."*

I noticed for the first time how shrill and desperate her voice was. At the time, it had sounded like a controlled whisper. On the recording, it sounded like a child's whine.

> *"Jess, really."*
>
> *"Do it! Start with the hair. Or the pants. Whatever."*
>
> *"No."*
>
> *"Do it!"*
>
> *"Stop, Jess."*
>
> *"Are you a fucking man? Or do you just beg and cry for what you can't have? Is that how you get off?"*

Then the crash.

Margie paused it. "We've heard the rest."

"Where did you get that garbage?" Rinaldo asked.

"You Tube," Margie said. "It had seven hundred views this morning. But let me refresh. Huh. Got about forty-two hundred now. Funny what people find entertaining, isn't it?"

"A woman asking for it," I muttered. Margie shot me a look, but I was spared the heel.

"She stole my phone." Jessica's her eyes bore into me.

"I have no idea what you're talking about."

"The singer."

"Go near her again, and I'll kill you."

Margie's heel drew blood. I would have to buy her flats for our next meeting.

"Like you did Rachel," Jessica said through her teeth. "Took sixteen years. But there's no statute of limitation on murder, even manslaughter, Jon."

Ryan Myers stood, closing his files. "We're done here. Ms. Drazen, you and your client can consider our offer. Get back to me when you have an answer. The photographs still stand, as well as the possible pattern of abuse with his current girlfriend, which we'll be sure to mention to the prosecutor."

"Thanks for the warning." Margie stood and shook his hand. Meeting over and, as usual, only the lawyers walked away unscathed.

Chapter 29

Monica

I wore bruise-hiding clothes for the meeting, but as I wrapped my scarf around my neck, I wondered if Jonathan would come back to me before or after they were gone. My eyes welled, but I choked it back. Self-control. A woman of grace. I had to be that. I could crash after the meeting.

The car was, in a word, themostfantasticthingever. Fuck Jonathan. I got to the meeting feeling as though I was the architect of a major planetary takeover. I would return the car as soon as I was done there, but until then, it was like a space pod in a science fiction movie. Up the elevator, I told myself the usual. *My name is Monica. I stand six feet tall in heels. I am descended from one of the greatest writers of the twentieth century. I sing like an angel and growl like a lion. I am music. I am a goddess.* I choked on the last word because it was his, but I believed it. I didn't think I ever had before.

I expected to be awed by the size of the lobby or the glass-enclosed conference room, but I wasn't. The dark wood floors, the receptionists' desk that put their heads six inches above the person they were talking to, the marble staircase to the executive offices, all of it would have given me an anxiety attack six months earlier. But on the day I actually had a meeting that would have sent my friends into fits of envy-laced congratulations, I felt not a bit of tension or worry. Everything was in its box. Every emotion, positive or negative, was put away.

I understood what Jonathan found so appealing about self-control. I was the master of my body, my feelings, my words. I was fully in the moment, keeping my shit together. I was unattached to the results of the meeting. I was only concerned with being *in* it.

I'd heard those sentiments before, but I only realized that I had internalized them as I waited to be brought to a meeting where I was but a single, struggling singer in a room full of people who could make my dreams reality. I had what they needed. I had the music.

Carnival Records didn't have a cutting edge reputation. They weren't "street." They recorded gangsters and drug addicts, same as anyone, but internally, they were old school and buttoned-up. The office was all business. They weren't there to create or be part of an arts community. They took care of business. That was all. So though I'd worn a yellow dress with cream shoes, a cream scarf to cover Jonathan's marks, my hair in braids, and red lipstick bright enough to stop traffic, the employees kept the colors toned down, the lipstick nude, and the arty affectation to a minimum.

I wasn't waiting long before the receptionist brought me up the stairs, her ass swaying like a pendulum in her Robert Rodriguez skirt, big cloppy shoes silent from practice. She led me into the conference room. "Would you like some coffee?"

Again, Los Angeles was spread before me from Wilshire to the haze of the horizon. "Tea would be great. Just plain."

She smiled and left. I didn't sit but looked out the window onto the city of Los Angeles and the miasma of smog over the east side. Windows looked out into the hallway and all the blinds were up, so everyone in the office could see where Harry was and who he was talking to. He came into my sight, flanked by an entourage, mid-conversation. He smiled and waved through the window to me, stopping to finish talking to Eddie Milpas and an older woman who had a very important point to make, apparently. Two younger women flanked with notebooks and smart suits. A young man with three days of facial growth and a plaid shirt with slacks, an intern from the looks of him, opened the door when Eddie pointed to it. The gaggle of them strolled in.

"Ms. Faulkner," Harry said.

We had handshakes and introductions. Eddie and I exchanged a meaningful look that acknowledged we'd already met. I tried to put an innocuous expression on my face to tell him I wasn't going to wrestle with him over Bondage Girl in front of his boss. Everyone sat.

We had almost exactly the same small talk as every other meeting I'd attended. Traffic first. Los Angeles neighborhoods next. Some personal family stuff from Harry about his kid's Little League. I avoided a conversation about baseball that could have gone on for days.

"Well," Harry said as if he was cutting in on his own conversation, "it was something else to hear you perform last week. Wasn't what I expected to see when I came out there."

"I'm glad you enjoyed it."

Jerry, the producer who first recorded me playing "Collared" with a theremin, blasted in wearing a navy jacket and a windowpane shirt with the top three buttons undone "Sorry, sorry." He winked at me.

Harry gave him a smile that could have been swapped for a glare with no change in the message, then turned back to me. "Everyone in this room has seen you play."

I hadn't expected that. I thought they might have all heard Jerry's recording, but apparently, they all stopped by Frontage at some point. Of course, Harry had heard me play the B.C. Modern.

"We're all very impressed," he said. "Eddie and I have been discussing some marketing strategies, and he's come up with some ideas that are out of the park."

Customer service smile.

If it was Bondage Girl, we were going to have a very short meeting.

If it was me pretending I was some sort of expert in the art of submission, I was taking my little F-type Jaguar home, picking up Darren, and going up and down Mulholland until I needed to hit a gas station. Then I would bring it right back to Griffith Park with an empty tank.

"Out of the park, huh?" I said. "I'm excited to hear it."

"Were you considering doing more work like you did at the B.C. Mod show?"

Without Kevin?

Could I? I wasn't visual. I had taste, I could put stuff together, but I didn't have what Kevin had. "I'd like to, but it's complicated. That was a one-off."

He waved his hand. "It's an attitude. The work will follow, if that's what you want. We want to brand you something like a Laurie Anderson. An all-around package. A musician, yes, but also an artist."

"We want to introduce you around to some of L.A.'s art patrons," Eddie broke in. He seemed on board with the new strategy. I hoped he'd thought of it, because if he was just along for the ride, it would be half-assed. "There's an event Thursday night at L.A. Mod. The Collector's Board gala. Very big thing."

"It's short notice," I said. I had work, but I could switch a shift. Work wouldn't stop me. Jonathan had been clear he wasn't going, but maybe that had changed. I didn't know how I felt about seeing him under those circumstances.

Harry picked up the thread. "It's very short notice, but this event is only once a year. Next year, it'll be too late. We want your face there, photographed with Carnival Records." He indicated Eddie. "An artistic partnership."

I don't know what expression I wore, but I wore it long enough for Eddie to break the silence.

"What do you think?" he asked.

"Can I get back to you on Thursday night?"

"No problem," Eddie said with the same tone he'd used the last time we met, as if *maybe* really meant *yes*. He held out his hand to one of the assistants, and she handed him a piece of paper. He passed it to me. "These are the terms we're offering."

I looked at the paper, but the words and numbers swam before my eyes. I bit my lips between my teeth to keep from smiling.

Chapter 30

Monica

I couldn't drive. I kept hitting the gas pedal too hard and taking unbelievable risks because that fucking car moved like a Serengeti cat. I had a heart-lightening exuberance I hadn't felt since, well....ever.

I needed a lawyer. The problem was artists didn't hire entertainment lawyers. I couldn't call someone out of the phone book or get a recommendation from a friend and hire an entertainment lawyer for a ridiculous hourly rate. Entertainment lawyers took on clients they believed in and either charged seven-fifty per billable hour or took a percentage of the contract's value. They didn't just look over a contract; they negotiated it, and negotiated hard. The big ones were picky. They weren't wasting their time on a negotiation where their client had no leverage.

I pulled over, parking by a meter on LaBrea. I called Jonathan but got a recorded message in a soothing female voice telling me the subscriber wasn't available. I'd never heard that one. I didn't go to voice mail. Just nothing. Fuck it. I played with my phone until the web told me the number I was looking for.

"Hi," I said when I got a pick up. "This is Monica Faulkner. I'm looking for Margaret Drazen."

"Hold please."

I waited. I was sure I'd be sitting at the side of the road in my white convertible for a good long time. Her firm was huge, her name was on the door, and I wasn't even a client.

"This is Margaret," Margie said.

I sat straighter, pausing because I didn't expect her to pick up. "Hi, uhm, this is Monica. Jonathan's..." I paused again because I didn't know how to describe myself.

"Yes. Hello. Nice to hear from you. How are you?"

"I'm fine. I really hate to do this. I feel like I'm imposing on you."

"You don't need me to help you move or anything, do you?"

"No. I need a lawyer."

"Fancy that," Margie said. "I'm a lawyer, and I got a staff of them running around here."

"I know, but I need an entertainment lawyer. I don't want you to think I'm trying to use Jonathan to get ahead. I'm just in a bit of... well, a great position, actually. And I need help with some contract negotiations. So I'm sorry, but—"

"My dear," Margie said, her voice warm and comforting, "don't you realize? You've turned my brother around. You may live to regret this, but you're one of the family now."

She seemed so happy, I couldn't tell her about the previous night.

Chapter 31

Monica

"That's Steinbeck country," I said, watching the waitresses work the floor.

"Yeah," said the blonde in the blue dress. Her friends were ten feet away. "They made us read all that in school. I'm more of a Heinlein, Ellison girl myself. You?"

She was lovely. The perfect vision of womanhood in a simple, short blue dress and heels. Not slutty. Fair hair twisted up. Warm smile through pink lips. Fingertips at the wine glass she sipped from. She was smart, and we were both sober, which was also nice.

"Modernists, I guess. Pynchon, that kinda thing. Ever read *Mason & Dixon*? It's hilarious."

"None of that stuff in the Salinas library," she smiled. "Sheriff Traulich would burn it himself."

I normally wouldn't talk to a woman at my own bar, and I'd promised myself I wouldn't sleep around. But that morning, I'd run over a silver heart Harry Winston keychain as I pulled out. Since it felt insignificant, like an out-of-place stone, I opened the gate and continued. I almost hit the white Jaguar parked across the driveway on the street.

The return of my gift had hurt, even though it shouldn't have. I should have expected it. Of course Monica wouldn't accept it after what happened. She was still honorable. I'd managed to leave that intact. I looked in the glove compartment for the navel ring and didn't find it. I was sure it would turn up on my desk.

But it didn't, and that confused me. I'd gone up to the bar to verbally pistol-whip Freddie about hiring a sixteen-year-old to carry drinks, and to think about not thinking about Monica. The first got done, the second was interrupted by the blonde in the blue dress.

"... and they all play country music," she said.

I'd missed something, and I didn't care. I'd never actually needed to care before, but that had changed. The woman in a blue dress was a nice person, by all accounts, but I had no interest in sleeping with her.

I couldn't hear my phone over the music, but I felt it buzz in my pocket. My first thought was the memory of Monica's song, but I'd blocked her. There would be no more songs. It was Eddie.

—Cancel Thursday night. I have to go to the
Collectors thing. You going?—

"Hang on a second," I said. "Let me take this." The woman in the blue dress nodded. She wasn't boring or easy. She was fine, but she wasn't a goddess.

—Nope—

—Ok. Monica said you weren't going.
Just checking.—

I dialed his number and walked to the hall with my finger pressing my free ear closed. "What does Monica have to do with it?"

"Carnival is sending her with me. Why? You don't trust me?"

"No, I don't. You're a lousy driver."

"She's driving herself. See, I knew you'd flip out."

"I'm not flipping out."

"You are flipping out," he said. I got into the elevator. "It's business. I'm not touching her, okay? Harry would have my ass, and God only knows you'd bean me in my sleep or something."

"I apologized."

"Whatever. I knew I had to explicitly say something, and that's what I'm doing. Don't flip out."

"Okay, Ed," I said as I walked into the hotel lobby. Michelle, the rooms manager, tried to stop me with something I was sure I didn't care about. I waved her off and headed for the exit. It was pouring rain, and I had no umbrella.

I was flipping out.

Chapter 32

Monica

Darren waved from the Frontage bar. It was crowded. I did some meet and greet before I made my way to him and Adam.

"Thank you," I said when he handed me the keys to my Honda. When Jonathan had said he'd replaced the starter, he obviously meant "with a new car" because the Honda had still been missing a piece.

"Came to three-twenty-five," he said.

"I'll have it for you tomorrow."

"Damn right you will. Because you owe him." He indicated Adam, who put his arm around my waist.

"I'm taking it out in kisses." He planted his mouth on my cheek, and I squealed. He held me harder and I laughed louder, playfully punching his shoulder and forgetting Jonathan for half a second. Adam was a good guy. I owed him and Darren for towing my Honda from the Stock parking lot to a repair shop, paying for the work, and driving it to me. Kisses and a few hundred bucks were the least I could do.

"It's in the lot," Darren said once Adam let me go before I got cooties.

"Where are you guys off to?"

"Loft party at the Family Four. You coming? Dizzy Roth wanted to talk about the B.C. Mod piece."

That sounded like the best offer I would get. "I'll meet you there."

Chapter 33

Jonathan

I'd tried to let the world spin on its usual course for two days. I tried to see what would happen if I just worked, stared at the ceiling, and avoided Monica. I didn't ask Eddie if he was *really* going with her, and I didn't ask Margie about Dad's attendance. That lasted twenty-four hours. I found myself in the pouring rain at Frontage, watching at her through the window.

She was smiling. Darren was there, but he didn't concern me. The other guy kissed her cheek, and she laughed. I stepped out from the bus shelter, into the rain. He touched her waist, and she permitted it.

I don't know what brought the clarity. It could have been the kiss. It could have been the touching. But the laughter put me over the edge. Seeing her with her friends, as free of me as I'd made her, without all the destruction I'd brought. Happy, while I could barely have a straight thought without her voice invading.

I had wanted to talk to her. That was it. Just tell her I didn't want her to go to the Collector's Board thing because my father would be there, and I simply didn't want her near him. I was soaking wet in the middle of Santa Monica Boulevard, wondering if I should hurl myself through the window or the door, as if those were the only rational choices.

I was on my way to the door when they were on their way out. I moved fast. That was always my advantage, not strength but speed and agility. I had the guy against the wall, crushed against the umbrella he'd started to open, before he'd even seen me.

"What the—"

"Jonathan!" Her voice. It sounded very far away. I had the guy's eyes on mine. He looked confused, and I wanted to kill him for not knowing what had upset me.

Monica. Even with the rain in her hair and in her eyes while she was snarling like a lion, I wanted her. What the fuck had I been thinking?

"God damn it. What is *wrong* with you?" She pushed me off the guy who had kissed her, then pushed me again. "You are fucked, you know that?"

I stepped back. She stood between him and me, hands out, ready to take me on. I couldn't get to him without knocking her over. "Move. Just move."

"Are you serious?"

"You're mine. No one puts his hands on you. No one."

The three of them stared at me for a second, then Monica jerked out her thumb. "This guy?"

"That guy."

"Okay, besides the fact that you walked out on me—"

"Enough!"

The voice that cut the rain was near as powerful as anything I'd heard. Had a car alarm gone off from the vibrations, I would not have been surprised. It was Darren. Little pipsqueak snapped me right out of it. I went from rage to shame before he was finished with the last syllable.

"I have *had it* with the two of you," Darren shouted. "I am sick and tired of the whining from you"—he pointed at Monica—"and the psychotic behavior from you." He pointed at me. "Stop acting like a dick and throwing money at her. Stop breaking up. Just stop. The next time I hear you two broke up, I'm sending out wedding invitations."

I was struck silent. A part of me smiled, but it wasn't my mouth.

Darren took the hand of the guy who had kissed Monica and pulled him away. Of course, the coupling had never been Monica and him but Darren and him. I opened my mouth to apologize, but Darren wasn't facing me. Rain soaked my shirt, dripping under my collar. I'd never felt so ridiculous. Losing my temper never had good results. Monica hugged them both and came back to me. Her skirt stuck to her legs and her shoes sloshed, but she took her time.

"Do you feel like an ass?" she said.

"Yeah," I said. "How did you get here?"

"Little black Honda."

"Can I walk you?"

"Did you bring an umbrella? Because you broke mine."

I took my leather jacket off and held it over her head.

"Chivalry will get you nowhere," she said.

I sensed she meant it. A drop of water fell from her nose to her lower lip, and I had to swallow the desire to kiss it away. "I need to talk to you."

"Really?" Sarcasm dripped from her.

She started walking, and I followed her. She kept too far away for my jacket, so I just rolled it over my arm. We walked down the block, getting ever more wet with each step.

Chapter 34

Monica

The neighborhood was residential, lined with single-family houses and the occasional apartment building. Wet, brown leaves covered every car, curb, and grassy patch. We said nothing the entire walk to my car. I was getting wet, but he was soaked. His hair was dark brown with water, and his eyelashes stuck together in points of four or five. He looked down, hands in his pockets. He must have been freezing.

I stopped by my car. "This is me. Thanks for walking me."

"You could have kept the car I got you." He put his hand on the wet bark of the parkway tree.

"I know. I drove it to my meeting because this one wasn't fixed yet. So, thanks for the loaner."

"I don't like us when we're formal. All please and thank you."

"What do you want then?" I crossed my arms.

He pursed his lips and looked at my feet, then back up to my face. "I want you to be real with me."

"You want me to be real?"

"Yeah."

"Real. You want real?"

"Real, goddess."

"You *blocked* me, you motherfucker!" I pushed his shoulders, and he stepped back into the tree trunk. "I wrote you that song, and you were so disgusted, you blocked me." I pushed him again, but he had nowhere to go.

"I had to."

"Oh, let's hear about that."

"If you kept sending me shit like that, I was going to come back to you."

"As opposed to what? This?" I spread my arms to indicate the block, the rain, our bodies almost touching, the fight over who was allowed to kiss me.

"I knew if I saw you again, I'd want you." He was pleading, leaning forward, hands out as if passing me a basketball pumped full of pain. "That fucking mouth. As soon as it opened, I knew I'd want to kiss you. And those wet clothes sticking to you. And the hair plastered to your face. You're custom made for me to hurt. Do you understand?"

I understood all too well. "Hurt me."

"Monica, that's not what I mean."

"Ruin me."

"Stop."

I stepped forward. "Destroy me, Jonathan."

He cursed under his breath and pushed his lips to mine. His movements were fierce, his tongue invading my mouth, his arms circling me. He tasted of fennel toothpaste and whiskey, the same as the first time I'd kissed him. The memories went down the curve in my back and settled between my legs. He pushed me into the car, pressing his erection into me, and I pushed back, letting his hardness find my cleft. I groaned into his mouth.

"God," he said, "I have to have you."

"Take me. Own me. Use me. Pick a verb. Just, please."

"Fuck you. I'm going to fuck you. That's my verb."

He pushed his hips into me hard, and I bent my neck in response. My legs wrapped around him, grinding. Water dripped from his forehead onto mine as he kissed me. The rain had gone from a heavy mist to a driving torrent. He straightened and pulled me off the car.

"Take me home," I practically had to shout over the weather.

He pushed me against the car and kissed me in the rain one more time.

Chapter 35

We fumbled up the steps with lips attached, past the porch swing where he'd tried and failed to break my heart, into the living room, where we dripped little pools of water like a reverse archipelago behind us. I took his hand and walked him into the laundry room.

The laundry room was a foul, filthy place, and I was immediately ashamed of it. When I cleaned the house, the laundry room was the last floor to get a mop-over and the last sink to get wiped clean. So nine times out of ten, I just didn't bother. And there I was, with a guy who had a team of people clean his corners with Q-tips, dripping onto gross, 1980s-era linoleum. It was the first water that floor had seen in months.

"It's a mess in here," I said, turning away from the towels I had strung up to dry, weeks ago.

He put his arms behind me and unzipped my dress. I noticed his chattering jaw and the ice of his fingertips as they grazed my spine.

"What does that have to do with me fucking you?" He peeled off my dress. My bra cups were heavy, soaked, hanging off me, and he slipped the straps off my shoulders, easily releasing me. I was down to panties and shoes, and he was still freezing in wet clothes.

Pushing him against the dryer, I unbuttoned his shirt, kissing down the center of his torso as I went. He was damp, and I warmed him with my mouth, licking his hard, tight, nipples. His arms came out of his sleeves like a molting caterpillar. I threw his shirt on top of my dress on the floor and worked on his pants while he kissed me.

"On your knees," he said.

I got down, eye-level to his crotch, and opened his pants. The zipper didn't work well wet, but I got it down. I hooked my fingers in the waistband and took his briefs down with the pants, arcing the elastic over his erection. He stepped out of the legs, kicking off his shoes while he did, and held up a foot. I peeled off his sock, then did the same with the other foot. He was naked. Perfect. I gazed up at him, his perfect, lean body with its cut lines and furrows making a triangle from his hips to the beauty between his legs.

I took his cock in my mouth, licking every surface as if to warm it. He put his hands in my hair and groaned.

"Let me feel you."

He held my head still and pushed his cock all the way down my throat, balls-deep. I breathed through my nose, the aroma of his wet skin filling me. He held me still, and when I looked up at him, he was watching me. He slid out slowly. I put my tongue against him as he did.

"Have I mentioned you're very good at this?" he asked.

"Yes."

"Stand up."

When I did, he gathered up the clothes and put them in the dryer. He stared at the buttons and smiled.

"You have no idea how to use this, do you?" I asked.

"Not the knobs, no."

I turned the machine on. Jonathan picked me up by the waist and put me on top of it. The dryer shook and rattled under me.

"Lean back," he said, "and spread those knees for me." He slid a finger under the crotch of my panties. I drew in a breath. His fingers moved from my entrance to my clit. "You're wet." He slid his fingers in me. They were cold.

"God, yes."

He pushed my knees farther apart with his free hand. "Tell me what you want."

"I want you."

"You want me, what?"

I wanted his cock in me. I wanted to come. I wanted him to do whatever he wanted to make me scream and beg for him. I looked at him, his perfect skin mottled with goose bumps, his nipples hard with cold, hair still wet. For the first time, I noticed the blue tinge around his lips. "I want you to dry off. You look hypothermic."

I snapped a towel off the line and put it over his head, leaning forward to dry his hair. He let me, drawing me closer as I caressed his head more slowly and gently as he got drier. I hopped off the dryer and ran the towel all over him, chest to back to glorious butt to muscular legs and the tops of his perfect feet. Wrapping the towel around his shoulders, I kissed him.

"I feel better already," he said.

"You need something warm to drink. I have tea."

"You? Tea?"

"You can pick a flavor. Come on."

He picked me up as if he was carrying me over a threshold, brought me to the kitchen, naked but for my underpants, and deposited me on the counter. I leaned to the shelf and got my teapot, then leaned the other way and filled it. I gave it to him, and he put it on the stove.

"The tea's on the shelf above," I said. "I have some assortment thingie in the back."

"Assortment thingie. Let me see." He found the box and brought it back, but he didn't open it. I put my legs around his hips, drawing him to me. He stroked my eyebrow with his thumb. "I'm sorry. I was cruel last night. I said terrible things."

"Yes, you did."

"And I blocked you. I knew it would hurt you, and I did it anyway. What you sent made me question my actions. I wasn't ready to question them. I thought I'd done the right thing, protecting you from me. I'm still not convinced otherwise."

"Does that mean you're going to leave me again? Because Darren's going to shit if you do."

"Fuck Darren."

"Don't leave me to protect me, Jonathan. I'm a grown woman, and I'm perfectly capable of ruining my life without your help."

"Yes, Mistress." A smile stretched across his face as he chose a black tea and held out the box for me.

"Not kidding." I snapped out a chamomile. "I mean it. I had to hold my shit together for a meeting the next day, and it was the hardest thing I ever did."

"But you did it."

"Yeah, but—"

"I'm proud of you." He put his hand on my cheek, and we kissed until the teapot whistled. He shrugged his towel tighter and poured the steaming water into two cups, dropping in the teabags.

"I called Margie," I said, crossing my legs and waiting for my tea to cool. "She's getting an entertainment lawyer from her firm to work with me. I'm sorry if that was wrong."

"It's fine. She likes you. You're the eighth sister she never had."

I cleared my throat. "And you know that thing? That collector's party?"

He glanced up at me, head bent toward his tea. "The Collector's Board at L.A. Mod. Of course."

"Carnival is a donor, so they're sending Eddie. They want me to go with him. It's part of presenting me as an artist." I saw him tense, changing the angle of the towel draped on his shoulders. "It's business."

"Absolutely not."

I was silent as I stared at him over the rim of my cup.

"Monica?"

"Jonathan."

"He wants to fuck you."

"I don't think you're actually threatened by Eddie Milpas."

He rubbed his eyes. "I'll tell you what. You'll go with me."

"Really?"

"Really."

"Oh, Jonathan, I'd so much rather go with you."

"I want you to be warned it's all Jessica's crowd. They're nasty. They're bored and rich. If you're with me, you're a target for their boredom."

"I don't care."

He put his face to mine. I smelled the tea on his breath. "They'll whisper about you."

"Fuck them."

"We found the whole audio on her phone, and we posted it online. It's gone crazy. Everyone knows."

I got closer, put my nose next to his, and whispered, "What part of 'fuck them' was unclear?"

"That's my goddess." He pressed his face to mine, his mouth open only enough to move them in time with me, giving me a kiss made purely of lips and skin. There was sex in the kiss, but only the wafting hint of his breathing. Then he slipped his tongue between my lips, and my spine tingled as if some unholy spirit used my vertebrae as piano keys.

I groaned. My mouth accepted his darting tongue, the command of his lips. I arched when his hand slipped down to my breast, grazing the back of his hand against my hard nipple.

"Take me," I whispered into his mouth.

"I'll do as I like," he said into mine, and I felt the force of his words in the pressure between my legs. The personality change that accompanied play was so stark that the first utterance in his stern, serious voice, made my cleft quiver like a plucked string. "Hands behind you on the counter. One on top of the other."

I did it. He put his hand at the small of my back and pressed upward until I was arched and facing the ceiling.

"You need to go back to Bordelle." He pulled my knees apart roughly. "This cotton shit is unworthy." Opening two drawers, he placed my feet on the edges so my legs stayed open. I heard the clink of silverware. "This thing," he said before I heard the soft crunch of fabric being cut. He'd sheared my panties with a steak knife. "It offends me."

"Yes, sir."

He ran his hand over me. I couldn't see what he was doing. I felt his dry skin awaken nerve endings, grazing over my breasts, belly, thighs. Even the slightest pressure sent shards of pain at the black-and-blue base of my rib cage and the soft meat between my legs, a punctuation for the pleasure of his touch.

"You're still bruised," he said. "That'll take time to heal."

"Don't stop."

"I'm going to be gentle where you're hurt," he said. "But everywhere else is mine."

"Yes."

"Now, you want your tea?"

"Yes, sir." Though my body was awake with desire, my voice was husky with heat and exhaustion. My vocal cords hadn't forgotten that it was close to midnight.

He pressed my mouth open with his thumb and forefinger, as if I was a kitten taking medicine. The teabag hovered over my face, dripping hot liquid over my mouth. I felt hot fluid on my lip and the dry, waxen taste of chamomile tea on my tongue. It traveled down my chin and my throat. I swallowed it like an offering of communion.

"Thank you, sir."

I closed my eyes, feeling the warmth of dripping tea down my chest. He must have dipped the bag back into the cup because the heat renewed on my nipples. Lines of molten liquid dripped down around my ribs to my back. I gasped when he put the bag on my belly and dragged it down to the edge of my triangle. I quivered in anticipation. That hot thing, on me. Soft and pliant, yet firm in its burning intensity. But he didn't. He leaned over, kissing and licking the tea from me. He sucked my nipple gently as his hand stayed on the teabag, which felt as though it as cooling too fast.

I groaned. I had never thought to put a hot teabag on my clit, but it was all I could think about. He had to do it. Had to. Before it got cold.

When he moved his mouth to the other nipple, cleaning it with his tongue and lips, he slid the bag down, pressing it against my clit with the heel of his hand while putting two fingers in me. I yelled. Hot. Not straight-from-the-pot hot, but hot enough. Ten times hotter on my clit than anywhere else, and the fire added exponentially to my desire. Hot tea dripped down my cleft. I shuddered everywhere, spreading my legs wider, pushing into his fingers. His tongue was still at my nipple, and I was bruised, yes, but I wanted him to bite it. I wanted him to hurt me. I was addicted to it.

He pushed his hand against me, heel on hot teabag on clit, fingers in cunt, and he rubbed them in circles. My pussy drank it. The bag got drier as the tea was squeezed out of it, making it rougher, like crackling leaves in the fall. The little scratches from hot, sticklike herbs drove me to the edge.

"I want to come," I cried.

"No."

"I can't." I opened my eyes to find him looking down at me.

"You're mine. No matter what happens. Your pleasure and pain. Your skin. Your lips. Your cunt."

He pushed the bag and his fingers into me. "Jonathan. You own me. I am yours. God, who else? Fuck. Please. My king. Please let me—"

"Come."

With a sharp movement, he brought me to orgasm in my kitchen again. I thrust against his hand, screaming, back twisting. He put his other hand behind my head so I didn't bang it on the cabinet, and when I found myself winding around to the point where I almost kicked out a drawer, he caught me, panting and naked.

"Thank you," was all I could say.

"You're welcome."

"God, I love you."

"And I, you," he said softly. "You still want tea?"

"It's cold," I said into his ear. "I don't like it cold."

"You have it all over you. Let me get you in the shower."

He took me to my bathroom and got me into the tub. I stood under the water, letting it run where the tea had.

Jonathan got in, exquisitely naked, taut, lean, skin over muscle over bone in perfect proportion. I didn't know if he worked out. I didn't know where he'd find the time. He could just be the way he was with no effort whatsoever, and that was all right with me.

"You just dried off," I said. "And I'm making you get wet again." I put the bar of soap to his chest and rubbed, working over his shoulders slowly, and back to his nipples, to his tight stomach. His erection was huge, waiting, a sign of things to come. I stroked it with the soap. I didn't want to rush. I wanted to take him in fully, in all his beauty, touch every surface, feel every bump and curve.

His eyes went over my body as I washed him. I cleaned his back by putting my arms around him, feeling his dick press against me. He took me by my hair and pulled my head back. The water got in my face, and I smiled. He wet my hair as he kissed my neck. He squeezed too much shampoo into my hair and massaged my scalp. The suds were everywhere. I laughed when they went into my eyes, and he laughed too, pressing his thumbs to my eyes to stroke the suds away. I was covered in shampoo, and Jonathan used it to bathe me, sliding his hands where the tea had gone. He went gently where I was hurt, roughly where I wasn't, until he got to where the teabag had made me come, and I groaned.

"Ah, goddess…" He slid his hand under my ass, his fingertips slipping into my folds. They were wet but not from the shower.

"Again, please."

"Put your hands up to the showerhead." I did, and his followed the line of my arms, cupping his hands over mine, sliding them to the pipe that held the shower head. "Hold that."

My arms up as if tied, he pushed me against the tiles and put one of my legs around his waist. The head of his cock sat at my entrance, waiting. I pushed against him, and where his member touched me, my body responded in waves of pleasure. He kissed me, hands at my ass, spreading me apart with his fingers.

"Please," I said. "I want you."

"I'm yours." He thrust into me. It felt like an electric shock through my body, pulsing as he thrust, every inch adding to the pressure. I was full, engorged, all surface area for him. "Look at me."

I opened my eyes. His hair was soaked. Rivulets of water dripped down the angles of his cheeks and neck as his hips worked into me. He pulled my ass open and slipped in a finger. Just a finger. Exquisite. The pleasure with none of the pain. I clenched around him.

"Soon, when you're healed, I'm taking this ass again," he said.

"It's yours."

He pushed another finger in, and his eyelids dropped a little. I groaned, feeling stretched and possessed, as though every part of me was under his control and protection.

"Look at me when you come," he said.

"I'm close." My arms ached, but I didn't move them, just held the pipe above me because he commanded it.

"Yes." He went faster, pushing into me. He used the fingers in my asshole to draw our bodies together fast and hard as he slapped against me.

My clit filled, my cunt opened with sensation, my ass sucked him in. "Oh, God Jonathan. Jonathan." I looked in his eyes, holding his face still in my vision.

"Come with me."

"Yes."

I released. The effort of keeping my face to his while I came prolonged the orgasm that washed over me. My arms were frozen. I couldn't arch or close my eyes. I just exploded in a controlled way, toes curling, my hands gripping the pipe. My cries echoed against the tile walls. My vision blurred. His mouth opened, and he grunted a long slow vibration, slowing, pulsing in a different rhythm. His eyes and mine watched each other, locked in pleasure, above and below.

Chapter 36

Jonathan

The house was as dark, and the rain and cloud cover had darkened it further. We tucked each other into bed, and I curled against her. I shifted her T-shirt and kissed her shoulder, moving my lips across it. She tasted of warm milk and canned peaches.

"My Jonathan," she groaned.

"I'm not making a pass at you."

She turned to face me. "Like hell."

"I think you'll help me sleep."

"You never sleep much."

"Well, I've been sleeping less, and I don't feel right. Not since the arrest. And since Rachel." I cleared my throat when I choked on her name. My neck and arms hurt as if the nerves were being squeezed. I broke out in a sweat. Ridiculous. I tried to get control of myself, but it was hard to breathe. I must have been coming down with something.

She turned around to face me. "You ever going to forgive yourself for that?"

"I'll get around to it."

"You're going to give yourself ulcers."

I didn't answer. Talking about my irrational emotional issues wouldn't get either one of us to sleep, and we both needed it. I stroked her eyebrows as I'd done before, getting her eyes to flutter closed. She sighed and let me touch her, relaxing. Our legs got heavy together as she released the spring of tension binding them. She seemed on the edge of sleep, breathing regularly and softly. Her eyes stayed closed when I stroked her hair. Then she opened them.

"You're wide awake," she said.

"It's all right."

She sat up. "No, it's not."

I tried to sit up with her, but she pushed me down. I was stronger, of course, but I let her press my shoulders to the mattress.

"Stay here," she said.

She rolled off the bed and padded away. I didn't know where she was going or what she intended, but I hoped it didn't involve Xanax or alcohol. I didn't want to fight about that or anything. She came back with a viola and bow slung over her shoulder like a batter coming off the on-deck circle. If I'd ever seen anything as sexy as Monica Faulkner in a stretched-out T-shirt and wielding a stringed instrument, I'd be at pains to remember it.

"You going to knock me unconscious with that thing?"

"One way or the other." She crawled on the bed, leaving one foot on the floor and stretching her body so the instrument fit under her chin. She drew the bow across, making it hum, then turned a knob at the top of the neck. I slipped closer until my lips touched her thigh. "Any requests?"

"Something bombastic. With percussion."

She laughed and played a measure. I recognized it right away as Mendelssohn's "Evening Song." She was all right, my woman. What she was trying wouldn't work, but the honest attempt wouldn't go unappreciated. I stroked her knee with my thumb as she played and rocked her body with the slow rhythm of the song. The piece was short, and when it ended, she riffed on the melody, smoothing it further. Her hips rocked the mattress like waves on the ocean. I stroked her knee, then stopped, placing my hand on her leg.

I listened with my eyes closed, feeling her sway, hearing her music, as it got farther and farther away. The sounds of the ocean outside the window grew louder, and the water rose, coming over the sill and flowing onto her floor. She must not have noticed the flood or care about the fact that her house would probably float right down the hill, because she kept playing and rocking. I was too heavy, too weak, too contented, to stop her.

The rain got louder and harder, dropping into my eyes, blinding me. My stomach was in complete upheaval, and my head swam as the waves pulled me out to sea. I had a dead weight dragging down my right arm. It was a person. A woman. Monica? I'd let her face go under while I fought the tide. I pulled her up, the effort twisting my stomach. Her mouth was full of water, and her eyes were glassed over.

The scene was mine. I'd been blacked out from half a bottle of whiskey, but things had happened, and my brain had stored them deep.

"Rachel, baby, come on!" But even saying the words took more energy than I had.

I looked upward, to safety, and saw only sheer cliffs between us and the street above. The beach had drowned under forty nights of rain, and we were about to as well. No one knew we were there. Most of the population of Palos Verdes was away for Christmas.

So it was on me. I had to do was keep our heads over the water and not drift too far out, a simple task that became more difficult as the minutes wore on. The car drifted away, the headlights getting dimmer as it drifted out to sea. I'd been thrown clear, saved by inertia and a body limber and pain free from conspicuous alcohol consumption. Rachel was sober and stuck, but somehow, I'd jumped in and pulled her from the car.

I looked up the cliff again, the rain dropping in my eyes. It was a black edge, cutting the starry sky in half. Hopeless. Going down had been as easy as a running jump. Getting back up would be impossible. I tried to keep our heads above water, and failed, and tried again, and failed again.

A light.

Two lights.

A car parked right at the edge of the cliff. I tried to cry out, but I had nothing left. The noise of the ocean and the rain would have drowned out even the most powerful scream. All I had was my body and my last bits of strength. I swam toward the lights, pushing against the current, and saw that the driver had found a way to crawl down.

The driver was my father.

He wore the khaki trench coat I'd looked for at Sheila's house. I'd wanted his keys so I could chase Rachel. I'd seen him out the window, going after her, and run out. That's how he knew we were there. Thank God for him. I'd never been grateful for my father before. I looked at Rachel. She'd become a dead weight in my arms, but I pulled her up. A wave caught us. A lucky break. I smacked against the rocks, managing to put myself between them and Rachel. My father got thigh deep in the water, grabbed my collar, and pulled me onto the ledge. I climbed with him, pulling Rachel. Dad grabbed her and helped us up. I collapsed at the top.

"This is going to cost me, son." My father's voice. "It's going to *cost*."

The world swam as if I was riding the teacups at Disney. I opened my eyes. In front of me, so close I had no context but a few blades of grass, the dark, rainy night, and my own nausea, was Rachel's face. She too had her cheek to the grass. Her eyes glazed over. Her mouth hung open. Her hair stuck to her face. She blinked, and a tear fell over the bridge of her nose.

She faded, like a movie going to black, and the sound of the rain in Echo Park replaced the sixteen-year-old remembrance. Monica breathed in my ear in the rhythms of sleep. Outside, I heard traffic, a bus on Echo Park Avenue, and the children playing in the Montessori school yard. I opened my eyes, as if waking not from a dream but a resurrected memory.

It was morning, and finally, Rachel was free.

Chapter 37

Monica

I wore one of the dresses he'd bought me in Vancouver, sleeveless black one with a skirt that fell half an inch from the floor. The neckline so low it required a special bra that had been hanging with it. He requested I wear it, and it was magnificent.

I covered the yellowing bruises with a little makeup, draping hair, and whatever accessories I could gather. I wouldn't stand up to a forensics team, but at night, in a dark party, maybe I wouldn't have to crack a joke or tell a lie.

I'd wanted to take my own car, but Jonathan insisted on letting Lil drive, so I waited on my porch for the Bentley. It was exactly on time. Lil let Jonathan out the back. He wore a navy suit and a tie of darkest pink. His shirt was white and pressed, and he was perfect. I started down the porch steps, and he held up his hand.

"Come on, Monica. Give a guy a chance to get you at the door."

I stopped and waited. He opened the chain-link fence that seemed cheap and worn next to his cleanly pressed self. He walked up the short, cracked concrete that led to my broken wooden steps.

"Are you ready?" he asked, taking my hand.

"It's just a party."

"No, it's going to be ugly."

I kissed him once on the lips. "I've been to high school."

"The stakes are higher."

"I'm not staying home. I got all dressed up."

"Ah, speaking of…" He removed a long, thin box from his pocket. I recognized the Harry Winston dark blue.

"Jesus, Jonathan, you're going overboard."

"Yes. I am. I don't have a viola." I took the box. Cursing him out while I was smiling would be hard. I undid the ribbon. He took it and rolled it around his fingers. When I looked at him quizzically, he said, "Might need this later."

"If the ribbon is the real gift, you could save a ton of money by just getting me empty boxes."

I lifted the top. Inside the box, a flat platinum chain curled around itself. I pulled it out. It wasn't a loop connected at the end but a long strand. It had to be five feet long, with jewel-encrusted drops the size of blackberries. One sparkled with sapphires, the other, emeralds.

"A lariat," I said. "My God, it's beautiful. Can you put it on me?"

He looped the strand around my neck once, draping it so the jeweled drops fell just below my breasts. "Green emeralds for sea. Blue sapphires for sky."

"Thank you." I kissed him. "It's perfect."

"I'm glad you like it."

"You're going to make it tough for me at Christmas."

"We'll figure out some kind of trade."

"And don't think I don't see what you're doing." I pulled the strand on one side, looped it around my neck a second time, and pulled tight. The smooth, flat links clicked against one another, easily tightening around my throat. "Makes a lovely collar."

He laughed. Taking the blue drop, he unlooped it and rearranged the necklace until it was loose. "Let's not rush." He took my hand, and we went to the car.

Chapter 38

Monica

He got a call on the way. He mumbled a few syllables and relaxed visibly. When he hung up, he squeezed my hand.

"What?" I asked.

"My mother isn't *feeling well*," he said, the last two words emphasized as if it was some sort of code. "We may actually have a good time if I keep you away from the harpies."

"I can handle harpies and your family."

"I'm not keeping any secrets about my parents that you don't already know. But I'd like you to be unsullied as long as possible."

"I won't think less of you because of them."

"Give me some time."

He didn't try to fuck me on the way, though our lips met so often that I had to reapply lipstick when we arrived. We stood in the parking lot as Lil drove away. Other sleek cars discharged people in expensive shoes and suits. The lights glared as I used the valet window as a mirror, lipstick hovering. Jonathan snapped the tube from my hand before it touched my face and kissed me again.

"'Soul meets soul on lovers' lips.'" He kissed me, then put his mouth to my cheek, and back to my ear. "Except when wax and pigment come between them."

"Barrett Browning?"

"Percy Shelley."

"And the second part?"

He turned my lipstick tube until the brand was visible. "Lancome, apparently." He fondled the emerald end of my lariat as if it was part of my body. "I can't wait for this circus to be over." He shifted closer and whispered, "I'm taking you home, and I'm going to tie your wrists to the

354

banister. I'm going to blindfold you, then I'm going to undress you slowly. I'll put my lips all over you until you beg me to take you, which I may or may not do."

"Jonathan," I whispered, his name a white flag of surrender.

"Did you just shudder, or is it cold in this parking lot?"

"Was there anyone before you?"

"You might have thought so at the time."

"I feel like no one's ever loved me before."

"I'm sure they did their best, but you always belonged to me."

The parking lot's lights were fluorescent and cold, but his gaze was more than warm—it was hot and fixed. I did indeed feel as though I'd never been loved before. At least not correctly. Not with purpose.

He broke our connection to glance over my shoulder, then back to my face. "Vipers descending."

I looked back. Jessica, wearing purple and cream, walked with a crowd, her hand clutching the arm of a man with an athletic build. I nodded at her. She did not nod back. She looked away to make conversation with a ruddy-cheeked man rather than engage me at all. A face I knew stood out from the crowd.

"Geraldine," I said. "Wow. Hi."

Trompe l'oile street artist Geraldine Stark looked at me, then Jonathan, and smiled. She'd let her curly brown hair go wild and wove sparkled strands through it. Her dress was a macramé shift of a thousand colors over a black satin slip. She gave me a Los Angeles hug, but I felt her eyes on Jonathan, who kept his hand on my back.

"Oh my God," she said. "Did you hear about Kevin?"

"No, I—"

To my side, Jonathan greeted Mr. Athletic. They shared words I couldn't concentrate on. As the crowd moved toward the elevators, I heard Jessica laugh behind me. Her voice was caught in the lilt of small talk and joyful greetings.

"He's stuck in Boise," Geraldine hissed. "Three years."

"What? Why?"

"His parole is real strict. He gets actual jail time. They're *pissed*. So…"

She glanced at Jonathan, then back at me as we stepped into the elevator. She thought I didn't know she'd been with him. She thought she would surprise me for dramatic effect. She thought wrong. Looking meaningfully at me, then at Jonathan, who spoke to the blond guy, she muttered, "Have you heard about your date? It's all over town."

"The thing about Kevin is terrible. Honestly." The news shook me. I didn't care if she'd fucked Jonathan a couple of nights back when I didn't know he existed. I didn't care if she wanted to rub my face in it for fun. Jesus Christ, I knew the guy wasn't a virgin. A hundred woman in the city could commiserate on my lover's prowess if I were the commiserating type. Which I wasn't. I was the type who got upset when her ex-boyfriend went to jail. "It's awful."

Geraldine looked away. I hoped she was ashamed.

"We incorporated light into the design," Jessica said to someone I couldn't see. "The right temperature of light was the hardest to achieve. We wound up finding old tungsten bulbs in a warehouse in Torrance."

The doors opened onto the patio at L.A. Mod, which had been decked out in hanging lanterns and silver streamers. The effect was beautiful, incandescent, as if a few dozen artists had collaborated on the décor.

"Five minutes," Jonathan said in my ear as the crowd filed out. "Stay in my sight."

Geraldine's date pulled her with the tide out toward the patio, but not before she grabbed my hand and said "*Do it...*" She laughed as she disappeared into the throng.

Photographers and reporters waited, and the flashing lights made me wince. I waved to her quickly to say good-bye, and she waved back. I wished she'd stayed, even to talk about sex or prison time, because I was alone. Jonathan was ten feet away by a serving stand, talking in serious tones to the light-haired guy. Jessica was surrounded by a gaggle of people, all laughing as if they didn't have a care in the world. Jonathan and the big guy looked as though they were going to come to blows. He glanced at me and held out his hand in a slight gesture that meant "stay away."

The elevator doors slid open and another group got out. I heard the phrase again, though Geraldine was far from me.

Do it...

It sounded recorded. I looked behind me. Two girls stared at a phone, the light glowing on their faces.

Do it...

One pocketed the phone when they stepped onto the patio, giggling.

Jonathan's conversation wasn't going well. I couldn't stand there. I just couldn't. I walked over.

"Hi," I said. Jonathan slipped his hand over my shoulder. "I'm Monica." I held out my hand. The blond guy didn't take it.

"You stole something from my house."

Jonathan pulled me closer. I felt his body inching between the other man and me. "This conversation is over."

"It hasn't started. I've got a lawyer."

He seemed aggressive and off-kilter. As big as he was, he was so non-threatening, I couldn't be scared. He was handsome and looked fine in his tuxedo, but he wasn't wearing it... it was wearing *him*. He had no presence, no voice, no significance. Then I realized who he was. Erik. The man Jessica left Jonathan for.

That woman needed a cunt transplant.

"All these phones look alike," I said. "It was dark. I thought it was mine." I pursed my lips, trying to keep my mouth in some kind of line that didn't resemble a smile. But I failed on some level. He didn't believe me. A four-year-old wouldn't have believed me.

"You know what he did?" Erik said. "To her?" He jerked his thumb in the general direction of where Jessica may have been standing.

"I hear she was asking for it." The elevator dinged behind me.

"You're both sick," Erik said.

"O'Drassen!" A voice came from behind us, at the elevator. Jonathan turned me around and led me toward Eddie. He wore a white jacket and black tie, his hair combed into a pompadour.

"Ed," Jonathan said, "take care of her." He pushed me toward the guy he'd objected to taking me to the event in the first place.

"No problem," Eddie replied. "And I'm doing great, by the way. Thanks for asking."

"I mean it. Not out of your sight."

Some guy thing happened between them, because Eddie stuck out his hand and Jonathan shook it, taking him by the bicep. Then he kissed me. "Be good." He turned back to Erik, who had been joined by a man with darker hair and ruddy cheeks.

"I feel like I'm stranded in Manland," I said to Eddie.

"You are."

As we went into the throng of photographers, I glanced back to find Jonathan and Erik talking heatedly as if I hadn't even interrupted.

"You ready to be Carnival's newest face?" asked Eddie.

"Unless you try to put me in a leather mask."

"Yeah, well that's off the table. Coulda made a lot of money. This new idea's a clunker."

"You could drop me."

"And let some douchebag from Vintage pick you up? Hell, no."

The flashing lights were blinding. Between the women in sequins and the men wearing black, it was a high-contrast world. I heard laughter and chirpy voices. I heard clearly one phrase had caught on. It was whispered and shouted and giggled over.

Do it...

I had my customer service smile ready. My hand was on Eddie's arm, but I kept my body far from his. I didn't want to embarrass Jonathan, and I didn't want to appear weak and needy. Those pictures would end up in music and art trades. If I acted like a piece of arm candy for a record executive, I'd have to explain, then prove that I wasn't.

The cocktail hour was a whirlwind of drinks, cameras, and questions. Who was I? Why was I there? I talked about the B.C. Mod show with Unnamed Trio, which brought Kevin to mind. I tried not to think about him. I talked about my gigs at Frontage, the possibility of a contract, and my education. There were no softball questions about music. The reporters were from art trades, so there was no talk of art itself, only the business of art. I brushed shoulders with Jessica once. We glanced at each other and moved on. It was business.

Eddie and I milled with the guests outside a huge pair of wooden doors. A woman in a red jacket had come by with a man behind her. He carried a silver tray filled with metal lapel pins. Gold, silver, and rhinestone. She asked our names, then selected a gold pin from her assistant's tray and gave it to Eddie. She gave me a rhinestone. I had no idea what it meant. Glancing around, I could easily tell the artists from the collectors. They were different from their postures to the make of the clothing. The colors, accessories, shoes, all spoke to social class. I caught Geraldine Stark's eye. She wore a silver lapel pin. My eyes found Jessica. She looked nervous and unhappy, tucking her hair behind her ear. She also wore a silver pin. Artists must get silver, except I had rhinestone.

A couple behind me said, "*Do it...*" together before giggling.

"We're sitting down in five," Eddie muttered. "I'll pass you back to your date."

"Thanks. That was fun."

"Get used to it."

"I thought we were all going to go broke because I didn't want to carry a riding crop."

"Not quite *broke*." He smirked at me and patted my arm.

The doors opened, and the crowd flowed into a huge room overlooking Los Angeles on three sides. Tables had been set in rows with white tablecloths and shining silverware. A longer table sat in front, by the window, Jonathan wasn't there. Chairs scraped. Voices bounced off the high ceiling. I could sit and start a conversation, but he'd been gone too long. Way too long.

Eddie and I held an animated conversation about the future of streaming with two men he introduced as website developers. I saw Erik talking to Jessica. I scanned the room. No sign of Jonathan. Between his hair and his height, he was a hard guy to miss. Seats were being taken, and the wait staff came out with water pitchers and wine. I slipped away from Eddie as he was making a point about subscription rates on internet radio, and I went out the big wooden doors back to the patio.

The staff had already started breaking down, and the area looked inelegant at best. The floodlights had been removed from the photographers' area already, making it appear flat and littered. Jonathan was nowhere to be found. The cameras had missed him entirely. I wondered if that was his plan from the beginning.

A man walked toward me with intention. He as tall, maybe six-four, and wore a black cashmere coat and scarf. He was in his sixties but well-worn, taut in the neck and jaw. He had sparkling turquoise eyes and white hair. "Have they gone in?"

"Yeah. The ladies in the red jackets give you your seat. You get one of these pins." I indicated my rhinestone, and he looked at it appreciatively.

"God forbid we should walk around without a status symbol," he said.

"Yeah. It's like a nametag but not as personal."

"Like you're only as good as the money you spend."

His voice sounded eerily like Jonathan's but wasn't. I must have looked worried because he put his hand on my shoulder. It wasn't an uncomfortable touch, just comforting. "Are you all right?"

"I'm fine, thanks."

He took his hand off me and straightened, pulling a silk handkerchief from his pocket. "You should wipe your eyes, then."

"I wasn't crying," I said, more in surprise than denial. I put my fingers to my face, but he put out his hand before I touched it. He pressed the handkerchief under my eyes. I let him. I didn't know why. He seemed nice enough.

"You're smudged, nonetheless. It wouldn't be right to have such a lovely woman look like a raccoon."

I put my hands on his and pressed the hankie down,. He brought his hand away.

"Thanks," I said.

"You look familiar," he said. "Did you come to this circus last year?"

"No."

"My God. You should have seen the place. It was a Damien Hirst homage with decapitated heads for centerpieces."

"Sounds awful."

"The forks had these hands already attached to them. With veins and nerves. I almost didn't come tonight. I was afraid they were going to try to top themselves." He wrinkled his nose, and I smiled. "Well, I'm glad you weren't here. Maybe I know you from somewhere else."

I looked up at him as if for the first time, trying to see if I could place his features. There was something about the shape of his eyes, the angle of his jaw, the way he tilted his head when he spoke.

Jessica burst out the big doors, on the phone. I angled myself behind the man in the cashmere coat. "Deny it," she said into the phone in clipped syllables. "It's not my voice. Just say no comment."

She stopped in the middle of the patio, still on her call, and stared at her shoes, then out over the mezzanine onto Wilshire Boulevard. The flights of stone steps on each side framed her perfectly, yet she still looked lost. If I felt sorry for her for half a second, the image of Jonathan getting put into a police car at Santa Monica Airport dismissed my compassion and replaced it with something much fiercer.

Jessica glanced at the wood doors then turned on her heel and went down a hall. Once she was far enough away, I handed the man his handkerchief. His back had been to her, and he didn't look around.

"Thanks," I said.

"Keep it." He smiled and went toward the wooden doors. I saw inside when he opened them. The room was crowded, and everyone was sitting. I checked my phone. Nothing from Jonathan. If he was sitting at our table, getting pissed, he would have texted me.

I went down the hall. I'd come to look for Jonathan, but I thought I might hear another snippet of phone call. I was sure he was fine. Just being mysterious, as usual. I followed Jessica into the ladies room. It was a standard museum bathroom. Clean, white and blue, with midlevel fixtures and flat, warm, white lighting. My shoes echoed on the tile. If she'd been on the call in the bathroom, she either stopped talking when I entered or she'd cut the call already.

The door opened behind me, and I heard Jonathan's voice, but it wasn't him.

"—my belt, loop it once, and slap it across those sweet white cheeks until you're pink as a rose and your face is covered with tears. I'll stop when I can stick two fingers in your cunt and feel how sopping wet you are."

I froze. It was undoubtedly him, from the floral metaphor, to the word cunt, to the dominant voice. Three women came in and stopped dead in their tracks when they saw me. The young woman with the phone in her hand had her hair done up like Audrey Hepburn, right down to the tiara. The second was tall and matronly with a sweater, flat shoes, and lines of disappointment permanently etched on her face. They both wore silver pins.

The third woman was Geraldine Stark.

The recording continued.

"Then I'll fuck you until you beg me to let you come, which I may or may not let you do. That going to work for you? Didn't think so."
"Do it."

The voice was shrill and desperate and definitely Jessica's. That must be it. The voice memo from her stolen phone.

Audrey Hepburn fumbled with the phone, shutting it.

"I want to hear it," I said. "From the beginning, if you don't mind."

She hesitated.

"I was telling them," Geraldine said, "he's really like this, and it's hot. Don't you think?" She raised an eyebrow. I didn't answer but stared down Audrey Hepburn. She was a nervous kitten, breakable and easily bossed.

"Do it," I said, my voice the exact opposite of Jessica's whine.

She shrugged as if she wasn't giving in as much as bored by the prospect of not continuing. "It's only really good when he starts this."

"I'll undo your jeans. I'll pull them down to the middle of your thighs so it's hard to walk. You'll be uncomfortable, and that will please me. Then I'll get behind you, and I'll grab a handful of your hair at the back of your head and bend you over that table. I'll take off my belt, loop it once, and slap it across those sweet white cheeks until you're pink as a rose and your face is covered with tears. I'll stop when I can stick two fingers in your cunt and feel how sopping wet you are. Then I'll fuck you until you beg me to let you come, which I may or may not let you do. That going to work for you? Didn't think so."

"Do it."

"Jess, really."

"Do it! Start with the hair. Or the pants. Whatever."

"No."

"Do it!"

Audrey cut it off. I knew what the joke was. The desperation. The pitch. An actress couldn't have reproduced something so raw. I pressed my lips between my teeth. We all knew who it was, and as it turned out, we all thought the idea of her desperately begging for a spanking was hilariously funny.

Geraldine snickered first. Then Audrey. Matronly looked as if she ate a lemon, and the crinkles in her brow sent me over the edge into laughter. Then we all broke up. Between peals of hilarity, someone would shout *do it!* in a shrill, pleading whine, and we'd laugh again.

"Do you want to hear the rest?" Audrey asked.

"No, thanks," I said. "I'll have plenty of the real thing later. Without the *do it!*" I shrieked the last two words, and we laughed again.

I checked my face in the mirror, stood up straight, and arranged my lariat. "I'll see you back in there." I looked at each of them in the mirror. "Thanks for the entertainment."

When I got back onto the patio, I stopped at the big wooden doors and turned around, stepping behind a partition. Despite the cool, collected person who had shown up in the bathroom, I was upset at hearing Jonathan promising sex to another woman. And I was upset that everyone knew. They wouldn't see him as mine. They'd look at me and either feel sorry for poor cheated-on girl or assume I shared him with other women.

"Stop it, Monica," I whispered to myself. "Stop caring." I clenched my fists.

The three artists left the bathroom, giggling and commiserating. Matronly opened one of the big wooden doors, and they were gone. Were they laughing at me? Was Geraldine talking about her nights with Jonathan, taking bets on when he'd dump me?

My name is Monica. I sing like an angel and roar like a lion. I am the owner and ruler of my mind. I keep my own counsel. I decide how I feel. I answer to no one.

I didn't realize my eyes were closed until I heard a sob and the scuffle of feet on carpet. Jessica ran out of the bathroom, crying. She stopped, and I ducked farther behind the partition. She fiddled with her phone, but she was upset and couldn't seem to get it to do what she wanted. She tossed it in her bag and rooted around in the purse, pressing it to herself so she could dig in the bottom.

For the second time, I felt pity, but I was overwhelmed. I'd known exactly what I was doing in the bathroom. I knew she was behind a stall or a wall, yet I'd egged the girls on because I could. For what? To hurt her feelings? Wasn't I better than that? I stepped out from behind the partition. "Jessica?"

She spun and saw me. "Get away from me." She used her *do it* tone. I didn't think she could even hear it.

"Are you ok?"

She ran, still clutching her open bag, heading for the stone steps. I went to the mezzanine railing and watched her go, feet shuffling. She lost her balance and the contents of her bag scattered. Papers and receipts fluttered down into the courtyard, lipsticks and pens clicked. A notebook opened like a butterfly three steps beneath her. She stopped and scooped up her things. Her sobs echoed off the granite walls, even as far away as she was.

"What happened to Eddie?" Jonathan stepped up behind me. "He was supposed to watch you." I put my hand on his face. He was cold and damp.

Jessica looked up, and seeing us both looking down at her, she left half her bag's contents and ran away them. She tripped, skidded, righted herself, and ran onto Wilshire without looking back.

"What happened?" he asked with short breaths.

"That recording." I didn't want to describe the bathroom scene. I didn't care anymore. He looked like shit, and Mister Drazen never looked like shit. "Are you all right? Where were you?"

"Looking for someone." He crunched his eyes shut.

"Who?"

"I haven't been feeling…" He leaned on the railing. "My back hurts and…" His knees bent. I took him by the arms and looked in his green eyes. He wasn't all right; he was panicking. No. That was wrong. I took out the handkerchief the man in the cashmere coat had given me and patted his face.

"You look like hell. You need to sit down." The nearest bench was a mile away, or four steps.

He took the handkerchief. "Where did you get this?" His breath heaved as if it hurt him.

"Some guy. Tall guy, it's fine."

It dropped from his fingers, and I saw the black and blue embroidered letters: JDD. It all came to me. The voice, the way he had looked and walked. It had been Jonathan's father. I was about to confirm that, but Jonathan put his head on my shoulder. I put my arms under his, and before long, I was holding him up.

"Jonathan!" I cried for help, the sounds shrieking and echoing off the granite walls.

He fell, sliding down my body. I bent over him, rolling him onto his back. I didn't know what to do. His face told me he was in pain, his hands reached for me, clutching my arms, keeping me from moving. All I could do was shout his name.

Why was no one coming?

My phone. I had to get my phone.

I dumped the contents of my bag onto the floor, searching through the contents. I looked at him, the love of my life, finally found, finally recognized, finally embraced, with his eyes toward the sky in surrender. I turned back to my pile of crap and found my phone through a curtain of tears. "Okay, I'm calling someone. Please just…"

His eyes closed.

"No! You shit!" I screamed his name and slapped his face.

His eyes moved under the lids.

I slapped him again.

People came.

I hit him harder.

I felt hands on me, clenching hard on the bruised parts of my arms.

I couldn't slap him if they held me.

So I fought, and they pulled me away.

I didn't remember anything after that.

To be continued…

The Submission Series
continues with
Sing Coda!

Out now!

About the Author

To keep up with what I think is sexy today, see **CD Reiss on Facebook**
Email me at **cdreiss.writer@gmail.com**

If you'd like to be notified of new releases, which are run at a discount during the first days of launch week, sign up for the mailing list by visiting the facebook page (click on the rainbow envelope button up top) or my website at **cdreiss.com**. I'll also be sending out bonus scenes, when appropriate, but only to people on the mailing list.

And, of course, if you have any feelings about this book you'd like to share, kindly leave a review.

CPSIA information can be obtained
at www.ICGtesting.com
Printed in the USA
FFHW020834070419
51584773-57015FF